The Rainbow and
the Rose

NEVIL SHUTE

The Rainbow and the Rose

HEINEMANN : LONDON

William Heinemann Ltd
15 Queen Street, Mayfair, London W1X 8BE

LONDON MELBOURNE TORONTO
JOHANNESBURG AUCKLAND

First published 1958
Reprinted 1960, 1966, 1972
© by NEVIL SHUTE NORWAY 1958

434 69918 7

873240

Printed Offset Litho and bound in Great Britain
by Cox & Wyman Ltd,
London, Fakenham and Reading

Acknowledgment

The sonnet by Rupert Brooke, 'The Treasure', from 1914 *& other Poems*, is printed by permission of Messrs Sidgwick & Jackson, Ltd.

When colour goes home into the eyes,
  And lights that shine are shut again
With dancing girls and sweet birds' cries
  Behind the gateways of the brain;
And that no-place which gave them birth, shall close
  The rainbow and the rose:—

Still may Time hold some golden space
  Where I'll unpack that scented store
Of song and flower and sky and face,
  And count, and touch, and turn them o'er,
Musing upon them; as a mother, who
Has watched her children all the rich day through,
Sits, quiet-handed, in the fading light,
When children sleep, ere night.

RUPERT BROOKE

Chapter One

John Pascoe must have created something like a record for a pilot in civil aviation, because he went on flying a D.C.6b across the Pacific from Sydney to Vancouver as a senior captain of AusCan Airways till he was sixty years old. The Department of Civil Aviation stuck their toes in then. They couldn't stop him flying because he was still perfectly fit and could pass every medical test they could think up. Perhaps they were afraid of what the papers might say if there should ever be an accident. At any rate, they refused to renew his licence for regular airline flying, on the score of age. He took his pension and bought three small aeroplanes out of his savings, and formed himself into a small aero club and superphosphate spreading company at Buxton in Tasmania. Flying was his whole life and he had few other interests, so he went on flying.

He was unmarried; back in the dark ages before ever I knew him there had been a divorce. He was the healthiest man of his age that I have ever met; at the time of his retirement he used no spectacles and still had all his own teeth. He was a very good tennis player. He was athletic in most ways; on his summer leaves he used to go on pack-horse trips into the Canadian Rockies for the fishing, and at Nandi in the Fiji Islands where he was based in his last year of airline flying he did quite a bit of skin-diving, using an aqualung. I knew him for nearly thirty years; in fact, he taught me to fly when I was eighteen at Duffington aerodrome near Leacaster where my father was a solicitor.

Buxton is a little place in north Tasmania where the aerodrome is a grass field with no runways. I went there once before Johnnie Pascoe's time. I was flying a D.C.3 from Hobart to Melbourne in the winter in deteriorating weather when an oil pipe on the port engine split just as I was starting on the crossing of the Bass Strait, so that I had to stop that engine. I didn't feel like going on across a hundred miles of sea like that and Area Control agreed with me quite quickly when I put my problem to them on the blower. Hobart had closed in by that time and Launceston wasn't too good, so they sent me in to Buxton which has dead flat country all around. I slithered in over the fence and put her down and boy! was I glad to be on the ground! So were the passengers.

I don't think the population of Buxton can be more than three thousand, though it is the centre of a prosperous grazing district. It has one hotel, so bad that the commercial travellers avoid it and drive long distances to do so. It's not a place that I would care to live in personally, but I'm not Johnnie Pascoe. There was quite a bit of minor flying to be done there, though, and I suppose that's why he went. He had a Tiger Moth fitted up with a canister for spreading fertiliser from the air and he did a bit with that, and he had two Austers for instruction and occasional charter flights. He had a ground engineer called Billy Monkhouse to look after these three aeroplanes, who was nearly as old as he was. He lived in a small house just by the aerodrome and got a woman in each day to do for him; he went duck shooting with the locals in the autumn and trout fishing with the Shire Clerk in the spring. He got the sort of life he wanted, I suppose.

He always looked about the same, from the time I first remember him when I was a boy. He would have been about five foot nine in height with partially grey hair, regular features, rather a fine face, very tanned, a little lined towards the end. He hadn't got a very great deal of humour in him, rather stiff. Women liked him, but I don't know that he liked them very much; at any rate, he gave the impression of being careful. "Once bit, twice shy," he told me once, and I suppose he was speaking of the divorce. "But that doesn't seem to stop one being bitten . . ."

He was born a Canadian, in Toronto I believe. He went to England as a flight cadet to train with the Royal Flying Corps in 1915 and he never went back to Canada —not to live, that is, though he must have passed through it often enough. He lived and worked in England and the Far East all the time between the wars, but it was as a Canadian that he got his job with AusCan after the Second War. All the pilots on that line had to be either Australian or Canadian for some point of politics.

Well now. I emigrated to Australia when I got married just after the Second War. I was in the motor trade at first, but then I got a job instructing with the aero club at Ballarat which got me back into the aircraft world. I joined Australian Continental Airways some time ago, and I've been a captain with them for the last five years. In July of last year I was on the Sydney-Melbourne run flying a Viscount with Dicky Powell as first officer. On that tour I used to take up Flight 82 in the late afternoon, get a three-hour break in Sydney, and bring the last flight back, Flight 156 that left at 20.25 and got to Essendon at half past ten at night. I didn't like that duty much, for several reasons. One got to Sydney after the shops shut and with too little time to go into the city for a movie. If possible I like to be at home in the late afternoon because of reading to the kids before they go to bed. One sees so little of them, otherwise. I like to help them making models, dressing dolls, and all that sort of thing. Instead, I had to stick around for three hours at Kingsford Smith airport five hundred miles away from them, reading a book in the pilots' room, listening to the radio, or just snoozing in a chair.

That year we had a terrible July. I was sitting there one evening half asleep, listening to the radio and the wind outside and the rain beating on the window. The seven o'clock news was just coming on, and I stayed to listen to that before going in to tea. I sat dozing through all the stuff about Egypt and the Middle East, and all the stuff about the floods along the Murray. Then there came a bit that jerked me suddenly awake. The announcer said something like this:

"It is reported from Tasmania that a pilot flying a small aeroplane upon an errand of mercy crashed this afternoon on a small airstrip on the west coast. The pilot, Captain John Pascoe, was attempting to land to bring a child into hospital, Betty Hoskins, aged seven, who is suffering from appendicitis. There is no practicable land route to the Lewis River and all communications normally take place by sea, but no vessel has been able to enter the river for the last ten days owing to the continuing westerly gales. Captain Pascoe is reported to have sustained a fractured skull."

I was a bit upset when I heard this news. We all knew Johnnie Pascoe because for a time Sydney had been one of his terminals and he still passed through now and then. The world of aviation is a small one in Australia. But I knew him better than anyone, of course, because I had known him off and on for thirty years, ever since he taught me to fly in England at the Leacaster Flying Club. In 1942 I had met him in Cairo when he was flying a courier service to England in a Hudson. In 1944 he had flown me back to Lyneham from Calcutta in a Liberator after I got shot up in Burma. I had met him many times since then,

4

particularly in Australia. All through my life I had known Johnnie Pascoe, quiet, grizzled, and competent. He was a part of my experience.

When I went for briefing and ran through the flight plan with Dick Powell I asked the Control Officer, "Did you get any more on Johnnie Pascoe than was on the news?"

"Not much," he said. "Hobart sent a machine out just before dark, but it didn't get far. It's clamped down over the mountains."

"Is it right he got a fractured skull?"

"So they say."

"They got that over the radio?"

"That's right. They've got a transceiver at the Lewis River."

I had already got the weather gen for my flight, but I went back and saw the Met Officer again. I asked him, "What's the form for tomorrow—on the west coast of Tasmania? I'm wondering how they're going to get Johnnie Pascoe out."

He turned to his chart, and stood tapping his pencil against his teeth, silent. Then he laid it on the chart. "There's this depression stationary at the eastern end of the Bass Strait. It's been there for four days. There seems to be another forming down to the south-west—*here*." He traced a little circle on the chart. "Might push it away."

"Get a clear interval before the second one comes up?"

"We might. I could tell you better tomorrow morning. If we do, it'll deteriorate again. It's like that at this time of year, of course."

I went out to the aircraft and put all this out of my mind. You must do that and I had got into the habit of it years before; when you're doing pre-flight checks you

5

only want to think about the pre-flight checks. It was a miserable night with a strong gusty south-west wind that was going to make us fifteen minutes late on schedule, with drifts of rain lashing against the machine.

Presently I got my clearance from the Tower and taxied out to the runway, and took her off. When we were on our way and climbing upon course I had time to think about Johnnie Pascoe again, and the more I thought the less I liked my thoughts. The west coast of Tasmania must be one of the most inaccessible districts in the world. It's only about a hundred miles from Hobart but there are no roads there at all and only one bush track that you can walk along, and that doesn't go within forty miles of the Lewis River. The mountains stick up in pinnacles all over the country, sort of haphazard, not in definite ranges. The valleys that meander in between and all around these islands of mountain are filled with bush so dense that you cannot penetrate it on foot but have to cut your way through yard by yard with a machete. When you get towards the coast you come upon occasional plains, but these are button-grass plains where no feed grows that will sustain a horse. You can't work a horse in that country at all. If you want to get in to the Lewis River you must go on foot packing all you need for the next fortnight on your back, hacking your way through the horizontal scrub yard by yard. Or you can go round the coast in a fishing boat if the weather is good enough for entering the estuary, which is uncharted and unbuoyed. Or you can fly in to their tiny airstrip. That was what Johnnie Pascoe had tried to do.

We flew at twenty-three thousand feet, and even at that height we had a rough trip. When we were half an hour from Melbourne I spoke to Essendon Tower and got clearance to let down. We were the only aircraft in the air that night, so when we were steady on the let-down I

6

spoke to the controller again and asked if there was anything fresh on Johnnie Pascoe.

"We've been monitoring their frequency," he said, "but there's been nothing fresh. I don't suppose there will be till the morning. The woman's there alone."

"What woman?" I enquired. "Over."

"They're tin miners," he explained. "Mr. and Mrs. Hoskins and two children. They've got a surface working. They just dig up earth and wash the tin out of the soil, I think. They've got a diesel-engined boat. Don Hoskins took it round to Hobart a fortnight ago to fetch stores, leaving his wife and children in the house. Now he can't get back."

I frowned. "They've got some neighbours? Over."

"There's not another house for thirty miles."

"For the love of Mike!" I said. "Who's looking after Johnnie Pascoe?"

"The woman is," he replied. "She pulled him out of the machine and got him to the house."

I thought very quickly. "What's the strip like?"

"They land an Auster there in fine weather," he said. "Somebody was saying it's only about a couple of hundred yards long, on top of a little hill."

"Is there a data sheet for it?"

"I think there might be. Would you like me to look and see?"

"I wish you would. I'll come up to the Tower when we land."

We got in to Essendon at about a quarter to eleven. I waited till the passengers were all off and then left the machine myself, hurrying through the rain to our office. The weather was even worse here than it had been at Sydney, as dark as pitch and with quite a high wind. In the warmth and light of the office I glanced at the movements board. There was a Dakota freighter scheduled to

7

leave for Hobart in Tasmania at one o'clock in the morning. I asked the night clerk if that flight was still on, and he told me they were loading the machine.

I left the office and ran through the rain to my car in the park, and drove to the Tower. The controller was up there waiting for me. He had the data sheet for the Lewis River airstrip on his desk, and he handed it to me. "It's not a licensed field, of course," he said.

It certainly wasn't. The plan showed it as one tiny runway six hundred and thirty feet long, little more than two hundred yards, and only forty feet wide. It ran approximately north-west and south-east, more or less across the prevailing wind. The approaches were quite unobstructed, and it had a hard surface. It was built upon a ridge because the ground fell away quite steeply towards the west; at one point it was marked: 'Cliff 50 ft.' only a few yards from the runway. To the east the slope was more gradual and here was the legend: 'Ground soft and uneven'. The homestead was marked upon the plan about a quarter of a mile from the strip, and a secondary plan showed the general position of this lot in relation to the Lewis River and the surrounding country. There was a mountain two thousand four hundred feet high about four miles to the north-east which might be a bit of a trap for young players in bad weather, and a lot of little hills and escarpments dotted about. The altitude of the strip was five hundred and thirty feet above sea level.

The rain beat and drummed on the glass walls of the control room all around us as I stood looking at this data sheet, taking it all in. "It's pretty small," I said at last.

He nodded. "They don't use it much. The Hobart club fly in to take them the mail once a week, but they don't very often land. Generally they drop the mail and parcels as they fly over. They *do* land light aircraft there, though, in fine weather."

8

I waved the data sheet. "This is the only strip in the vicinity?"

He nodded again. "They used not to have a strip at all. Then they made this about two years ago. I suppose it was the best that they could do. It's a big job, of course, just for one man and his wife."

I stood there, thoughtful, looking down on Runway 260, still lit up. "Any more on Johnnie Pascoe?"

"Not since I spoke to you. I should say they've closed down for the night. They'll be speaking on the morning schedule, at seven o'clock."

I turned to him. "How did all this begin?"

"The kid got sick two days ago," he told me. "The mother got on the radio about it, and they got the doctor on the other end. He diagnosed appendicitis, and said she'd got to be brought into hospital at once."

"Easier said than done."

"That's right. Rhys-Davids knows the form out there better than anyone. He's the pilot-instructor at the Hobart club. Actually, he's the only man who's ever landed an aircraft on that strip, and he's the one who always takes their mail. He's in hospital with a hernia, and they won't let him out till next week. He had the operation on Monday."

That's the sort of thing that always happens, of course.

He went on, "They sent a machine out from Hobart, twice. They couldn't make it over the mountains either time, and they hadn't got the range to go round the south coast in anything that could make a landing on the strip. Then Pascoe said he could make it from Buxton. It's about a hundred and ten miles from Buxton, flying down the coast from the north. He tried early yesterday morning in an Auster. It was clear when he took off, and raining heavily by the time he got there—visibility less than

9

half a mile. He waited for it to clear, circling over the sea until his fuel was getting low, and then came back to base. He went off again yesterday afternoon." He paused. "The woman said that he made three attemps to land—touched his wheels each time and took off again. The fourth time, she said, the machine turned upside down in a gust and fell off the edge of the runway."

"Over this place where it says, 'cliff'?"

"Could be."

I glanced down at the paper in my hand. It was several hundred yards to the homestead. "She got him to the house?"

He nodded. "She couldn't carry him, of course. But she must be a pretty good kind of a girl. She had the child out there at the runway in her arms ready to pop it into the machine, so that the pilot wouldn't have to leave his seat. She put the child down and pulled Pascoe out of the wreckage. She says he's got a big dent in his head where the skull's caved in, a broken thigh, and possibly other injuries."

"Christ!" I said softly. I could imagine the scene—just one woman in the rain and the wind, with all that on her plate. "What did she do then?"

"She did all right," he said. "She left him lying on the ground and ran back with the child to the house. Then she ran back again with a couple of hot water bags and blankets. She knows about shock, apparently. Then she ran back to the house again and got on the blower to Hobart. She's got the standard medicine chest and they told her what to give him—morphia or something. She gave him that and then she went and got their tractor and a sled, and put him on the sled, and got him to the house and into bed."

It was just about as bad as it could be. "He's unconscious?"

"Semi-conscious. He asked for a cigarette and smoked it while she was getting the sled."

"What's the form about the weather?"

"They're hoping for a few hours clear tomorrow. Then it's likely to close down again."

A sudden gust of wind whistled about the Tower. "Do you know what they're planning to do?"

"I haven't heard," he said. "If it clears they'll almost certainly send out a machine from Hobart. They'll probably take a doctor."

"Is there anyone at Buxton now? I mean, if it *doesn't* clear? Any other pilot who could fly an Auster down from there?"

He shook his head. "I haven't heard. They may be sending somebody up there tonight. So far as I know, Pascoe was the only experienced pilot there."

I stood in thought for a moment while responsibility descended squarely on my shoulders. Johnnie Pascoe had taught me to fly, and whoever they had at Hobart in the absence of Rhys-Davids it was quite unlikely that he'd have one half of my experience. I couldn't let this rest. I'd have to go over and do what I could to help.

I turned to the controller. "Mind if I use your telephone?"

I got on an outside line from the Control Tower and rang Peter Fosdick at his house, our operations manager. He was in bed, but I got him out of that. I told him what the form was, and asked if he could spare me for a day or two to go over on this thing. He grumbled a good bit, but he'd got plenty of time to rearrange the crews because I wasn't flying till the afternoon. He couldn't very well refuse, and besides, he knew Johnnie Pascoe, too.

The controller had heard all of that, of course, because I was speaking from his desk. I replaced the telephone. "I'm going over on Flight 117, the freighter," I told him.

11

"There'll be a change in the flight plan. I'm going to ask them to go in to Launceston and drop me off before they go on to Hobart. I'll go straight to Buxton and see what the form is. I believe that's the best place to be. When you're speaking to Hobart, would you tell them that's what I'm doing, and I'm on my way? I'll be talking to them on the land line first thing in the morning."

I folded the data sheet about that rotten little airstrip and put it in my pocket, and went down to the car. I looked in at the office and told the clerk about the freighter stop at Launceston. I grabbed one of the Tasmanian maps and went out to my car again, and drove off home. I live in the suburbs at Essendon not very far from the aerodrome, in a fair-sized single-storey house on the corner of two streets. I left the car out in the road instead of driving into the garage, and went into the house.

Sheila had gone to bed; she came out in her dressing gown to meet me in the hall. "You're late, Ronnie," she said. "Did you have a bad trip?"

"Not too bad," I told her. "But there's been a bit of drama in Tasmania. Johnnie Pascoe's bought it."

"I heard it on the news. I'm sorry. Why did you leave the car outside?"

"I'm going over there," I said. "See if there's anything that I can do. There's a freighter in about an hour's time. I want my leather coat and helmet."

She stared at me, astonished. "Your *leather coat*? I haven't seen that for years."

"We haven't given it away?"

She wrinkled her brows. "I don't think so." She stood in thought. "I remember wrapping it up in newspaper so that it wouldn't make other things dirty . . . I put mothballs in with it . . . I think it might be in the trunk under Diana's bed, underneath my stole."

"Would the helmet be with it?"

"It might be. Peter had that last, two years ago, when he went to that fancy dress party at school."

Diana woke up when we pulled the trunk out from under her bed, and sat up sleepily, "Wha's the matter?"

"It's all right, darling," Sheila told her. "Go to sleep again. We just want Daddy's coat. He's going flying."

At eight years old one is easily satisfied. "Is that all?" she said. She lay down and turned on her side; I pulled the bedclothes over her and tucked them round her shoulders for the night was chilly, and she went to sleep immediately. The coat was there in newspaper and we found the helmet in the chest of drawers in Peter's room. Sheila said softly, "He puts it on sometimes, in front of the looking glass."

We closed the door quietly behind us. "You'd better have something, Ronnie," she said. "Dripping toast and cocoa?"

It was a good idea, because I should be up all night. She went into the kitchen and I went into the bedroom and stuffed a little haversack full of pullovers and warm clothes. There wasn't room for pyjamas but I could do without those in favour of long woolly underwear. Whatever things were like at Buxton, I was going to be damn cold at some time or another. I could see that sticking out a mile.

Sheila was busy in the kitchen. I put the haversack down in the hall beside my coat and wandered out into the workshop. Peter and I were planning a surprise for Diana, because we were going to build her a doll's house, a big one with six rooms, for Christmas. I had got the plywood and the lengths of small, sawn timber, and we had laid out the baseboard. I stood looking at the drawing, pondering this thing. I had another project on hand for Peter for Christmas, a flying model aeroplane with a small diesel motor, but that I was building in a corner of the workshop at the aerodrome to make it a surprise.

I stood pondering the doll's house in the workshop, savouring my home. Sheila came to me in a few minutes. "Don't stand mooning there," she said. "The toast's ready."

"What colour shall we have the drawing room?" I asked.

"Pink," she said. "Pale pink walls. She likes pink. Now come and eat your toast."

I left the workshop and went through to the kitchen and ate the little meal she had prepared for me. Presently I glanced at my watch, and it was time to go.

She said a little anxiously, "Don't go and buy it yourself, Ronnie."

"I won't do that," I promised her. "There's trouble enough over there already."

I put my old leather coat on in the hall, and kissed her; she came to the door with me. "Will you be able to ring me?" she asked.

I thought for a moment. "After dark," I said. "I'll ring you after dark tomorrow night and let you know the form."

I drove back to the airport and locked the car up in the park. In the office the flight crew were getting ready to take off the freighter. We exchanged a few words about Johnnie Pascoe and went out to the machine; we took off on time and settled down to a long flight against the head wind. I sat on the floor with my back against the freight, dozing a little; it was very cold and draughty and noisy in the unfurnished shell. I was glad of my leather coat. It was nearly half past three in the morning when they put her down at Launceston and taxied in.

We had radioed the airport control to ask them to get a car to meet us, to drive me sixty miles to Buxton. It was waiting for us with a very sleepy driver, and I got in beside him and we started off. It was a quarter past five when we got near the little town, and the driver asked me where I wanted to go.

"Better take me to the hotel," I said. I remembered it from my forced landing, years before. "What's its name?"

"The Post Office Hotel," he said. "They won't be open yet. They don't get out of bed till about nine."

We drove into the deserted street, black and silent and wet. "Well, take me there, anyway," I said.

He stopped in front of the hotel. I got out and knocked on the door for a few minutes, with no result. Then I went exploring round the back with my small torch and found that the kitchen door was unlocked. I went back to the street and paid off the taxi, returned to the hotel kitchen, and switched on the light.

It was a pretty dirty sort of place, and smelt a bit. It was warm, though, with the residue of heat from the stove. I was hungry again and there was nothing much to do for an hour, so I started ferreting around and found the larder, smelling a good deal worse than the kitchen. There was an electric cooker there, so I made myself a cup of tea and boiled a couple of eggs and cut some bread and butter.

It was still dark outside at half past six, and there was still no movement from upstairs in the hotel. The controller at Essendon had said that the woman at the Lewis River would be speaking on the morning schedule at seven o'clock; before then I must get to a radio and find out what was happening. I wrote a note for the hotel on a page torn from my diary and left it on the table with a ten-bob note to soothe any ruffled feelings there might be, and went out to the yard, and so to the street. I could see the length of it now in the faint light, but the wind was still high and there was a little rain with it.

It didn't take me long to find the police station. There

was a light on in the front office, and when I opened the door a young constable got up from a desk. Behind him on a table was the black metal case of a transceiver. I had come to the right place.

He said, "Guid morning," in a strong Scots accent. "And what can I do for you?" He could not have been in the country very long.

"My name is Clarke," I said. "Have you heard anything about me?" He shook his head. "Well, I'm a captain with Australian Continental Airways." I went on to tell him briefly why I'd come to Buxton. "They told me at Essendon that Mrs. Hoskins would be speaking on the morning schedule at seven o'clock. Mind if I listen in?"

"Not at all," he said. "There'll be others coming to hear that. Mr. Monkhouse, the ground engineer, for one, and Sergeant Farrell from the house. Nae doubt they'll be making a great effort to get him out of it today."

I nodded. "Have you heard a weather forecast this morning?"

"Only what came through on the six o'clock news."

"What was that?"

"Stormy, with low cloud and rain."

I offered him a cigarette and we stood smoking for a time, not saying very much. Presently a very old Ford Anglia drew up in the street outside; the constable glanced out of the window. "Here's Mr. Monkhouse."

He was an oldish man, shaved and presentable, dressed in a roll-neck sweater under a soiled sports coat. He had once had red hair, now turned mostly to grey. He had a merry face and, I guessed, some affinity for beer that might have prevented him from rising higher in his life than ground engineer at a small Tasmanian aero club. His face struck a faint chord of memory in my mind; I introduced myself, and then I said, "We've met before, haven't we?"

16

"Burma," he said. "Cox's Bazaar and Akyab. I was with the Army, servicing L.5.s of 82 Div. You were in 607, Spitfires."

"You've got a memory," I remarked.

"Cor," he said, "I remember you before that. I was a G.E. with the Yorkshire Club at Sherburn-in-Elmet back in 1930. You came over for a Pageant one time, in a Bluebird. You learned to fly at Leacaster."

I smiled. "That's right. Captain Pascoe taught me to fly. He was at Leacaster instructing."

"So he was."

I glanced at him. "You're English?"

"Not me—I'm Aussie. But I been all over. Went to England after the First War and never come back till 1946, except one time. I'm from West Australia."

"You've been in aviation a long time."

He nodded. "Pretty near as long as Captain Pascoe, and that's saying something." He glanced at me. "You come to fly him out?"

"We'll see what the form is," I replied. "The Hobart club may have got something laid on by this time. What have you got here?"

"There's an Auster and a Tiger," he said. "Tiger's got a super canister in the front cockpit."

"Take you long to get it out?"

"Three or four hours. But the Auster would be better. Got a blind-flying panel. Stick a stretcher down in the rear fuselage of that, too."

"It'll take a stretcher?"

He nodded. "Captain Pascoe had it modded, special. Both of them. We got a special stretcher, narrow each end like a coffin lid. Take out the front passenger seat and it fits just nice." He paused a moment in thought. "He had it with him yesterday, so I suppose it's bust. Knock you up another one in half a day, do for the time being."

17

"Is the Auster okay?"

"Filled her up and did the daily last night," he said. "Case anybody wanted her."

The sergeant came in from a door that led into the house, buttoning his jacket. He went to the transceiver and turned it on to warm up, and we stood silent, listening. Presently it came to life, and Hobart came upon the air. The sergeant adjusted the tuning a little.

The announcer said, "This is 7 HT. 7 HT calling all regular stations. Good morning, everybody. This morning I'm taking 7 KZ first, and after that we'll take the regular schedule. 7 KZ, if you are listening, will you come in, Mrs. Hoskins."

There was a momentary pause, and then, "This is 7 KZ," said a woman's voice. "How are you today, Mr. Fletcher?" And then, "Over."

"I'm fine. How are your two patients? Over."

"Well, Betty's better, Mr. Fletcher. There's no doubt of that. Her stomach doesn't feel so rigid, and she drank a little milk. Captain Pascoe, he seems just about the same. I gave the second injection at midnight, like the doctor said."

"Is he conscious?"

"Well, it's hard to say, you know. I don't think he can say anything. I don't think he's feeling much pain, though. Sometimes his eyes are open, and then it's as if he's looking at things in the room, you know. It's hard to say. Over to you."

"I'll put you through to the doctor in a minute, Mrs. Hoskins. Before I do that, tell me about the weather. What's it like with you this morning?"

"Just the same, Mr. Fletcher. There don't seem any difference to what it was yesterday."

"There should be a fine spell this morning, according to the Met. It ought to be clearing soon from the west, away over the sea. Is there any sign of that?"

"Well, to tell the truth I haven't looked, Mr. Fletcher, only just out of the window. If you'll hold on a minute I'll go out and see."

"I'll wait, Mrs. Hoskins. Take your time; there's no hurry."

We waited silent, staring at the set. If it was true there was a break coming, I would try and make it in the Auster. That was, if Hobart had nothing better to suggest. I said as much to Monkhouse in a low tone, and he nodded.

In a few minutes she came on again. "Mr. Fletcher? This is Mrs. Hoskins here. It's quite right what you said. It's showing a little line away over on the horizon, like as if it was clearing behind the rain."

"Good-oh. They forecast a fine morning and it looks as though you're going to have it. I'm going to switch you through now to the doctor; he's waiting on the line. Before I go off, though, we shall want to speak to you again before the machine takes off, to get the latest weather from you. Can you be listening again at half past eight?"

"I'll be listening at half past eight. After I've spoken to the doctor, can I speak to Don? Over to you."

"He's here with me, Mrs. Hoskins. I'll put you through to the hospital now, and Don will speak after that."

I lit another cigarette and we stood listening to the consultations. The doctor took the child first, and from the tenor of the conversation there seemed to be no doubt that she was better. The pain and the inflammation were less than they had been, and the temperature was now below a hundred. So far as Pascoe was concerned, there did not seem to be much change. The doctor was principally concerned about infection of the head wound, and he gave her very elaborate directions about dressing it, making her write them down as he dictated slowly.

In the end he said, "Well, that's all for now, Mrs. Hoskins. I'll be speaking to you again from the airport at half past eight, before the machine takes off. It's just possible I might be coming out with the machine. But anyway, I'll speak to you again then. Now back to the control."

We listened while the woman talked to her husband, but there was nothing much in that. He was weatherbound, as all the fishing boats were in Recherche or Southport at the entrance to the D'Entrecasteaux Channel; the report from the Maatsuyker lighthouse on the south coast showed the weather to be quite impossible for small craft. Don Hoskins was still in Hobart tied up at the quay, judging it better to remain available rather than to be lying anchored somewhere out of touch.

The announcer allowed them two or three exchanges, and then he cut them short. He said, "Before we go on with the morning schedule, has any other station anything to say about Lewis River?"

At the set the sergeant touched a switch and spoke into the microphone. "This is 7 PC, Buxton. There is a Captain Clarke here wants to speak. Over."

"Okay Buxton. Put Captain Clarke on."

I went to the microphone and said, "Clarke speaking. Have you heard anything about me from Essendon? Over."

"Yes, we had a message to say you were coming. We're very glad to hear that there's a pilot at Buxton. What aircraft have you got there?"

"There's an Auster fuelled and serviceable," I said. "There's a Tiger with a canister in the front seat that could be made serviceable in half a day."

"Okay. Did you hear me talking to Mrs. Hoskins?"

"We heard all of that."

"This break in the weather that's coming won't last

longer than two or three hours, according to the Met. After that it's going to clamp down again for an indefinite period, days perhaps. The Met don't think there's going to be much reduction in the wind velocity. If that's right, we shan't be able to go round the south coast from here unless we take the Proctor, and that's not got a hope of landing on that strip. We shall try it with an Auster taking the doctor as a passenger, with his operating gear. We don't expect to be able to land properly, but in this wind force we hope to be able to fly so slowly across the strip into wind that he'll be able to jump out without hurting himself. But we'll have to go over the mountains to get there at all, and that may not be possible. Over to you."

"Clarke here. The wind's dead across the strip, is it? Over."

"It is at present, and not likely to change much, according to the Met."

"It's a job for a parachute doctor, surely?" I said. "Over."

"I know it is, but we haven't got one. The R.A.A.F. are sending down a Lincoln with a parachute doctor and a parachute nurse, but it's got to come from Brisbane and I don't think it's taken off yet. It can't be here before the early afternoon, and then we'll have to brief them. It doesn't look as though this break will last so long as that. Over to you."

"I can make the Lewis River down the coast," I said. "Tell me what you want me to do, and I'll do it. Over."

"Are you willing to try and put a doctor down?" he asked. "Over."

I paused before replying. It was years since I had flown anything like that, but I had been good on Austers once, when I was instructing at Ballarat before I joined the airline. "I'm game to try it," I said. "I know what you want. Whether I'll succeed in landing him—well, that's another thing."

"What's the weather like with you, now?" he asked. "Any sign of this break?"

"Hold on." I spoke rapidly to the sergeant, and he led me outside. Twenty yards up the street there was a gap between the houses and a view across flat country to the west. There was a line of blue sky down on the horizon.

I hurried back to the police station and the microphone. "Clarke speaking," I said. "It's breaking over to the west, about twenty miles away. With this wind it might be clear here in half an hour. Over."

"The Met only give it about three hours before it clamps again," he said. "I'd like to fly our doctor up to you, but I don't know that there's time for that. Have you got a doctor there with surgical experience, who would be willing to try it?"

"I don't know," I said. I turned to the sergeant and asked him. "Is there a doctor here?" He replied, "Dr. Turnbull." I said, "You'd better speak," and he took the microphone.

"This is Sergeant Farrell," he said. "Dr. Turnbull lives here. He does surgery on accidents and that."

Hobart said, "I don't know him. Is he young and active, or is he an old man?"

The sergeant said, "He's young. Only come out of medical school two or three years."

We left it that the sergeant should take me to see the doctor and we would speak again at half past eight. Hobart went on with other stations and the constable sat down to monitor the conversations. I turned to Billy Monkhouse.

"We'll have to hop around now, Mr. Monkhouse," I said. "Will you go to the aerodrome and run that Auster up? I want to do two or three landings on her before I

22

take off for the Lewis River. I'll go with Sergeant Farrell now to see this doctor, and I'll come out to the aerodrome immediately after that. Then we'll come back here and see what the form is at half past eight."

"Take the dual out?" he asked.

"Oh—yes. We shan't want that."

He went off and got into his little car and drove away, and I went with the sergeant to the police car. As we got in I said, "Tell me about Dr. Turnbull. We're going to his house?"

"He hasn't got a house," he said. "He lives with the Reverend Haynes—he's the vicar. He has two rooms in the vicarage and Mrs. Haynes does for him."

"He isn't married?"

"No."

"Does he have his surgery in the vicarage?"

He slipped the gear in and looked over his shoulder as he backed the car out. "He's got a surgery in a room in the office building, over Woodward's shop. That's where he sees people mostly, but he won't be there yet. I'll take you to the vicarage." He swung the car round into the road. "We never had a doctor here in Buxton till he came, two years ago," he observed. "He's squatting, you might say. We used to have to get a doctor out from Devonport before."

"Do people like him?"

"Oh, aye. He's Tasmanian—his father has a fruit farm on the Huon River. He's only a young chap, you know."

We drove about a quarter of a mile up to the church. It was a stone-built church with a square tower, very like an English church as many in Tasmania are. Beside it was a forbidding, two-storey vicarage with Gothic windows and a slate roof. There was a brass plate on the gate leading into the front garden, unpolished for a fortnight. We parked the car and went up the front steps of the house and knocked on the Gothic, ironbound, hardwood front door. We pressed a button and a clockwork bell rang on the inside of the door.

Presently the handle clanked, and it was opened by a boy of ten, in grey shorts and a sweater. The sergeant asked if we could see the doctor. He stared at us without speaking, and then he ran back to the kitchen at the rear of the house, leaving the door open. We heard him say, "Mum, there's people to see Alec."

The vicar's wife came to us at the door, a little grey, a little portly, with a good-natured face, wearing a rough apron over a black dress; she smoothed worn hands upon it as she came because she had been getting breakfast. "Good morning, Sergeant," she said. "Did you want to see the doctor?"

"If we can," he replied.

She stood smoothing her hands on the apron. "I was letting him lie," she said. "He was out till four in the morning with Mrs. Jardine's baby. Is it anything urgent?"

"It's Captain Pascoe," the sergeant said. "We want him to fly down to Lewis River."

"Oh . . . Had I better wake him, do you think? He's only had three hours in bed."

"I think you'd better, Mrs. Haynes. There's not much time to lose."

"Well, come upstairs." She turned and led the way up polished and uncarpeted stairs to the top floor. Here the boards were out of sight of the front door, and were unpolished. She opened a door for us. "Just wait in there and I'll tell him."

It was the doctor's private sitting room, and it wasn't much. There was a square of threadbare carpet in the middle of the floor, an oval table with a knitted doily in the middle of it and an ashtray upon that. There were two upholstered chairs with broken springs before a fireplace in which no fire had burned that winter, and one small wicker-seated chair at the table. There was an antique, horsehair sofa with one leg missing, supported on a chunk of wood. A faded print of the Good Shepherd hung above the fireplace. A small bookcase housed an array of medical volumes, some copies of the *Australian Medical Journal*, and three or four paper-backed novels.

We stood in the cold room, waiting, listening to the murmur of voices in the next room followed by the creak of bed springs. We heard the woman go downstairs again, and presently the doctor came in at the door in his pyjamas, bleary-eyed from sleep, hair tumbled, doing up the cord of his dressing gown. "Morning, Sergeant," he said thickly. "What can I do for you?"

He looked incredibly young. I learned later that he was twenty-eight, but that morning he looked about fifteen. He was only about five foot seven in height and he had the clear skin and staring red hair of a boy, that generally darkens quickly in the twenties. He was slight in build; both the sergeant and I seemed to tower over him.

"Sorry to wake you, Doctor," said the sergeant. "But it's Captain Pascoe."

"That's all right," he muttered. "What about Captain Pascoe?"

"This is Mr. Clarke," the sergeant said. He corrected himself. "Captain Clarke, I should say, with A.C.A. We're waiting on a call from Hobart now about flying in a doctor to him there. It don't seem possible to get him out just yet, but there's a clear patch of weather coming for a few hours now, so Captain Clarke could maybe fly you in."

The boy rubbed a hand over his face and shook his head a little, shaking away his sleep. "What's he got? Fractured skull, isn't it?"

"He's got a fractured thigh as well, they say."

"What about the other one? The appendicitis?"

"There's that, too," the sergeant said. "But the report on the morning session was to say she's better."

The doctor stood in silence. Presently he plunged his hand into the pocket of his dressing gown and produced a packet of cigarettes. He offered them to us and we both took one. He lit them for us, and lit his with another match. "I asked Mrs. Haynes if she could bring us up some tea," he muttered.

"That'll be nice," the sergeant said politely.

We stood in silence till the doctor spoke again. "I couldn't do two major operations there," he said irreso-lutely. "It's like asking anyone to set up a hospital with—nothing. And no help. It's not a reasonable thing to ask of anyone. You'll have to get them out to where the job can be done properly."

"There doesn't seem to be much hope of getting them out," I said.

"Why not? There's an airstrip there."

He was stalling; that was evident. I couldn't help being a bit sorry for him in his predicament. He looked so young, so inexperienced. He was tired, too. I was tired for I had had no sleep at all, but then I was a lot older than he was. "Do you know about aeroplanes and fly-ing?" I asked.

He shook his head. "I thought of learning to fly once, but it costs too much."

"I'll try and explain," I said. "The Hoskins could only make a very short strip there, only about two hundred yards long and about forty feet wide. It's really no more than a little bit of road on top of a ridge of hill. To land even the smallest aeroplane on that you'd need to have perfect weather and the wind blowing straight along the strip. Well, now we've got a wind that won't be less than thirty miles an hour any time today, and blowing dead across the strip, at right angles to it. I can't land in a cross wind like that. No pilot could, upon a lightly loaded aeroplane, the sort of a slow aeroplane you'd have to take to use that strip and not run off the end. Johnnie Pascoe took a chance and tried it yesterday, to get the child out. He bought it."

He looked at me, a little sullenly. "If you can't land there, what's the use of talking?"

"There *is* one thing that we can do," I said. "We've got a patch of clear weather this morning, that won't last longer than a few hours. I can take an Auster there and fly slowly across the strip, with any luck, heading in to wind. I won't be more than five feet up—I may even be able to touch my wheels. We'll be flying at about forty miles an hour into a thirty mile an hour wind, so we shan't be doing more than ten miles an hour across the strip. I might even be able to hold her stationary for a few seconds, with the wheels upon the ground. An active man could just step out on to the strip. In any case, it won't be much of a jump."

We stood in silence, and in the silence Mrs. Haynes came clumping up the stairs and into the room. She had a tray with three cups of strong tea on it, and a bowl of sugar. "I brought you some tea," she said comfortably. "It's still blowy outside, but it looks as if it's fining up. We might be going to have a nice day."

We thanked her mechanically, and she went out. "You could break a leg trying to do that," he said. "Anything could happen."

He was the only doctor that we'd got. "I wouldn't ask you to break a leg," I said patiently. "We don't want any more casualties there. If I can't make it so that you can just step out, we'll come home again."

"Suppose I were to do that," he said. "I couldn't hope

to do much for either of them." He stared up at me with some hostility. "You know all about aeroplanes. Well, you don't know much about medicine. Am I supposed to do a wonder-operation on a fractured skull with nothing but a blunt penknife and a kettle of muddy water? Or take out an appendix? There's not a hope of a successful operation. I can tell you that. I can tell you another thing. If I try it, both patients will die."

The sergeant said quietly, "A cup of tea, Doctor." He passed a cup to him and gave me one, and passed the bowl of sugar.

"If I can land you, I can land anything else in reason," I said. "It may be necessary to drop it. But I can land your instruments, and anything else you'll need, provided that the weather holds if a second trip is necessary. A steriliser, perhaps."

"Don't talk rubbish," he said irritably. "There's no electric current . . ." And then he said, "There's only one thing to be done. They'll have to send a party in to them by land. They can fly in to Lake Pedder, can't they? Well, it can't be more than thirty miles from there."

I shook my head. "I doubt if they'd make Lake Pedder," I said. "Not with all this low cloud. It's in the middle of the mountains." I turned to the sergeant. "I think they ought to start a land party, though. How long would it take them to get through?"

He rubbed his chin. "They can get a truck as far as Kallista," he said thoughtfully. "Then there's a track to the Gordon River—that would be how they'd go. That's about twenty miles. After that, it might be about another forty miles over the mountains and through the bush to reach the Lewis River." He paused in thought. "I'd say it might take a land party four days," he said.

I asked the doctor, "Would they be alive in four days' time?"

"The girl will," he said. "From what you say, her appendix is subsiding. That often happens. She'd probably be able to walk out by then."

"What about Captain Pascoe?"

He was silent. We all stood looking at each other.

At last I said, "Well, that's the position. Hobart are coming on the air again at half past eight. They're going to send out an Auster with a doctor to try and get through; if they do they'll try to land him in the way I said. But I don't think they'll make it over the mountains, in this cloud. And they've not got the range to go by the south coast."

"Who's the doctor?" he asked.

The sergeant said, "It would be Dr. Parkinson. He does air trips for them now and then. Did one last year, to Maria Island."

"Well, why can't they fly up here and take on more petrol, and then fly down the coast from here?"

"They've got to get here, for one thing," I said. "They'd have to go pretty well to Launceston to avoid the mountains, and then due west another sixty miles against the wind. It'd be a three-hour flight before they could be here to start the job, in an Auster. From what the Met say this clear patch is only going to last about three hours."

He stood in silence before us. "I don't want you to think that I'm afraid of jumping out there," he said at last. "That doesn't sound too bad. It's what comes after that that I don't like. I can't see any hope of a successful operation, in that place. And if I operate and then he dies, just think what the papers will say!"

It seemed to me that it was time to be brutal, and I was getting a bit tired of this. "The papers will be on to this already, by this time," I said. "You'd better think what they will say if you refuse to go, and then he dies."

He stood there biting his lip.

"We're all in a bit of a jam over this," I said. "You, most of all, perhaps. We'd better go through the motions of doing the best we can."

"There's another way to look at it," the sergeant said. "I know the chance is that you won't be able to save him, everything against you as it is. But you might save him. He might recover. Just think of what the papers would say then."

He stood irresolute. "I'll add a bit to that," I said. "I'll give you a good break with the Press. I'll tell them you insisted on going to do what you could, at the risk of your own life."

He looked up at me. "You'd tell them that? Even if he dies?"

"I will," I said. "Especially if he dies."

He still hesitated. "All my other patients . . ." he said. "There's no telling when I could get back from the Lewis River."

The sergeant asked, "You got anything urgent? Babies coming down, or anything of that?"

"Not exactly . . . But I can't just run out and leave the practice."

"The district nurse is here," the sergeant said. "And there's plenty of doctors in Devonport, come out in an emergency."

"I suppose so. If I went I'd have to take an awful lot of things with me. Some of them in bottles—liquids. They'd all get broken, wouldn't they?"

"We'll just have to do our best," I said. "That's all we can do. Pack them with a lot of padding in an old suit-case, and see what we can do."

He stood there silent, and I guessed that he was trying to think up a few more objections. It was time to cut him short. "Well, that's all fixed, then," I said positively. "I

30

think you've made the right decision. Look, I'm going out to the aerodrome now to look over the machine. I'll be back in the police station at half past eight, to hear what Hobart has to say. You'd better meet us there then. There's not much time to lose, because this clear weather isn't going to last. Have all your stuff down at the police station at half past eight, and we'll make a quick getaway while the sun shines. That's in fifty minutes' time." I moved towards the door, and the sergeant followed me. "See you then."

In the car on our way out to the aerodrome, I asked the sergeant, "He does do surgery?"

"Well, yes," he replied. "He hasn't done much since he's been here, because there's not been much to do. All the motor accidents, they go to Devonport. We haven't got a hospital here, you see. Derek Hepworth, he fell off a roof about six months ago and broke his leg, and the doctor set that all right. He's a Bachelor of Surgery."

"Has he done any operations since he came here? An appendicitis, or anything like that?"

He shook his head. "Not that I know about. Anything like that would go to Devonport."

I was worried. "Look, Sergeant," I said. He turned to me. "Look, stop the car a minute. Just park here." And when he had done so, I said, "What do you really think about all this, yourself?"

"I don't like it," he said flatly. "I don't think he wants to do a fractured skull—at the Lewis River or anywhere else."

"I don't think he does," I said. "This is his first practice, isn't it?"

"That's right."

I bit my lip. "He must have done a fractured skull or two, in hospital."

"Aye," said the sergeant. "But that's different to doing it upon the kitchen table at the Lewis River."

"Is there any other doctor we could get? Anyone more experienced?"

"We'd have to try in Devonport," he said. "Dr. Simpson—he might be the most likely. He's a good surgeon, and he's not so old. He still goes ski-ing. But whether he could drop everything and come away at five minutes' notice—that I wouldn't know. He does a lot of surgery. He might have two or three lined up to be operated on this morning—maybe some as urgent as Captain Pascoe. It's just a chance if you could get a man like that to come."

"By the time we got him here, Dr. Parkinson could have flown up from Hobart. He's all set to go. But either way we lose about three hours."

"That's so."

He evidently wasn't going to help me much; he had nothing constructive to suggest. If a decision had to be made quickly, and apparently it had, the onus rested squarely upon me. I was rushing into this, bullying an unwilling and inexperienced young doctor into doing an operation which he clearly felt to be beyond his capacity. I was doing this purely on the score of time, because Johnnie Pascoe had a fractured skull and there was no time to get a better surgeon. But what if I was wrong? What if the weather forecasters were wrong, as they so often were? What if it should be a brilliant, sunny day, all day, with a light, gentle breeze that would permit a proper landing on that strip?

I looked up, and the sky was blue to the west right down to the horizon, with every promise of a brilliantly fine day.

I made up my mind. "I'll fly Dr. Turnbull in," I said. "I'll land him if I can, and get back here as quick as I can. While I'm away, we'll try and get a better surgeon here, and if it keeps fine, then I'll make a second trip and fly him in as well. That's what we'll do."

"Aye," said the sergeant, "that's a good idea." We went on to the aerodrome.

The aerodrome at Buxton is a square grass field only about a mile from the town, about six hundred yards long in any direction. No scheduled air service flies to it because there isn't the demand; sheep graze on it from time to time and have to be herded off before a landing. There is one corrugated iron hangar with a tattered wind-sock on the gable, capable of housing four or five small aeroplanes. This hangar had a board on it, PASCOE FLYING SERVICES PTY. LTD., rather in need of a new coat of paint.

Billy Monkhouse had got the Auster out and was running it up outside the hangar in the strong, gusty wind; he had two boys to help him, hanging on to the wing struts to prevent it blowing away. The conditions were not good for flying a light aeroplane, and I hoped that my hand hadn't lost its cunning. I had a short talk with the sergeant and sent him back to the police station to ring up Dr. Simpson in Devonport and see if there was any chance that he could come to help us; the ground engineer would run me back into the town.

I moved over and stood by the wing tip of the Auster in the cold, bleak wind. Presently the ground engineer throttled down; I looked at him in enquiry and he raised one thumb. I moved to the door as he got out. "I'll do about three landings and bring her in," I said. "Get the boys to stay on the wing struts while I taxi out down-wind."

I sat in the machine for several minutes, trying to accustom myself to the size again after years of flying air-liners. There my seat when the machine was on the ground was nearly twenty feet up; a landing at that height

33

was a good landing. Here it was about three feet from the ground. I sat there savouring it all. The horizon came just *so* upon the windscreen; that was how it must be when landing. The grass looked *so*. With a glance down I could actually see one wheel upon the ground; I did not think that that would be a help, but it was possible. There was the throttle and the mixture control, there the flaps. I was glad to note that the machine had navigation lights and a blind-flying panel of instruments; that was a benefit that I had hardly dared to hope for.

Presently I waved the chocks away and nodded to the engineer, and we began to taxi out down-wind at walking pace.

I turned her in the strong, unpleasant wind, waved the boys away, and took her off at once. She was just like all the Austers that I had flown before, lightly loaded and so wallowing a bit in the wind turbulence, but light on the controls and easy to fly. I did one circuit, for the time was short, and came in for a landing. I pulled down the lever for a little flap but she was coming down so vertically that I eased it slowly back again. In that strong wind I brought her in at fifty, and we came down a flight path that must have been close on forty-five degrees to the ground, moving forward very slowly. I rounded off too high, gave her a little throttle and floated on till the far hedge looked about right on the windscreen, and then cut it as she rolled on to the grass.

I did another circuit and another landing. The third time I brought her down on to the grass tail up at a very slow speed over the ground, and touched the wheels. I shot a quick glance down; they were well and truly on the ground and only moving forward a few miles an hour. I throttled very carefully a little more, and we were motionless, flying at about a quarter throttle, tail well up. I held her on the ground like that for a few seconds; then a gust

34

came and I jammed everything forward, and took off again.

I brought her round, landed just outside the hangar where the boys were waiting to catch the wing struts, and taxied her in. It was a quarter past eight. I stopped the motor and got out of the cabin on to the ground, and helped to push her into the hangar. It was too rough a day to leave her standing unattended on the tarmac.

The break in the clouds now was practically overhead; to the west there was blue sky with a little light cirrus. The sun, of course, was in the north-east and low down, so that it was still overcast and cold, and the wind was no less strong. I was very conscious that I had had no breakfast, but there was no time for that. I got into the old Ford with Billy Monkhouse and he started it, and drove out on the road towards the town.

"With any luck we'll get the doctor in to them this morning," I said. "If this weather holds till dinner time, we'll be right."

Chapter Two

When we got to the police station it was a few minutes after half past eight, and Hobart was already speaking to Mrs. Hoskins at the Lewis River. Dr. Turnbull was there, dressed and looking very sour. I listened with one side of my mind to what was coming out of the loudspeaker, but crossed directly to him. I said in a low tone, "I've been thinking about what you said this morning, Doctor. Would you like it if we could get in somebody to help you at the Lewis River? There's just the chance, of course, that this clear weather may last longer than we think. It's possible that I could put you down there, and then make a second trip, fly somebody else in. There might be time enough for that, you see."

The loudspeaker was saying, "Well, it's a lovely day here now, Hobart. The sun's shining and everything. The wind's still strong, though. It looks rough out at sea, and it's breaking very hard at the mouth of the river. I wouldn't want to see Don try it in the boat."

The doctor said, "It's a job that needs some help, somebody who knows what to do. The district nurse wouldn't be able to land like that . . . There just isn't anyone round here."

"How would it be if I asked Hobart to fly Dr. Parkinson up here? I'd have to fly you in first, while the weather holds good. But by the time I got back he might be here, and then if it's still clear I could fly him in to help you."

His face lightened. I knew what he was thinking as well as if he had told me, that in that case Parkinson would do the operation. It would take him an hour or two to get the

patient ready, or he could spin it out so long, and then there was a very good chance he wouldn't have to do it at all. He would be the junior surgeon, and would stand by to assist Parkinson.

"That's quite a good idea," he said. "I know Parkinson. He's got a great deal more experience than I have, with head injuries."

"Has he?" I enquired. "I don't know anything about him, except that he's a surgeon and he's volunteered to go upon this job."

"He does a lot of this flying work," he told me. "I don't say he's the best in Hobart, by a long chalk. But he's got a great deal of experience of injuries."

The loudspeaker was saying, "Well, Hobart, it's still cloudy over the mountains. It often is like that, you know. Sunny here, and then cloudy up against the hills."

"How are the patients, Mrs. Hoskins? Over."

"Betty's easier, Hobart. There's no doubt of that. I think she's sleeping now. Captain Pascoe, he seems much about the same. He seemed to be cold, so I filled the hot water bags about half an hour ago."

"Thank you, Mrs. Hoskins. I'm going to call Buxton now, but I want you to stay listening in case I want to speak to you again. 7 PC, this is 7 HT calling. If you are listening, 7 PC, will you please come in. Over."

The sergeant touched the switch. "This is 7 PC answering 7 HT. Over to you."

"Thank you, Buxton. If Captain Clarke is there, will you ask him to speak? Over."

I took the microphone. "This is Clarke speaking. Over."

"What's the weather like with you?"

"It's clearing," I said. "Quite clear over to the west, cloud still to the east. Wind about thirty knots. What's it like with you? Over."

"We've got low cloud here still, ceiling about eight hundred feet, mountains well covered. Wind 250 degrees, twenty knots."

"Not much hope of getting through from your end?"

"Not from here. How is it with you?"

"I can make it," I said. "Dr. Turnbull here, he's going to try and jump out as I fly slowly across the strip. He'll make it if anybody can. There is one thing, though. Dr. Turnbull would like help if he can get it, with the operation. Could you fly Dr. Parkinson up here while I'm away? Then if the weather holds I'd fly him down and land him the same way, making a second trip. Over."

"Hold on, Buxton." There was a long pause while they consulted at their end. I stood holding the microphone and looking out of the window. There was a hard brightness in the weather that didn't look too good; it was sunny now, but there was no warmth in it. Hobart came on again. "This is 7 HT. That's okay, Captain Clarke. We're going to fly Dr. Parkinson up to you in the Proctor, leaving in about half an hour. It should be about two hours' flight, so that you can expect him at eleven o'clock, or soon after. Over to you."

"That's good," I said. "I should be back by then, or not much later. Have you got the latest Met report?"

"Not very satisfactory," he said. "There's another depression coming up. They think it may clamp down again about midday on the west coast."

"We'll have to do the best we can," I said. "I can fly round the coast from here at sea level. It's just a question then of being able to get up to the strip."

I asked to speak to Mrs. Hoskins and they put her on. I told her that we were coming and that I hoped to have the doctor with her in about an hour and a half. I told her that we would fly over and drop the doctor's suitcase first, and I asked her to pick a soft spot of turf or heather close beside the airstrip and pin a sheet down on it with stones, so that we could see where to drop.

Then I handed the microphone back to the sergeant, and we were ready to go. The doctor had a medium-sized fibre suitcase with him, heavily laden. "I packed a lot of towels round the bottles," he said. "I think they should be all right." He was wearing a woollen overcoat but underneath that he was quite sensibly dressed, in ski-ing trousers and ski boots, with a roll-necked sweater.

We left the police station and drove out to the aerodrome again with the ground engineer. The sun was bright and the sky blue so that everything looked cheerful, though the wind was still very strong for a light aircraft. We drove up to the hangar and got out. Before we pushed the aircraft out I crossed to the ground engineer's desk and laid out the course upon my map, marking it with a thick pencil line; in that weather I could fly it direct. It was about a hundred and fifteen miles, course 178 degrees magnetic, practically due south. It was going to take us all of an hour and a half to get there in that wind, and the machine had fuel for less than four hours. We shouldn't have much time in hand for messing about. I studied the map again. There were mountains up to four thousand feet along my route; I could dodge them by flying down the Arthur River to the coast but that would add another twenty-five miles to the distance. In that clear weather it would be better to go over them.

I folded the map with the airstrip data sheet and put them both in the diagonal map pocket of my old flying coat. Then I took the doctor to the aircraft and sat him in it with the suitcase on his knee, strapping him in with the safety belt. I showed him what he had to do. "We'll drop the suitcase first," I said. "When I give you the word, just open the door a little, like this, and hold it balanced on the edge, like this. Then when I tell you, just

39

push it through and let go." I paused. "I shall go up and we'll make another circuit then. While we're doing that, undo your belt and get out of your coat—I'll drop that to you afterwards. I'll come right down on to the strip and hold her there while you get out. You'll have to make it snappy, because I shan't be able to hold her there for long. But you'll have time enough, I should think. Anyway, we'll see. We might do a dummy run first, and see how it goes, and then make another circuit before you get out."

He licked his lips, and nodded. I was sorry for him, because he'd obviously never had to do anything like that before. "You'll find it quite easy to get out," I said.

He pushed the door open, lifted and turned his body, put his foot down on the metal step that hung below, and got out. "That's easy enough," he said bravely. "It'll be easier without this coat."

I nodded. "You won't have any difficulty."

He got back into the machine and I gave him the suitcase to hold upon his knee, and then we pushed the machine out into the wind. On the tarmac I got in beside the doctor, closed the door, and nodded to the ground engineer. While the two boys held the wing struts he swung the little propeller for me and the engine caught; I let her run for a minute and then ran her up, trying the magnetos. Everything was in order. I nodded to him and they pulled the chocks away. With the boys upon the struts I taxied out a little way across wind, turned into wind, waved them away, and took the machine off.

In the air it was very bumpy, of course. The doctor sat gripping his suitcase, tense and obviously anxious. I turned on course and held the machine on the climb because not far away were mountains that we had to cross. They lay across our path, snow-covered in the sunlight. To the east the cloud hung down upon them still, to the west all was clear with sunlight and blue sky. I pulled out

40

my map and set to work to identify the peaks, and the course that I must make good over the land. We had about fifteen degrees of drift.

My business finished, I turned to the doctor. "Pretty, isn't it?" I said.

He lifted his head and looked around, relaxing a little. "Yes, it is," he said. "Awfully pretty." And then he said, "You know, this is the first time I've ever been up."

I was startled. I suppose I should have thought of that. On the airline, of course, it is common to go down the cabin and find passengers who have never flown before. I generally pause and chat to them, ask them where they are going, let them talk a little, offer them a cup of coffee and tell the hostess to bring it. It had simply never entered my head that this doctor, young and active as he was, was totally unused to flying. With my mind set on other things, upon the need to get a doctor to the Lewis River, I had treated him pretty rough.

I dared not weaken him with any sympathy, however. "You've missed a lot," I said. The thing to do now was to get him interested. "Do you sail a boat?"

"Yes," he replied. "I do that a good bit. We've got a sailing dinghy at home." I remembered that his home was on the Huon River, a deep inlet of the sea to the south of Hobart.

"This is just like sailing a boat," I said. There was no dual control in the machine, for the ground engineer had taken it out. I took his hand and put it on the stick beneath my own, and flew the machine like that for a time in the rough weather, so that he could get the feel, explaining the motions to him as I had so often done before upon the first flight of a pupil. In a quarter of an hour he was doing it on his own, and seemed to have relaxed.

It got bitterly cold. We had to go up to about five

thousand to get over the hills, and it must have been well below freezing there. I had my leather coat and helmet and a muffler and even so I was cold; my feet chilled and my hands blue. In his normal overcoat he must have been much colder. However, over Macquarie Harbour I started to let down and it got warmer. We came to the coast and flew on southwards at a thousand feet; it was still sunny but the sea was grey and rough, and we were crabbing along with a big drift.

I identified Mount Osmond, and began looking for the Lewis River. Several small rivers run down from the mountains to the sea in that part of the country, and we were uncertain for a few minutes which it was; they all looked equally impossible for a boat to enter. Then Turnbull saw the house, and pointed it out to me. There was no other house upon the coast for thirty miles, so this one had to be it.

It lay in the middle of a sort of undulating moor. Part of this moor round about the house had been cut like a peat bog over a fairly wide area; here there were one or two pools of water, and tumbledown wooden structures, and a few concrete tanks, and pipes running about the landscape. That would be the tin working, where they washed the metal out of the surface soil. The house was a white wooden building, single storey, standing in a fold of the land for shelter, with a little stream beside it and a kitchen garden. As we circled round, a woman came out on the step and waved to us.

Then I saw the wreckage of the Auster Pascoe had flown in, and that led me to the airstrip. Used as I was to proper runways, I could hardly believe my eyes at first. It was difficult to see because the button grass was thin upon the ground around it, and so this thing looked more like a little fortuitous line of soil where no vegetation grew. I brought the machine round and dropped off height to fly along it and have a good look. It was no better than a little bit of cart track that led nowhere. That was what the data sheet had told me, of course, but I suppose I hadn't really believed that it could be so bad.

I went up again and circled round. The woman had come out of the house with what looked like a bundle of washing in her arms and she was doing something a bit to one side of the south end of the strip. I circled closer to see what she was up to, and saw that she was putting up a windsock on a little flagstaff; Rhys-Davids must have given her that. It was a help, definitely, for there was nothing else to tell you the wind direction except the run of the seas. When she got it up it stood out stiff and horizontal from the mast, making an angle of about seventy degrees to the strip.

She was now laying a sheet out upon the ground, pinning it down with stones. I turned to the doctor. "I'm going to do a dummy run over that sheet," I said. "Don't put the suitcase out this time. Next time."

I brought her round and headed into wind over the sheet, flying at fifty or sixty on the clock and throttling to lose height. It was turbulent, of course, but not too bad; we passed fairly slowly over the sheet ten feet up and I knew that I could get her slower than that. I put on power and went round again, thinking that I should have to watch for the increased drag on the machine as he opened the door, and not let that fox me. "We'll put it out this time," I said. "Wait till I tell you and then open the door a bit and hold it balanced on the edge, ready to shove it out. Don't drop it till I say."

I took a longer run-up this time, to give him plenty of time. He got the door open a bit and seemed to have some trouble with it; it was hinged at the front side, of course, and for the first time a doubt flitted through my mind. It seemed to require a good deal of pushing to get it open, and when the trailing edge was standing a few inches proud the effect on the machine was very noticeable. However, he got the suitcase down on to the sill and partly out, and then glanced up at me and nodded.

I brought her in more slowly this time, and lower, flying at fifty minus. She still had plenty of control and we were going quite slowly over the ground; I could have run pretty well as fast. I reckoned he would take a little time, so when we were fifty yards from the sheet and about four feet up I shouted, "Shove it out now!"

He had a great struggle to do so. The case was only a foot deep, but he had the greatest difficulty in opening the door so far as that, and the machine yawed a bit, and I had to open up the throttle a little. I had to keep my eyes on what I was doing, and I could only sense what was going on beside me. He was working in an awkward attitude, of course, sitting down and strapped in. We sailed over the sheet while he was still struggling and I went on as slowly as I could, four or five feet up, intent upon the flying. Finally I think he levered the door open with the suitcase and managed to get it out; it fell on the low scrub a hundred yards beyond the sheet. I shoved the throttle forwards and went up again.

I turned to him. "I'm sorry about that door. I didn't think that it would be so difficult, at this slow speed. I ought to have lashed the case on outside somehow. Then we could have cut the lashing."

He looked down at it as we circled round. "I think it fell pretty soft," he said. "Anyway, it didn't come open."

I was very worried about the door now. "I'm going to make another dummy run," I said. "I'm going to put her on the ground if I can, and hold her there for a few seconds. While I'm doing that—when I tell you—just see if you can open that door wide enough to get out. But don't get out this time. Just try the door, and see."

44

I brought her round again; the woman had gone to the suitcase and was examining it. The ground on each side of the strip fell away most smoothly at the south end. Here the air turbulence would be least, and I made my run-up on that. As I approached the strip that lay crossways before me I brought her in more and more slowly, flying by the feel of the drop of the tail behind me. Five feet, three feet, one foot up; we crossed the near edge of the strip and I put her on the ground, throttled a bit more and put the stick forward a little. We were motionless on the ground now, with the tail well up and a good bit of engine power. I shouted. "All right, try that door!"

He lifted the catch and shoved it open. The blast of the slipstream was strong upon it, and to make things worse I had to open up the throttle to counter the increasing drag. I shot a glance at him as he struggled. With one hand he could only open it a few inches; with both hands only an inch or two more. With a sick feeling in my throat I realised that we were up against something here that I had not reckoned on. With all my skill in putting down upon that strip, the doctor might not be able to get out of the cabin of the aeroplane.

I shouted to him to shut the door, and took off again. When we were well up and circling, I turned to him. "This is my fault," I said. "Do you think you'll be able to push it far enough open to get out?"

"I could get out all right if it wasn't for the door," he said. "We weren't moving at all. It's the wind holding it or something."

"It's the slipstream from the prop," I said. "I have to keep the motor going pretty hard."

"If you could stop it for a moment," he said, "I'm sure I could get out."

I shook my head. "I can't do that." I sat there weighing up the position. There was a red lever at the door

45

hinge; it was there for the purpose of jettisoning the door as an emergency exit. If I pulled that down the hinge pins would be withdrawn and the door would fall out and fly away, leaving a great empty space where it had been. If I did that while we were flying it would probably hit the tail, and we might both be killed. If I told him to do it while I held her on the ground it might fall away safely or we might tie something on to it to keep it from the tail— my scarf, perhaps. Then he could get out. But after that I should have to take off with just a great big hole where the door had been, and fly her home like that.

Would that Auster fly safely without the door in place? I had never flown one like that, nor had I heard of anyone else doing so. It might be quite all right. Probably it would. I studied the fuselage. It was a little narrower at the front end of the door by the instrument panel than it was at the rear end, in way of our seats; the fuselage tapered forward to the engine. That meant, with the door removed, a great blast of air would come into the cabin as I flew, building up a pressure. I turned and scrutinised the structure behind me. The main frame and the wings would probably be all right, but the big sheet of perspex that roofed the rear end of the cabin might well go, and take with it the fabric covering of the rear fuselage. The cover of the fin might go. I did not think that the machine would be unflyable, but it might be very much damaged. Anything that was going to happen would probably happen at a very low altitude, just as I was taking off. That wouldn't be so good, for there would be no time to think, no time for a recovery of any control lost.

On the other hand, I could put the doctor on the ground, and Johnnie Pascoe had a fractured skull. And it might all be perfectly all right, no damage to the aeroplane at all.

I bit my lip and went on circling round. This was my

46

fault, fairly and squarely. I was the one who was supposed to know about aeroplanes, and I had boobed, fallen down on the job, with all my years of experience behind me. In all those years of flying I had had things happen to me in the air from time to time, sufficient to warn me; I had always had height, and luck; and perhaps skill, and I had always got away with it. This time I might not do so, for there would be no height. It would come at fifty feet or less, a great cracking noise behind me, followed by a jammed elevator or a jammed rudder, no landing possible ahead, no control, no time to try anything, no time even to think before we hit the ground, the engine came back into my lap, the fire broke out. Too bad on Sheila and my children, and I thought what she had said, "Don't go and buy it yourself, Ronnie . . ."

All this passed very quickly through my mind. The doctor said after a moment, "It's sitting like this makes it difficult to shove it open. I think if I was getting out and put my backside against it, I could squeeze through."

"Do you think you could?"

"I could try."

I glanced around, and now there was a new development. It was bright and sunny where we flew, but over to the west I saw fresh cloud low down upon the sea at the horizon. I glanced at my watch; it was five minutes to eleven; before long we must be on our way home or we should be out of fuel. The Met had been quite right. More bad weather was coming up; it would be overcast here in an hour and probably low cloud and rain after that. There would be little prospect of a second trip today.

"All right," I said. "Let's try it. Undo your belt and take off your coat. But look, Alec. Be ready to hang on and get back into the machine if I tell you. I shan't be able to stay down on the ground for very long."

It was the first time I had called him by his Christian name.

I thought for a moment as I turned downwind if I dare throttle back upon the ground for a few seconds while he got out. The windsock stood straight and stiff and horizontal from the mast, and the air was very bumpy. The wind was still at least thirty miles an hour, perhaps more; it was around the stalling speed of the machine. I could not depend upon the woman to help me; for one thing, there was no means of communicating with her. If I throttled back, if once I let the tail go down, the machine would lift in the wind and blow over backwards. I put the thought out of my mind, and turned on final.

He was out of his coat now, and ready to try it. I thought as I brought her in that I had two things now to think about at the same time, the aircraft and the doctor. Hitherto the safety of the aircraft had been my main concern, but now I had to think about the safety of the doctor and watch what he was doing. Still, in the previous run the aircraft had been pretty stable on the ground . . . I was uneasily aware, as I brought her in towards the strip, that this was getting near the limit. The chance that I had taken in putting this little aircraft on the ground across the strip and holding her there had proved to be a reasonable one. Now, however, things were getting dangerous. I was asking a lot of this young doctor, though perhaps he didn't know it. I could quite easily kill him.

Five feet—slower now—three feet—it was bumpier than ever. A little slower—one foot—and she was on the ground and motionless with the tail up. It was more turbulent than it had been before; I could not hold her so for very long. I shouted, "Try it now!"

He lifted his legs underneath him and screwed his body round. The seating side by side was very close in that small aeroplane; to get out backwards he had to put his head pretty well in my lap; my hand upon the throttle was in his way, and I dare not let that go. I raised my elbow high and he put his head under my arm, and at the same time I think he pressed the door back with his body and put one leg out. I dared not look what he was doing because as the door opened things were happening to the machine; I had to keep my eyes ahead, my left hand delicately on the stick, my right hand delicately making tiny movements with the throttle in spite of his head under my arm jerking my elbow. This was getting very dangerous indeed.

He forced his body backwards and opened the door further, and put his left leg down and found the step. The door was now more than a foot open and the effect on the machine was very bad. Elevator control seemed much reduced, she needed quite a bit of rudder, and I had to open up the throttle making things still more difficult for him. All this I did without thinking, instinctively, only conscious that this aeroplane was in a bad way. He forced the door still further open with his backside, searching for the ground with his right foot.

Then the gust came. I knew that it was coming; I suppose I saw it blowing the rough herbage. I opened up the throttle a trifle, I think, but I didn't dare to put her nose down further for fear of hitting the propeller on the ground. I shot a glance at him, half out of the machine and searching for the ground with his foot, and in that instant while my eyes were averted the gust came down on us more strongly, lifting the machine. By the time I got my eyes back to the windscreen we were five feet up.

There was only one thing to do then, and that was to go off again. I gave her a little more throttle and put the nose down a little more. The doctor was half out of the machine, his stomach on the doorsill, but he still had his left foot on the outside step. I said as quietly as I could, "Get back in again, Alec."

I flew on straight towards the sea, heading in to wind, at a low altitude, flying as slowly as I dared to make less pressure on the door. The machine handled like a pig, the door held wedged well open by his body. I hooked my right hand under his shoulder to help him struggle into the machine again, but the pressure of the air upon the door was pinching his legs. I shot a glance forward, and then leaned across him and forced the door open with my right hand, freeing his legs. With that help he managed to struggle back into the cabin and close the door; the control became normal again, and I put her into a slow climbing turn.

"You all right?" I asked, metaphorically wiping the sweat from my brow.

"*I'm* all right," he said. "I could have got out easily but for this damn door."

A shadow passed across the machine and it grew suddenly cold. I looked up, and a cloud was passing across the sun. It was only a small, isolated cloud and the sun would be shining again in a minute, but others were coming up from the horizon, now dark and menacing. The weather would not last more than an hour longer at the most; in any case we should not have fuel to stay so long. I glanced at my watch and was surprised to see how late it was. In five minutes we must be on our way back to Buxton, or we wouldn't get there.

I circled for a minute or so, torn with indecision. I could land him if I jettisoned the door. When I took off again, without the door . . . I turned round again and looked at the perspex sheet, the fabric covering of the rear fuselage. It looked terribly frail, accustomed as I was now to a large, all metal airliner. It would be dicy. With a heavy heart I came to my decision, wondering if this was cowardice or good sense. It certainly wouldn't help to have another crash, perhaps another badly battered pilot. There comes a point, I thought, when cowardice merges with good sense. I turned to the doctor beside me. "This isn't any good," I said. "We'll have to go back to Buxton and try something else."

"I'm quite ready to have another go," he replied. "Let's try it again."

He didn't realise the risks that I was running, of course. He didn't realise that our lives had been balanced on a knife-edge of danger. When I was a younger man I wouldn't have cared two hoots for that, of course, but now I was forty-six years old. For many years as a prudent airline captain I had avoided dangers, and to do so was now second nature to me. The sort of flying that I had been doing in the last twenty minutes cut clean across everything that I knew to be right. Now it was time to pull up and stop behaving like a crazy teen-ager.

I shook my head. "It's just not good enough. I'm sorry, but we'll have to go back."

He resigned himself. "I suppose there isn't any way of picking up that suitcase?" he enquired. "It's got all my instruments in it."

I said, "I'm afraid there's not," and set a course for Buxton, angry and mortified, feeling that I had failed. We flew in silence after that. Cloud was forming again over the mountain tops so that I had to deviate and go towards the coast, flying over the shoulders close beneath the cloud to make the distance as short as possible, the coastal plain on my left hand. Finally we came off the mountains and the flat land to the north lay before us. The petrol gauge was jumping on the zero stop, which meant we had about two gallons left, but there were flat paddocks now in front of us. I started to let down, found Buxton, and came in to land. The Proctor did not seem to have arrived from

Hobart yet. I put down just by the hangar and taxied straight forward into wind; the boys came out to catch the struts and I taxied her right inside.

When I killed the motor we sat motionless for a moment in the silence. "I'm sorry we couldn't make it," I said at last. "I thought we'd have been able to. It was worth trying."

He said, "I'm sorry I was such a fool about the door." He hesitated, and then said, "I'm a bit new to this."

"You were all right," I said. "It was too difficult for anyone."

Monkhouse, the ground engineer, came up to the machine as I opened the cabin door on my side to get out. "No go?" he enquired.

I shook my head. "I put her down, but she needed quite a bit of throttle. With the slipstream on the door the doctor couldn't get out."

He nodded slowly. "You didn't jettison the door?"

I shook my head. "I thought of that, but I didn't like to try it. Tell me, will these things fly without the door in place?"

" 'Course they will," he said. "Captain Pascoe took up a parachutist in this one last year, time of the Pageant. We flew it hours and hours without the door. They fly all right."

I bit my lip. "I didn't know that. I was afraid to jettison it."

"It's an airworthiness requirement for all sorts of aircraft," he observed. "Anything that can be jettisoned, the aeroplane's got to fly safely without it. These fly all right without the door."

I got out of the machine in silence. Now that he mentioned it, the airworthiness requirement struck a faint chord of memory. I have never been a test pilot, never had anything to do with flying of that sort. I had never had to fly an aeroplane with an escape hatch open, and I had never bothered my head about it. I should have done, perhaps. Because I hadn't, Johnnie Pascoe now might die.

I walked a few steps out on to the tarmac. The sun had gone and lingered as only a faint indication over to the north-east. It was overcast and grey and bleak, the cloud ceiling at about fifteen hundred feet, and descending. The wind was much as it had been before, but in the west it looked dark with more rain coming. I went back into the hangar and walked round the machine to where the doctor was getting out. "Mr. Monkhouse tells me this machine will fly all right without the door in place," I said. "Would you be willing to go out again, at once, and have another stab at it?"

"You mean, take the door right off?" he asked. "I wouldn't fall out, would I?"

The question was a reasonable one, because the door comprised practically the entire side of the cabin; in that little aeroplane it was an enormous hole. "You wouldn't fall out," I said. "You're strapped in with your safety belt. But I'm afraid it may be cold for you."

"I don't mind that . . ." He looked up at me. "Now we've started on this thing we'd better see it through. Most of my equipment's in that suitcase, so I can't do much here. We'll have to be quick, though, won't we? Because of the weather?"

I nodded. "I'll get the machine refuelled right away." I turned and spoke to Monkhouse, and then I asked him, "Is there anything to eat here? I've had no breakfast." I was hungry, cold, and getting very tired. I had been up all night, and I had done a lot of flying since I had slept last.

"There's my sandwiches for lunch," he said. "Over on the bench there, with a thermos of coffee. You can have

53

those." I protested a little, but he said, "I'll go and get some more when you've taken off."

I offered to share his lunch with the doctor, but he refused; the vicar's wife had given him breakfast before we started. I stood by the bench eating mutton sandwiches and drinking coffee from the thermos, thinking what an awful fool I was. I, the great airline captain, the self-acclaimed expert who had barged in to take charge of this affair, and put up a black right away. Even Billy Monkhouse, ground engineer in a pipsqueak show like this, even he had known the fundamental fact I had forgotten in my arrogance and pride.

Tired as I was, the only thing now was to go on with it. Johnnie Pascoe would have had a doctor with him now but for my ignorance. The food and the hot coffee were putting new life into me, and I braced myself. I could repair the damage I had done. If we got off at once, we could still beat the weather down to the Lewis River, though I might have a sticky time getting back.

It took about ten minutes to fill up the aircraft with about fifteen gallons of petrol from the old, hand-operated pump, and to put in a gallon of oil. Then we got in again. I saw that the doctor's safety belt was properly done up, for there was little else now to retain him in the cabin in bumpy conditions. "I feel a bit like the young man on the flying trapeze," he said.

"Quite happy?" I asked.

He nodded. "I'll be able to get out all right this time."

"Okay," I said. "Let's go." I nodded to the ground engineer and he swung the prop. I ran her up a bit and tested the magnetos, and then taxied out on to the aerodrome with a boy on each wing strut and turned her into wind for the take off.

I lifted my eyes to look around after my pre-flight check, and saw a car drive in off the road and up to the hangar. It crossed my mind that it might possibly be Dr. Parkinson who was supposed to be flying up to us in the Proctor, and I paused for a moment, watching. Then I saw it was a taxi by the sign over the windscreen, and the door opened and a woman got out. Billy Monkhouse could deal with her, I thought, and I nodded to the boys, opened up the throttle, and took off.

It was bad in the air, very turbulent, the cloud ceiling down to about twelve hundred with a clammy coldness of approaching rain. With virtually no side to our cabin the grey wisps seemed to come right into the aircraft, and perhaps they did, for the map grew soggy in my hands. I had to deviate towards the coast much more than previously, and as we went the cloud forced us lower and lower. By the time we got to Trial Harbour I was flying down the coast at about seven hundred feet in the increasing murk. I knew then that it would be touch and go if we could get up to the tiny airstrip at the Lewis River, which was five hundred and thirty feet above sea level. If we did, there would be nothing to spare.

I found the entrance to Macquarie Harbour, crossed it to the south shore, and flew round Cape Sorell, the top of which was in the cloud. I checked the time, and did a bit of navigation, working with one hand upon the map upon my knee. It was another sixty-eight miles to the Lewis River, and we were making good about eighty-seven miles an hour over the ground. I calculated in my head. If we were doing ninety we would have forty-five minutes to go, but it was three per cent slower, so call it forty-seven minutes. I pencilled the time upon my map off Cape Sorell and the E.T.A. Lewis River, and went on, keeping the coast in sight upon my left. Ten minutes later it began to rain.

I must have known that it was pretty hopeless then, but I went on. It was my fault that Johnnie Pascoe hadn't got

55

the doctor with him, and there was always the faint chance that the rain might stop and the clouds break when we got to the Lewis River. We went on down the coast with visibility less than a mile, and as we went the cloud forced us lower till we were flying at about two hundred feet well out to sea, the coast just visible on our port hand. It was a desolate, deserted coast fringed with black reefs that had a very heavy surf breaking upon them, shooting up in places almost a hundred feet high. If our motor had packed up in that place our chances of survival would have been absolutely nil.

It was raining all the way from Cape Sorell. The water ran off the windscreen on the doctor's side and blew from the edge straight into his lap. In ten minutes he was soaked, but there was nothing we could do about it. We went on, trying to check each river mouth and identify it as we passed. On the west coast of Tasmania, however, the maps are very inaccurate because nobody lives there; we soon lost track of where we were and had to go on till we had run our time.

When we were on our estimated time of arrival we had been flying for an hour and forty-three minutes. We should be a little faster going back, I thought, but the margin on our fuel was short and we had no more than ten minutes in which to find the strip and land the doctor. I approached the coast in the murk well throttled back. It was featureless, fairly low, but the cloud ceiling was only about four hundred feet. There was no sign of any river mouth. I turned right and flew along the coast, getting a bearing of its run; south of the Lewis River it turned sharply east, but here we were still flying on a course of about 160°. We were probably still to the north of it, and I went on southwards, one eye on my watch. Things were getting terribly tight for us.

It began to rain harder than ever, and the visibility

grew worse. I had stopped talking to the doctor, and he to me. The cliffs got higher till their tops were in the cloud; I sat tense and anxious. Then they dipped down, and there was a river entrance between black reefs boiling with surf. It didn't look a bit like the entrance to the Lewis River as I had seen it about three hours before, but it probably was the same, seen from a different viewpoint, under different circumstances. If that were so, the doctor was now within a couple of miles of Johnnie Pascoe.

I flew across the river entrance at a safe distance in case there was a headland sticking out in front of us, and then I turned back and flew across it somewhat closer in. I pulled the little data sheet of the airstrip out of my pocket, that the controller at Essendon had given me. It showed the river entrance. It was probably the same, but it was hard to say. If it were, the course from the entrance to the airstrip would be about 110°.

Over the sea the cloud ceiling was now about three hundred feet. It might be a little higher over the land, I thought; there is usually a hundred feet or so of clear in weather like that. It's only in a calm that the cloud descends on to the ground in the form of fog. I turned westwards and flew out to sea for a couple of miles on the reciprocal course, and then turned in again and flew towards the coast on 110°, climbing into the murk till I could only just see the sea.

The first rocks passed beneath us and I sat tense, ready for anything. We came to the cliff and crossed it, and now button grass was very close beneath my wheels. There was no clear air, or if there was, I was not game to try and find it. With my heart in my mouth I thrust the throttle hard forward, eased back on the stick, and climbed up into the murk. I sat waiting for the crash till the altimeter showed seven hundred feet. Then I relaxed and put her in a slow turn to the right to find the sea again, flying completely blind between the hills.

I said to the doctor, "I'm afraid this is no good, Alec. I think we're right over the Lewis River, but we shan't be able to make it."

He said, "If there was a beach, perhaps I could get out on that."

"I haven't seen one," I replied. He didn't know what he was suggesting, although, as a Tasmanian, perhaps he did. If so, he was just brave and that's all about it. I couldn't have guaranteed my position within ten miles; we might be playing about over some other river, not the Lewis River at all. If I found a level patch where I could put him out as I had tried to on the airstrip, I should be leaving him stranded in quite uninhabited country in the worst weather with no provisions or equipment at all. That wasn't practical.

I started to let down towards the sea when I judged that it was safe, watching the altimeter. "I'm going back," I said. "Back to Buxton. We'll have to wait until this weather moderates again."

We came out at about a hundred and fifty feet over a black, rough sea and started flying northwards. We were going a bit quicker, but the visibility was worse than ever, and it was raining harder. I could only see a few hundred yards; I went on for ten minutes keeping the coast in sight on my right hand, seen dimly through the rain.

Then it suddenly loomed up dead ahead of us; we seemed to be flying straight into a cliff. I flung the machine round in a violent turn to port, and we missed it by about a hundred feet. We were so close that I could see the mutton birds on the rocks; I even fancied I could see their little eyes and their claws. It was as near as that. I steadied on a course westwards, straight out to sea, and pulled out the map. "That was Penguin Head," I said as calmly as I could.

If we went on following the coast like that we should be dead before we got to Buxton. We had practically no fuel for deviations, but they would have to be made. A course of 315° for eighty-six minutes would take us clear of all dangers and would land us ten miles out to sea off the mouth of the Arthur River, with Buxton about sixty miles away downwind to the north-east and all low country in between. I explained the position to the doctor and showed him what I was going to do, and then I started in to fly my compass course about a hundred feet up over the sea.

We were pretty cold and miserable by the time I made my turn, nearly an hour and a half later, and I was getting very worried indeed about the fuel. However, in a few minutes we passed over the beach and went on across an undulating country. The clouds were rather higher here than they had been further south, and we could fly at about seven hundred feet most of the way. We went on at a good speed over the ground, but now the gauge was jumping on the zero stop again. I said to the doctor, "Tell me if you see anything you recognise."

I decided to give it another five minutes, and glanced at my watch. There was still a light rain falling, but we could see more than a mile ahead. At four minutes we came to a weatherboard farmhouse, white-painted. It stood in flat paddocks, and it had a few trees round it as a windbreak. I could probably land here, and when I realised that, I knew that I wanted very much to be down safely on the ground. A line of poles ran from it to a road; I looked again, and saw another set of poles; it was on the telephone. I went into a turn and said to the doctor, "Do you know that place?"

He said, "I'm not sure, but it looks rather like Jeff Duncan's property. If it is, they're patients of mine."

"How far would that be from the aerodrome?"

"I should think about twelve miles."

The needle of the gauge was solid on the zero stop. "I'm going to put down there," I said.

There was a little plume of wood smoke from the kitchen chimney, which was a help, and a paddock of ten or fifteen acres downwind from the house; the trees would make a shelter for the aircraft on the ground. I dropped off height and turned low over it; there were some sheep there but the surface looked all right. I picked a clear patch between the sheep and brought her in and put her down, thankful to be out of the air. Some people came running out of the house as I taxied slowly forward to the shelter of the trees, the doctor got out and went to one wing strut, a young lad to the other, and we got her into shelter and tied her down to a harrow and a disc plough.

It was Jeff Duncan's farm all right, and they all knew the doctor. He was soaked to the skin, and stiff with cold, and trembling. We all went into the kitchen and stood by the wood stove; they gave him dry clothes to wear and hot whisky and lemon to drink. I drank tea because there was more flying to do, and rang up Billy Monkhouse at the aerodrome and asked him to bring over a jerrican of petrol. He told me that the Proctor had arrived and Dr. Parkinson had gone in with his pilot to the police station to speak upon the radio. I told him to call in on them on his way out with the petrol and tell them that, again, I hadn't been able to land the doctor.

When I got back to the kitchen after speaking on the telephone I found the doctor standing by the stove; they had opened up the front of it and stoked it up with wood so that it made a warm blaze. He had his second whisky with hot lemon in his hand, half consumed, and he was looking a great deal better than he had a quarter of an hour before.

He said, "I'm sorry we couldn't manage it, Captain. The weather wasn't very good, was it?"

I shook my head. "It wasn't . . ." It seemed to me an understatement.

"What will we do now? Wait till it gets better and try again?"

I had very nearly killed him twice, at least, that day. "Do you want to try again?" I asked. "Dr. Parkinson's in Buxton."

"He'd be much better at dealing with a fractured skull than I would," he said. "He's had much more experience. But I'd be quite willing to try again, so far as the flying goes." He smiled. "I've got a sort of thing about this now," he said. "I want to see it through."

I nodded. "So do I. I'll have to get my head down for a bit, though, before going out again. We'll find out what the Met has to say, and then go for the next clear patch."

After a time Billy Monkhouse arrived in his old car. We all went out with him to refuel the machine for me to fly back to the aerodrome. I asked him, "Have you heard anything from the Met? Any more breaks coming?"

"They won't say," he replied. "Nothing in sight immediately, anyway. They've started a ground party to walk in through Kallista."

"I'll have to get a room at the hotel and get some sleep," I told him. "Who flew the doctor up from Hobart?"

"A young chap called Phil Barnes," he told me. "Assistant instructor at the club—came out of the R.A.A.F. about a year back. He knows the country."

I nodded. "He can carry on while I get some sleep. I suppose I can get into that hotel?"

He rubbed his chin. "I don't know that you can. They let four rooms. They've got the boss's mother in one and his wife's sister and her little girl in another. Then there's Dr. Parkinson and Phil Barnes, each got a room. They turned out the little girl for one of them and put her in her

61

ma's room." He paused. "The best thing you can do is to go in Captain Pascoe's house," he said. "He wouldn't mind."

"Where's that?"

"Last house out of town before you get to the 'drome," he said. "You'll be all right there."

"I'll be all right anywhere, so long as there's a bed," I said.

As soon as she was refuelled I got into the machine to take her off light from that paddock and fly her back to Buxton. The doctor was to go back with the ground engineer in his car. The Duncans herded the ewes over to one side of the paddock and I got into the air and flew back to the aerodrome. I landed just outside the hangar, the boys came and caught the struts, for the wind was still high, and we put her inside. My job was over for the time, and I could rest. Great gusts of rain were blowing across the fields.

I got out of the machine and stood on the damp concrete floor, cold and unhappy. There was no car there, for Billy Monkhouse had taken his over to me with the petrol, and he was not back yet. I rang up the police station while I was waiting for him and spoke to the sergeant, and told him the position. He said that the Met report was discouraging. There was no break in sight. Dr. Parkinson and his pilot had gone for dinner at the hotel, with the lady.

"What lady?" I asked.

"A lady came just after you took off," he said. "A Mrs. Forbes. Something to do with Captain Pascoe, I think. She flew across to Launceston from Melbourne first thing this morning, and got a taxi here. She's going to stay at the hotel."

"Is she a relation?" I asked.

"I don't know that," he said. "She might be. I

62

didn't give her much attention, what with other things."

I rang off, and soon after that Billy Monkhouse drove up with the doctor. I told him what I had done, and that a woman had arrived. "I know that," he said. "She come just as you were taking off."

"Do you know who she is?"

"She didn't say. A cousin, perhaps. I dunno."

There was no point in bothering with her; she couldn't help us. I said, "Show me which is Johnnie's house. Can I get something to eat at the hotel?"

He glanced at his watch. "Not at this time, you can't. Dinner 'll be off. Mrs. Lawrence 'll fix you up something. She does for Captain Pascoe—lives next door. I'll take you there."

I got into his little car with the doctor. He said that he would look in at the hotel and see Dr. Parkinson, which would save my going into town. I think he saw that I was just about all in from the strain of flying in difficult conditions and the lack of sleep, and indeed I think I actually fell asleep in the three or four minutes that it took us to drive from the hangar to the first house on the edge of the little town, because I know I woke up with a start.

We went and spoke to Mrs. Lawrence in the next house, a fat, comfortable woman washing up after their midday dinner. "I think he's got some bacon and eggs in the house," she said when the position was explained to her. "I could come over in a minute and do that, if that would be enough." I said anything would do. "I'll bring over some bread and some milk," she said. "If you're going to be in tonight I could go in and get a bit of steak." She paused, and then she said, "We're all so sorry about the captain."

"We'll get a doctor in to him before long," I told her. "As soon as this weather lifts."

63

She nodded. "I never knew it be so crook. It's been like this for days. You go on over and make yourself at home, and I'll be over in ten minutes. There's a fire laid all ready in the lounge." She took a key down from a nail over the sink and gave it to me. "That's the back door key."

Monkhouse drove the car on to the town with the doctor, splashing on the dirt road through the sheets of rain, and I went over to the other house. The door opened into the kitchen and I shut the rain out. I was cold and wet, and the house seemed chilly and unlived in. I went through into the lounge and dropped down on my knees before the fire, and lit it. There was wood in the wood box and a good pile outside the back door. There was no need to stint myself of warmth; I stayed on my knees in my leather coat for some time piling on the twiggy bits and then the rather larger pieces and finally the logs. With the shelter from the weather and the increasing glow from the fire a little warmth began to creep back into me, and presently I noticed that my coat was dripping water on the fire-irons and the fender. I stood up stiffly, and took it off, and went and hung it on the back of the kitchen door. Then I came back to the fire and looked around.

The sitting room was a pilot's room, the walls covered with photographs of a long flying life. On the wall above the mantelpiece was a wooden propeller with queer, curved blades, hung as a trophy like a pair of antlers. There were little bits of aeroplane all over the place, most of them old and quite unfamiliar to me. On another wall among the photographs there was a complete instrument panel hanging like a picture, but the only instruments on it were a clumsy airspeed indicator, an equally antique aneroid, an oil-pressure gauge, and spirit cross and fore-and-aft levels. I wondered idly what sort of an aircraft

64

that had come out of, but I had no time for his mementoes at that moment. What I wanted was a bed, and I went out into the little corridor.

There were two bedrooms in the house, one on each side. I opened the door on the left, and found myself in Johnnie Pascoe's bedroom. It was a very large room, much larger than I should have expected to find in a house of that nature. I glanced around and saw that it was quite well furnished, and then backed out and tried the other door. It would be better to use his spare room.

It was his spare room all right, but it wasn't up to much. There was a bed there with a mattress on it, but there were no bedclothes and no pillows. There was a dressing table but the dust lay thick upon it. There was no chair. There was a short strip of worn carpet on the bare, unstained boards beside the bed and thin, faded curtains joined by a few cobwebs shrouded the closed window.

I was tired, too tired to set about cleaning up his spare room and getting it in order. I went back to his own bedroom. It was spacious, well furnished, and comfortable; the bed made up neatly and covered with a bedspread with an eiderdown on top of that. His razor, his hairbrushes were all there on the dressing table, his washing things were on the basin by the gleaming taps. His dressing gown hung behind the door, his slippers were under the bedside table with the reading lamp; I opened the door of the built-in wardrobe idly, and it was full of his clothes. Like the sitting room, the walls of this room were covered with photographs and souvenirs, but what riveted my attention was the bed. It looked just marvellous, exactly what I needed. Johnnie Pascoe wouldn't mind my sleeping there, I knew. It would be some time before he would use it, anyway, for when we got him out from the Lewis River he would certainly go into hospital.

I put my haversack of warm clothes on the bed and then Mrs. Lawrence came in at the back door and began to organise a meal for me in the kitchen. I had a word or two with her, and went back to the sitting room and put more wood upon the fire. My flying was over for the day; I was still cold, and started to look around for a drink. I hadn't far to look; there was a corner cupboard in the sitting room with three unopened bottles of Scotch in it, and one half empty. I went and got a glass and some water from the kitchen and gave myself a drink of his whisky. Glass in hand, standing by the fire, warm and comfortable for the first time that day, I had leisure to examine the room.

On the wall over the cupboard that housed the whisky there was a studio portrait photograph of a very pretty blonde girl. It was inscribed across the corner in a round, flowing hand, "For Johnnie with oceans of love, from Judy," but the ink had faded and some of the words were hardly legible. The photograph had gone a bit yellow, too, but there was nothing on it to indicate the date.

I looked around the corner, and there were other photographs of the same girl upon the walls, and of aeroplanes, all biplanes except one, which was a triplane. This was a corner of the room that was devoted to Judy, it seemed, and I studied the photographs curiously as I stood there, drink in hand, before the fire. They all seemed to have been taken at the time of the first war. There was a very young man in the double-breasted 'maternity' jacket of the Royal Flying Corps standing in front of the triplane—could that be Johnnie? I moved over for a closer look, thinking of the pilot instructor who had taught me to fly nearly thirty years ago. It was Johnnie all right—a much younger man than I had known, but the same. In the photograph he was very young indeed, no more than eighteen or nineteen. The drooping wings upon his chest had no ribbons beneath them. The triplane was a single-seater with a rotary engine and an open cockpit; it had R.F.C. roundels on the fuselage. I searched my memory for pictures I had seen— could that have been a Sopwith?

There was one of Judy driving a golf ball off the tee. There was something wrong about that one, but at first I couldn't place it. It looked faked in some way, too good to be true. Then I got it. It was like a photograph of an actress or a model playing golf in one of the glossy magazines, perhaps in an advertisement, posed carefully by the golf pro in exactly the right position at the end of the swing, and holding the pose while the photographer did his stuff. The clothes were very old-fashioned.

There was a very pleasant photograph of Johnnie and Judy in front of the rotary engine of some fighter. It was a biplane, a very small machine. The portion of the under-carriage that was visible looked terribly flimsy, the tyre on the one wheel that was showing unbelievably small. He had his arm around her shoulders and they were laughing together at the camera, both very young. The drooping wings had two medal ribbons underneath them now, and the arm around her shoulder had a thin bit of gold braid vertical above the cuff. One of the ribbons seemed to be the Military Cross, but I could not make out the other, nor could I identify the aeroplane. The wooden propeller behind them had the same curved leading edge, and I turned and looked at the one over the mantelpiece. The boss, I saw, was stamped with a lot of letters and numbers and the one word 'CLERGET'. I wondered if that propeller was the same as featured in that merry photo-graph, if Johnnie and Judy had once leaned against it, forty years ago.

There were other photographs of ancient aeroplanes, one of them an enormous biplane pusher that I thought might be a Farman, but no more of them featured the girl Judy. I poured myself another whisky and studied the portrait, wondering if that had been the marriage that went wrong. It could quite well have been; the date was about right. It was a very pretty face but rather a hard one, perhaps; the face of somebody who knew exactly where she was going. The lines of the chin and jaw were very firm, in spite of the softness of youth. She was very young in the portrait, but it was quite possible, I thought, that by the age of thirty she might have developed into a real hard piece. Perhaps she had, and that had been the trouble. Or again, it might have been his fault. You just can't say.

Mrs. Lawrence called me to the kitchen for my meal, which Johnnie Pascoe evidently had normally upon the kitchen table. She had done bacon and eggs and fried potatoes; there was bread and cheese and a pot of jam, and a big pot of hot coffee. I thanked her, and she said, "That's nothing. Just leave everything upon the table when you've done. I'll come in again later."

"I can wash these few things up," I said.

"Captain Pascoe leaves them and I come in," she replied. "You'd better do the same." She looked out of the window. "I never saw such rain," she said. "I do hope you can get a doctor to him soon."

"One or other of us will be flying down to him the minute the weather clears," I told her.

She went away, and I sat down to my meal. It was about four o'clock in the afternoon, and already the light was beginning to fade; I got up half way through and put on the kitchen light over the table. I ate heartily and drank several cups of coffee with a lot of milk. Then, taking Mrs. Lawrence at her word, I got up from the table and went back to the sitting room. The fire was burning well. I switched on the light and stood in the warm glow,

68

thinking now of bed. Better give the meal time to settle, however, and I lit a cigarette. I wondered if there would be time to put a call through to Sheila before I slept, and decided that I ought to. I crossed to the telephone, lifted the receiver, and put in the call. I asked what the delay would be, and told them to ring me back if it was going to be long.

I put the instrument down, and raised my eyes to the wall above it. There was a photograph there, and after nearly thirty years my heart turned over because it was a photograph of Brenda Marshall. It was Brenda Marshall as I had known and loved her from a distance when I was a boy, when I was eighteen and she was nearly thirty. It was taken outside the hangar at Duffington aerodrome, where I learned to fly in the same year that that photograph must have been taken. She was standing beside her Moth in the white boiler suit she always flew in, smiling a little shyly at the camera. She had her white flying helmet in her hand, showing her short, curly hair. It was Brenda Marshall as I had known her in my youth.

It brought me up short, and I stood staring at it, full of sad memories. The corner of the hangar that showed just behind the Moth was the corner she had died in, on the stretcher, as I well knew. I was only eighteen at the time, and hers was the first fatal crash that I had had to do with. I stood staring at the photograph, remembering her vivacity. Brenda Marshall . . . Johnnie Pascoe must have got hold of that photograph, and he had kept it all these years. He had taught her to fly, too.

A car splashed to a standstill in the rain outside the house. I looked out of the window in the semi-darkness, and it was the taxi. A woman got out of it and spoke to the driver, who indicated my house. She pushed the gate open and came up through the neglected front garden to the door. I cursed her inwardly because I wanted to go to bed, but she knocked and rang the bell. There was nothing for it, and I went to the front door and opened it for her.

"Captain Clarke?" she asked.

I said, "Yes." I did not invite her in, though she was standing in the rain.

"I just came down to talk things over with you," she said. "I'm Marian Forbes."

She was a woman about forty years of age. I did not move from the door. "Is this anything urgent?" I enquired. "I got no sleep last night, and I'm just going to bed."

"You poor thing!" she exclaimed. "I know. I shan't keep you more than two minutes."

Very reluctantly I let her in out of the rain, and she pushed forward past me into the sitting room. "What a lovely fire you've got!" she said. "And what a cosy room!" She turned to me with a winsome air that might have been attractive twenty years ago. "You know, there isn't anywhere at all to sit in that hotel, except the bed-room! Don't you think that's dreadful?"

"What can I do for you?" I asked. "I'm just going to bed."

"I know—I know," she said. "I shan't keep you more than two minutes." She took off her raincoat and laid it on a chair at the back of the room, and moved over to the fire. "I just wanted to have a little talk."

"What about?"

"Oh dear," she said. "You *are* in a hurry to get rid of me, aren't you? And I've been waiting such a long time to see you. I got here just before you started off on the last flight but I was too late to talk to you then."

The telephone rang, and I picked up the receiver. It was the exchange to say that there was a two hours' delay to Melbourne. I told them to cancel the call. There was now nothing but this woman to keep me from my bed, and I turned back to her. "Let's cut this short," I said rudely. "I'm going to bed in about thirty seconds. Who are you, anyway?"

She said, "Well, I'm John Pascoe's daughter."

Chapter Three

I stood silent for a moment. "I'm sorry," I said. "I never knew he had a daughter."

"I don't suppose you did," she said. "He's probably forgotten it himself."

It didn't seem to be any concern of mine, anyway. "We're doing everything we can to get a doctor down to him," I said. "There's nothing to do now but to wait until the weather clears."

"That's what they told me," she replied. "I suppose you've known him a long time?"

"He taught me to fly, back in England in 1931," I said. "I can't say that I know him very well, but I've certainly known him a long time."

"That's what they told me in the hotel." She paused, and then she said, "I live in Adelaide." Later on, I learned that her husband was one of the leading surgeons of the city. "I told Dennis when we heard it on the news last night, I told him that I'd have to come over and see that everything possible was being done. After all, he *is* my father."

I wrinkled my brows. "You weren't very closely in touch with him?"

She laughed shortly. "Good Lord, no! I don't suppose he knows I'm in Australia. I don't suppose he cares where I live. He left my mother when I was two years old and after that we never heard a word from him. I knew that he was here because I saw it in the paper."

It seemed a funny sort of relationship, but it was nothing to do with me. "Well, everything that's possible is being done, Mrs. Forbes," I said. "While this weather lasts we can't do much by landing at the Lewis River, but there's a Lincoln of the R.A.A.F. on its way with a parachute doctor and a parachute nurse. It ought to be at Hobart by this time. Apart from that, a ground party started off about midday today, but it's going to take them three days to get there over the mountains. The doctor's been talking to the woman, Mrs. Hoskins, over the radio every two or three hours and telling her what to do. Everything possible is being done."

A gust of wind whistled around the house and beat upon the window.

"They tell me you're a married man," she said.

I was surprised. "That's right."

"Any children?"

"Two." I wondered what on earth she was getting at.

"I wouldn't want to see anything happen to a man like you," she said flatly. "Not for the sake of a man like Pascoe."

There was a hostility in that remark, of course, hostility to her father, and I didn't quite know what to say in reply. I was evidently dealing with a spiteful woman, and I wanted to go to bed. She had, however, settled down in front of my fire. I wasn't inclined to let her stay there after that. She would have to go back to the hotel, uncomfortable as it was.

"Johnnie Pascoe's all right," I said. "In any case, I can look after myself."

"Are you a friend of his?" she asked.

"Not a close one," I said. "He taught me to fly, and I've known him off and on since then."

"Well, I've known him better, and much longer," she retorted. "He's an out and out rotter. I don't want to see anybody taking any risks, real risks, that is, over a man like that. You or anybody else."

73

"I thought you said that you had come to help him—from Adelaide."

"That's right," she said. "I'm his daughter. If there's anything needs doing—nursing home or surgeon's fees or paying him an allowance till he's fit to earn his living again—I've got a sort of duty to him, I suppose. Dennis feels like I do about that—we'll have to see him right. That's why I came over. Apart from that, I don't want to have anything to do with him."

"Well, you may as well go back to Adelaide right away," I said curtly. "He seems to have plenty of money for anything he needs, and he's got friends who'll look after him."

She was silent for a moment. Then she said, "You don't like me much, do you?"

"Lady," I replied, "I don't like you because I've been up all night and I've done quite a bit of flying and you're keeping me out of my bed. I'll be in a better frame of mind to talk to you tomorrow, if there's anything to talk about."

She got to her feet; she was on the move, anyway. "If you don't want to listen to what I've got to say—well, that's the end of it," she said.

"I don't, if it's just grumbles about Johnnie Pascoe's character," I replied. "That's not material at the moment. The thing we've got to do is get a surgeon to him."

"If it's worth it." She paused, and then she said, "I had lunch in the hotel with Dr. Parkinson and Mr. Barnes, who flew him up from Hobart. Dr. Turnbull came in afterwards and he was telling them about the two flights that you've made today down to the Lewis River."

"What about them?"

"When Dr. Turnbull told them what you'd done, they were horrified at the risks that you'd been taking.

74

Dr. Parkinson says he doesn't want to fly with you."

I was very angry. "I never heard such nonsense. At a time like this things have to be stretched a bit."

She picked up her bag. "I don't know anything about flying," she said. "I only know what they were saying in the hotel—people who do know about it. They think you're crazy. I think that, too, because Johnnie Pascoe simply isn't worth it. That's what I came to say, and now I'll leave you to your bed."

She moved towards the door, but I stood motionless. I didn't like her spite against her father, but there might have been a twisted element of kindness in her visit, kindness to me and to my family. I stood in thought for a moment, and my eye fell upon the portrait photograph on the wall behind her. "Was your mother's name Judy?" I enquired.

She looked at me curiously. "Judy Lester," she said. "That was her stage name. You must remember her."

Vague memories of childhood flitted across my mind. "I think she was a bit before my time," I said. "I've heard the name."

"Our real name was Lichter," she said, "but she didn't use that on the stage. Why did you ask?"

"Only because there are three photos of her in this room," I told her curtly. "That's a funny thing, if he's the sort of man you say."

She was startled. "Where?"

"On the wall behind you."

She turned and looked at the many photographs, and then her eyes fastened on the portrait. She moved close and squinted at it a little; she seemed to be short-sighted and afraid of the disfigurement of spectacles. "That's my mother," she said. "I've got a copy of that photograph somewhere."

I did not speak. I stood there thinking what a fool I

75

was to have interested her in the pictures. She would probably stay half an hour longer.

She looked at the picture of the girl posed in a golfer's swing, and said, "That's her, again. Of course, she was much younger, then." And then her eye wandered to the one of Johnnie and Judy in front of the rotary engine of the biplane fighter, the laughing one. She looked at it for a moment or two, and then indicated the laughing boy in the R.F.C. jacket with the drooping wings and the two medal ribbons. She turned to me and asked, "Is that him?"

"Of course it is," I said. "That's Johnnie Pascoe. Don't you know him?"

"I was only two when he deserted us," she said. "I don't remember him."

"Didn't you ever meet him—when you grew up?"

She shook her head. "We lived in Gardena, Los Angeles—that's where I was brought up. Ma went there for the movies, and then when her contract ended she kept a rooming house. That was after she divorced my stepfather." She paused, and then she indicated the photograph. "*He* lived in England in between the wars."

"You've never met him at all?"

"I flew by AusCan once from Vancouver to Sydney," she said. "Coming back from England, about three years ago. He was the pilot from Honolulu to Nandi in Fiji. They change crews there, or something."

"Did you make yourself known to him?" I asked.

She laughed shortly. "I wouldn't demean myself. Dennis thought I ought to say something, but I said, better not. All I'd have had to say would have been that he deserted my mother, her and me, and we'd got on very well without him." She paused. "But it was interesting, seeing him. I saw him once upon a newsreel, too. Opening the airline, from some place to another."

I made another effort to unstick her so that I could go to bed. "Well, there it is," I said. "He's kept those photos forty years."

Her lips curled a little. "Evidence of a conquest." She glanced around the room. "He's got quite a few others to keep her company. Evidence of other conquests, I suppose."

She was looking over to the photograph of Brenda Marshall, standing by the Moth in her white overall with her smile and her short, curly hair. I disliked this woman very much, her attitude, her cynicism, her whole way of looking at things. I didn't like any part of her, and she was keeping me out of bed. "He's over sixty years old," I said. "If he likes to keep photographs of women who've been kind to him all through his life, that's nothing to do with us. We've no right to be in this house anyway, but I've got to use it because I've got to get some sleep. I'll have to ask you to go away now, and leave me to it."

She asked, "Can I use your telephone to call a taxi?"

I glanced out of the window; momentarily the rain had stopped, but the clouds were still scudding low before a high wind. "It's not raining now," I said. "You can walk it into town in ten minutes."

She flushed angrily. "All right, I'll go and leave you to sleep. When you wake up you'd better think of going back to the mainland. I don't suppose any of the doctors here will want to fly with you."

I showed her out, and she marched up the road picking her way between the puddles, an arrogant, slightly absurd middle-aged woman in a blue suit and high-heeled, black patent leather shoes, most unsuitable for country walking. I went back into the sitting room and poured myself another whisky from Johnnie Pascoe's bottle with a hand that shook with irritable anger. I sat down in his chair before the fire and lit a cigarette, to cool off for a few

77

minutes before I went to bed. I knew I wouldn't sleep if I went to bed as angry as I was just then.

That was a bad, spiteful woman, and I mustn't let her get under my skin. Be objective, recognise her for what she was, and then the barbs would cease to rankle. To tell a pilot of my age and experience that his flying was unsafe, that doctors didn't want to fly with him—that was a shrewd one, the stab of a woman in the habit of hurting. The worst of it was that it was very nearly true. I had stretched things to the limit of safety that morning, and perhaps a little bit beyond. Surely one had a right to do that when a man's life depended on it? Surely one had a right to call up all one's capital of skill? If I was prepared to take a chance myself, surely I had a right to make the doctor take it with me? He hadn't seemed to mind about it at the time.

I took another drink and blew out a long cloud of smoke. In spite of my efforts I had achieved nothing, nothing at all. All I had done had been to lose the doctor's suitcase with all his instruments in it. God only knew when he would get that back.

To take my mind off my own troubles I got up and moved around the room. I set his barometer, and then I went on looking at the pictures. There were other photographs of Johnnie Pascoe in the First World War that I had not examined. There was an informal group of about a dozen pilots standing in a meadow in summer weather, probably on the edge of an aerodrome because a quaint, old-fashioned Nissen hut with a boarded end showed in the background. All the men were very young, and all of them were in Army uniforms. Three of them wore the R.F.C. tunic, double-breasted. One seemed to be an American, for he wore a single-breasted khaki tunic buttoned close up round the neck and the wings upon his chest were the unswept wings of the American Army.

The rest of them wore normal British Army tunics with wings, and these wore khaki collars and ties; three of them wore Sam Browne belts, and one was wearing riding breeches and puttees. Scrawled on the bottom of the photograph were the words, ST. OMER 1918, in white ink that had faded to yellow.

I looked at it closely, and decided that Johnnie Pascoe was standing on the right, one of the pilots in an R.F.C. tunic. He had something round his neck that flopped down in a light streak on one shoulder, and I puzzled over this aspect of his uniform for a few moments. It looked for all the world like a silk stocking.

There was a very good photograph of a rotary-engined biplane fighter, taken broadside-on and in flight. It had the R.F.C. roundels and a design of black and white chequers on the engine cowling and the front fuselage. It was a very small machine, to judge by the size of the pilot's head, with a single pair of struts between the wings. I guessed it to be a Sopwith Camel, but I was by no means sure, because I never saw one. It had two machine guns mounted on the top cowling. The pilot's head was turned towards the camera and it might have been Johnnie Pascoe, though it was difficult to say. The aeroplane was doped a khaki colour, very clean and smart. It looked like a brand-new aeroplane, taken by some official photographer.

So many photographs of the First War, all framed and hung close in a group upon one wall! There were too many for me to take them all in. All dated from before my earliest flying days, but they brought back for me the memories of that first enthusiasm that has lasted from my boyhood. They brought back memories of slow-revving engines blipping on the switch, of clouds of castor oil sweeping in blue clouds of the slipstream over the grass, of taut doped fabric drumming beneath one's fingers, of the smell of acetone in the hangar. They brought back memories of the rush of air over one's head beyond the leather of the flying helmet, of the freshness on one's face as one put up the goggles before going in to land, of carefully judged gliding turns on the approach, of the final sideslip in over the hedge, of soft landings upon grass. So many joys that lay behind me, half forgotten, a part of my youth.

They had been part of Johnnie Pascoe's youth, too, even more than mine. He must have learned to fly, I thought, in 1916 or thereabouts, fourteen years before I did. If I still sensed the drama, the adventure of it all— how much more must he! Probably that enormous pusher two-seater with the engine behind the pilots was what he had learned to fly in—would that have been a Farman? A Rumpety? That thing with the long skid in front of the undercarriage—well, I knew that one. That was an Avro 504K. I had been up for a joyride in an Avro when I was a boy of twelve, the first flight that I had ever made. When Johnnie Pascoe learned to fly it was probably still a front-line operational type, with a top speed of about seventy miles an hour.

When he had learned to fly, flying had been the greatest adventure the world had to offer, an adventure that led almost certainly to death. In the First World War the casualties in training pilots had been staggering, because the aeroplanes were cheap and easily made, the pilots were needed in a hurry, and nobody understood much about flying training. When they were sent to France they were sent as soldiers, and the duty of a soldier was to fight and go on fighting. In that war there was no relief for a pilot after a fixed number of missions. A pilot went on flying two or even three missions on every fine day till he was killed, or else so seriously wounded as to need a spell in hospital. That had been the pattern of Johnnie

Pascoe's youth—the greatest and most stimulating adventure in the world leading to death willingly accepted. That had been the mental pattern of his life when that laughing photograph with Judy had been taken, in front of the rotary-engined fighter. Everything that he had done in his first youth must be related to that pattern. I could just get an inkling of it, perhaps, because I had entered the same world myself fourteen years later. Marian Forbes would never have a clue, not if she lived to be a hundred.

She was a bitter, spiteful woman, but she was so because it was beyond her capacity to understand. Whatever had happened between Johnnie Pascoe and his Judy had happened very soon after the First War. It must have meant enormous readjustments in his mind when the war ended. When the promise of death, willingly accepted, was withdrawn—what had there been to take its place? Johnnie Pascoe had gone on flying, anyway; I had never heard that he had done anything else.

I was growing sleepy now, and ready for bed. Marian Forbes had ceased to worry me, for she was something different, like an Eskimo. I threw the butt of my cigarette in the fire. There were a couple of thick logs smouldering together but there was no flame; the fire was safe and it would probably last till morning. There were still a couple of mouthfuls of whisky left in my glass; I stood there finishing them, looking at the photos in that corner. *That*, the single-seater with the top wing of the biplane sprouting from the fuselage at the pilot's seat—that must have been a Sopwith Dolphin. *That*, with the backward stagger, might have been a D.H.5. How he had loved those days of early youth, to keep so many photographs!

I went through into his bedroom, for I was very sleepy by that time. Unknown to me, Mrs. Lawrence had been in the house, for someone had removed the bedspread and turned down the bed; there was a pair of clean pyjamas, Johnnie Pascoe's, laid out on the folded sheet. I had brought with me only a haversack filled with warm clothing and a few essentials and my flying helmet; there had been no room for pyjamas and I could get on without them for a night or two. Now Johnnie Pascoe was providing them for me, as he was providing everything else in this room.

His razor, his hairbrushes, his washing things, his towel, were there for me to use if I wanted them. His pictures were there for me to look at and to savour his early life, even in this room. There was a very large framed photograph of the earliest Handley Page bomber, the 0.400, with a Camel flying beside it, perhaps to show the scale of the big aircraft; the Camel had the same chequered markings that I had seen on the photo in the other room. There were two pictures of biplane fighters that I could not identify at all, and one of an S.E.5. His bed was there for me to sleep in, his pyjamas for me to wear.

I threw off my clothes and got into his pyjamas, washed my teeth at his washbasin, and got into his bed. I put out his bedside light and settled down to sleep, tired after thirty-six hours on the go. Outside the wind was high and the rain still beat against the side of the small, exposed house, and drummed on the corrugated iron roof. Later on I would ring Sheila, when I woke again. She wouldn't be worrying yet because it was only about five o'clock, though it was now quite dark.

We must get help to Johnnie Pascoe the instant there was a break in the weather. I didn't know how long a man with a fractured skull could live without attention, but no more than a day or two. I should have asked the doctor, I thought, how much time we had, and yet it would not have made any difference to events. I had failed in my first mission, failed because I had forgotten about the door. I knew that Johnnie would not hold that one against me, for we all have finger trouble now and then, but the onus was on me to get help to him and repair the error. I would do so even if I had to tie that doctor hand and foot and shove him in the aeroplane, for Johnnie Pascoe was dying.

I was very near to sleep now, in his bed and on his pillow. If he were to die, at any rate he would know that we were doing everything we could to help him, for he would come back to this small house beside this minor aerodrome, if a man goes anywhere beyond his death. This was his home, the only home he had, the shrine that held the treasured relics of his life. Somewhere in this bedroom with me would be . . . would be the Military Cross, in one of the drawers of his chest, perhaps. Somewhere there might be souvenirs of Judy . . . a silk stocking he had worn around his neck when flying, forty years ago.

Those rotary engines . . . the Le Rhones, the Monos, and the Clergets! They made a sort of crackling hiss, and always the same smell of castor oil spraying backwards down the fuselage in a fine mist over your leather helmet and your coat. They were delightful to fly, the controls so light, the engines so smooth-running. Up among the sunlit cumulus under the blue sky I could loop and roll and spin my Camel with the pressure of two fingers on the stick beside the button switch which I used as little as possible. Looping, turn off the petrol by the big plug cock upon the panel just before the bottom of the dive, ease the stick gently back and over you go. The engine dies at the top of the loop; ease the stick fully back and turn the petrol on again as the ground appears so that the engine comes to life five or six seconds later.

She would climb at nearly a thousand feet a minute, my new Clerget Camel; she would do a hundred and ten miles an hour. She would be faster, I thought, than any-thing upon the Western Front. There was the aerodrome, turn off the cock and put her into a volplane. Turn it on again to try the engine at a thousand feet, and turn it off. Volplane turns downwind from the hedge, S turns keeping the aerodrome in view. Try the engine once more with the cock. A turn to the left in the bright sun, keeping the hedge in sight through the hole in the top plane. A turn to the right. Now turn in, a little high, stick over and top rudder, the air squirting in upon you sideways round the windscreen. Straighten out, over the hedge, and down on to the grass. Remember that the Clerget lands very fast, at over forty miles an hour, and with that great engine in the nose the tail was light. Watch it . . . Lovely.

I came to rest upon the grass in the bright sunshine; for an April day it was terrific, right out of the box. I turned the petrol half on, set the mixture, and pulled my goggles down again to taxi in to the tarmac. She was throwing a light mist of castor oil over the fuselage, the windscreen, and me, just the right amount, not too much and not too little, but you don't want to get it in your eyes or you know it for the rest of the day. I glanced over my shoulder and took off again, and flew her over to the hangar in little blips of engine on the switch, my foot working hard. I put her down right on the edge and rolled forward on to the gravel and stopped just outside the Bessoneau. Cochran was doing that at London Colney in a Spad but he was going too fast and ran into a support of the hangar and brought the canvas roof down on top of him, and then the gas tank burst behind his back and the whole lot went up in flames. There wasn't much left for the funeral. Was the C.O. mad!

I let the motor die and pushed up my goggles and wiped the oil off my face with my silk scarf. Donk was on the tarmac with a lot of other people, girls, some of them. I jumped out of the cockpit and the oil was just right, even all the way round the cowling. It made her glisten, so that she looked wonderful. I told the mechanics to wipe her down before the dust got on it, and then to drench out each cylinder with paraffin.

Donk and Bose and Jerry came up with the girls. Bose said, "Meet the Hounslow Wonder. Flies upside down a darn sight better than right side up. Flies backwards, too, so the breeze can cool——"

Donk said, "Don't listen to him. He's not got over last night."

"I wasn't," said one of the girls. "I know it." She turned to me. "You were just wonderful."

"Don't tell him that," said Jerry. "Now he'll go and drop it. Remember Butch?"

"He didn't drop it," I said. "One wing came off. Introduce me."

Donk said, "This is Daisy, and this is Lily, and this is Judy. This is Johnnie Pascoe. He's as mad as—well, as mad as holes."

The others were in ordinary clothes, but Judy was in uniform, a W.A.A.C., and she was lovely. Even in the two-tone drab buttoned up to the neck she made the others look like two pennyworth of muck. My face was oily, so were my hands, and my old maternity just reeked of it. I turned straight to her. "I'd like to shake hands, but I'll make you in a mess," I said. "You doing anything tonight?"

She laughed up at me, and it was perfect. "Yes."

"Any of these hoodlums here?"

"No."

"Then put him off and come and have dinner with me at the Savoy."

She laughed again, and shook her head.

Donk said, "She's in *Picardy Princess*. You remember

85

the little French girl at the *estaminet*?"

I turned to her again. "You're not Judy Lester?"

She nodded, laughing.

I touched the sleeve of her uniform, and started walking on air. "But what's this in aid of?"

"Part time," she said. "I drive General Cadell in the mornings."

"Nevertheless," I said, "will you have dinner with me?"

She laughed. "I can't. I'm on in the First Act."

"Will you have supper with me after the show? I'll make a party."

"When?"

"Tonight."

She laughed again, adorably. "All right. But I go home at midnight."

"You won't tonight," I said. "What do you like to eat best?"

"Smoked salmon and ice cream."

"Tournedos in between?"

She nodded. And then, on the tarmac by the Sopwith Camel, she clasped her hands together, bent a knee, put on a woebegone air, and said, "Oh sir—I am but a simple village maid. I know not what you intend by these fine gifts, so far above my station in life."

I blinked at her, and then the others burst into a roar of laughter. Donk said, "You'll know before the evening's out."

She drew herself up now with regal dignity, and said icily, "Sir, though my father earns his living underground at the corner of the Edgware and the Harrow Roads, I still have that which a maid values more than anything on earth."

Donk said, "You won't have it long."

I was getting the hang of this now. "Lady," I said, "I

thought of asking this lot to my party, but I'm not so sure now. What about you and me just dining alone?"

She laughed at me. "Not much. I go with the party."

"In words of one syllable," said Bose, "if you feed her you've got to feed us all."

"It's worth it," I said. I turned to her. "Can I pick you up at the stage door?"

She nodded, and when she smiled at me my heart turned over.

"What time?"

"Ten past eleven." And then she asked, "Is this your new aeroplane?"

I nodded. "I only got it yesterday."

"Are you pleased with it?"

"It's a beauty," I said proudly. "It's as fast as an S.E.5 and much handier. It's a hundred and thirty horse-power."

"That's terrific." She came apart from the others with me and I showed her the engine, dripping a little clear yellow oil and making little sizzling noises. "Are you taking it out to the Front?"

I nodded. "We're forming up a new Squadron now. I'm to lead one of the Flights."

"Captain Boswell was saying that you shot down seven Germans."

"The eighth shot me down. I was lucky and got down behind our lines."

She glanced at the one gold stripe upon my sleeve. "Is that how you got your wound stripe?"

"I'm going to cut it in half," I said. "It wasn't worth a whole stripe."

"Have you ever crashed?"

"Six times," I said. "The seventh is the lucky one. Do you drink champagne?"

She laughed. "Kind sir, I know not what to say!"

87

"You don't have to talk to it," I said. "Just drink it."

She said, "Jiminny! Here's the General coming. I'll have to go."

I looked, and saw all the high brass coming, but they were the length of the hangar away. By side-stepping a couple of paces we could get behind the fuselage. "Come this way," I said. "I want to give you a kiss."

She laughed. "Not much."

"Why not?"

"You're all oily. You'll mess up my uniform. I wear this in the Third Act, for the Grand Finale. Besides, I don't know you."

"First part makes sense," I said. "Last part—that's damn nonsense."

"I must go. They're coming."

I let her go, reluctantly. "Ten past eleven?"

She nodded, and ran quickly to the dark green Crossley tourer parked by the hangar and swung the starting handle. When the General came up she was standing stiffly to attention. She saluted him just as she saluted in the Grand Finale in the footlights with the orchestra crashing and banging away before her feet, and opened the back door for him to get in, while we stood laughing. Then she went round to the driver's seat and got in, let the clutch in too hard, and stalled the engine. The others were all laughing fit to burst, but I ran over and grabbed the starting handle and swung it for her. She gave me a lovely smile and got away with a jerk and a crash of gears.

That afternoon I got my Flight together for a dog-fight. For the first ten minutes Donk and Jerry and Tim Collins, a New Zealander, were to set on me and try and get me in their sights, and then I'd pull out while Jerry and Tim set on Donk and I watched. I wanted Tim to have a good work out because he'd only just come down to us from the School of Aerial Fighting at Ayr. The first ten minutes

88

went all right and then I pulled out at about ten thousand and Donk started in. Donk was a good pilot on a Camel and he had them all tied up; over and over again they got behind him but when they went to line up on him he just wasn't there. I sat around a little way away watching their mistakes to tell them on the ground, and so I saw it happen. I suppose they got mad or something because they both came in at the same moment, Tim only looking ahead and Jerry with Tim in the blind spot underneath the engine as he dove in on the same line. Jerry's wheels took Tim's top plane clean away and the rest of the wings collapsed, and there was just a heap of wreckage in the air, and Tim going down in the bare fuselage without any wings, Jerry flying round without any wheels, and Donk and me fluttering about like a couple of wet hens. Tim went into some greenhouses near Hanworth and made a hole four feet deep, and Donk and I shepherded Jerry back to Hounslow where he made a belly landing in the middle of the field and stepped out of it unhurt; his Camel was repairable. All we wanted was one new Camel and one new pilot. Jerry was all cut up and talking a lot of nonsense, so I put him into my machine and sent him up to practise aerobatics, telling him I'd have his hide if he bent it, while I went off to see the C.O. We fixed the funeral for Friday at Feltham and I said I'd write to his folks in New Zealand and see about a wreath from the Squadron. I waited till Jerry got down in my Camel, with a bottle of egg-nog in each pocket of my overcoat, and when I'd satisfied myself he hadn't done my Camel any harm we had an egg-nog in the hangar. Then Donk came along and we had another, and then Bose came so we had another, and by that time things didn't look so bad. We all went into Town by tube and got out at Piccadilly.

We got a beautiful wreath for Timmy at the florists', from the Squadron, ten guineas, and I told them where to send it. And then there were so many lovely flowers in the shop I got a bright idea, and I told the Duchess who was serving us I wanted a bouquet. A really nice one, carnations and things. She said in her funeral voice, "To go with the wreath, sir?"

"No," I said. "This is another thing again. This is for a lady on the stage. In *Picardy Princess*. I want it to hand up across the footlights, so let's make it good."

She gave me a dirty look as if she was the Second Gravedigger, but she'd had ten guineas off us and she could see another five coming so she got busy with the carnations and the fern. We got behind a stand of pot-plants where I thought she couldn't see us and had another egg-nog. When I got my bouquet it was gorgeous, all pink and white and green and done up with silver paper round the bottom. Donk and I had a service flat in High Street Kensington and we took Jerry home with us for the night. Bose went off to book a table at the Savoy and dig up a red-head that he knew for Jerry to take his mind off things, which she did, and arranged to meet for dinner at Murray's. I had a bath and changed into my best uniform and sat looking at my bouquet.

They hadn't got any seats for *Picardy Princess* that night, not one in the whole house, but they'd got a box so I took that. I might have filled it up with the others but I didn't; I wanted to look at her alone. So I didn't tell them anything about it but just said I'd join up with them at the Savoy, and went and dined at the R.A.C. and sneaked out to the theatre alone. I felt awfully conspicuous alone in the box and wished I'd brought the others with me, and I think she knew that, because she spotted me almost immediately and sang her two songs straight at me, so that the audience began to turn and look at me in the box, and laugh about us, because they could see I was in the Flying Corps and that I'd got the M.C. and the Croix de Guerre.

To top it off, after the Grand Finale when the attendant took my bouquet up and handed it to her across the foot-lights she buried her face in it, and then looked up laughing, and blew a kiss at me. I stood up in the box and blew one back at her, and that brought the house down of course. Then I was round at the stage door in the alley at the back, waiting for her, in my new trench coat.

She came hurrying out and dragged me back into the dressing room she shared with two other girls, to show me the bouquet as her dresser had put it out in a great vase. I had never been back-stage before, and it was all new to me, the shabby walls, the brilliant lights, the half-dressed girls. She insisted on giving me a buttonhole from the bouquet to wear at the Savoy, but my maternity hadn't got a buttonhole to put it in, so she tucked the carnation into the strap of my Sam Browne and secured it with a safety pin just underneath the strap. Then I waited while she did up her face, and helped her into her fur coat, and then we were off chattering and chi-hiking together to the taxi I had waiting, walking on air.

The crowd were all at the Savoy when we got there and the party was in full swing, and they chipped us about having tarried on the way, which we hadn't—much. The red-head was there with Jerry, but my grandmother told me always to steer clear of a red-headed woman in black underwear, so I did. I took Judy in my arms for the first time as we danced together, and we liked it, and did it again, and again, with only a pause now and then to nibble a bit of smoked salmon or take a gulp of champagne as we rubbed knees under the table. Then, before we'd hardly got started to get to know each other, the band was playing 'God Save the King', because it was two o'clock.

Jerry must have been a bit lit up by that time, I suppose. I forget what made him do it, but in the foyer of the Savoy the red-head stooped to pick up something and he gave her a resounding smack on her black behind. She was a much bigger girl than Judy, but Judy went into one of her acts. She faced up to Jerry, eyes aflame. "You contemptible cur!" she said. "How dare you strike an innocent child like that! Poor little Evie, only six years old, and her mother still in the home for delinquent girls! Oh, how I despise you! Why don't you hit somebody your own size? Why don't you hit me? O—oh. . . . Ow!" And she flung herself on the floor of the foyer of the Savoy just as if she had been knocked down, her hand to the side of her face, the other pointing dramatically at Jerry, who was all at sea. A crowd gathered round, of course, and we were all laughing fit to burst, and then the manager came out and wasn't sure if it was going to make a legal case or not, and we picked up Judy who was moaning and saying that the brute had broken her jaw, and the hall porter with a couple of bell-hops pushed us all out into the Savoy Court where the taxis were. I got Judy into a taxi and took her to the flat in St. John's Wood that she shared with another girl, and she lay in my arms all the way while we kissed each other, and it wasn't nearly long enough.

I was writing to Timmy's mother in Palmerston North, wherever that may be, next morning, and saying what a terrible loss he was to the Squadron and how he'd died fighting the Germans just as if he'd been at the Front, and all the other things—the standard sort of letter—when Donk came in with the news that Chuck Patterson was killed, up at Waddington. Chuck was flying in a Bristol Fighter in the gunner's cockpit and they had a forced landing. The pilot, an English boy called Jenkins, tried to get into a field and hit the fence and turned it on its back. Chuck was thrown out, and when he came to, the machine was burning and the pilot in it, trapped. So

Chuck went in to try and get him out, and then the petrol tank exploded. Chuck died in hospital next day. He and I were in the same year at McGill together doing first year Engineering, and we joined up on the same day. This sure was a rough sort of war.

Judy.

Flowers, lots and lots of them. The Duchess smiling when I went into the shop.

Funerals, and firing parties. "Rest on your arms reversed . . ."

The bright sunlight in the chasms of the cumulus, the brilliance of the white clouds, the blueness of the sky. The blipping engines and the smell of castor oil and cordite from the guns.

Dancing with Judy, and the softness of her breasts against my uniform. The whispers in her ear as we danced, that never seemed to get finished.

The fun of that early summer, and the laughter, and the deaths.

Judy.

The day we had together down at Henley in the punt, when we changed into bathing things among the bushes and went swimming in the river, and I took one of her stockings so she had to take the other off and go back to London without any stockings on at all, Judy Lester, in *Picardy Princess*. The footlights, and the songs . . .

Dancing with Judy. "If you were the only girl in the world . . ." The Bing Boys, and George Robey.

Sandy McPhail diving on the target in Staines Reservoir just ahead of me when the C.C. gear failed and shot off one blade of his propeller. The engine falling out of the machine, the Camel fluttering down in weaves and spins into the water with the two machine guns running wild and spraying the whole countryside with bullets, the white plume of gas that showed its track. Sandy swimming

93

ashore fit as a flea with nothing to show for it but a cut lip and a bruised eyebrow, and the colossal binge we had at Murray's to present him with a medal for saving life—his own. The laughter, and the kisses, and the drinks.

Judy.

The investiture at Buckingham Palace, with Judy watching from the gallery. The King in naval uniform, the Sailor King, the little pointed brown beard close to my face as he pinned on the silver cross, the firm handshake. The party we had afterwards on that fine summer day when we should all have been flying and weren't because of the investiture, the lunch at Gatti's, the drinks, the kisses, and the dinghy race on the lake in Regent's Park. Taking Judy back to the flat in High Street, Kensington, to give her a cold bath so that she'd be sober enough to go on in the evening.

Judy.

The day we got our orders for going to France in ten days' time, the day I didn't have a drink all day but picked up Judy at ten past eleven at the stage door and walked her out under the trees of Leicester Square amongst all the tarts, and took her in my arms and told her, and asked her to marry me.

Judy.

The exhibition of formation flying and stunt flying that we put on for a bunch of brass hats from the War Office, nineteen of us at full squadron strength. The pilot from South Africa with ginger hair who got his fin and rudder taken off by Ben's propeller and went spinning slowly down doing everything he knew to get control again, although he must have known that you can never hope to fly a Camel without rudder because of the gyroscopic torque. The explosion when the tank burst as he hit the ground and the great column of black smoke that acted as a windsock for us all to land by, all eighteen of us. The

94

Australian from Bendigo, Tom Foreman, who 'went crook' in front of all the generals because we don't have parachutes and the Germans do . . .

The special licence. Judy.

The military funeral at Feltham in the morning, the Union Jack over the coffin on the gun carriage, the Dead March, the muffled drums, the firing squad, the prayers. The frantic rush back to the flat for a bite to eat and a couple of drinks before getting married to Judy in the afternoon, the flowers, the old slipper, the confetti at the railway carriage. Skindle's at Maidenhead, the calm summer evening, and Judy.

Judy.

The relief and the release from tensions in the morning, the little secret smiles, the breakfast tray in bed with the sun streaming in on us. The familiar hiss and crackle of a flock of Clerget Camels that brought us hopping out of bed and out on the verandah in our night things as the Squadron peeled off one by one and started in to beat up Skindle's. Jerry doing a full roll below the level of our window, Donk running his wheels along the river so that they made two light furrows on the water for a hundred yards and set the moored punts rocking. Bose going through the telephone line and taking away a length of it streaming from his undercarriage. The blipping engines, the waving pilots, the startled onlookers, and Judy waving at them in her nightie in the sun . . .

Judy.

Judy back in the show that evening, and the whole Squadron in the stalls chi-hiking at us and Judy ad-libbing back at them across the footlights, the laughter, and the fun. The four of them that set on me during the Grand Finale and dragged me out and through the little door and shoved me on the stage beside her, the glare of the footlights, the welcome from Daisy Holmes, the leading lady, as she gave us the centre of the stage, the orchestra switching from the Grand Finale to the 'Wedding March', the shouts and the laughter and the cheers from the audience, the many curtains. The impromptu supper on the stage with all the cast and all the Squadron, the champagne, the toasts.

The quiet of the night drive through the moonlit streets of London in an open taxi to the flat in Kensington that I had for the next four days alone, with Judy.

Judy.

The hectic rush to get the Squadron fit for operations in the next three days, the lining up of sights upon the new machines, the swinging of the compasses. The new pilot who was posted down to us from Ayr to replace the South African, a pink and white boy called Phil Thomas with only twenty-six hours' solo flying up in all, only twelve on Camels. The row I had with the C.O. when he was posted to my Flight, because it would be just like murder out in France, the efforts that I made to find something wrong with his flying, the failure to do so. The C.O. pointing out that I had gone to France with less experience than that. Trying to make him see that that was different, that was 1916 and on Pups while this was 1918 and on Clerget Camels. The cheerful face I had to put on it to give Phil confidence, the secret worry and the strain, even with Judy.

Judy.

The early breakfast on the last morning, the serious last kisses, the little gifts, the promises to write. The parade upon the tarmac with all the machines lined up, the speech from the General, the girls and the relations in the background. Taking off for Lympne to refuel before the Channel crossing, the major in front and the three Flights behind him, each in a V formation. Curtis in A Flight getting in Donk's backwash on the take-off and sticking in

96

a wing and cartwheeling upon the aerodrome. The dive upon the hangars and the crowd and the zoom up in farewell, the turn on course beneath the low grey clouds, the excitement and the pain of leaving. The sense of stripping off the non-essentials before battle.

The sea-crossing from Lympne, with Calvert turning back when we were five miles out because his motor quit, and going down into the sea with no boat near, a couple of miles off shore. We couldn't do a thing to help him, but Bose and Roger circling round for ten minutes, hoping somebody would see. Calvert all right, but the Camel slowly sinking when they had to leave. Hodson cracking up in landing at Gravelines. The new hut for a mess, the search for furniture for it, the air raid the first night, the letter to Judy.

Judy, who now seemed so far away.

The first patrol across the lines, leading my new Flight. The three Fokkers two thousand feet below, the dive in to attack with our six Camels, the hideous surprise when they just put their noses up and climbed away from us till they were on top and in the sun and diving down on us. These new D.7s can certainly outfly our Clerget Camels. The dog-fight and the turning, turning, covering Phil Thomas and trying to work our way back to our own side of the lines before another lot of Fokkers came along and made the numbers even. The one that I got in my sights and fired ten rounds at till the gun jammed, the sight of Jerry firing straight into a Fokker while another one was on his tail, with Phil on his. The infinite relief when they climbed away from us and made for home, probably short of fuel. Jerry cracking up on landing with his plane shot all to hell, and mine the worse for wear with two bullets in the lower port front spar.

The working out new tactics with the Major to exploit our better manœuvrability in a dog-fight. Bose bringing

97

back his first patrol with Roger missing, shot down by a Fokker somewhere to the east of Kemmel Hill. Bose telling us the Fokkers were at twenty thousand feet, a good five thousand feet higher than we can get. The Dolphins and the S.E.5s can get as high as that, but not our Camels. The knowledge that we've got to make up with our better piloting and fighting the advantage that they've got upon us in performance.

Writing to Judy, telling her about the piano we got for the mess to play her songs on.

Phil Thomas dead. Diving on a two-seat L.V.G. over Sailly that was escorted by two Fokkers, and then jumped on by four or five more Fokkers that came down out of the clouds. Jerry got the L.V.G. and sent it down in flames; he said the observer jumped out and went down in a parachute. Dick saw that, too. I was busy with a Fokker that went down smoking and out of control, a probable. Then I saw another Fokker on Phil's tail as he was flying straight and trying for a hopeless shot, miles away. Trying to get over to the Fokker to relieve Phil, and Hodson trying, too, watching the Fokker shoot him down. Hodson got the Fokker for a certain kill just after he got Phil. Passing pretty close to Phil as I pulled out and seeing half his face was shot away, certainly dead. Telling the Major when we landed that I'd said he wouldn't last a fortnight, and he hadn't.

Sam Cooper missing.

Writing to Judy, telling her what a pretty little town Gravelines is. Waiting for a letter from her, but she hasn't written yet.

Writing to Phil's mother at a place called Northwood somewhere near London.

Writing to Sam's wife at a place called Kidderminster. She's having a baby.

Writing to Judy telling her about the wildflowers here,

and the grand party we had with 74 on Tuesday when it rained all day.

Bose missing, and Bose turning up again after being shot down in flames. The ground machine guns got him going home from a patrol across the lines at about five hundred feet. The engine went on fire so he stopped it, and got out on to the wing. He found he could volplane it without engine by reaching in to grab the stick among the flames although his hand got burnt. He tried to land it but there was a hedge and he went into that and got thrown into it. He sure was lucky. He'll be in hospital a week or two, and in the meantime Peters has his Flight.

Jim Peters killed, his first patrol as Flight commander. The rear gunner in a Rumpler got him. These high-flying two-seaters are just murder because you have to fight them up at fifteen thousand feet where we have no performance. It takes three Camels to tackle a Rumpler at that height. The rumour that we may be going to get Dolphins.

Andrews and Davies, both in Donk's Flight, killed. Donk's Camel like a cullender. He says he's getting ulcers. Fokkers.

The arrival of four pilots straight from Ayr. All English, all under twenty, one of them, Peter Stanley, with only thirty-one hours' solo. God help him, because we can't do much about it.

A letter from Judy!

Judy.

Four pages, but she writes pretty big. She says everything's very dull, and I never tell her anything about the war. She's not sure, but she thinks she's going to have a baby.

I sure wish I hadn't done it. Writing to Judy to say that's marvellous.

Peter Stanley killed upon his first patrol. A Pfalz. God didn't help him and I couldn't. But I got a Fokker, certain, which makes nine. Drinks in the mess.

Writing to Peter Stanley's mother at a place called Clifton. His father was a ship's captain, killed last year. Torpedoed.

Getting the woofits now, because I don't sleep so good. Bose back and flying with his hand in bandages—they tried to send him home but he won't go. The little black-haired Irish girl that he got tangled up with at the hospital. That's bad luck, because it takes your mind off flying and you can't have that when you're on Camels in this year of grace.

Pancaking my Camel coming in to land after a patrol and wiping off the undercarriage. Saying it was because I got shot up, and knowing it was really just bad flying. The third Camel that I've used up since we came out here. Hoping that we'll come to the end of them, and get on Dolphins.

Jim Sanders killed.

I got another Fokker, which makes ten. I just got mad and went for him with three of them on my tail, all missing. Turns were a bit funny till I found that the port ailerons were shot up, not working, the controls shot through. Donk says that brandy is the best, last thing at night. But still not sleeping.

Writing to Jim Sanders' wife, in Taunton.

Reading the English newspapers. "The Fokkers saw a Flight of Camels coming down on them, so they turned and raced for home." Cutting it out and pasting it up on the wall by the bar. Good for a belly-laugh.

Bose missing, believed killed. He had his Flight out on patrol and jumped a solitary Pfalz, but it was there as a decoy and about ten Fokkers came down out of the sun. Don Curtis was shot down and killed, and Bose last seen going down with smoke pouring out and two Fokkers following him down to finish him off. Nobody saw him crash, but he won't get away with that one. They got one

Fokker. They say one of the Fokker pilots got out with a parachute. He fell about a thousand feet before it opened.

Writing to Mrs. Boswell. He was older than the rest of us, and had two kids. A schoolmaster. Every time I get to sleep I wake up with a jerk, and then I can't sleep again until I've had a drink. Going to the hospital to tell the little Irish nurse. I think she'll be consolable.

Going out alone before dawn and sneaking across the lines hedgehopping in the first light. Found a Jerry aerodrome with a Rumpler taking off and took it head-on at about five hundred feet, put a burst in its belly and went underneath. Saw it crash in flames. Eleven. Ground fire very bad all round the aerodrome and lucky to get back for breakfast. Drinks in the mess. A General came in a blue uniform to give us a pep-talk about our fine offensive spirit, and to say we'd got to get us new blue uniforms like his because we're Royal Air Force now. Called himself some kind of marshal.

Trying to write to Judy, but my hand was shaking so I gave it up and anyway I couldn't think of anything to say. Sandy McPhail got shot up and crash-landed just behind our lines. In hospital, but they say that he'll recover. Took off one leg.

Getting five Fokkers in one day, and losing the Major and Tom Foreman. Five must be pretty near a record. They're sending us Cy Hampton from 74 to be our new C.O. Of all nineteen of us who flew to France two months ago there's only Donkin and Jim Curtis left, and me. I hardly know the names of some of the mess, they come and go so quick. Cy thinks they'll send us back to England to get re-equipped with Dolphins. If so I'd see Judy and get to know about the baby. I've only had one letter but I've written a lot of times, I think.

Lying awake from midnight until half past three and

then going out in the moonlight with a bottle of gin to try and get another Rumpler. Waiting with the mechanics till the first streaks of light showed down on the horizon, watching the Handley Pages coming back from some night raid. Like great cathedrals, two Rolls Eagles, seven hundred and fifty horsepower and four men in them. The heavy dew upon my flying boots, the gin in my mouth. Contact, and the men swinging on the prop, the swish and crackle, the spitting back, the blipping till she warmed. The chocks away, the take-off down the field in the half-light. Testing the guns hedgehopping across the lines, four or five rounds from each.

The ground fire, much worse than before. Machine guns everywhere, all spitting flame at me. God, this is bad. Must, must keep low. They hit then, several times, but not me. Over those trees and down low to the fields. Gunners ahead of me, so let them have a burst. They're everywhere. Hit again then, and now smoke coming from the engine. That'll be an oil pipe, heading west now from this shambles towards our lines. Full bore, but the motor dying—only seven hundred revs. Hit again in the tail, several times, can hardly keep her in the air. Wham—my leg. Motor stopped, prop stationary, this is it.

Switches off, petrol off, down into this field. The firing has stopped. Too short and all shell-holes. Pancake down, undercarriage collapses, skidding along, the cracking of the timbers. Tip on the nose and crack my head upon the guns, then she falls back right side up. Blood streaming down my face, blood in my flying boot and down my leg. The grey-clad, running soldiers in the grey dawn.

The man speaking broken English that I could not understand, the stretcher bearers helping me out, the first aid station in a farm stable, the bandaging. The three German pilots giving me cigarettes and asking questions that I mustn't answer. Telling me that I was over G.H.Q. and asking what I hoped to gain by strafing it alone, asking if there were bombs in the machine. Not answering. If they can learn anything that's any good to them by looking at a Clerget Camel they're welcome.

The ambulance, the hospital at Ghent, the German nurses, the morphia, the deep, peaceful sleep. Waking only when they came to dress my leg and my face, and then sleeping again. Sleeping for three days and nights, they said.

The Red Cross visitor, the messages through Switzerland to Judy and to mother back in Hamilton, Ontario. The old German soldier on guard at the end of the ward, the other prisoners, the naval seaplane pilot burned all over, dying on the night he was brought in. The Halberstadts that flew by overhead in the bright sun, and the desolating knowledge that I was a prisoner, that I should never fly again.

The long journey to the prison camp at Burgwedel near Hanover.

The prison camp.

The weary months.

The weary months.

The letter from Judy in October that had taken three months to reach me, telling me the baby would be born in February.

The cold, the weary days, the snow, the prison camp.

The Armistice, the cheering and rejoicing, the sullen German officers, the train to the Dutch frontier town, the English and American voices. The sea-crossing to Harwich, the room at the Piccadilly Hotel, the trunk that I had left with Cox and King's with a new uniform in it, the tube journey to Golders Green, the bus to the small house where Judy was living with her mother.

Judy.

Judy, changed and pale and irritable and out of work. Her mother hard and hostile, pointing out that I was out of work, too. Judy refusing to come up to Town or to be seen anywhere until the baby arrived, because of her career.

Judy refusing to come back to Canada with me for my demobilisation because of her career in London.

Judy refusing to come away with me for a short holiday.

Judy crying and in a temper.

Judy.

The Piccadilly Hotel, and Donkin, Major Donkin now. Hearing from Donk about Jerry and Bose, and going down with him to Roehampton to see Sandy walking on his dummy leg. The talk of ghosts, the whiskies and the gins. The second visit to see Judy, worse than the first.

Judy.

The crossing on the overcrowded ship to Halifax, four in one cabin, the poker and the drinks. The visit to the Air Force Headquarters in Ottawa, the demobilisation, the gratuity. Arriving home at Hamilton, the crowded platform at the depot, the reporters, the photographers. Mother, and Sis, and home, so little and so very much the same. The demands that I should tell them all about it, all the neighbours. The demands that I should tell them about Judy.

Judy.

The great weariness of home, with nothing there to do. The visits to the aerodrome, the desolating sense of being out of place.

The plain clothes instead of uniform, so commonplace, so strange.

The suggestions that I should go back to college, back to school again, a married man.

The snow, the thoughtless, untouched people. The boredom of it all.

The ship back to Liverpool, third class, husbanding my little store of money.

The journey down to London, the small hotel near Euston, dirty, cheap. Judy, irritable and waiting for the baby, with the nursing home fixed up. Judy evasive when I said I'd have a flat for her to come to from the nursing home, with the baby. Judy suggesting that I'd better try and find a job. Judy full of plans for a new show as soon as her figure was back to normal.

Judy.

The desperate search for a job, with all the other ex-officers. The high ideas to start with, seven hundred a year, the demands for qualifications, for experience of business, the drop to four hundred, to four pounds a week. The visits to the aerodrome at Hounslow and at Croydon, the putting one's name down—'We'll let you know.' The job in Great Portland Street selling second-hand cars on commission that did not pay expenses. The insurance agency. The windscreen-wiper job. The tyre re-capping job. The many visits to the aerodromes, Hendon, Cricklewood, Stag Lane.

Judy in the nursing home, better tempered, thankful it was over. Judy preparing to park the baby with her mother till she could afford a nurse for it, the baby red and wrinkled, unattractive. Judy full of plans for a new show. The sense of being out of things, completely.

Judy in the showroom at Great Portland Street, dressed to kill, looking younger and more attractive than ever. Judy wanting to lunch at the Savoy so that she could be seen, and offering to pay. Judy and Herbert Schiner, actor manager. The desolating sense of being out of things.

Judy with a leading part in *Lucky Lady*, musical, seventy pounds a week. Judy taking on a nurse and moving with her mother to a flat in Hampstead. Judy with her name in lights in Leicester Square.

Judy.

The air-minded Jew clothier at Streatham, prepared to buy an Avro to do seaside joy-riding if I would fly it for him. Three pounds a week and twenty per cent of the takings after expenses were paid. The joy of the chance to get flying again. The trouble with Judy.

Judy offering me seven pounds a week as her publicity manager.

The quarrel with Judy.

The success of *Lucky Lady*.

Judy.

The Avro with its blipping, Monosoupape engine, purchased for scrap price, seventy pounds. The one ground engineer and the one boy. The tent beside it, on the beaches, in the fields. The aged Commer truck, the Primus stove, the frying-pan meals. The placards with my picture on them, the dare-devil ace, the eleven victories, the Military Cross. The warm-hearted little Jew from Streatham, delighted with the success of his first venture into show business. The one visit from Judy, half an hour, her lip curled a little.

Judy Lester, in *Lucky Lady*.

Judy.

The crowds, the blipping engine, the smell of castor oil, the ceaseless take-offs and landings over hedges in small fields, the seven-minute flights, the gaping crowds, the endless photographs in front of the machine.

Judy with a Hollywood contract, reading about it in the *Daily Mirror* in the tent in a wet field on a wet day. Telephoning Judy.

Judy.

Judy leaving for America, with her mother and the baby and the nurse. The stilted good-bye at Waterloo station, the sense of being out of place in the theatrical crowd to see her off. The knowledge then that we might never meet again.

The warm-hearted little clothier at Streatham. "You forget her, see? She got no use for you. She come to a bad end, boy. You just wait."

Judy.

The second Avro, and the second pilot, the third engineer.

The film of *Lucky Lady*.

The letter from the lawyer at Reno, Nevada, telling me that Judy Pascoe (Lichter) was suing for divorce citing desertion, asking if I intended to contest the suit.

. Judy.

I woke in the darkness in the little windswept house beside the aerodrome in Tasmania. My face and Johnnie Pascoe's pillow were all wet with tears.

Chapter Four

In the ordinary way I never have bad dreams or any dreams at all; I had not cried since I was a boy. I was ashamed of myself, and I was struck by the grim idea that this was a new manifestation of fatigue. All pilots must grow old like other men; when the fatigues of flying start to bear too heavily upon them it shows at the next medical examination. I was not an old man and I had kept myself pretty fit, but bad dreams and crying were probably a warning.

I got out of bed and went into the other room. It was about nine o'clock; I had slept for about four hours. I must sleep again, but now I was restless and awake. The fire was still glowing in the hearth; I poked the logs together and threw on more wood. The wind was still high, but the rain seemed to have stopped. I thought about Sheila, and crossed to the telephone and put in a call to my home at Essendon.

They told me that the call would be through in a few minutes, so I put down the receiver, went back to the bedroom, and put on Johnnie Pascoe's dressing gown. He seemed to use it a good deal, for there was a packet of cigarettes in the pocket, open, with a few still left in it, and a box of matches in the pocket on the other side. I lit one of his cigarettes and went and stood before the fire, waiting for the call. I glanced at the photographs of Judy. Since I had slept she had become very real to me, far more than a monochrome image on a fading bit of sensitised paper. I knew the way she turned her head, the feel of her against me. I could have picked out her voice amongst a hundred others on a gramophone record. My imagination had been running wild in my dreams, and that was not a very good thing. When a pilot gets to a certain age, I thought, he should begin to live a very regular sort of a life—get up at the same time, go to bed at the same time, work at the same time each day. If you did that, you could go on flying for a long, long time, as Johnnie Pascoe had. If you didn't, you would fail a medical at forty-five, and that would be the end. I had departed from my regularity in the last day or two, and I had received the warning. Still, nobody knew of it but me.

The telephone rang, and there was Sheila. "Evening, dear," I said. "I just rang to say it's okay over here. How are things with you?"

"We're fine here," she said. "How are things with you, Ronnie?"

"I made two trips down there this morning with the doctor, in an Auster," I said. "It's a shocking little strip, and I couldn't land him either time. The second time it clamped right down."

"It said on the wireless that the R.A.A.F. had sent a Lincoln down to Hobart with a parachute doctor and a parachute nurse," she remarked.

"I believe they have," I replied. "They may be able to get in for a drop tomorrow, but I wouldn't bank on it. They'll have to have clear weather for the drop. There are some pretty high mountains round about, up to about four thousand feet."

"They could jump above the clouds, couldn't they?" she asked. "I mean, if it was clear for a few hundred feet underneath?"

"I don't believe they'd do that," I said. "It's too close to the sea. And the country's quite uninhabited you know, and very wild. I don't think that would be a reasonable risk. No, if it was like that I think we could do better in the Auster. Come in low over the sea and nip in underneath the clouds."

"How is he now?" she asked. "Johnnie Pascoe?"

"I haven't heard for the last few hours," I told her. "I've been asleep since five. I'm going to ring the police station in a minute and find out what the form is. He's got a fractured skull, and that's not quite so good."

She said, "Oh, the poor man . . ." And then she asked, "How is the child? The one that's got appendicitis?"

"She seems to be recovering. The urgent case is Johnnie Pascoe now."

"I know." There was a pause, and then she said, "Don't go and take *too* many risks, Ronnie."

I laughed. "I won't do that." We had been married for twelve years, and I knew what she was thinking. One day Ronnie Clarke might be in the same boat, and want help from another pilot. "I'm going to have another stab at it at dawn if the conditions are at all possible. One or other of us should be able to get in to him tomorrow, one way or another."

"When do you think you'll be able to ring me again?"

I thought for a moment. "I'm hoping to be home tomorrow night. If I can't make it, I'll ring you tomorrow evening."

"All right, dear," she said. "Good luck."

"My love to the kids," I said. "And you. Good-bye for now."

I rang off, and lit another of Johnnie Pascoe's cigarettes while the line was clearing. Then I picked up the receiver again and rang the police station. The sergeant answered. "Captain Clarke here," I said. "Speaking from Captain Pascoe's house. I've been asleep. Tell me, what's the latest on the weather?"

The sergeant said, "Well, the wind's dropping, so they say. I've not noticed it here—blowing as hard as ever.

They don't think there'll be any more rain for the time being."

"What about the cloud?"

"Continuing low cloud all day tomorrow. They think there might be a break tomorrow evening, and a fine night."

"What about Captain Pascoe?"

"He's still alive, but he's worse. Deteriorating, you might say."

"Where's Dr. Parkinson?"

"He's at the hotel, with his pilot. If I may say so, Dr. Turnbull is the one you want."

"Why? Dr. Parkinson flew up here specially to do this job."

"I know. But now he's here, he don't seem so keen on it, somehow. Dr. Turnbull, he's roaring to go."

I laughed shortly. "I thought I'd have given him a sickener of flying."

"I don't know about that," the sergeant said. "He was telling them what you'd been doing in the hotel. It's Dr. Turnbull wants to go with you again. He's got a nurse, too."

"A nurse?" I thought very quickly. A nurse was what the doctor had wanted with him for a head operation. If he had found one now . . . well, the Auster would seat three people, though she would be more heavily loaded, less easy to handle in extreme conditions. Still, if there was a nurse it was clearly up to me to take her in with the doctor. "Where did he get a nurse from?"

"She arrived about seven o'clock. Friend of Captain Pascoe, or something. She's a qualified hospital nurse all right. Works at the Alexandra Hospital, in Melbourne."

"Just a moment," I said. "This isn't a woman called Mrs. Forbes, is it? A middle-aged woman, from Adelaide?"

"No," he replied. "Mrs. Forbes, she came this morning.

She's staying at the hotel. This is a younger woman, a Sister Dawson. Under thirty, I'd say."

I thought for a minute. "Look, Sergeant," I said at last. "I'm going to get a good night's sleep, but I want to go down to the Lewis River again at dawn if the weather's anything like fit, taking the doctor with me, and this nurse. If I can't land them, I'll come back and wait an hour or two, and try again. It's the only way—we've got to keep on trying. The doctor's on the telephone, isn't he?"

"That's right," he said. "He lives at the vicarage. The number is two six, Mr. Haynes. You'd get him there now, unless he's out upon a case."

"How can I get hold of the nurse?"

"I think she's with the doctor. Mrs. Haynes was going to give her supper."

"I'll ring them in a minute. How can I get hold of Mr. Monkhouse, the ground engineer?"

"He isn't on the telephone. I could send a message over, ask him to come down to see you."

"I don't think that's necessary. I'm just going back to bed . . ." I thought for a moment. "Look, it starts to get light about seven. Tell him I want the Auster refuelled and ready to take off at six o'clock in the morning. I'll be down at the hangar then. If it's a reasonable night I'll take off in the dark and get down to the Lewis River about dawn, with the doctor and the nurse with me. Tell him I shall want a few kerosene flares out on the aerodrome for the take-off—he'll know what's wanted."

The sergeant said, "You want everything ready to fly at six o'clock, kerosene flares, and everything. I'll take that message over myself."

"Thanks a lot, Sergeant. If you're speaking to Hobart again, see if they can get me any sort of Met report by half past five. And tell them to warn Mrs. Hoskins at the Lewis River I'll be down again soon after dawn."

"Will you be speaking to Dr. Parkinson, sir?"

I hesitated. "I suppose I ought to. But you say he doesn't want to do this job?"

The sergeant hesitated in turn. "Well, I don't know anything officially."

"Tell me what you know unofficially," I said. "Is it that he doesn't want to fly with me?"

The sergeant laughed awkwardly. "Well, that's about the strength of it, I'm afraid. I was off duty after dinner, after you come back, and I went into the hotel to meet these gentlemen and have a beer. While I was with them, Dr. Turnbull, he came in and told them about the first flight you made when he couldn't get out of the door, and about the second time when you was messing about in the rain in among the cliffs and running out of petrol. Dr. Parkinson and his pilot, they got quite upset at what he told them. Of course," he added hurriedly, "Dr. Turnbull, he wouldn't know what was safe and what wasn't."

"What did Dr. Turnbull think about it all?" I asked.

"He come out on your side," the sergeant said. "Dr. Parkinson, he said as he'd prefer to fly with Mr. Barnes, that flew him up from Hobart. Dr. Turnbull, he turned round and told them what he thought. Said he'd fly with you again. Said it was reasonable to take a chance when somebody was dying, and anyway you'd brought him back safe and sound, not once, but twice. The two doctors had a proper dust-up there in the hotel. All very quiet and polite, you know. But very awkward."

I thought about it for a minute. "We'll have to take turns with this Auster," I said at last. "I shan't speak to Dr. Parkinson tonight. If that's the way he feels about it, he certainly won't want to take off in bad weather in a single-engined aircraft in the dark to fly down the coast without any navigation aids, and no alternative strips to land on. If you should see him again tonight tell him what we're doing, and that we'll be back by breakfast time if we can't make it. Phil Barnes can have the Auster then and have another stab at it with Dr. Parkinson in daylight, while we're resting. That way we'll have another doctor and another pilot trying to get through. We'll take it in turns all day tomorrow."

"That's a good idea," the sergeant said. "Real tactful, I would say. If I don't see you before you go, sir, the very best of luck."

I rang off, and stood thoughtful for a minute while the line cleared. His first experience of flying seemed to have done Dr. Turnbull a bit of good.

I rang two six, and Mrs. Haynes answered the phone. I waited while she fetched the doctor from upstairs, and then I told him what I wanted to do. "It's going to be a bit early in the morning, and it's going to be a bit dicey in a single-engined aircraft in the dark over that sort of country," I told him. "But as I understand it, it's getting really urgent now."

"I think it is," he said. "It sounds like sepsis to me."

"Could you do anything for that?" I asked.

"Oh, if I could get down there I could lift some of the damaged bone and do something about it," he said. "That's quite a normal procedure. Whether he'd recover ultimately—well, that's another matter."

"Would you mind flying down so early as that?" I asked. "We'd have to fly without the cabin door again."

"No, I don't mind," he replied. "I think we ought to. There's just one thing, though. I've got a nurse here now, a proper nurse experienced in surgery. Could we take her with us?"

"I know," I said. "The sergeant told me about her. There's room for her in the aircraft, in the seat behind. The only thing is, she'll have to get out in the same way that you do. If there's a strong wind I'll try and hold the aircraft stationary on the ground for a short time like we did this morning, so that you can get out. Then I'd probably have to take off again and cruise around while she changes into your seat, and then come in and put her out in the same way. Do you think she could do that?"

"I think she could."

"What sort of a woman is she?" I asked. "Is she active and athletic?"

"She's here with me now," he replied. "We've been talking about this already. She's quite ready to try it. I think she'll be all right."

"She'd better not wear skirts," I said. "Can you fit her out with a pair of trousers? Trousers without turn-ups at the bottom?"

"I can borrow a pair of ski-ing trousers for her."

"That's just the thing. Get her some ski boots, too—something to support the ankle. No high-heeled shoes."

"I'll look after that."

"Fine. Tell me, how did you get hold of her?"

"She just turned up to see if she could help. She knows Captain Pascoe. She worked for a year as an air hostess for AusCan, flying between Sydney and Vancouver. She met him then. Then she went back to the hospital."

"Well, she couldn't have turned up at a better time."

"One thing," he said. "I'm having a bit of trouble finding somewhere for her to sleep tonight. The hotel's full, and we're full up here. Have you got a spare bed in Captain Pascoe's house if I bring her down?"

"There *is* a bed," I said, "and it's got a mattress on it, but no bedclothes and no pillows, and it's all a bit dirty. She's welcome to that, but you'll have to rustle up some bedclothes for her."

He thought for a moment. "I've got a sleeping bag," he said. "I think she'd better use that. You don't mind if she sleeps in the house with you?"

"Not if she doesn't."

"It'll make it a bit more convenient for getting out early in the morning if she's there with you," he said. "She's just going to have supper. Be all right if I bring her down in about an hour?"

I hesitated. "That'll be all right," I said at last. "I'm sleeping in Johnnie Pascoe's room, and I'm going back to bed now. That's the room on the left as you go into the passage from the living room. She'll be sleeping in the room on the right—I'll leave the door open. The thing is —it's rather important that I should be on the top line tomorrow morning and I want to get a really good night's sleep. I'm going to take a Nembutal. When you come in, try not to make a noise."

"I understand," he said. "You've got a Nembutal, have you? I can let you have one if you haven't."

"No, I've got all I want," I said. "Just try not to wake me up when you come in. I'm setting an alarm clock for five o'clock, and I'd like to sleep through till then."

I rang off, and stood for a moment looking round the room. I was wakeful and thirsty, and the thought of another whisky crossed my mind. Alcohol, however, is a stimulant and might not be a very good thing to take if one wanted the hypnotic drug to work. A glass of milk would be better, and I went through to the kitchen and found milk in the refrigerator, and came back to the living room with a glass of ice-cold milk and a couple of biscuits.

Cold milk. Cold milk at a party. Ice-cold milk with Crème de Menthe. What bell did that ring in the distant past? Something to do with flying, certainly—but what? Ice-cold milk and Crème de Menthe? What pilot had that been?

And then it all came flooding back into my memory, the inquest that the Coroner, my father, had held on Brenda

Marshall after she died in the hangar of the club. Me sitting in the body of the court and Johnnie Pascoe on the witness stand, and Dad asking him questions about the accident, and writing down his answers all in longhand so that the enquiry stretched out, painful and apparently interminable. "Have you any reason to suppose that the deceased had taken any alcoholic liquor before she went up on this flight?" And Johnnie Pascoe answering, "No, sir. As a general rule, she never drank anything but cold milk in the clubhouse. Sometimes in the evening at a party she would drink a Crème de Menthe, but I never saw her do that before flying. I shouldn't think that alcohol had anything to do with it." Johnnie Pascoe on the witness stand, the pilot instructor, bronzed and athletic, very grave and serious.

Brenda Marshall.

I crossed the room and stood looking at the photograph again, immersed in memories. It must have been taken in 1930 or 1931, about the time I learned to fly. I remembered the Moth behind her in the photograph so well. She had it painted white, and because the registration letters were G-EMLF she called it Morgan le Fay. Over her shoulder in the photograph I could see the beginning of the word Morgan, painted below the engine.

Johnnie Pascoe had taught her to fly in 1930, the year before he taught me. Brenda Marshall, with her short, curly hair, her shy and friendly smile, her white flying suit, her Moth. Brenda Marshall, who was kind to everyone, who made a home for her sister's baby when her sister had to go to India with her husband. Brenda Marshall, at Duffington aerodrome in 1930. Brenda Marshall, of Duffington Manor, the big house in the village. Brenda Marshall, who had had bad luck with her husband, who lived alone in the big house with her mother till her sister wished the baby and nurse on her. Brenda Marshall, the first woman I was ever in love with, though I was eighteen and she nearly thirty. Brenda, that everybody in the Duffington club had been in love with including Johnnie Pascoe, pilot instructor. But nobody knew that but me, I think, and I never told a soul. Brenda Marshall, who had taken me up in the front seat of her new Moth one day and let me fly it, long before I learned to fly officially.

I blew a long cloud of smoke as I stood looking at the photograph twenty-eight years later. At that time and for some years afterwards it seemed to me that Dad had never been so stupid. He could be very dense sometimes. Before the inquest I had tried to make him understand something about aeroplanes, with the superior knowledge of about five hours' solo to my credit. I had said to him that the accident needed a good deal of sifting and investigation; she had got into a spin at six or seven hundred feet right over the middle of the aerodrome, and that sort of thing just didn't happen to an experienced pilot like Brenda Marshall. But Dad had been pig-headed and legal that day, and had refused to listen to me. He just said that aeroplanes were very dangerous things for women pilots, that she must have fainted, and that anyway I couldn't possibly know what had happened in the machine. He had taken that line at the inquest, too. He had asked the standard, rather stupid, questions about the airworthiness certificate of her Moth and about the validity of Brenda's licence and about her general state of health, and he had written all that down in longhand. He had examined Dr. Haughton who had given him an account of her multiple injuries, two broken legs, fractured pelvis, three fractured ribs, fractured right forearm, fractured jaw, and fractured left clavicle, and had told us that the cause of death was shock, and Dad had written all that down. He had examined the police sergeant who turned up on a bicycle just before she died and had a long account to give that told us nothing, and he had written all that down in long-hand, too.

By that time the inquest had lasted for an hour and a half, and I suppose Dad felt that he had done his stuff. He shuffled his papers together and announced that after a full investigation of this very sad affair he found that the deceased had met her death by accidental causes in a flying accident. He expressed the sympathy of the court with the dead woman's mother and with her husband who was shortly to come out of hospital. With that he closed the court, and at home he refused to discuss the case with me at all. As he had been so stupid about it all, I didn't pursue the matter. Soon after that Johnnie Pascoe left Duffington to take a job with Imperial Airways in India and the club got another pilot instructor. Her mother went away and took the baby with her but it died a short time later, someone told me. Within six months there was another tragedy at Duffington when Derek Marshall who had had shell-shock in the war and had been in and out of hospital ever since, got himself involved in a particularly unpleasant case of rape and blew his head off with a shot-gun. After that the house was sold and some people called Forsyth came to live there, who bred goats.

It was years before it gradually occurred to me that possibly Dad hadn't been so stupid after all. But he was dead by that time, and I never had a chance to verify my hunch.

The cold milk was beginning to work, and I was feeling more relaxed. I stubbed out my cigarette and went into the bedroom, glass in hand, and found the little bottle of hypnotic pills in my haversack, and swallowed one down with a mouthful of milk. The unmade bed was beginning to look inviting, but I went back to the sitting room for a few minutes to stand by the fire and finish my glass of milk. The time was half past nine.

Johnnie Pascoe, I thought, must know much more about Brenda Marshall than I did, because I had seen him kissing her in the half-light late one evening in the hangar, behind the Blackburn Bluebird. I remember that evening particularly because it was the evening she came back to Duffington from France. She had been away in France for the whole of the winter, and in those months her Moth had been down at Heston for a C. of A. She had stayed in London for a few days on her way home, and had picked up her Moth after its overhaul and flown it home. When she came back to Duffington that April afternoon we had none of us seen her since the previous September, and it was grand to have her back. I was in the air with Johnnie Pascoe doing dual when she came in. He saw her first, a little speck in the south-east just above the horizon, coming towards us, and we flew to meet her, and turned and flew alongside her Moth in formation, waving at her as she waved back to us. From the air we watched her landing and landed ourselves immediately, cutting short my lesson, and taxied in behind her. I hung around till dusk examining her Moth after we had pushed it into the hangar, because it had had Sperrys put in it at the overhaul and I wanted to ask one or other of them how you used them. But they were both too busy to have time for me. It hurt a bit to see him kissing her although I was able to laugh at myself, for she was nearly thirty and a married woman and I was only just eighteen. But they both looked so happy I was glad for them, and after all her husband had been in the loony-bin for years.

I stood there wondering, as I had wondered for the last two years since chatting with him in the pilots' room at Sydney airport, whether the baby had been his, the one that died. When I was eighteen it never entered my head and if it had it would have been incredible. But now, with greater knowledge of the world, I wondered . . .

Presently I finished my glass of his milk, went back sleepily into his bedroom, threw off his dressing gown, and got back into his bed. The Nembutal was beginning to work, and I was drowsy now. The time was about twenty minutes to ten. His travelling alarm clock was on his bedside table by my side; I reached out for it and set it for five o'clock. With any luck now I could get to sleep before the doctor brought the nurse into the house, and I settled down upon his pillows with his bedclothes round my shoulders.

Twenty-eight years later, for Johnnie Pascoe the wheel had come round the full circle, for he was now a pilot instructor at a little flying club again teaching young men and women how to fly an Auster or a Tiger Moth. Successive waves of sleep were passing over me and sinking me down into forgetfulness of present things, and as I went I wondered if he had ever had another pupil such as Brenda Marshall. I knew how it had happened; it was all as clear as if it had been yesterday. She lived with her mother in the big house at the entrance to the village, and she drove an Alvis sports saloon. In a way she owned the aerodrome because it had been requisitioned in the war from one of her husband's farms, and the Air Ministry were still leasing it. For a year after I arrived in Duffington I saw nothing of her. I lived at the hotel, the Seven Swans, and I was busy working up the club, and I was getting most of the enterprising young men and women of Leacaster as members. I knew the Marshalls' car and I knew who she was by sight, and I had heard that her husband was in some hospital. It was a surprise to me when the Alvis drew up outside the hangar one bleak morning in January and she got out. I had never spoken to her but I knew that in a way she was our landlord, and I went out of the office to meet her.

She came towards me. "It's Captain Pascoe, isn't it?" she asked.

I smiled. "That's right."

She said, "I'm Mrs. Marshall."

"I know," I replied. "I'm very glad to meet you."

She said, "I ought to have met you a long time ago, but we don't go out a great deal." She hesitated, and then said, "I felt I must come down here and see what's going on. After all, we're such near neighbours."

"I'd like to show you everything there is to see," I said. The January wind whistled around us from the north. "Would you like to come into the office? There's a coke stove in there. We've got a fireplace in the club room, but we don't light the fire unless we know that there are people coming out. Only the week-ends. Things go a bit flat in the winter in a flying club, you know—although the hours are keeping up quite well. We did a hundred and five hours in December."

"That's splendid," she said vaguely. I showed her to the office, and the hot air and the stink from the coke stove hit us like a blast. She threw back her fur coat. She was bare-headed, and the short reddish-brown curls were massed all over her head, boyish. She was rather pale, and I thought she did not look well.

"Have you got a lot of members here?" she asked.

"Two hundred and ten flying members," I told her, "and about three hundred associate members. Would you like a cup of tea?"

"Oh, please don't bother."

"We usually have one about this time." I went out and spoke to the ground engineer, and asked him to slip over to the clubhouse for another cup, with a saucer, unusual in the hangar. Then I went back to my visitor and found her standing in the office door looking at the aircraft. "They're so much bigger when you see them close up," she observed.

"These two are Moths," I told her. "That's a Bluebird."

She walked over and looked into the cockpit of the nearest Moth. "All these clocks mean something, I suppose . . ."

"That's the most important one," I said. "Tells you how fast you're going. Have you ever flown?"

"Just for ten minutes, about two years ago," she said. "A man was here giving joyrides."

"Would you like to go up again?" I asked. "I can take you up any time. We charge two pounds ten an hour."

She brightened. "Could you do that?"

"That's what we're here for. We could go up this morning, if you like, but you might enjoy it more when it's sunny. I'd like to take you, any time you say."

She looked out of the hangar door; it had begun to rain a little. "I'd love to go up again, but it's a bit piggy now. I'd like to go when you can see something."

I laughed. "Quite frankly, Mrs. Marshall, so would I. Creeping along in the rain just above the tree tops, trying to find one's way back here by recognising the cows, isn't really my idea of fun. There's a change forecast for this evening, though. We might get a fine day tomorrow."

We went back into the office for our tea. "Esmé Haughton's a member of this club, isn't she?" she asked.

"The doctor's daughter? She's been doing quite a bit of dual. She'll be going solo in a week or two."

"She was telling me about it last night. She said that everybody has such fun down here . . ."

"We get quite a crowd here at the week-ends," I said. "It gets to be a bit of a riot sometimes, I'm afraid, but we do our best to keep things under control. Everybody's fairly young, you see. Still, I got the Lord Mayor as a member last week and the Chief Constable the week before, so they can't think too badly of us."

"Esmé told me Colonel Chance had joined. She says he's learning to fly."

I nodded. "He's had two lessons. He's going to be all right." The Chief Constable had two sons in the Royal Air Force, and he wanted to learn the craft that was important in their lives.

"He's awfully old to learn to fly, isn't he?"

"I think he's about fifty-eight. It's not difficult, you know, so long as you've got good eyesight."

"Can a person really learn to fly when he's as old as that?" she asked. "I always thought you had to be frightfully young."

I smiled. "Not to fly this sort of aeroplane. Of course, if you want to fly the latest Air Force fighter, then you do have to be young. The Avro Avenger and the Hawker Fury—they do two hundred miles an hour and they land at over sixty. But anyone can fly this sort of aeroplane."

"Women also?" she asked. "Could you teach me to fly?"

"Of course, Mrs. Marshall. Would you like to learn?"

Her eyes sparkled. "It would be marvellous! But I thought I'd be too old."

I smiled. "You must be under thirty, surely."

She nodded. "That wouldn't be too old?"

"Of course not. Your eyesight's all right, isn't it?"

"I think it is. I don't have to wear glasses."

"Your heart's all right? There's nothing the matter with you? It doesn't look as if there is."

She laughed, and blushed a little. "I think I'm quite all right."

"Of course you can learn to fly," I told her. "You'll probably get a lot of fun out of it."

"I believe I should. I used to sail a boat. It's like that, isn't it?"

"A bit," I said. "You're keen on sailing?"

She nodded, and put down her cup. "Would you like to come outside and sit in the machine?" I suggested. And as we walked over to the Moth I said, "If you're going to learn to fly you'll have to join the club. That'll cost you three guineas."

She laughed. "That's really what I came here to do. I didn't mean to learn to fly at all."

"I know," I said. "One thing leads to another."

I showed her the footholds on the fuselage and helped her into the back cockpit. When she was settled down and comfortable I started in to show her the controls, using the Gosport patter. I found that she was rather above average of women pupils for her comprehension of things mechanical. That was probably due to her position; she was used to driving a fast car and interested in it. The oil-pressure gauge and the rev counter were familiar to her, and she readily grasped the starting-up procedure to avoid kicking back. She learned the idea of the main controls without much difficulty, and when she had got that far it seemed to me that she had had enough for one day. She sat on for ten minutes longer in the machine, getting the feel of it, and to assist her we swung the Moth round to face the rain-swept aerodrome through the open door and lifted its tail up into flying attitude upon a trestle to make the look and feel of the machine realistic for her.

Presently she got out of the machine, made an appointment for a lesson the next day, and drove off in the Alvis.

It was sunny and cold next morning, with a touch of frost in the air and not much wind. I fitted her up with a helmet and headphones, lent her my leather coat and goggles, put her into the back cockpit, strapped her in, and saw that she was comfortable. Then I got into the front seat and the G.E. swung the prop for me, and I sat explaining to her over the phones what I was doing in the pre-flight checks. Then we taxied out to the far hedge, and got into the air.

She wanted to see her home, Duffington Manor, from the air, so we did a circuit over that, and then went up to a thousand feet for her to learn to fly straight and level, while I gave her the patter. She got on all right, and at the end of half an hour I took over the control and told her we were going in to land. She was to rest her hands and feet lightly on the controls and just watch what I did.

She said, "Before we land, do you think we could loop the loop?"

I was surprised. "Would you like me to loop it?"

"Not if it's any bother. But I would like to loop the loop one day."

"We can loop it now," I said. "We'll get a little bit more height, first." As we climbed I made her check her safety belt. Then with her hands and feet resting loose on the controls I dived the thing a bit and sailed it over in a loop, telling her what I was doing all the time, cutting the engine when the ground came down from the ceiling. When we were flying level again I twisted round to look at her, and she was flushed and laughing. "That was marvellous!" she said.

I turned back to the voice pipe. "Did you have your hands and feet on the controls?"

"Yes. I felt everything you did."

"Okay. I didn't feel you." I learned then that she had a very gentle touch, very sensitive hands. "Keep them there while we land."

I brought the Moth on to the circuit and in on final to the hedge with a bit of sideslip, talking my patter all the time. I put it on the ground and taxied into the hangar, and stopped the engine. I got out and helped her out of the machine, and when she was on the ground she said, "I don't know when I enjoyed anything so much. How long were we up for?"

"Half an hour," I said. "That's enough for one

lesson." She was flushed and bright-eyed, looking ten times better than she had the day before.

"It seemed like five minutes. Can I have another one tomorrow?"

"Sure," I said. "If you're going to learn to fly, it's quite a good thing to go on and do it every day, if you can manage to. You don't forget things in between."

"How long would it take me before I could go solo?"

I smiled, and thought for a moment as we walked towards the office. Women usually take longer than men, but she had very good hands and some knowledge of motor cars. Still, I'd have to be very sure of her before I let her go. Navigation would probably be a weakness; she might lose sight of the aerodrome and get lost. "Most people take ten or twelve hours dual," I said. "Twenty or twenty-five lessons."

"Three weeks," she said. "Then one day you just get out of the front seat and tell me I can go alone?"

I laughed. "That's right. Would you like a cup of tea?"

"I'd love a cup of tea."

We went into the office and I sent the boy for tea, and she took off my coat and helmet and ran a comb through her short, curly hair. She was full of questions about the machine and her instruction, really interested and very much alive. I took twenty-five bob off her for the lesson and three guineas for her membership, and seven and six for a book of flying instruction that I thought would do her good. Then the tea came, and she took a cigarette off me.

As she was smoking it, she asked, "Tell me, Captain Pascoe—are you English? I'm afraid that's a frightfully rude question."

I laughed. "It's a very natural one. I'm Canadian. Have I still got an accent?"

"Not an accent," she said thoughtfully. "It's more of a

rhythm. I thought at first you were American, and then I didn't think you were. Forgive me for asking."

"I come from Hamilton, Ontario," I told her. "I came to England in 1915 to join the R.A.F., and I've hardly been home since. I don't suppose I'll ever get to talk quite like an Englishman."

"You'd rather be here than in Canada?" she asked.

I nodded. "I've grown into things here. I'd probably feel like a fish out of water back at home now, after all these years."

"I've never been out of England," she said. "It must be fun to travel."

I was very much surprised, for she was evidently well off, to live in a house like Duffington Manor. I would have expected her to know the south of France, and Italy. "You've never been to France?"

She shook her head. "I've never been anywhere. I suppose you've been to France a lot of times."

"As a matter of fact, I haven't. Only in the war, and that doesn't count."

"Esmé said that you were flying fighters in the war."

"That's right."

"Were they very difficult to fly?" A shaft of the January sunlight came in weakly through the office window and made a golden aureole around her in the blue haze of the coke stove.

"They were much more difficult than a Moth, although they only had about the same performance. They had rotary engines without any proper throttle control, most of them. It was much more difficult to learn to fly in those days than it is now."

"What you taught me today wasn't very difficult."

"You seemed to get hold of it all right."

"Will it be more difficult when I get further on?"

"I don't think so," I said. "It's like everything else—

don't try and learn too much all at once. Don't bother about that loop, for example—put that out of your mind for the present. I'll teach you that later. Just concentrate on what you've done, and then next time we'll do a little bit more, and so on. You won't have any trouble."

She finished her tea, and made an appointment for another lesson next morning, at the same time; she asked me to ring her up if the weather should be too bad. As she was leaving, she said, "I'm not sure that I'm dressed right, Captain Pascoe. A skirt isn't very convenient. Would it be better if I wore a pair of trousers?"

That was a very daring suggestion, and I was surprised. "Well—yes, it would," I said. "It might make you a bit conspicuous, though."

"I could change here, couldn't I?" she asked. "In the Ladies' Room?"

"It would be better," I said. The Lady of the Manor had a position to keep up in Duffington. "Have you got a pair of trousers?"

She shook her head. "I know a shop in London where they sell them for ladies, ready made."

"If you're going to do that," I said, "I think I'd go the whole hog and wear an overall, a boiler suit. There's always liable to be a bit of oil about an aeroplane. We try and keep them clean, but they aren't like a car. If you wore a boiler suit over everything, it might save your clothes."

She nodded. "I believe you can get white ones in London. One could have them laundered, then."

"That's right," I said. "You *can* get white ones, and they look very nice. You could come in your own clothes and change over at the clubhouse."

She got into the Alvis and drove off, still bright and excited, and looking very pretty. That afternoon it was sunny, and Colonel Chance came out for a lesson, the

Chief Constable. He had had four or five before, and he was doing turns. I had him up for half an hour, and when he landed we stood smoking outside the hangar for a few minutes.

"I got a new member yesterday," I told him. "Mrs. Marshall joined. She had her first lesson this morning."

"Mrs. Derek Marshall?" he asked. "From the Manor?"

"That's right."

He smiled. "How did she do?"

"All right. She might make a good pilot."

He stood thoughtful behind bushy grey eyebrows, the short, clipped grey moustache. "I should think she might. She drives that car too fast, but she drives quite well. Pity about her husband."

"He's in some kind of hospital, isn't he?"

He said shortly, "He's in The Haven."

"I'm sorry," I said. "I didn't know." The Haven was a very expensive private home exclusively for mental cases, on the outskirts of Leacaster.

"He got shell-shock in the war," he said. "When they were married everybody thought he was cured, but then he got a relapse. He's been in and out of The Haven ever since." He paused, and then he said, "Of course, it wasn't the shell-shock. There was a weakness there before. The Marshalls all used to marry their cousins."

"Is he in there permanently?" I asked.

"I think so. He's certified now, anyway. They keep on trying every new thing, of course." He drew on his cigarette, and then he said, "She's had a time with him."

I was grateful to him for telling me. It's better to know the scandal about members, and then one can avoid saying the wrong thing. I think that was in his mind, too, and that was why he told me.

"They must be pretty well off," I said.

"Wool spinners," he replied. "Marshall and Collins.

They've got a big mill in Halifax. His brothers run the business."

I wrinkled my brows; now was the time to find out everything I ought to know. "Who's the old lady—Mrs. Duclos, that lives at the Manor?"

"That's her mother," he told me. "She came to live there after Marshall was certified. I suppose it was lonely for Brenda living in that big house all alone."

"Are there any children?"

He shot a glance at me. "Children? Oh, no. I suppose they had more sense."

He went away, and I went back to writing up the log books and digested my new information. Next day my pupil came again for another lesson, and told me she was going down to London. There was a gap of a few days then, and when she came for her third lesson she had a brown paper parcel in her hand as she got out of the car.

I smiled. "You got it?"

"I got three of them," she said, "and a white flying helmet. Look, are they all right?" She undid her parcel on the bonnet of the car and spread her purchases out, child-like, for my approval.

I turned the flying helmet over in my hands. "That's all right," I said. "I've got a spare pair of headphones we can put in this."

"I asked about that," she said. "They told me these ear flaps were designed to take the standard R.A.F. phones."

"That's right. It should look very nice when you're wearing it."

"I got a pair of goggles, too, like yours," she said. She showed them to me. "And I got this leather waistcoat to go underneath."

I turned the garments over, smiling. "You've got everything. You must have spent a lot of money."

She said simply, "I had a lot of fun. Shall I go over to the club and put them on?"

I nodded. "I'll get the machine pushed out while you're changing, and fit a pair of headphones in the helmet for you."

When she came across the tarmac to the machine in the weak, frosty sun she was dazzling in white, boyish with her short, curly hair. She put on her new white helmet and I adjusted the headphones for her; with the strap done up beneath her chin the white fabric framed her face giving her, queerly, the appearance of a nun. I stood back and looked at her, and then went round behind her and did up the strap of the boiler suit behind her back. "That's better." And then I said casually, "You look like a million dollars."

She laughed self-consciously. "It feels very business-like."

"Well, let's get to business. We'll try a turn or two today."

"How do you do a turn?"

"I'll tell you when you're in the air. Can you remember how to do your belt up?"

"I think so."

"Well, get in and do your belt up while I get my coat, and then I'll come and see if you've done it right."

When we were in the air I told her about climbing and gave her the machine to hold on a straight climb. When we got up to a thousand feet and she was flying straight and level I found that she was doing it quite well; over the gasworks and the railway station the air was a bit bumpy, but her corrections were quick and accurate. I turned the machine and set her to fly back through the bumpy bit for practice, and then I started in to show her Rate One turns. By the time that her half hour was up she was doing those quite nicely, and I was reflecting that I'd have a job to spin out her instruction for twelve hours, the time I always like to give a woman pupil as a minimum.

When we landed and got out of the machine I told her, "That was very good, Mrs. Marshall. You were doing those turns quite nicely. You were slipping outwards just a bit on one or two of them. Holding off a little too much bank. Try and think of your behind when you're in a turn. Get the feel of it so that you don't feel you're slipping either way upon the cushion."

"Isn't that what the little bubble is supposed to tell you?"

"Don't think about the bubble. Think of your behind. I'll tell you about the bubble later. The only instrument you want to use at present is the airspeed indicator."

She nodded. "I do like flying in this boiler suit. It seems to make it so much easier."

"Does it?"

She nodded. "My skirt was always blowing up before."

I wondered if a boiler suit would help Esmé Haughton, whose progress had been slow. "None of my other women pupils fly in boiler suits," I said. "I wish you'd show it to them."

"I never see them," she said. "Nobody's ever here when I come."

"That's because you've always been here on a week-day," I told her. "There's a crowd here all the time on Saturday and Sunday—all three aircraft going hard. If you want a lesson tomorrow or on Sunday I'd better put you down for a time now. We're liable to get booked up."

She hesitated. "Do none of the other women wear boiler suits like this?"

"They don't yet," I said. "When they've seen you, they'll all be getting them."

"You don't think it looks a bit conspicuous?"

"It looks swell," I told her. "It *is* conspicuous, but it's so very practical. I think you'll set a fashion here when they see that."

I was surprised when she came to the club next day to find how few members knew her. Leacaster is a fair-sized city and she lived in one of the biggest houses in the neighbourhood, but she came shyly, as a stranger. She came with Esmé Haughton and they both had a lesson, the doctor's daughter wearing one of Mrs. Marshall's spare boiler suits. It didn't make a lot of difference to her flying, but the owner of the suit was getting on quite well. I was too busy that afternoon to be able to give them much attention after their lessons, but I introduced my new member to young Peter Woodhouse, the honorary secretary. When darkness came and I landed for the last time that day with the last pupil, I went into the bar for a can of beer and found Peter there. He told me that they had both changed back into their ordinary clothes directly they had finished flying, and he had given them afternoon tea in the club room. Then they had watched the flying for a little and had gone away. Mrs. Marshall had put her name down for a lesson next afternoon.

"I thought she was rather nice," he said. "She thaws out after a bit. At first I thought that she was snooty, but I'm not sure that she isn't just shy."

I nodded. "She doesn't know many of the members."

"I'd never met her before," he remarked. "I've seen the car, sometimes. It's a wizard car. If I had that I wouldn't wash it. I'd lick the dirt off it."

"She seems to live a very retired sort of a life," I told him. "Nobody knows much about her in the village. Her mother does most of the shopping. The vicar says she was a concert pianist before she married, and she plays beautifully."

He took a drink of beer. "I suppose it's natural," he

said. "For any woman who's a bit sensitive, after that hoo-ha with her husband."

"Hoo-ha?"

He nodded. "It must be three years ago now, but it caused quite a rumpus at the time, and made a lot of talk. They had him in court for it."

"What for?"

"Little girls," he said. "After that they put him in the bughouse."

I was grateful for the information, but I changed the subject and ordered him another can of beer. "She's going to make a very good pilot if she goes on with it. I don't know when I've had a woman that got hold of it so quickly."

He grinned. "Looks all right, too."

"See if you can introduce her to a few people," I suggested. "When there's an opportunity. I don't like to see a couple of women coming here and knowing nobody, and having tea alone."

He was a good secretary, Peter Woodhouse, and he took up my suggestion. He didn't introduce her to the motor racing crowd, not just at first. I dashed into the clubhouse for a quick cup of tea next afternoon between lessons while the Moth was being refuelled, and I saw her having tea with Ronnie Clarke. Ronnie was mad on flying. He was only just seventeen and still at school, in the fifth form of St. Peter's College. He spent all his spare time out at the aerodrome watching the flying and going up as a passenger whenever he got the chance, but his father wouldn't let him learn to fly till he was eighteen and had passed his matriculation. I thought then that Peter had made a good choice, because she wouldn't be shy with Ronnie and he was a pleasant sort of boy, and he was always there at the week-ends. Later, she could get to know the tougher guys.

We got a spell of bad weather after that, with westerly gales and rain, but she still made an appointment for a lesson each day, though frequently I had to ring up in the morning and cancel it. Once when I did that she said, "The clouds are quite high, aren't they?"

"They're all right," I said, "but there's a wind of about thirty miles an hour, and very gusty. You wouldn't be able to learn anything on a day like this—it's much too rough."

"Could you fly in this?" she asked. "Safely, I mean?"

"Oh yes," I replied. "Have to have someone on the wing tips, taxi-ing. It's just that it's too rough for instruction."

"If I came out, could you take me up?" she asked. "Just so that I can feel what you do in rough weather, resting my hands and feet on the controls?"

"We could do that, if you like," I said. So I took her up and flew her round a bit, battling with the Moth and using full aileron now and then. At the end of twenty minutes I asked her if she would like to try it straight and level by herself, and she did, and did it fairly well. After that she never let me cancel a lesson unless I could assure her that I wouldn't fly myself. We flew in mist and rain, groping our way around the countryside at a few hundred feet. I was glad in a way because it gave me an excuse to prolong her instruction to my twelve hours minimum for women; otherwise she'd have been fit to go solo at seven or eight.

She went solo early in March. She had been ready for a week or two, but I kept her doing landings and little cross-country trips around Leacaster till we got the perfect day. Then one morning it was bright and sunny, cold with a northerly wind and a rising barometer. We did two landings together, and then I undid my belt and turned to look at her. "Like to try it alone?"

136

She nodded.

I got out on to the wing, and closed the door of the front cockpit, making sure my safety belt was secured across the seat. I got down on to the ground and stood beside her in the slipstream of the slowly running engine. "Take your time," I said. "Do a circuit or two at a thousand feet till you feel comfortable, and then bring her in to land. If your gliding turns don't come out just the way you want them, put on engine and go round again. You're flying very nicely this morning. If you feel quite comfortable after the first landing, do another one. If you're not quite happy, bring her in and we'll do a bit more together. Okay?"

She nodded, and smiled at me. "Don't get heart failure . . ."

I grinned at her. "I shan't do that." I turned and walked across the grass towards the hangar, not looking back because it fusses a pupil when he sees the instructor looking at him. It was not until I heard the engine open up that I turned to watch her rather wobbly take-off.

She climbed away straight from the aerodrome till she was at about seven hundred feet, then levelled off and did a wide turn to the left. She flew back over the aerodrome and did a couple of steeper turns, and by that time I knew that she was gaining confidence. Then she went over downwind and commenced the gliding turns that would bring her close up to the hedge. She came in rather high but carried on and touched down about the middle of the aerodrome, bounced two or three times, and came to rest. I saw her looking towards me as I stood upon the tarmac, and I signalled to her to go on and do another.

When she taxied the machine into the hangar she was flushed and excited. I walked up to the cockpit as she came to rest. "That was all right," I said. "Were you quite comfortable?"

She pulled her helmet off. "It was marvellous," she said. "The first one was a rotten landing," I'm afraid."

"It wasn't too bad," I told her. "The second one was better. You came in a bit high on the first one. Did that upset you?"

"Yes, it did," she said. "I wasn't sure if I ought to put on engine and go round again, and I dithered a bit over that, and then I decided there was plenty of room. I think it put me off."

"That'll all come right with a bit of practice," I said.

She nodded, and got out of the machine. And then she turned to me and said quite seriously, "I don't know how to say what I'm feeling, Captain Pascoe. But I do want to thank you for all you've done in teaching me. I felt so *safe*."

I laughed. "I'm glad of that, Mrs. Marshall. It's what I'm here for, after all."

"I know," she said. "But there are ways and ways of doing things." And then she said, "If I come out again this afternoon, could I have another go?"

"Of course," I said. "It would be a very good thing. I'll do one circuit with you first, and then if everything's okay you can take it by yourself again."

She came for her appointment at three o'clock. I was in the air with another pupil and glanced at my watch when I saw the Alvis on the road, but she was ten minutes early and I finished my half hour. When we landed I found her sitting in the other Moth, the one that she had flown that morning, savouring it, thinking about flying.

"I won't be a minute," I said as I passed her.

She smiled. "Don't hurry. I'm quite happy."

I came out five minutes later and got into the machine, and sat there while she took it off and did a circuit of the aerodrome and landed it again. Then I turned and nodded to her, and got out of the machine, and stood beside her. "She's all yours," I said. "Don't stay up longer than half an hour—I don't want you to get tired. Do four or five landings. Don't get out of sight of the aerodrome, but if you should lose sight of it just come down low and look around the horizon till you see the gasometer. All okay?"

She nodded and smiled at me, and I turned and walked away across the grass.

I watched her from the office window as I had a cup of tea. Some of her landings were better than others, but none of them were really bad. Stan Hudson, the ground engineer came in and watched one or two of them. "Doing all right," he remarked. "Pleased as a dog with two tails, she is."

I nodded. "Going to make a good pilot."

When she came in at the end of her half hour I strolled out to meet her at the entrance to the hangar. "That was all right," I said. "Feeling happy with her now?"

She nodded. "I feel that I could take her anywhere."

"Well, you can't. We'll have to do some navigation if you're going to go places. But you're flying it all right."

She said, "I feel we ought to celebrate, or something," she said. "It's been such a wonderful day."

I laughed. "There's nobody else coming out this afternoon for a lesson. I'll open up the bar and we can have a drink to mark the occasion."

She said, "Oh, do let's do that! I'll go over and change."

When she joined me I had opened the roller shutter and stood behind the bar. "What are you going to have?" I asked. "This one is on the club."

She said, "I'd like a gin and French. But I'll pay for it. What will you have, Captain Pascoe?"

"I'd like a beer," I replied. "But you get one free drink upon the club for going solo. Only one." I served her drink, and pulled the barman's stool up, and we sat down with the bar between us.

She sipped her drink, and I lit a cigarette for her. "I tried to tell you this morning what all this has meant to me," she said presently. "I put it very badly. It's been like stepping out into another world. A terribly exciting world, a much wider world. A world where one could hurt oneself in lots of ways, or even kill oneself. What I was trying to say this morning is that you've made it all so *safe*. I'd never have dreamed three months ago that I should ever fly an aeroplane. If I'd thought about it at all I'd have thought I'd never have the nerve, that I'd be too old, and too frightened. You've made it all seem so safe and easy, and showed me how to step out into the wider world. That's why I'm so terribly grateful to you, and I always shall be."

"There's nothing to be grateful for," I said. "I've just been doing my job. The thing is, that you didn't know the job existed."

"I suppose so. Captain Pascoe, if we did some navigation and cross-country flights together, I could really go to places, couldn't I? I mean, I could fly to France, and Italy?"

"Amy Johnson's just flown to Australia," I said. "I'd like to see you with fifty hours solo and fine weather before you fly abroad."

"It's all right to fly across the Channel, is it?"

"Oh, yes. You go to Lympne and refuel there, and from there it's only about twenty-five miles over to Boulogne. You want a nice fine day for it, and get up high, and wear a life jacket. Lots of people do it."

"I couldn't do that in a club machine, though, could I?"

I shook my head. "You wouldn't want to do it in the winter, and in the summer the machines are all in use.

Most people who go over to the Continent have their own machines."

"Is it difficult to own an aeroplane yourself?"

"Not more than a car, or not much more," I told her. "You could have a Moth of your own and keep it here. We'd maintain it for you."

"How much would a Moth cost?"

"A new one costs about seven hundred and fifty—depending on the equipment, you know. You could get a good second-hand one for about five hundred. Most private owners find it costs about three hundred a year to run."

"If I wanted to buy one, could you help me buy it?"

"Of course I would."

She stared into her empty glass. "I must be going crazy . . . Not on one gin and French, either Intoxicated with going solo. To talk of buying my own aeroplane . . ."

I took her glass and filled it up again. "If you've got the money, I should say it's not a bad thing to do. Get you out into that wider world that you were talking about."

"I've got the money," she said. "As for the wider world, I'm not sure I'm not in it now. Up till the time I joined this club I'd done nothing that I want to remember, except music. Now, I just want to remember every minute of every day, as long as I live."

I smiled. "You'd better start and keep a diary."

"I don't need to." The second gin must have given her confidence, because then she asked, "Have you got great bits of your life you never want to think about again? Somebody once told me that everybody has."

It was a new idea to me, and I thought before replying. "Yes, I think I have."

"Very long bits—years and years?"

"Two years," I said. "The last year of the war and the year after that."

"Did you have a very bad time?" she asked softly.

I nodded.

"Was that when you were shot down and taken prisoner?"

I suppose the beer had loosened up my inhibitions, too. "It wasn't that," I said. "I got married, and it wasn't a success."

"I'm sorry," she said. "It's rotten when that happens."

"It's a long time ago now."

She asked, "Are you still married?"

I laughed shortly. "To tell you the truth, I don't really know. She divorced me for desertion, in America, at a place called Reno where divorce is pretty easy. I'm not sure if that's valid here in England. I don't think it is."

"Why did you desert her?"

"I don't think I did. I think it was the other way about, but it would take a lawyer to find out. You see," I explained, "she was much better off than I was, in her job." I hesitated, and then asked, "Did you ever see Judy Lester?"

"The actress? Judy Lester? Of course I did. Was she your wife?"

"For just a bit," I said.

"She was in *Picardy Princess*, in the war. And then she was in *Lucky Lady*. She was awfully good."

"Too good for me," I said a little bitterly. "She was earning two hundred pounds a week when I was earning three, after the war."

"Is that what broke it up?"

"That, and other things. She got a job in Hollywood and went out there, and then she got tied up with a band leader, and divorced me."

142

"I'm very sorry," she said quietly. "Women can be terribly silly in these things, sometimes."

"Not only women," I said, laughing. "So can men."

She laughed with me. "I suppose so. All fools, all the lot of us." She finished her drink, and got up from her stool.

"Will you have another?" I asked. It was a long, long time since I had been able to talk to anyone like that.

"Not me. I should be tiddly, and then I'd crash the Alvis." We walked towards the door. "May I come out and have another go on the Moth tomorrow?"

"Sure. Half past ten?"

"That'll be fine." We walked to her car and I opened the door for her. "I'm going to think about that Moth—a private one," she said. "It's rather a revolutionary idea."

"This place is a bit of a snare, I'm afraid," I said. "One thing leads to another."

She laughed. "Don't I know it!"

When she came again I let her do a little more solo, and then started in to teach her something about aerobatics. She wasn't much interested in loops and spins after the first excitement, and she said that flick rolls made her feel sick. I kept her at it, however, because they would accustom her to getting her machine out of any attitude it might get bumped into; she saw the force of that, but seldom did them afterwards upon her own.

Then I started in to teach her navigation. She wasn't greatly interested in that at first; to her it was a lot of tedious sums that seemed unnecessary when you had roads and railway lines to follow. So one day I told her to fly me up to Leeds for lunch at the Yorkshire club, and to work out the course and fly there. She put on the correction for variation the wrong way and she forgot all about the wind, but it was a nice fine day. When we'd been flying for about an hour and a quarter a big town showed up ahead of us and a bit to the right, with a very large river in front of it. She said down the speaking tube to the front cockpit, "Is that Leeds, Captain Pascoe?"

"You tell me," I said. "I'm just the passenger."

"It looks like Leeds," she said, "all except that river. That's not shown upon the map."

"I can't help that," I said. "I want my lunch. You've got about two hours' fuel left."

She flew on to the city, and there were docks and trawlers and ocean-going ships and an indication of the sea over to the east. Presently she said in a small voice, "Captain Pascoe."

"Yes?"

"I think we've come to the wrong place. I've been looking at the map, and I think this must be Hull."

"You take me to Leeds," I said. "I'm hungry and I'm getting very cold. You've got about an hour and three quarters' fuel left."

She turned and began to fly north-west. Presently she said, "It's thirty-five miles to Sherburn, so that'll take us twenty-six minutes, but I can't remember about the variation. Do I take it off or add it on?"

"Add it on to get the magnetic course," I said. "What are you doing about wind?"

"I'm not doing anything. I can see the smoke from a train and it's just about straight ahead of us."

"Sure we're going to get there in twenty-six minutes, then?"

"Oh . . ."

"You've got about an hour and a half's fuel left."

She found the aerodrome in the end and made quite a smooth landing. We taxied in and met the pilot instructor. She said to him, "We came rather a long way round, but we got here in the end." And then she turned to me and said, "I'm terribly sorry for being so stupid."

144

"You weren't stupid," I said. "Everybody's got to start."

"I got so muddled," she explained. "The noise of the engine, and the wind, and nothing to write on. I didn't seem to be able to think properly."

"That's the big difficulty," I told her. "You want to work it all out before you start and put a nice thick line upon the map."

"I put the nice thick line," she said. "But the ground wasn't the same as on the map."

"Come into the clubhouse, and bring the map and your ruler. I'll show you what you did wrong."

In the club I offered her a soft drink. She said, "Do you think they'd have any milk?" I went and asked in the kitchen, and got her a glass of very cold milk, and over that we held the post-mortem. Then she worked out the course to take us home again, and got it right this time.

Over lunch she said, "I'll have to do a lot more of this. Could we do another one tomorrow?"

"Saturday," I said. "I'll have lessons all day. We'll have to get back quick, because I've got two this afternoon."

"Oh dear. Sunday . . . Monday's the day off. Could we do one on Tuesday?"

"I'll have to look at the book," I said. "Now that the weather's getting better we're getting a bit booked up. We should be able to fit one in on Tuesday or Wednesday."

"That's nearly a week."

"It's a bit difficult taking the club machines away in the summer," I said. "They get booked up."

"I know. I've been thinking a lot about having a machine of my own."

"Airwork usually have a few second-hand Moths, if you're really thinking about it."

"A second-hand one would be better, to start on, wouldn't it? I mean, I'm not very experienced."

"It might be. Would you like me to ring up Parkes and find out what's available?"

Her eyes fairly danced. "Could we do that when we get back, this afternoon?"

"Of course."

"Come on. Let's go now."

I laughed. "I haven't finished my cheese."

"You don't want your cheese. It'll make you fat. Let's go, and ring up Airwork."

She dragged me away from my lunch, and we got into the aeroplane and flew back to Leacaster, straight as a die down her pencilled line upon the map. When we landed and got out of the Moth, she said, "Was that better?"

"Perfect," I said. "That's because you wanted to get back here. No wandering away to Wigan this time."

"Let's ring up Airwork."

When I got through Parkes told me that they had two Moths, one with a Genet motor and one with a Cirrus Mark II. The Cirrus one was what would suit her best; it was in the shop for its C. of A. inspection and would be finished in about a week. By my elbow she said urgently, "Ask him if I can have it painted any colour I like."

"What colour do you want?"

"White," she said. "White, with red registration letters and a red leather seat."

"Take a lot of keeping clean."

"Never mind. Ask him."

I did so. "He says that's all right, but he wants to know pretty soon. It'll cost you a bit more."

"I don't mind that. When could we go down and see it?"

I thought for a moment. "Monday?"

"But that's your day off!"

"I'm not doing anything particular. We could fly down on Monday, if you like. Give you a bit more cross-country practice."

"That would be marvellous," she breathed.

We flew down to Heston on the Monday morning, about a two-hour flight. The Moth was all dismantled in the workshops, of course, and it looked a bit of a shambles to her, but I welcomed it because it gave me a chance to have a good look at the condition of the structure. It was quite all right; it had been kept under cover all its life and not parked out in the rain. I told her it was a good buy, and the salesman showed her one that they had just reconditioned, all new-looking and shiny, and she was as pleased as Punch. The salesman took me aside and told me that he had reserved two and a half per cent commission for me for the introduction, and I told him that I didn't want it, that he was to take it off the price that he had quoted her. I don't know why I did that because it was fair business, but it seemed like making money out of her great pleasure.

We went into the office and dealt with the questions of the extras, her red leather seat and the turn and bank indicator that I made her have, and she wrote a cheque and paid it over there and then. We went over to the restaurant for lunch.

Colin Hicks was there, the chief pilot. I introduced her to him and he offered us a drink; as we were flying back I had a ginger ale and she had her glass of milk. I told him that she had just bought a Moth from the firm, and he asked the registration. When I told him, he said, "Major Struther's old Moth. That's a good machine. He sold it because he was posted out to India." She was interested, of course, and he turned to her. "We're having a rally at

La Baule in June with the Aero Club de Paris," he said. "You must come to that. Your Moth knows the way—it was there last year."

She asked, "In France?"

He nodded. "On the Bay of Biscay, not far from St. Nazaire. We generally land at Le Touquet and collect the party and have lunch, and fly on from there. It's quite an easy trip, and the week-end's a lot of fun."

"I'll have to think it over," she said. "I'm not very experienced yet."

We went to our table for lunch. Between courses she sat staring out over the aerodrome, immersed in her thoughts. Presently I asked, "Happy?"

She turned to me. "Terribly," she said. "So happy, it just can't be true."

"It's fun having something new," I said. "A new car's just the same."

She nodded. "It's not only that. It'll be terribly exciting having the Moth, but it's—it's going to places. You see," she said, "I've never been anywhere, hardly. And now, to go to France for the first time, and fly there by myself in my own aeroplane—it's incredible. I don't know that I'll ever have the courage to do it, and I know that I'll regret it all my life if I don't."

"You know some French?" I asked.

"I did French at school," she said, "fifteen years ago. I've forgotten most of it, and anyway they never taught us what to say to French ground engineers upon an aerodrome."

I smiled. "You'll have to start looking for a passenger who knows the ropes. Lots of the club members would jump at the chance of going to La Baule."

"Maybe." She sat thoughtful for a time, and then she said, "What were the registration letters, again?"

I told her. "G—EMLF."

148

"MLF," she said. "Morgan le Fay. That's what I'm going to call her."

"Who was Morgan le Fay?"

"An enchantress—King Arthur's sister. She's enchanted me already."

"Morgan le Fay," I repeated. "It's not a bad name for an aeroplane. Would you like to have it painted on the nose, just underneath the engine? Quite small red letters, on the white paint?"

Her eyes danced. "That would be lovely. Could have that done?"

"Of course. We'll go back to the office and add it to the order, before we take off."

We did that after lunch, and then we got back into the club Moth and she flew me back to Duffington. She was getting much better at cross-country work by that time, because as we passed Bedford she said down the voice pipe, "Captain Pascoe."

"Yes?"

"I put on five degrees drift for wind 280, but that train down there seems to show the wind from the east. Ought I to change the drift?"

I glanced down. "That's right. It's not very strong. I'd put on about two degrees to your basic course. You're over to the west a bit, and that's another sign."

"It's horrid of the wind to change like that."

When we landed back at Duffington in the late afternoon there was nobody there, of course, because the club was closed on Mondays. She taxied up to the closed hangar door, and we got out and unlocked the hangar, and pushed the big doors open, and pushed the Moth inside. When that was done she turned to me. "I'm so grateful to you for giving up your day off for me," she said. "It's been a lovely day for me, but I'm afraid it's been at your expense."

"That's all right," I said. "I wasn't doing anything particular—only a bit of shopping. I can do that any time."

"Had you got anything fixed up for this evening?"

"No."

She said a little diffidently, "Would you care to come and have dinner at the Manor? It's not very exciting, I'm afraid—it'll be just Mother and me."

I said, "That's very kind of you. I'd love to come. What time?"

"Seven o'clock? We usually have dinner about seven-thirty."

I nodded. "That's fine. I'll write up the log books and go back and change, and I'll be with you about seven."

I walked up to the Manor that evening newly shaved and in my best grey suit. I had never been to the house before, though I had seen it every day from the air. It was an old house, part of it Elizabethan. On the ground that night the drive seemed longer, more impressive, the house larger. A maid in a white starched apron opened the door to me and showed me into the drawing room. Mrs. Marshall and her mother got up to welcome me and I was introduced to the mother, Mrs. Duclos.

I knew her by sight, though we had never spoken. I found her to be a somewhat formidable old woman, very direct and straight-spoken. They offered me a drink and I chose sherry, and while my pupil was getting sherry and glasses for us all the old lady engaged me in conversation.

"Brenda tells me that she bought an aeroplane," she said.

I smiled. "She did." And then I asked, "Do you approve?"

She gave a sort of snort. "It wouldn't make much odds if I approved or not. But—yes, I approve. So long as she doesn't go and kill herself in it. You won't let her do that?"

"Not if I can help it."

"Well, stand back and let me take a look at you."

I stood back for inspection, and I suppose I passed, because the next thing she said was, "She tells me that you shot down eleven Germans in the war."

"Yes," I said. "I'm afraid I did."

"What have you got to be afraid of?"

"Nothing," I said. "Only it doesn't seem now quite such a good thing to have done as it did then."

"You're turning pacifist, are you? What's your name, anyway? I can't keep calling you Captain Pascoe."

I laughed. "My name's John. My friends call me Johnnie. I don't think I'm pacifist. I suppose I'd do it again if there was another war. One sort of goes nuts."

"Everybody goes a bit mental in a war," she said. "But we don't talk of things like that in this house, Johnnie."

I nodded. "I understand that."

My pupil came back with the drinks, and we talked about the new aeroplane, and the club members, and the Chief Constable, who had just gone solo. Presently we went in to dinner, very well served with silver gleaming on a polished oak table, the maid who had opened the door waiting on us. After dinner we went back to the drawing room for coffee, and presently I said, "They tell me you're a fine pianist, Mrs. Marshall. Would you play something for me?"

She laughed a little awkwardly. "I'm not as good as that."

"I'd like it if you would."

"Would you?"

I nodded.

Mrs. Duclos got up from her chair. "If Brenda's going to play I'm going to write some letters." I got up. "If I don't see you again, Johnnie, I'll say good-night.

Come again and cheer us up. It's not very exciting here, two women living alone."

"I'd like to do that," I said.

I opened the door for her, and Brenda crossed over to the piano and opened it. "Make yourself comfortable by the fire," she said. "What sort of music do you like?"

"Not too classical," I said, "and not too lowbrow. Something about ten per cent better than tea-room music." She laughed. "But you play what you want to."

She sat down at the piano and began to play a cheerful little melody that she told me was a Hungarian dance by Brahms, and she went on to bits of Chopin and Tchaikowsky. She played beautifully, and she was catholic in her selection, mixing in things like 'Tip-toe through the Tulips' with old English airs like 'Greensleeves'. I sat smoking by the fire, enjoying every minute of it. In the life I led, flying all day and living at the village inn, I very seldom had the chance to sit and listen to music; I could have sat and listened to her all night.

She went on for over an hour, and finished with a spirited and brilliant rendering of 'Sur le pont d'Avignon'. Then she got up from the piano and came over to the fire.

"That was perfectly delightful," I said. "That's made my day."

"Has it? I'm so glad, because you've made mine. Let me get you a drink."

"Are you having one?"

"If you are. Whisky?"

"I'd like a whisky. Let me get it."

"No, you stay there." She went out and presently came back with the decanter and the siphon and the glasses on a silver tray. She poured me out a drink and gave it to me, and then gave herself one. She sat down with me by the fire.

Presently she said, "I want to tell you about my husband."

"Don't if it's upsetting," I replied. "I know a certain amount already."

She nodded. "I suppose you must. I suppose everybody in the village knows all about it. He's in The Haven, you know."

"I know. I'm very sorry."

She nodded. "It's an illness, just like any other illness, really. Only he has to stay in hospital, whether he's well or ill. I go and see him twice a week. That's why I go on living here."

"They tell me it's a very good place."

"The best in the country for this sort of thing. Dr. Baddeley—he's awfully good. People come to him from all over the world."

"He's been there for some time, hasn't he?"

She nodded. "He's been certified for nearly three years now."

"Bad luck," I said.

"Yes. But it's the sort of thing that happens, and you've just got to make the best of it."

I asked, "Is he happy?"

"I think so," she said. "He's perfectly all right for weeks on end, you know, and while he's like that he knows it's better for him to be there. He loves his golf, and they've got a nine-hole golf course in the grounds. Then he gets another fit, and then it's—well, it's difficult. But when he's well, I think he's quite happy, though it's a very restricted life. He plays a good deal of bridge."

"Is there any chance of a cure?"

She took up the poker and scraped a little ash from the surround of the glowing fire. "I don't know. None of the ordinary things seem to be much good. There's an American doctor in Cincinnati who's got good results with some kind of spinal injection, and he's coming here in about six months' time. Dr. Baddeley thinks we should try that." She raised her head. "Of course, we'll try anything."

"He's quite co-operative, is he?"

"Derek? Oh yes—when he's well. At other times—it's difficult." She paused. "It's not very easy to be optimistic," she said. "We've had so many disappointments. Before he was certified we'd try something new and it would seem marvellous, and he'd be wonderfully well for months, but the relapse always came. Dr. Baddeley says now that he'd want to keep him certified and in The Haven for two years after any new treatment, to make sure. You see, when he was out before there was—well, trouble."

"I know," I said.

"I know you do," she replied. "All these months while I've been learning to fly you've never said a word to make me feel awkward. I knew that you must know a good deal about Derek, and so I wanted you to know the whole thing."

I nodded. "How do you feel about it all, yourself?" I asked. "Could you get a divorce, if you wanted to?"

She shook her head. "There's no grounds for a divorce. A member of Parliament is working on a new divorce bill —A. P. Herbert, who writes in *Punch*. He wants to make incurable insanity grounds for divorce, but that won't come for years and years—if ever." She was silent for a moment, and then she said, "Even if that was possible, I don't know that I'd ever want to do it. When you marry somebody you marry them for good, for better or worse, for richer for poorer, in sickness and in health, till death do us part. I'd hate myself if I ran out on Derek while he's sick. That's the time a wife ought to stand by and help him all she can. And after all, I've had the 'richer' part."

She glanced around the room. "This is all his money—the piano, and my new Moth—everything."

"Does he know you bought a Moth?" I asked.

"I told him I was going to, the day before yesterday, when I went to see him. I tell him everything. I think it helps, because then he doesn't get fussed that things are going on behind his back."

"How does he like the thought of you flying?"

"Oh, he's all for it. He's very well just now. He gets worried that I'm having a dull life, you see. He thought it was a great idea that I should join the club and learn to fly." She added softly, "He's very sweet—when he's well."

We sat in silence for a time. At last I said, "It's a bad-luck story, all right. I suppose it's going on for ever?"

She nodded. "I think so. One gets accustomed to things, though. People can adjust themselves, you know. Take up new interests. Like flying."

I nodded. "If I may say so, you're looking a lot better than you were in January."

"Everybody says that," she replied. "I *am* a lot better—sleeping better, eating better, feeling younger. I think flying must be good for people."

I laughed. "It's terribly good for you to get scared stiff now and then. Stimulates the flow of adrenalin, or something."

She laughed with me. "Let me give you another whisky."

"Just a small one," I said. "Then I must be going. Flying tomorrow."

She refilled my glass, and I got up and took it from her. "What are you going to do about collecting your Moth from Heston?" I asked. "Are you going to fly it up yourself?"

"Do you think I'm fit?"

155

"I think so," I said slowly, "if it's a nice fine day. I wouldn't like to see you try it in bad weather, not just yet. The only thing is—it's just out of the shops. You might get a forced landing for some silly little thing. Why don't you get them to deliver it up here for you?"

"Would they do that? Fly it up here for me?"

"Oh, yes. It might cost you a tenner. It wouldn't be more than that. I think that might be best, and then you can get to know it flying round the aerodrome before you take it across country."

"You're a very safe person," she said quietly. "The safest person that I've ever met. You think of everything to make things easy for me. Yes, let's ask them if they can deliver it up here."

I nodded. "I'll give them a ring in the morning."

I finished my whisky and put down my glass, because it was time for me to go back to the inn. She was too attractive, and I was too lonely. "I must go," I said. "Thank you for a perfectly delightful evening."

"Thank you for a perfectly delightful day," she said. "I shan't sleep tonight, for thinking of my Moth."

She came with me to the door, and I walked down the drive and out on to the moonlit road that led a few hundred yards into the village. I didn't sleep that night, for thinking about her.

She flew most days that week upon the club machines, and then came the great day when her Moth arrived. I got a telephone call to say that it had taken off from Heston and I rang her at the Manor, and she came hurrying to the aerodrome in the Alvis. It was a bright, sunny day and she was excited, looking about eighteen years old and terribly attractive. She was an hour early, and we stood on the tarmac looking at the sky towards the south, scanning the clouds. Then we saw it as a little speck coming towards us, and presently we heard the engine.

It grew larger, dropping off height as it approached, and presently it flew over the aerodrome. The pilot saw us on the tarmac and showed the machine off to us, doing a few right and left hand turns at a couple of hundred feet. It was a very pretty little aeroplane, white and crimson, gleaming in the sun.

"Take a good look at it," I said to her. "It's probably the last time you'll be able to."

She stared at me. "The last time?"

"You'll always be in it," I remarked. "Unless you lend it to somebody you'll never see it flying again."

"Oh . . ." She stood with her eyes glued upon it. "Doesn't it look *lovely*?"

The pilot landed it and brought it to us on the tarmac, stopped the engine and got out. They had made a very good job of it, and it looked like a new aircraft. She signed a delivery note, and then drove him to the station in the Alvis; while she was away I had Morgan le Fay refuelled and made a bit of an inspection myself with the ground engineer. When she came back in haste from Leacaster it was all ready for her to fly.

She hurried to change into her clean white overall, and when she came to the machine she asked me to go with her on her first flight. "Not much," I said. "It hasn't got any dual in the front cockpit. When you pile it up I'd perish miserably. No, you take your own machine alone for the first time. It's just the same as the club Moths."

She laughed. "I'm not going to pile it up."

"Of course you're not. I was just joking."

"Don't joke about serious subjects," she said. "If I pile it up I'm going to cut my throat."

"Try it on a gliding turn or two before you come in to land," I said. "They're all just a little bit different on the glide, according to the rigging."

She smiled at me, and got into the cockpit. When she

was comfortable I swung the prop for her and she ran it up, waved the chocks away, and taxied out. I went into the office and stood watching from the window as she took off, a little depressed. This was the end of two months that had meant a lot to me; from now onwards she would be flying as a pilot in her own machine. She had no need of further dual from me.

She flew it for some time, came in for a quick lunch of a sandwich and a cup of tea in the club, and flew it again. Then in the late afternoon she taxied in and we pushed it into the hangar and put it away for the night. She brought the three log books into the office and I showed her how to write them up.

She turned the pages of the journey log book. "She's been everywhere," she said. "Just look at this."

We bent together over the book, her head close to mine. "Paris, Dijon, Cannes," she breathed. "And look—here's Avignon, where the *pont* is. She's been there. Milano, Venezia—she's been to Venice." She turned the pages. "Le Touquet, Dinard, La Baule . . ."

She raised her head, and I moved back a little. "I'll have to go to some of these places this summer," she said. "I mean, it would be letting her down if I just stuck in England."

I smiled. "I should start in now and put in time on her for the next month. How many hours solo have you done?"

"Fourteen," she said.

"La Baule in June would be an easy first trip on the Continent," I said. "That gives you two months from now. You could go to the Pageants at Sherburn and at Cramlington in May, get a bit of experience. We shall be sending club machines to those."

"Will you be going to La Baule?" she asked.

"Not unless the club decide to make a thing of it and

send all three machines," I told her. "They did that last year for Deauville. I don't know about La Baule. It depends how many members want to go."

She said, "Do try and work it. Then we could go together."

I nodded. "Have a Flight of the three club machines and yours. It might be possible. I'll have to talk to the Committee."

She came every day to the aerodrome in April, and flew her Moth whenever the weather was fit to fly. She got into the habit of coming to the office for a cup of tea with me if I wasn't up after she had done her flying for the day, and twice she asked me up to dinner at the Manor on my day off. We talked no more about her husband; apparently she was satisfied with having told me what the position was. Once she brought her mother down to the aerodrome, and we put the old lady in the front seat of Morgan le Fay and her daughter took her up for a short flight. Ronnie Clarke, of course, would fly with anyone and she took him up two or three times. Towards the end of the month she was doing cross-country flights upon her own.

Late one afternoon, when it was raining cats and dogs and she had flown to Cambridge, she rang me up. "Johnnie," she said, "I'm at Peterborough, on the aerodrome. I started back and it began to rain and it got very piggy, so I put down here. What's it like with you?"

"Horrible," I told her. "Looks as if it's set in for the evening. I wouldn't try to fly back here tonight. I should get into a hotel and stay where you are till tomorrow. Would you like me to ring Mrs. Duclos?"

"I ought to get back," she said. "I'm seeing Derek in the morning. I think I'll have to try and hire a car."

"Would you like me to drive down and fetch you in the Alvis?" I asked.

"It's eighty miles," she said.

"I don't mind," I told her. "There'll be nothing more doing here today."

"Of course, I'd love that. But it would be terribly tiring for you."

"That's all right," I said. "I'll start right away, and be with you about half past six. Can you get Morgan into a hangar?"

"I don't think so. She'll have to stay out in the open."

"I'll bring down some screw pickets and your engine and cockpit covers," I said.

"Oh, thank you. And Johnnie, would you bring my raincoat and my skirt? They're hanging in the Ladies' Room. Then we can have dinner somewhere before driving home."

I started off at once, after ringing her mother to tell her what was happening, got on to the Great North Road, and drove down southwards in the pouring rain. It was dark by the time I got to Peterborough, and raining harder than ever. I found her waiting for me in a sort of barn upon the aerodrome; she had taxied her Moth into the lee of a shed and covered the cockpit insecurely with a couple of sacks. She was very wet, and very glad to see me. We put on the cockpit and the engine covers and folded the wings and picketed the machine down; while I finished off the job she took off her overall in the back of the barn and got into her skirt and coat.

"Let's go somewhere where we can have a drink," she said. "I'm miserably cold."

"What about the Dog and Duck at Thorganby?" I suggested. "We can get a meal there, and it's seven miles on the way home."

"Anywhere," she said, "so long as it's somewhere warm."

We pulled into the yard of the Dog and Duck ten

minutes later and ran in through the rain. Thorganby is quite a little village and the Dog and Duck is a very old house; on that wet evening there was a bright fire in the saloon bar with chairs in front of it, and nobody there but us. I knew the landlord slightly and while she was tidying herself up I ordered a meal.

"Ham and eggs and cold blackberry pie," I said when she appeared. "That all right? They're going to let us have it on a table here, in front of the fire."

"Oh, lovely!"

"I said we'd like to have it in about half an hour. What would you like to drink?"

"I'm cold," she said, shivering.

"Would you like a hot rum toddy, with some lemon in it?"

"Oh, Johnnie!"

Behind the bar the landlord nodded, and went out and fetched a very big, black kettle and put it on the fire, where it began to sing. We had a toddy and felt better, so we had another one, and then because the kettle was there boiling, we had a third. Then it seemed time for some blotting paper and we had our ham and eggs and blackberry pie in front of the fire. And finally we had another hot rum toddy for the road.

It was fine and very dark when we went out into the yard to find the car, and much colder than the saloon bar. We had had too many rum toddies, of course, because the sudden change of temperature made my head swim a little. She was affected, too, because in the darkness she stumbled on the uneven paving, and I caught her arm, and then she was in my arms and I was kissing her, and she was kissing me in return. We stayed like that for a minute, and then she said quietly, "This is very bad."

"Too many rum toddies," I said thickly. "I'm sorry."

"Too many rum toddies," she repeated. "I'm not."

And then she said, "We'll have to think about this, Johnnie."

"Yes," I said. "We'll have to think about it." She released herself gently from my arms, and we found the car. "Which of us is going to drive?" I asked. "We're both about as bad as each other."

She said seriously, "Yes, we're both about as bad as each other." Then she laughed a little, and said, "You drive, and let me think. You're less likely to crash it than me, anyway." So I drove the Alvis out of the yard of the Dog and Duck and out on to the Great North Road for home.

We drove on in silence through the night, through occasional showers of rain, running easily at about forty-five. The Alvis was a sports saloon and her seat was very close, her shoulder rubbing against mine. We were both busy with our own thoughts. I hadn't wanted it to happen because it was bound to make trouble for us both, two lonely people, neither of whom was in a position to marry. Now that it had happened, I was glad, and so, I think, was she.

When we had passed through Blackford and we were about ten miles from Duffington she spoke for the first time. "Let's park a minute by the side, Johnnie," she said.

I drew up off the road a little under some trees and turned off the headlights; the rain dripping off the branches made little patterings upon the roof. She said, "I want to talk."

I smiled. "I think we'd better."

In the dim light she nodded. "I want to ask you a horrid question, Johnnie."

"Go ahead," I said.

She asked, "Do you do much of this? Do you have many girls?"

"No," I said. "You're the first girl I've kissed since Judy."

"Honestly?"

"Honestly."

She sighed a little. "That's what I wanted to know. I thought it was like that, but in a way it makes things worse."

"We can try and forget about it, if you like," I suggested.

"We shan't be able to," she said. "I don't think that's the answer."

She sounded so unhappy that I reached out and took her hand, and she let me have it. "Don't worry," I said gently. "It's been coming on for a long time, this has. It was bound to happen, one way or another."

She turned to me. "I know. If things were different this would be the sweetest day of my life. But I'm a married woman, and you're a married man. I'm not the sort of woman who does this sort of thing. And I don't think you're the sort of man to do it, either."

"We're neither of us so much married as all that," I said.

"You may not be, but I am," she replied.

I sat stroking her hand. "I didn't mean this to happen, but I'm glad it has," I said at last. "Too many rum toddies, and a damn good thing." She smiled a little. "I know we're running straight into a packet of trouble. But nothing that's worth having can be got without a lot of trouble in this world."

I paused. "I want to tell you something," I said. "Since we met I've been to a solicitor. I can divorce my wife, he tells me, and we're putting in a petition."

"Divorce Judy?"

I nodded. "She's been living with another chap for the last eight years, as his wife. In Hollywood. It's going to be pretty expensive and it's going to take a long time. But I can do it, and I will. There's half our tangle untied."

She sat silent for a minute. Then she said, "What would you do if I untied the other half?"

I turned to her. "I should want you to marry me."

She nodded slowly. "Now that you've said it, I don't want you to say it again, Johnnie. Not ever. Suppose I were to get divorced from Derek, and I don't think I could, it would still be years and years before you could say that to me. And people change. We've been thrown together a good deal in the last few months, and you've been terribly kind to me, kinder than any man has ever been in all my life. I've looked forward every day to meeting you again, counting the hours." I pressed her hand. "I've been very silly and rather cruel in return," she said. "If I wasn't prepared to go on with you, I ought not to have let things come to this. You've been very kind to me, and in return I've got to be unkind to you, and hurt you. I want you to try and forgive me."

"There's nothing to forgive," I said. "I wouldn't have missed a minute of it."

She said, "Nor would I."

We sat again in silence, and presently I said, "We've started something, and I don't know how it's going to finish. Whatever happens, we shall neither of us forget this. But if you'd rather that we didn't see so much of each other for a bit, we could try that. I could get another job now, fairly easily. Imperial Airways want pilots."

"You mean, you'd go away?" she said dully.

"I'd do that, if you want me to," I said.

"Would you have to do that?" she asked.

"If I don't," I said, "this'll probably happen again."

"I know," she replied.

Presently she said, "I'm tired, Johnnie—too tired to think properly. I can't imagine what we're going to do— I'll have to sleep on it. But when all's said and done, there's only one person that really matters in this thing."

I turned to her. "Who's that?"

"Derek," she replied.

I was silent. She said gently, "You and I are well. We're fit, and healthy. If sad, unpleasant things have to be done, we can do them and battle through. But Derek's not like that. He's ill, and he's my husband. He's the one we've got to think about. Not ourselves."

I was silent, not wanting to hurt her, thinking of the man who had assaulted little girls and got had up in court for it. She was quite right, of course, but I couldn't find anything to say. If she abandoned him, that might not be too good.

At last she said, "Take me home, Johnnie. I'll make up my mind and I'll do something in the next day or two. And then I'll tell you."

I nodded. "There's no violent hurry, Brenda. I shan't change. I'm going on with my divorce, and get that moving." I pressed her hand. "Don't take things too hard."

She said softly, "Dear Johnnie . . ."

I pressed the starter, and got the car out on the rain-swept road again in the black night. We went to the deserted aerodrome for me to get my own car, and I got out there. "I'll see you in the morning," she said, and drove off. I stood and watched her tail-light disappear, and she was very dear to me.

The next day was a fine one; she rang me early in the morning and went down by train to Peterborough after her visit to The Haven to fetch her Moth. She flew in in the late afternoon but nothing passed between us; she did not want to talk and till she did I would not try and force her. Several days passed; she came once or twice to the aerodrome and flew her aeroplane. Then one Sunday she suggested we should meet for lunch at Huddlestone, a village about thirty miles away. "It's difficult here," she said a little awkwardly, "with people talking."

I nodded. "I flew over Huddlestone Woods a day or two ago," I said. "The bluebells must be a sight. You can see the whole ground blue from the air, in the glades. Would you like to take a picnic lunch?"

She brightened. "Oh, that would be lovely! I'll get the lunch for both of us." So we arranged to meet in the village square at noon on my day off.

We did that, and we parked her car and drove into the woods in mine. It was a bright day and the woods were marvellous, carpeted in bluebells, and the air like wine. We left the car and walked on through the woods until we found a fallen tree to sit on for our lunch, and she unpacked the basket I had carried from the car.

Presently she said, "I had a talk to Dr. Baddeley last week."

"What about?"

"Derek," she said, "and us. I didn't say you. I just told him there was someone else."

She had been quite frank with her husband's doctor. She had told him that whatever she decided to do would be dictated by her husband's interest; that if he felt that a dissolution of the marriage would give him a great setback, then the marriage would go on. They had, however, talked of this once or twice when Derek had been completely in possession of his senses, and he had said that the marriage ought to be dissolved. It would never be safe for them to have a family, and while she was a young woman she should be free to marry again if she wanted to. He had been emphatic about it. What did Dr. Baddeley think?

The doctor told her that her husband had talked of this to him, and had expressed the same views. He had pointed out to him that the marriage could not be ended just like that; there would have to be a divorce, and grounds for a divorce. Until one of them misconducted themselves the marriage would have to go on, and since he was in The Haven and couldn't very well commit adultery, the initiative lay with her.

The doctor said his patient had been very much distressed by that aspect of the matter, and had said that it ought to be possible to end the marriage in her interest. From that time the doctor had avoided the subject, but his patient had referred to it several times. It was evidently worrying him. He thought, on the whole, it would ease his patient's mind if the marriage could be brought to an end, though if that were to happen he would like her to continue her visits.

"He was awfully nice about it," she said.

"What prospect is there that Derek will get well?" I asked.

She shook her head. "Very little. I asked him again about that. There's been no change. He said he'd have to keep him certified for at least two years after the last attack."

I nodded. "What's the next thing?" I asked.

"I want to have a talk to Derek," she said. "I'll have to pick my time a little bit. It might take a week or two. Would you mind if I tell him who you are?"

"Not a bit," I said. "We'd better have this all out in the open."

"I think so, too," she said seriously. "I'm sure it's better like that."

We had our lunch sitting together on the log. She told me about her childhood in Guildford, and I told her about my early life in Canada, and the hours passed like minutes. It was three o'clock before we woke up to the time. She had to go back for tea, and we began picking up the remains of lunch and packing them in the basket.

When we were ready she stood up, slender in the afternoon sun against the bluebells, and she said, "There's just one thing, Johnnie."

"What's that?" I asked.

"If this goes on," she said, "and Derek agrees to divorce me, I shall have to give him grounds for divorce."

I had been thinking the same thing. I reached out and took her hand. "With me?"

"I don't know who else," she said seriously.

I smiled. "Would that be very terrible?" I took her other hand.

"No," she said. "Not with you. But it's a bit smutty, and I wouldn't have wanted to start off on anything in that way."

"It can be play-acting," I told her.

"Play-acting?"

I nodded. "It's a bit of a smutty play, but it's play-acting all the same. There are hotels in London that cater for this sort of thing. Not the sort of a hotel that you'd care to go to normally. We can book a room and register as man and wife. We go up there at bed time making sure the porter notices us, and play cards all night in front of the gas fire."

Her eyes danced. "Dominoes," she laughed. "I love dominoes."

"All right, dominoes. Then at seven o'clock in the morning we tumble the bedclothes a bit and undress and get into bed, and ring for morning tea. Make sure the maid notices us and give her a good big tip. She goes to court and gives evidence, and you get your divorce without any strings on it."

"Would you do it that way, Johnnie?" she asked. "Without any strings?"

"I know you'd rather," I said, "and I think I would, although it means waiting a long time. When we've both got our divorces and we're both free people, then I'll ask you to marry me and we'll start off clean."

She came into my arms and we kissed, standing in the sunlight on the carpet of the bluebells, in the dappled shadows of the trees. Presently she sighed and said, "We oughtn't to be doing this. We're not free people yet."

I released her. "No," I said. "We'll have to watch our step. It's going to be the thick end of two years before we're free. But it'll pass."

Next week she told Derek the whole thing. He took it very well and said that he was sure that a divorce was the right course. He could not go himself to brief a solicitor and he asked her to see his solicitor in Leacaster and ask him to come and see him, and get the whole thing going with somebody to act for her. I had offered to go to see him if he wished but he didn't want that; he told her very sensibly that matters of this sort were always easier if they were kept as impersonal as possible. She saw his doctor later and he congratulated her upon the way that she had handled it; he said his patient seemed much easier in his mind.

It was up to us then to provide the evidence. I scouted round and got the name of a hotel in Bloomsbury that seemed to do a good bit of that sort of thing, and telegraphed to book a double room. I got a couple of days' leave from the club and went down to London, and met her at St. Pancras Station, under the clock. "I don't know if this is going to work," I said. "I've been and looked at the hotel from the outside, and it looks all right."

"I expect it'll work," she said. "If it doesn't, we'll have to try again. I feel as if I was playing the leading part in a dramatised version of a rude story."

I laughed. "That's exactly what you are doing."

She nodded, laughing. "I'll try everything once. Let's go and register at that hotel."

We took a taxi to the hotel and registered as Mr. and Mrs. Pascoe. She had taken some pains over her luggage and had got herself a new suitcase with the initials B.P. on it, and she had marked some of her clothes, *Brenda Pascoe*. In the bleak, utilitarian bedroom with the double bed and the gas stove she showed me these with pride. "It's getting ahead of the game a bit," she said. "But I can leave them lying about, and somebody might look."

We went down and had lunch in the hotel dining room, and then we went out. She wanted to go and see some herbaceous plants in Kew Gardens, so we went there and walked round the borders all the afternoon while she made notes in a little book for her garden at Duffington. "Though I suppose it's rather silly," she said once. "I mean, I shan't be living there very much longer."

I touched her arm. "We'll have a garden of our own, somewhere. Not so big as the Manor garden, though."

"I don't want another one like that," she said. "I'd like to have a little garden in a suburb, that we could do all ourselves. It'd be much more fun."

We went back and had dinner at the hotel. I had booked a couple of stalls for *Lilac Time*; she had never seen it and she liked Schubert, and this was a sort of compromise to please us both. It did, and when we went back to the hotel for the serious business of our visit to London we were very happy together.

In the bedroom we settled down to dominoes. There was only one tub chair and one upright one; we pulled the suitcase stand out as a table and put a suitcase on it and played dominoes on that. By two in the morning we were both dropping asleep, and I didn't care if I never saw another domino again in all my life. "Go to bed," I said. "The bed ought to be slept in, anyway. I'll sleep in the chair."

"You wouldn't mind if I did that? It's a bit hard on you."

I laughed. "Go on and go to bed. I won't look."

She did, and went to sleep at once. I sat on dozing intermittently in the chair till dawn came grey over the London roofs, and people started stirring in the corridors. I got up stiffly and turned out the fire, and opened the window to let fresh air into the room. She woke as I was doing that, and turned over sleepily, and sat up in bed. "Did you have an awful night?" she asked.

"Not too bad," I told her. "This is the last act, now."

I undressed and put on my pyjamas and got into bed with her. She bubbled into laughter. "Johnnie," she said, "what marvellous pyjamas!"

"I know," I said. "I chose them very carefully. There was a pair with naked women all over them, and I nearly bought those."

"It wouldn't have been in the part," she said. "We're supposed to be a respectably married couple, aren't we? I wasn't quite sure if we were or not. I wondered if I ought to have a flannel nightie buttoned up to the neck, and then I thought that it would be a waste of money, because I'd never use it again."

"I'm not quite sure what we're supposed to be," I said. "I ought to have asked the solicitor. Anyway, you're all right as you are."

She leaned towards me. "You're looking much too tidy. Let me rumple your hair."

"Not much," I said. "I'll rumple it myself. One thing leads to another."

She laughed. "Would you like me to get out and get the dominoes?"

We sat in bed together for half an hour, laughing and talking happily till we heard the rattle of teacups in the passage. I pressed the bell. "Now for a cup of tea."

She laughed. "I'd love a cup of tea."

A maid about forty years old came in, a horse-faced

woman with a slightly humorous expression. I ordered tea, and then I winked at her, as I had been told to do. She smiled, and crossed the room to close the window, taking a good look round the room as she did so. When she brought the tea she took a good look at us both in bed.

As the door shut behind her, Brenda asked, "Is that all, Johnnie?"

"That's all," I said. "I'll go out in a minute and get her name."

"It seems too easy."

In the corridor on my way to the bath I found the chambermaid hanging around. "Thank you for looking after us so well," I said. "In case I don't see you again, here's something to remember us by." I put two five pound notes into her hand.

She smiled, and said, "Thank you, sir. My name's Doris Swanson. If you should want to get in touch with me at any time, I live at 56 Kitchener Street, North Harrow."

"I'll remember that."

"I'm sure I hope that you and the lady will be very happy."

"Thank you," I said, and went on to my bath.

When I got back to the bedroom she was dressed and packing her suitcase. I dressed and we went down to breakfast together. We had decided we had better not go back to Leacaster by the same train; we left the hotel in a taxi and put her suitcase in the cloakroom at St. Pancras Station. She would do some shopping and go home in the afternoon.

In the bustle of the station she turned to me. "Thank you for everything," she said. "I was rather dreading this, but it's been lovely, all the time."

I grinned at her. "Like to do it again, one day?"

She laughed. "Not just like this. But I should never be afraid again."

April came to an end, with Brenda coming out to fly her Moth practically every day. We started on a mass of legal work. There were three solicitors engaged in our divorce proceedings, one for Derek in The Haven, one for Brenda, and one for me; mine was also working on my own divorce. All three had their offices in Leacaster and all lunched together at the Conservative Club; I suppose each of them suspected that the divorce was a put-up affair, but we all went through the motions. Whenever I wasn't flying at that time I seemed to be in a solicitor's office.

The Pageant at Sherburn-in-Elmet, the aerodrome for Leeds at that time, came early in May. We took up two club machines, and Brenda took her Moth, and a young man called Peter Dawson flew up in his private Comper Swift. He won the Sherburn Stakes that year. I didn't want Brenda to fly in a race just yet but she went in for the landing competition and won it by a most colossal fluke, finishing up her landing run with one wheel slap in the middle of the two-yard bullseye marked out at the centre of the circle. She also won the *Concours d'Elegance*, but I suspect that the white boiler suit and the short, curly hair had more to do with that than Airwork's careful work on the machine. She flew back to Leacaster in the evening with two silver cups in the luggage locker of her Moth, bursting with pride of achievement. At Cramlington a fortnight later she won another one for coming in on the sealed time in the arrival competition, and had it presented to her by the Lady Mayoress of Newcastle who made a little speech about Women in the Modern World.

Derek's solicitor got in touch with Doris Swanson and she came to Leacaster one Sunday to identify Brenda. Derek signed the papers petitioning for his divorce, and the case went down for hearing in the autumn. At a committee meeting of the Leacaster Aero Club I told them that more members than we had seats for in the machines wanted to go to the Rally with the Aero Club de Paris at their own expense, and suggested that we should close down the club for that week and take all three machines; Mrs. Marshall also wanted to go. The Chairman said that he thought it was a good thing to show the flag in this way once a year, but questioned whether Mrs. Marshall had enough experience to fly abroad. I said we couldn't stop her flying anywhere she wanted to in her own aircraft, but suggested that I should fly with her in the front seat of her machine and lead the club Flight from that. In that way we could look after her and see she didn't get into trouble. They thought that was a very good idea, and told me to lay it all on.

The Rally at La Baule was held on the first week-end in June that year, the machines being timed to arrive between two and three in the afternoon. This was all right for the Aero Club de Paris who had about a hundred and fifty miles to fly and could do it comfortably in the morning, but not so good for us with over five hundred miles to fly at an average ground speed of about seventy, with two refuelling stops. I decided that we would leave Leacaster at ten o'clock on Friday morning and fly in loose formation to Lympne on the south coast of England at the Straits of Dover, and have lunch there, and refuel. Then we would take off again and cross the Channel by the shortest route with everybody wearing life jackets, and fly along the coast of Normandy to Dinard, landing there to enter the French Customs and spend the night. It would then be only a short flight on to La Baule next day.

With the long hours of daylight at midsummer this was a good flight plan, because it gave us plenty of daylight on the ground. The Moth of those days wasn't as reliable as it became later, and the engines in our club machines had all done a good many hours. I wasn't worried about the Bluebird or about Brenda's Moth, but the other two machines had a habit of shedding their exhaust valve seatings from the cylinder head, which wasn't quite so good. I made sure that the pilots of those two machines were good, experienced chaps who were accustomed to forced landings, and I took a selection of cylinder heads, engine parts, and tools distributed between the machines, in case of trouble.

Brenda was thrilled at the prospect of this small excursion into France. She had never been abroad before. When it became definite that we were going to La Baule she got herself a set of gramophone records teaching French, and set herself to learn the language. She collected all the maps and drew thick blue pencil lines on them with distance and magnetic course carefully pencilled against each, and she got a Baedeker and read it. She came out to the aerodrome one day with four suitcases of different sizes on approval from the shop and made me sit in the front cockpit of her Moth while she chose the biggest that would go between my knees. One evening at the Manor she displayed a new evening dress that she had got for the occasion, for my approval.

We started off from Duffington on the Friday morning, all four machines fairly heavily loaded. The weather was good when we started, but the forecast was a bit doubtful, with a low coming up from the Atlantic and a chance of rain later in the day. The quicker we got across the Channel the better. I briefed my four pilots with the course, and with the hand signals I would make, and appointed Knox-Turner, who had been on Bristol Fighters in the war, as deputy Flight commander to me. Then we took off one by one and got on course for Lympne, flying in loose formation with Brenda and myself leading in the white Moth.

Everything went fine as far as Lympne, where we landed and refuelled the machines, and had a quick sandwich lunch in the club. Then we took off over the sea for Cape Gris Nez, as I had taken off with the Camel Squadron twelve years before, and passed over the spot where Calvert went down in the sea. I sat for a few minutes with sad memories of those days revived in me. Then I turned and glanced back at the rear cockpit at Brenda, bright-eyed and excited pointing at the coast of France ahead, and came back to the present.

We turned when we were over land and flew on down the coast at about fifteen hundred feet, passing Boulogne, Abbeville, and Dieppe. When we had passed Le Havre and I was starting to think about Dinard and our landing, Knox-Turner in one of the club Moths suddenly started to lose height. His engine was vibrating like a jelly and shooting tongues of flame out of the exhaust, and I knew just what had happened. He throttled back and started in on the approach for a forced landing.

I signalled to the other two machines to keep on circling around, and spoke to Brenda down the voice pipe. She throttled back and went down after Knox-Turner, keep-ing well out of his way. He picked a good big field and put down into it and made what seemed to be quite a smooth landing. We circled round at about two hundred feet and saw them get out; Knox-Turner pointing at the motor. We waved to them and started to climb back towards the other two machines; as we went I pin-pointed the position on my map. It was near a place called Unverre, a small village about ten miles from Bayeux.

I signalled to the other two machines when we got up to them to fly on, and I led them on to Dinard. We landed there and taxied in to clear the Customs, and I told the *Douane* officers about the machine that had forced-landed near Unverre, which would make a complication. They were very nice about it, but refused a lift back there in one of the machines with me; they didn't seem to care for flying. So I hired a car to take one of them to Unverre, and saw him start off.

Brenda offered to fly me back in her machine, so we told the other four club members to fix themselves up in the hotel for the night and we would rejoin forces either late that night if we could get Knox-Turner's Moth repaired in time to fly that evening, or else early in the morning. I collected all the engine parts and tools from their machines and put them into Brenda's, and we took off to fly back to Unverre. As it was to be a forced landing in a field she suggested I should fly it from the back cockpit, and so we went like that.

When we got back to the other machine I found that they had picked quite a good field, and I had no difficulty in landing beside them. They had got the cowling off the engine and had diagnosed the trouble, a valve seating, as I had suspected. The weather was fine and we had everything we needed for the job, and so I got to work. We borrowed a couple of chairs from a cottage about half a mile away to stand on, and with an increasing audience of French countrymen and children I started in upon the engine, while Brenda practised her French upon them down below. Presently the officer of the *Douane* from Dinard arrived, and we had to take time off for him.

The engine was a simple one, but we had to change the head and the gasket and remove the cylinder to make a very close inspection of the piston. It was about four hours before we got it all together again, and the sun was setting. We did a ground run then, using the branch of a tree for chocks, and the engine seemed all right, but it was getting too dark by then to do the test flight that I ought to do before club members flew it. We should all have to spend the night at Unverre, and fly on to Dinard in the morning.

We were very tired by that time, and we had had nothing to eat since lunch. Knox-Turner had gone into the village and had ordered a meal for us at the one inn, which Michelin didn't seem to think much of but which turned on a good meal for us. He had discovered that it had only one bedroom, with two double beds in it. That seemed a bit matey for us all, so he had got the landlord to ring up the next village, a place called Coudray three miles away, which had a much bigger hotel with three bedrooms. He had booked two of these rooms for Brenda and myself.

We picketed the two Moths down and went into Unverre in the local taxi to wash and eat. The whole thing was a delight to Brenda, who had never before seen a French village or a French meal. She had changed into a skirt in the taxi while we were dealing with the aeroplane and she was enjoying every minute, and so was I.

We had a very good meal of thick, country soup, and roast duck, salad, and cheese, washing it down with a couple of bottles of burgundy. Then the landlord suggested that they went to bed early at Coudray, indicating that they did so also at Unverre, and so Brenda and I took our bags and got into the taxi and drove off to La Belle Moisson hotel at Coudray.

When we got there, it became apparent that there had been some confusion, probably due to Knox-Turner's knowledge of the French language. There was only one bedroom vacant, though it had two double beds in it.

I said, "We can go into Bayeux."

She said, "It's so late, Johnnie. We might not get in there. Don't you think we'd better take this?" She smiled. "After all, it's not as if we'd never done it before."

"It's as you think," I said.

She turned to Madame at the door. *"C'est bien,"* she said.

The old lady smiled at us. "*Bonne nuit, monsieur et madame, et bon repos.*" She closed the door on us.

"If we keep on doing this," I remarked, "something's going to happen, one of these days."

She came into my arms. "We'll be free people before long, and, after all, we're getting our divorce for this. Does it really matter if it does?"

Chapter Five

The trouble when you take a Nembutal, or any of the barbiturates, is that you must go on sleeping for the allotted time. However great the distress that dreams impose upon you, you cannot jerk yourself awake, fully awake, that is, till the effect of the drug has eased. I think I may have been partially successful in my struggle to awake because I can remember the whistle of the wind around the exposed little house, and the rain beating on the window. Or perhaps it was some noise that Dr. Turnbull made that roused me partially, when he brought in the nurse. Whatever it was, I had to go on sleeping with a dream that turned to nightmare.

I lived in the Seven Swans, the inn at Duffington, and I went down to the saloon bar for a beer before my meal. I was a little weary, because we had taken off that morning at seven o'clock from La Baule to fly to Dinard, and then up the coast of France to Boulogne for the short sea-crossing to Lympne. We carried with us in the luggage locker of Morgan le Fay another silver cup which Brenda had won in the Ladies Race. We had had a cup of coffee at Dinard and lunch at Lympne, where I took over the piloting because Brenda was getting tired. We landed back at Duffington at about five o'clock in the afternoon with all four machines present and in good order. As we got out on the tarmac, a little apart from the others, she said, "It's been marvellous, Johnnie. The most wonderful week-end I've ever had."

She stood unbuckling her helmet. I smiled at her. "We're going to have a lot more like it."

"Right away from everything . . ." she said. "You don't know what it means. I've been so happy . . ."

"I've been happy, too," I said. And then we had to cut it out, because the others were getting out of their machines and coming up to talk about the flight.

When I went into the saloon bar Sam Collins, the landlord, was behind the bar, and Sergeant Entwhistle of the police was there, and Tom Dixon from the garage. As he gave me my beer Sam asked about the trip, and I told them all about it, the forced landing and the valve trouble. "Mrs. Marshall did very well," I said. "She won another cup—a great big silver one. For the Ladies Race. Two other Moths were in for it, flown by French girls—one of them with over five hundred hours up. Mrs. Marshall won by a short head. She flew a very good race."

They were pleased and interested, but presently there was a pause, and Sam Collins said, "Did you know Dr. Baddeley, at The Haven?"

I had to be cautious here. "I've met him once or twice," I said.

"You heard about him?"

"No?"

"Sorry to say he got murdered," the landlord told me. "Chap jumped out at him as he was going home from the hospital after midnight, beat him to death with a bit of iron bar."

"Good God!" I exclaimed. "When did that happen?"

"Friday night," he said. That was the night that we had spent at Coudray. They all stood looking at me with sympathy, and I wondered how much they knew.

They told me all about it. It seemed that he lived in a suburban house two streets from The Haven. Normally he would have occupied the Medical Superintendent's house inside the grounds, but he had three young children and disliked the thought of bringing them up in the sur-

181

roundings of a mental home. He put his deputy, Dr. Somers, into the Superintendent's house and lived outside himself, but near at hand. Because he was not on the spot he was meticulous in turning out at night to visit any patient who required attention, though a less conscientious man would have left the night work to his deputy. He was walking home through the deserted streets soon after midnight when an ex-patient, recently released from the mental hospital at Coatley, sprang out on him and beat him to death. They had got the man without much difficulty.

"He'll be for Broadmoor," the police sergeant said. "Should have been there years ago."

Little more was said about the doctor, and presently I went and had my supper, wrote a letter or two in the commercial room, and went to bed. I knew that Brenda would have heard the news from her mother. It was difficult for me to telephone to her from the Seven Swans or from the office in the hangar on the aerodrome, because both telephones were public and conversations were liable to be overheard. I had a sense of impending disaster all that night, but there was nothing I could do about it.

She came to the aerodrome next day, and we walked together on the grass up the boundary hedge towards the north-east windsock. "It's terrible," she said, and all the brightness of the last few months seemed to have gone out of her. "Poor Dr. Baddeley . . ."

Presently I asked her, "Do you think it will make any difference to us?"

She asked in turn, "Have you met Dr. Somers?"

"No," I said. "I only met Baddeley once."

"He's so terribly *righteous*," she muttered. "I'm pretty sure he doesn't approve of this divorce."

"What makes you think that?"

"I don't know. Something Dr. Baddeley said once, I think. He's a very different sort of man."

"In what way, Brenda?"

"More up to date. More modern. More—rigid, sticking by the rules." She turned to me. "Like a young schoolmistress in a very modern school, who's learned it all up out of a book." She paused, and then she said, "Dr. Baddeley was so *kind*. That's what made him so good."

I asked, "Do you think this chap Somers will get the job? Or will they put in somebody over his head?"

She said, "He's got an awful lot of letters after his name. He's studied in Austria and in America."

We were a long way from the hangar now. I stopped and took her hand. "There's nothing to worry over," I said. "It's all in train now. We're just waiting our turn for the case to come up in court."

"I know," she said. "But when I went there to see Derek this morning, it was—difficult."

"With Dr. Somers?"

"No—Derek. Sort of bad-tempered." She paused. "He'd taken everything so well before we went away."

There was nothing I could do to make things easier for her, except to give her the assurance of my love. And presently we walked back to the hangar and got out her aeroplane, Morgan le Fay, and started it up, and she took off and went up to the sunlit cumulus above the aerodrome, and I saw her playing in and out of the clouds for nearly an hour, never out of my sight for more than a few minutes at a time. When she landed and taxied in, her eye was bright and there was colour in her cheeks. "It was simply glorious up there," she said. "Like something out of this world."

"Not worried any more?" I asked.

She shook her head. "Not worried any more."

In the next few weeks her visits to The Haven were

never easy for her. She told me very little about Derek, and I did not press her, but I gathered that he had turned sullen and uncommunicative with her, and she had difficulty in keeping up a conversation with him for the forty minutes that was the duration of her usual visit. "I'm sure it will be easier when this divorce goes through," she told me once. "I'm sure that he'll be happier when that's over." Whenever it was fine after her visit to The Haven, and it was fine most of that summer, she used to come out to the aerodrome and fly her aeroplane, always among the clouds if there were any there. It seemed to ease her mind, and drive away the tensions and anxieties of the morning.

There came a morning in late July when she rang me at the aerodrome. She said, "Johnnie, I want to meet you for a talk. Not here. Could we go somewhere this afternoon?"

I thought quickly. "I've got a lesson at three and another one at four. I could meet you anywhere after that."

She said, "Could we meet at Huddlestone, like we did before?"

"Fine," I said. "I could be there by half past five. Is it anything serious?"

"A bit," she said. "I'll tell you when we meet."

When I drove into the village street at twenty past five she was already there and waiting for me, rather pale and quiet. I apologised for being late, and she said, "I was early. Let's go into the woods." So we left the cars parked and walked down the lane together and into the woods, fragrant and cool and silent. When we were out of sight of the last house, I took her hand, and said, "What's the trouble, Brenda?"

She turned to face me. "Three troubles," she said. "The first is, Derek's withdrawn his petition for a divorce."

"That's a bad one," I said quietly. She had had a letter

from her solicitor, who wrote with evident sympathy, but quite definitely. She showed it to me, and I read it carefully. There could be no ambiguity.

"What's behind this?" I asked.

"Dr. Somers," she said.

"Dr. Somers?"

She nodded. "I went to see him this morning. That's the second trouble. I asked him if he knew anything about this change of Derek's mind, and he said that he thought a doctor shouldn't try to influence his patient's mind in matrimonial affairs one way or the other. He said that perhaps he took a different view from his predecessor—he meant Dr. Baddeley. He said he thought that Derek was quite well enough to make his own mind up on matters of that sort without any assistance. And then he went on to talk about Derek. He said that in the nine months that he had had him under observation he had not, himself, detected any symptoms that he would describe in court as mental illness. He said that there had been fits of bad temper, sometimes associated with violence. He said that these could occur with any strong-willed person kept under indefinite restraint."

I stared at her. "Does he mean to say there's nothing wrong with him?"

"That's more or less what he said."

"But what about the case—the case he was in court for?"

She nodded. "I know. I asked him about that. What he said was that there were two sorts of people who would do a thing like that, criminals and criminal lunatics. He said that nothing that he had observed confirmed the supposition that Derek was a criminal lunatic. He said that he intended to keep him under observation for a further period, but that he was beginning to feel that the certification was due for a review."

I pressed her hand. "Does this mean that he's going to let him out?"

She nodded. "That's what he was hinting at. I think he's been putting the same idea into Derek's head, and that's why he isn't going on with the divorce."

I thought quickly. It was bad, very bad, whichever way you looked at it. The worst of it was, I could see it from Dr. Somers' point of view, because since I had known Brenda I had kept my ears open for gossip about Derek. I knew the efforts that his family had made to keep him out of prison; I even knew the amount of the fee marked on the brief of the eminent King's Counsel who defended him. If Dr. Somers now said that he wasn't going to have his mental home cluttered up with ordinary criminals who ought to be in prison just because they had the money for a first-class defence, one couldn't help feeling a little sympathy for him in his attitude.

I asked her, "What's the third trouble?" I knew the answer to that one, of course.

She faced me. "I'm in the family way."

I grinned at her. "That's not a trouble," I said. "That's a damn good thing. I was hoping for that."

She stared at me, bewildered, and then she smiled, and then she burst into tears. I had never seen her in tears before; I took her in my arms and let her cry. And when her sobs had eased, I said, "Maybe we shouldn't have done it, but I'm glad we did. We've wanted to have a family, and now we're going to have one. It's going to make things just a little bit more complicated at the start, but we'll get over that." I wiped her eyes with my handkerchief.

"Just a little bit more complicated," she sobbed. "That's an understatement."

"There's two of us now to work things out together," I said. "Two of us, because I'm in this now up to the neck.

I can take some of the dirty work off you now, because I've got a legal standing in this thing." I paused for a moment in thought. "First of all, I think I ought to go and have a talk with your mother."

She dabbed with my handkerchief. "She doesn't know anything about this yet."

"Does she know what Dr. Somers says about Derek?"

She nodded. "She knows about that, and about the divorce."

"Will you let me tell her about us, and about the baby?"

She stared at me. "Do you want to?"

"I'll be scared stiff," I admitted. "But I think I ought to. After all, I'm responsible."

"I'm not so sure of that. It was more my fault than yours."

"It wasn't anybody's fault," I said. "It was a damn good thing. But I think your mother might think better of me if I told her about it."

Presently we went back to our cars and drove home independently.

When I got back to Duffington I went to the aerodrome. The secretary and ground engineers had gone home so the telephone was private; I let myself into the deserted office and rang up Mrs. Duclos at the Manor. She said that Brenda wasn't home yet, and that I knew, because we had arranged it so. I told her that I wanted to have a private talk with her about the divorce, and she told me to come along at half past eight that evening.

When I went to the Manor I was shown into the drawing room. Mrs. Duclos was there alone; she got up to meet me. "Brenda came in, but she went to bed," she remarked. "Said she was tired."

I nodded. "I know," I said. "I arranged that with

her." She drew herself up a little. "I wanted to have a talk with you privately about this divorce."

She said a little testily, "Well, *I* can't do anything about that."

I nodded. "I know." And then I said, "There's something new now, that you'll have to know about. Brenda's in the family way, and I'm responsible."

She stared at me, erect, angry, and formidable. "You've got a nerve, young man, to come and tell me that!"

"Well, I wouldn't be telling you if I hadn't," I remarked.

We stood staring at each other for a moment. "When did this happen?" she asked.

"When we flew to France. She saw Dr. Haughton today."

"You ought to be ashamed of yourself!"

"I suppose so," I said wearily. "But I'm not. We both wanted this to happen some time, but it's a pity it had to be so soon."

"Sit down," she said.

We sat before the fire in silence for a time. When she spoke again she sounded much older. "I won't pretend to you that this is a surprise," she said. "I may have hoped you'd have more sense, but I don't know that I really thought you would. What are you going to do now?"

"Do you think Derek would go on with the divorce, in view of this?" I asked.

She shook her head. "Not unless he sees some advantage to himself."

"It's like that, is it?"

She nodded. "I think so."

"He wouldn't give any consideration to Brenda's position?"

"He might, but I don't think he would. If Dr. Baddeley

had been alive, he might have talked him round."

There was a short pause. "Brenda tells me that Dr. Somers is talking of letting him out."

"So she told me."

"We'll have to try and get Derek to go on with the divorce," I said. We talked about it for a few minutes. "Which of the three of us would be the best person to go and see him? I'm quite ready to."

She shook her head. "Not you. I'll go and see him myself."

"Would you do that? I'd be quite ready to go, but I don't think it ought to be Brenda."

She shook her head. "Not Brenda. I'll go and see him. Perhaps I'll have a talk with his eldest brother George first, up in Halifax. He's got a very good head on his shoulders. He might help."

Presently I said, "Suppose that doesn't come off. Suppose he won't have a divorce. Suppose Dr. Somers lets him out. We've got to think of what would happen then."

"Yes," she said drily. "We may as well start thinking about that."

I nodded. "I've been thinking about it. There's only one thing we could do, that would solve everything. I'd have to get a job abroad, and Brenda would have to come with me as my wife." She made a gesture of dissent, but I went on, "We could do that. Imperial Airways want pilots for their Far Eastern service. It means living in New Delhi, or Rangoon, or Singapore. But I could get a job with them, I think." I paused. "I don't suppose they'd want to see our marriage lines. I don't suppose they'd be interested."

She shook her head. "It wouldn't do."

"Why not?"

"Brenda wouldn't go," she replied. "She's Derek's wife."

I was silent.

"You don't know her very well," she said. "A divorce when a continuation of her marriage was hopeless—yes. She accepted that. I think she would go on with the divorce now, for the sake of her child, and for you, even if Derek were to get out of The Haven." She stared into the fire, at the sparks that we call 'gypsies' wandering in the soot at the back of the grate. "But to leave her husband and go away with you, unmarried—Brenda would never do that."

That one had never entered my head.

"I think I shall go up to Halifax tomorrow," she said, "and have a talk with George. He might be able to talk Derek round."

There was really nothing more to discuss, but I stayed ten minutes longer before getting up to take my leave. As I said good-bye to her, I said, "I'm very sorry about all this."

"No good being sorry now," she observed, a little curtly. And then she said, "Do you read poetry?"

I was startled at the change of subject. "I'm afraid I don't."

"Arthur Hugh Clough," she said. "I used to read a lot of poetry when I was a girl, and it keeps coming back. He wrote a poem about the Ten Commandments." And then she said,

"Do not adultery commit,
   Advantage rarely comes of it."

"He was dead right," I remarked, and went back to the Seven Swans.

I had a long talk with Brenda next day, out at the aerodrome. She had heard from her mother that she was going up to see George in Halifax—in fact, Mrs. Duclos had already gone. Her mother had told her that she wasn't to tell Derek anything about the baby; she or George would tell him when the time came. She had agreed, but she didn't like it. "I've never deceived him before," she said quietly. "I don't like doing it now."

There was so little I could do to help.

George Marshall came down next week-end. It was the Bank Holiday week-end, and every machine we had was flying about eight hours a day. I had ten or twelve lessons every day, and six hours of instruction day after day makes quite a strain. He went to The Haven on the Saturday morning, and on the Saturday afternoon Brenda brought him out to the aerodrome.

He was a big, heavy man about fifty years old, considerably older than Derek. He was very Yorkshire, with an air of solid, burly prosperity about him. I only had time for a few words with him of no importance before I had to go up with a pupil again. Brenda wanted to take him up in her Moth so I told the ground engineer to get it out and run it up for her, and then I had to go off to give my lesson.

She flew him round for half an hour or so, I think, and then they sat in deck chairs on the lawn of the clubhouse. I went and had a word with them once between lessons, but they were quite prepared to wait until the rush was over. I landed for the last time at about six o'clock, jotted a few times down upon a pad upon my desk in the hangar office, and then walked over to them at the clubhouse. The crowd was thinning now, and the cars were beginning to roll away. We walked a little way up the aerodrome hedge in the evening light.

"Ye've got a champion little club, Mr. Pascoe," he remarked. "D'ye get many accidents with all this flying that goes on?"

"We haven't had one since I've been here," I replied. "I don't believe in them."

"It's an active little business," he said. "Do ye make it pay?"

"It makes a profit every year," I told him. "Not a very large one, because we keep the cost of flying as low as we can for the members. When we look like making money, the Committee drops the rates."

"Aye," he said. "That's one way of doing it." And then he said, "Ye'll be wondering how I got on this morning. Well, I've no good news for you. Derek will have nowt to do with any divorce."

I glanced at him. "You told him about Brenda?"

"Aye, I told him about that. Couple of scallywags, the pair of you, that's what I say. Still, what's done can't be undone, and the only thing is, make the best of it. That's what I told Derek this morning. But he'd have nowt to do with it."

"Did he say why?"

"I dunno. He can be obstinate, can Derek. I wouldn't say that anything he said was very sensible. Said he'd be getting out of The Haven before long, and then he'd make his mind up what was best to do."

"*Is* he going to get out soon?"

"If that Dr. Somers has anything to do with it, he will. Proper ninny that one is, alongside Dr. Baddeley. But there's two needed to sign the certificate, and two needed to unsign it. It's not unsigned yet."

"You think he should stay in?"

"Aye," he said heavily, "I do. Always queer, was Derek, ever since he was a little lad. Always doing things he shouldn't do, we had to cover up."

"How soon would he be likely to get out?"

"Well now, it wouldn't be very soon. There's nothing started yet, and these things take a while. I wouldn't think that it would be before October, at the earliest."

Brenda was there, but this man talked good sense; he had influence in this affair, and I might not have another chance to talk to him. I said, "October's a bad time for a miscarriage."

Brenda flushed and looked annoyed, but George Marshall stopped and slapped me on the shoulder. "Eh! lad," he laughed, "I like a man that calls a spade a spade." He turned to Brenda. "Don't look so put out, lass. He's got the rights of it, and he' said nowt but what has to be said some day, by somebody. It wouldn't do for you to be in Duffington when Derek gets out of The Haven, not the way things are. Ye'll have to go away for the sake of the baby, and live quiet until this is all over. When's it to be?"

"March," she said.

"Well now, what about America? It's a fine place, New York. I was there two years back. There's fine hospitals there, and good doctors. I'll see you right for brass, if Derek won't. What do ye say?"

She was silent. This loud-spoken, positive man meant very well indeed, but he was driving her along more quickly than he should. He didn't know her well enough. There wasn't a chance that she would agree to go to America to live and have her baby; it was too far, too unknown, too different because she only knew it from the pictures. But she recognised the goodwill in George and struggled to keep up with him. "It's all so new," she said. "I want a little time to think it over. A series of rows with Derek might not be a good thing, just at that time. If I've got to go anywhere, couldn't I go to France?"

I might have known that that would be her choice. She had been to France and loved it; she had discovered that she could speak the language a little. People had helped her and she had been happy there. It was there that we had made love.

George Marshall frowned. "Dunno about the French doctors, lass. Scruffy lot, from what I hear."

She smiled. "Don't be absurd. Babies get born in France just as well as they do anywhere else."

"Aye," he said reluctantly. "I'd sooner ye were having it in Leeds Infirmary. But that's not to be."

We talked about France for a little while. In the months immediately before her confinement Normandy would be cold and bleak; if she had to go away she might as well go where it was warm and sunny, to Cannes, perhaps, or Nice. For her reputation in the district, too, it would be better for her to go before her condition became apparent. She could give out that she was going to spend the winter in the south of France, with her mother. If she then came back to Duffington in the spring with a baby— well, that was a bridge that we could cross when the time came. Everything might have changed by then.

George Marshall repeated his offer to finance her if Derek cut off her allowance. She was grateful, but I walked in silence while this was going on, not too well pleased. When they were leaving, I got him on one side to talk to him alone. "It's very good of you to offer to find the money she'll need, Mr. Marshall," I said. "But I can look after that. I've got a bit saved up."

"How much have ye got?" he asked directly.

"Nearly five hundred pounds." I was including the value of my car.

"And ye'll need every penny of it if you're going to set up as a married man," he said. "I tell ye straight, Mr. Pascoe, I'm right sorry for the lass, and so is my wife. She's had a rough spin from the Marshall family and that's a fact, for all that Derek's my brother. If now she's got herself in trouble with the right kind of a man, well, human nature's what it is, and it's not for the Marshall family to turn their back on her. No, leave the brass for this to me, and save your money till you're setting up a household. Ye'll need it then."

I could only thank him.

He went away with Brenda in the Alvis, and we went on much as we had before. The first time Brenda went to visit Derek in The Haven there was a violent scene, so that she had to leave after ten minutes. She went once more, and there was another one. After that Dr. Somers asked her to suspend her visits for a time till Derek had got used to the present state of affairs, till he expressed a wish to see her. After that she didn't go to the hospital again, and the lack of occupation was a distress to her. She said once that she felt that she was living in the Manor under false pretences.

In the weeks that followed I dined with her at the Manor many times. We were still careful about being seen about together, but on Mondays when the aero-drome was closed we used to go off separately in our cars, park one of them in some village ten miles away, and go on in the other up on to the heather-covered moors, happy to be together, walking or sitting talking in the sunshine, forgetting our troubles for a few hours.

Towards the end of August one Monday, up on the backbone of England on the purple hills, she asked me, "Do you think I could fly to Cannes?"

"When?"

"Now, in Morgan le Fay." She turned to me. "I'd like to go there and spy out the land, find a nice quiet hotel where we could stay all winter, and find out about nursing homes and doctors. I thought perhaps I could fly down to Cannes in easy stages, stay a week, and fly back again."

"You'd go solo?"

"You couldn't come, could you?"

I shook my head. "Not at this time of year." There was really no reason why she shouldn't go, because she was getting quite good at cross-country. "You wouldn't take anyone with you?"

She shook her head. "I'd rather go alone, and do it all by myself." She paused, and then she said, "I've been thinking, this may be the last chance I'll have to do a proper long flight, on my own. Later on, the weather will get bad, and anyway I wouldn't want to fly much when the baby gets well on the way. And after he's born—well, everything may be different. I might be anywhere. Perhaps I won't be able to fly at all then. I would like to have one really good, long flight behind me to look back upon and think about."

"You could do that," I said. "You wouldn't have any difficulty, provided that you aren't in a hurry. I wouldn't fly in bad weather, if I were you. If it's raining, or if the Met say that it's going to, wait till next day and have a look at the town." I got down to it with the maps with her that evening, planning her flight to Cannes in easy stages of not much more than a hundred miles each that she could take as she wished. From Duffington to Heston, from Heston to Lympne, to Le Touquet for Customs, to Le Bourget for Paris, to Auxerre, to Dijon, to Lyons, to Avignon, and so to Cannes. She pored over the maps with me, entranced. "I'll never get to Cannes," she saids "I'll want to stop so long at all these places—Paris, Dijon. Avignon . . . Johnnie, if I want to have the plug, checked, what do I say?"

"I'll get a couple of sets of new ones for you to take, and some other things," I said. "Then all you've got to do is, ask them to *changer les bougies*."

"*Changer les bougies*," she repeated. "I must get a little book and start writing all these things down."

The excitement of this journey was very good for her;

she was brighter and more cheerful than she had been for weeks. In the next few days I marked all her maps with a thick blue line from place to place, with the distance against it in red pencil, with the magnetic course to steer going out in blue and the magnetic course to steer coming back in green. I got her a course-and-distance calculator and showed her how to use it to check drift, and got her a fuel *carnet* and an aircraft *carnet*. Then, with her passport, she was ready to go. I put her bag of spares and tools in the front cockpit with her suitcase and strapped them down, her log books and clean overalls in the rear locker. She got in and I swung the prop for her; she ran it up, waved the chocks away, and taxied out, as pretty and excited as she had been on her first solo. I stood watching as she took off, got on course, and vanished to the south.

It was lonely at Duffington without her, and I knew that it was going to be lonely all the winter. She sent me telegrams from every place where she night-stopped, and a letter every couple of days. I wrote to her every day, and because it took her eight days to get to Cannes there must have been quite a packet of them waiting for her there. She flew home more quickly, in three days, and one afternoon towards the end of September she flew in and taxied to the hangar.

She unfastened her helmet and got out of the machine, her overall smeared a little with dirt and oil. "It was simply glorious," she said. "Like something out of this world. Nothing went wrong, I never got lost—I never touched the spares. And I could make them understand me, Johnnie!"

She was very happy, and looking very well. She had taken a cheap little folding Kodak with her and had taken a lot of photographs, and had had them developed and printed in Cannes. She wanted me to go up to the Manor for dinner that night so that she could show me them. I drove her home and then went off to wash and change before going up to the big house.

When I got there she was waiting for me in the drawing room with her mother. The radiant happiness had all disappeared, and she was looking white and drawn. "Things have been happening in the last few days, Johnnie," she said. "Derek."

"Important things?" I asked.

Mrs. Duclos said, "He's applied for his certificate to be annulled. Dr. Somers rang me up about it on Monday. As Brenda was coming home so soon I thought I wouldn't spoil her holiday."

"How soon shall we know?" I asked.

"The Commissioners in Lunacy are coming down to examine him," she told me. "Dr. Somers didn't know when, but he said he'd let me know."

It seemed that Derek had made a formal application to the visiting committee for a review of his case. He had put it to them personally on one of their periodic visits, acting in a very restrained and sensible manner. Dr. Somers, apparently, had backed the application, which had gone to the Commissioners in Lunacy. The procedure now was that two of the Commissioners, one of whom had to be a doctor and one a barrister, were to come down and examine him. If their report was favourable, the certificate would be annulled and Derek would be free.

Brenda said listlessly, "Dr. Ford-Johnson will probably be one of them. He's a specialist, in Harley Street, and he's one of the Commissioners. It was he who certified Derek, with someone else—some barrister, I think."

The photographs, the flight, her happiness, were all forgotten, and we were back in the same dreary mess. We talked about it all evening. Mrs. Duclos had rung George Marshall and had told him the news, and she thought that he was doing something in London. She didn't think that the Commissioners were coming for a week or two, but she didn't really know.

When we had been over and over the miserable business, I said, "I think you both ought to go to Cannes." Brenda had found a pleasant and inexpensive hotel just off the promenade at the east end.

"When?" she asked thoughtfully.

"Now. Before the Commissioners arrive."

"You mean, in the next week?"

I nodded. "As soon as you can." I paused. "You won't be able to go so well when Derek is just due to come home. Better go now, at once."

Brenda sat in thought, her chin cupped in her hand. "Of course, for myself I'd love to go. It's such a lovely place. But what would Derek have here to come home to? I mean, there'd just be the servants."

Mrs. Duclos said, "I think that's a matter for the Marshalls, dear. One of them would have to come and live here and keep house for him. After all, there are plenty of them. Myra could come down, or Janet."

Brenda said, "Not Myra—she's got the old lady to look after. Janet might come."

Her mother said, "He's right, dear. I think you ought to get away from here."

Brenda said, "It's like running away."

She knew that she would have to go, but she fought for a long time against a decision. In the end, at about eleven o'clock, she finally agreed. Her mother was for it; she had travelled widely in her youth and knew Cannes quite well. There seemed no point in making any delay. We arranged that they should go to London in about three days' time, stay there a little while to make what purchases they needed, and then go on across France with sleepers on the train.

Brenda said, "It's going to be a miserable way of travelling, after Morgan le Fay."

I smiled. "It's going to be quicker."

"I know. But the other was such fun." She turned to me. "You'll look after Morgan for me, Johnnie?"

"I'll look after her," I said. "If you stay away all winter she'll have to have her certificate of airworthiness renewed. I'll be in touch with you about that. We'd better get that done while you're away, and then she'll be all ready for you to fly next summer."

She said wistfully, "I'd like to fly to Spain. Could we do that together some day?"

"Next summer," I promised her. "I'll get leave, and we'll go together."

She came out to the aerodrome and flew her Moth once more. Then we put it at the back of the hangar and folded the wings. She brought down a lot of dust sheets and we spent an afternoon covering most of it up with these. "You'll be sure they turn the engine every week?" she asked me anxiously. "It says you have to do that, in the book."

I pressed her arm. "Don't worry. I'll look after her myself."

A couple of days later I saw them off at the station. It was terribly, terribly lonely when they'd gone.

Some time after that George Marshall rang me up from the Manor, and asked if I would run up there to see him. I had no idea that he was in the district. I went up there at once, and had a talk with him. It seemed that Mrs. Duclos had been in touch with him in London, and that he had undertaken to see that the house was ready for Derek when he came out of The Haven, with some member of the family living there to run it for him. I said something about his kindness.

"That's as may be," he said gruffly. "I've changed my

mind since Mrs. Duclos went to France. I'm laying off the housemaid. The cook will be staying on as housekeeper through the winter, to keep the house right for them when they come back here in April."

I glanced at him. "What about Derek? Isn't he coming out?"

"The Commissioners are coming down here on the sixteenth of October," he said. That was a fortnight hence. "We shan't know till they've examined him and made their report. But—no, I'd be surprised if they should let him out."

"I thought it was a certainty," I said.

"It never was that . . ." He stood and thought for a minute, and then he said, "Ye've a right to know how things are, Mr. Pascoe. When Derek was in trouble and was certified three years ago, the court and the Commissioners didn't know the half of it. We didn't see the sense in making a bad matter worse by raking up old troubles when he was a boy, things we'd been able to cover up and no scandal, and all forgotten about. But now, it's different. He's happy in The Haven and well looked after. We wouldn't want to see him given the responsibility of living his own life again."

He paused, and then said heavily, "I went and saw Mr. Justin Forbes, in his chambers, and told him everything that had happened, ever since Derek was a little lad. He's one of the Commissioners, the barrister. We don't want any more trouble, and he's happy where he is."

"He took it seriously?"

"Aye, he did that. Got his clerk in for a shorthand note, and had it typed out as a formal statement. I went back and swore to it that afternoon."

We stood in silence for a time. I was sorry for this man, sorry for all of them. It was obvious to me that George Marshall was afraid of another crime if Derek was released. If that should happen, he might go to prison for it. They were paying very high fees for him in The Haven, and it was better that he should stay there.

"You spoke pretty frankly to him?" I asked.

"I did that. Want to leave well alone, that's what I said."

I thought about it for a moment. "If the Commissioners decide to keep him in, then, Brenda and Mrs. Duclos could come back here if they want to?"

"Aye," he said, "they could do that. But she'll be four months gone by then, and better she should stay quiet where they are, and save the scandal. I was thinking, when all this has blown over, say around Christmas time, I'd come down and see Derek again and see if he'd go on with the divorce. Maybe Mr. Forbes would help in that. But all that's in the future."

"Does Brenda know you've seen the Commissioner?"

He shook his head. "I'd as soon you didn't tell her, either. Just leave it be, and tell her what the Commissioners decide. You can tell her after, if ye think it necessary. But least said, soonest mended."

Things seemed to be improving again so far as Brenda was concerned, and I went back and wrote to her cheerfully. Thereafter life went in a normal, routine sort of way. I wrote to her every other day and she wrote to me; I know that I lived for her letters, and I think she did for mine. Presently the Commissioners arrived, examined Derek, deliberated, and decided that he had better stay where he was. My solicitor heard about it first, and rang me with the news, saying that Dr. Somers was rather upset. I telegraphed it to Brenda.

The Leacaster Flying Club were fairly generous with leave; they gave their pilot-instructor three weeks every year provided that he took it in the winter months. I had taken no leave at all the previous year, my first year with the club, and I had little difficulty in getting the Committee to agree that I should take two spells of a fortnight each, one in January and one in March. We had several members with over five hundred hours of war-time flying in the distant past, and two with current B licences for commercial flying, who could act as assistant instructor while I was away. I spent all the early months of winter arranging that the work should go on steadily while I was on leave, and early in January I left for France.

That fortnight was a delightful time. Brenda was very well, and more composed than I had expected to find her. She had had no contact with her husband in The Haven since she had left Duffington, and though she was growing tired of the hotel life with her mother she was well adjusted to it. She could not have a piano but she went to every concert that took place in Cannes, and on the second day she showed me, rather shyly, two or three water colour paintings, landscapes. Encouraged. she produced another water colour that she was attempting of her Moth in flight. This was in an early stage; she had traced the drawing from an air photograph of a Moth similar to hers but had got it a bit wrong in spite of that assistance. She knew that it was wrong but she didn't know where the error had crept in. I was able to help her there; I could not draw but I did know very certainly what her Moth looked like when it was in flight. We worked at this together for a couple of mornings, and it was tremendous fun.

She had acquired a little car, a Renault, through the generosity of George Marshall and we made two or three long drives in this, to Grasse and up into the Esterelles. She was becoming very interested now in her coming baby, who she had quite decided was to be a boy, and she had two or three books on infant welfare in her room. She was very optimistic about a divorce; perhaps in Cannes it was easier to be optimistic than it was in the grey Midlands of England. She thought that Derek must agree to a divorce before very long, since it must now be clear to him that their marriage could not go on. She thought it would be better, when that happened, if I could get a job abroad as a commercial pilot so that when we married we could start off fresh in a new place, away from England. She realised that that meant the tropics in all probability and she welcomed that for herself, though she was puzzled about the baby. What were the special problems of a baby in a hot country? Did I know of any book about it? She spent every evening after dinner sewing little clothes.

She was going to call him Johnnie.

Once she said, "I suppose we'll have to go back to Duffington, shan't we? After the baby's born?"

"Nobody has to do anything," I told her. "I could give up my job there. But if I was going to do that, I ought to tell them now, so that they could get another pilot in the saddle before the summer rush comes on."

She asked, "Could you get another job with some other club, in some other part of England?"

"I don't think I could," I said slowly. "It would get around why I had left Duffington. The wives of members aren't so keen on a pilot who's a co-respondent."

She bent her head over her sewing. "The Wives' Trades Union," she murmured. "I see that."

"The only thing that I could do would be to get into air transport," I told her. "I'll have to do that one day, anyway. But that means India or somewhere."

"We'd never see each other then," she said. "I don't think I could face this all alone."

I took her hand. "I know. I think I ought to go on at Duffington for the time being, anyway. But that doesn't mean you'd have to come back there."

She sat motionless for a few moments, her sewing on her

lap. "It hasn't been a very happy place," she said quietly. "The club, and flying, and you, and everything we've done together—that's been just a dream. But not the rest of it."

"I know," I said. "Would you like a little house somewhere not too far away, but not in Duffington? In Oxford, say?"

"I don't know," she said slowly. "If I didn't go back to Duffington it would be like running away because I was afraid." I was silent. "Let me think about it, Johnnie," she said. "We don't have to decide anything for the next couple of months."

"It might look a bit odd if you went back there with a baby," I remarked. I was very disinclined for her to go back there, even then.

"That doesn't matter," she replied. "People gave up calling, after Derek's case. Nobody ever comes to the house anyway. A baby more or less won't matter." She paused. "I thought perhaps that I might say he was my sister's baby."

"Have you got a sister?" I asked.

She smiled. "No. But one has to say something, even though you know that people won't believe it."

She had her own way of looking at things, and her reputation didn't seem to worry her a bit. I left her at the end of the fortnight reasonably happy in my mind about her. In this very difficult time she was quiet and composed, enjoying her little life of waiting, with her concerts and her painting and her country drives. I went back to Duffington refreshed with the short holiday, and there I found a letter waiting for me from George Marshall.

He told me, very briefly, that he had failed again to make Derek consider a divorce. Derek seemed to consider that George was responsible for his failure to get out of The Haven, which indeed was true, and he was actively hostile to any proposal that his brother put up. It seemed very probable to me that Dr. Somers had been talking.

I was barely two months back at Duffington, and then I was off again to Cannes. Brenda had picked a pleasant little hospital on one of the hills behind the town, and two days after I arrived she went into this place to have her baby. A couple of days later, it was born, and it was a girl.

I saw her for a few minutes that evening, weak and exhausted. She was terribly disappointed. She had convinced herself that it was going to be a boy and that he would be a pilot, like his father. I tried to cheer her up. "Girls are fun," I said. "I'd rather have a girl."

A tear trickled down her cheek. "I did so want a boy."

I wiped it away gently. "Girls can be pilots, too," I said. She smiled faintly, and squeezed my hand. Then the French sister came and made me go away.

She recovered her strength quickly, but the sense of disappointment persisted. During the last week of my leave I raised the question of the baby's name once or twice; she had decided to wait to have her baptised till they returned to England. I wanted to call her Brenda, and she agreed to that without much interest. She was fond of the child, but decided to wean her at an early stage, before they came back to England. Her mind was set more on flying her Moth that summer than it was on nursing her child. If it had been a boy, I think things might have been different.

My leave was up, and I had to go back to Duffington before she left the hospital. At that time English nursemaids were not uncommon in Cannes, and Mrs. Duclos had already been in touch with one and was to interview another. They planned that when Brenda came out of the hospital they would go back to the quiet hotel where they had lived for six months and stay there for another month, getting the baby weaned and accustomed to a good English nurse. Then they would all come back to Duffington, arriving at the Manor about the end of April.

I went back to my job, and on my first Monday I flew her Moth down to Heston for the renewal of the certificate of airworthiness. In the year that she had owned it it had only flown about a hundred hours, but under the regulations of those days it had to be pretty well pulled to pieces for inspection every year, and that meant quite a lot of work. I left it there for this work to be done, and wrote to her in Cannes about it. In her reply she said that she would fly it back herself from London on her way home, which would save me another journey.

She flew in one afternoon at about tea time. I knew that she was coming, for her mother and the baby and the nurse had arrived by train the day before; she should have come on the same day but something had happened at Heston to delay the delivery of her Moth. I got a telephone call from Heston in the middle of the afternoon to say that she had taken off for Duffington; it was a fine, sunny afternoon with all the promise of spring, so I knew that she would be all right. Young Ronnie Clarke was learning to fly at that time, having taken his matriculation with an effort, and he was coming out for a lesson at four o'clock. He was a very quick pupil as such boys usually are; he had soaked himself in theoretical knowledge for years before he actually commenced instruction, and he had flown so many hours as a passenger in club machines that I could have sent him off solo quite safely after about three hours' dual. The insurance regulations demanded that he have eight hours, so rather than keep him at the dreary round of circuits and bumps I had been teaching him aerobatics. We were up at about three thousand feet that afternoon in a clear sky and I was showing him how to roll off the top of a loop; each time we came upright and climbed for another one I scanned the horizon to the south, looking for Morgan le Fay. I saw her as a faint speck in the distance about half way through the lesson and pointed her out to Ronnie; we broke off the lesson and he flew towards her and came round into loose formation with her while I told him what to do, and so we flew together the last five miles towards the aerodrome waving at each other. I held Ronnie off and made him do a circuit while she went in to land; I watched her till she was down and taxi-ing towards the hangar, and then let Ronnie land behind her.

She met us, radiant, upon the tarmac, and it was just like the old days of the previous summer. Ronnie switched off the engine and we sat unbuckling our helmets, and she came up to the machine beside us. "Johnnie, it's simply glorious to be back," she said. "How's Ronnie getting on?"

"Getting on all right," I said. "He could make anybody sick now. He'd have made me sick if you hadn't come along. Have a good flight up?"

"Beautiful," she said. "Morgan's flying a bit left wing low, I think."

I nodded. "I'll take her up and check her over for you. She may want a bit of fine adjustment on the rigging. Landing all right?"

She nodded. "Not too bad. I did two or three at Heston before leaving. It's so lovely to be back . . ."

"Lovely for us," I said quietly. Ronnie was there, of course, and the young don't miss much. We got out on the tarmac and pushed the machines into the hangar, and we all went into the office for a cup of tea. Brenda was radiantly happy, with colour in her cheeks and brightness in her eyes, looking younger than ever. I had a look at her aircraft log book for the rigging check, and then I took her out to look at the machine, leaving Ronnie in the office.

Behind the Bluebird we were out of sight, and I took her in my arms and kissed her.

"We oughtn't to be doing this," she murmured. "Not in the hangar. You'll lose your job."

"Wives' Trades Union," I laughed. She laughed with me. "We won't do it again. But this is a special occasion."

I had had her Alvis checked over at the garage and made clean for her, and I had brought it to the hangar the day before when she was to have come home. She got into it, and it was just like the old days as I stood chatting with her at the window. "I'll be out tomorrow morning," she said, "or I'll give you a ring. I'll have to see what's happening in the domestic situation, but if it's all under control will you come up for dinner tomorrow night?"

"I'd love to," I said. "We'll have to fix up something now about the christening."

She nodded. "I'll see the vicar about that. I think he'll do it privately for us, up at the Manor." I nodded. "I registered the birth, of course. In Cannes."

"What name did you give her?"

She smiled. "Brenda. Brenda Margaret. I thought she ought to have two."

I went up to the Manor for dinner next evening. Already the spontaneous gaiety of her arrival had been dissipated by the constraints of Duffington. The vicar had proved difficult over the christening; apparently he disapproved of the whole thing. He said that her baby should have been christened in Cannes by the resident Church of England clergyman, and he couldn't understand why it hadn't been. He could not refuse baptism to a child presented to him, but he would do it in the village church and nowhere else. Brenda had had to explain to him the general position of affairs and the necessity to avoid a public scandal if she were to go on living there. He had said that in the circumstances he would require the permission of the bishop before baptising the child privately, and he would let her know. It had all been rather unpleasant.

She had rung up Dr. Somers and had asked if her husband would like her to visit him. He had been reasonably cordial, but had warned her that the subject was a delicate one and he would have to approach it tactfully. He would ring her as soon as he had done so, probably before the end of the week.

I went back to the Seven Swans that night deeply troubled in my mind. It seemed to me that we had made a vast mistake in bringing her back to Duffington with her baby and that nothing but trouble lay ahead of us. It seemed to me that I should have insisted on a little house at Oxford or some place like that where no one knew her. even if it meant that I could only see her once a week for a time. If we had done that, this christening trouble would not have arisen, for one thing. In Duffington Manor she was now living with my child in an entirely false position from a twisted sense of loyalty to her husband, and the worst of it was that I could see no way to put things right.

I had adjusted the rigging of her Moth and had test-flown it for her, and she came out and flew it for a time next day. It seemed to put her mind at rest, and she came down far more composed and cheerful than she had been when she had taken off. On the following day she came out and flew it again, but she had heard nothing from the vicar and nothing from Dr. Somers. And that evening she rang me up just as I was leaving the aerodrome.

She said, "Johnnie, can you come up here at once? I've got to talk to you."

"Of course," I said. "What is it?"

She said dully, "Derek's escaped. He got out of The Haven."

"My God!" I said. "Where is he now?"

"They don't know. They're out looking for him."

"All right, darling. I'll be with you straight away."

When I got to the Manor I heard the whole story, so far as she knew it. It seemed that there was a gate to the high-walled grounds of The Haven, an iron grille affair which was kept locked. That afternoon the gardener had un-locked it to push a barrow through; at the same time one of the nursing sisters of the women's side of the place was fiddling unskilfully with the motor of her car in the garage about fifty yards from the grille. She moved a chafed lead, and the horn began to sound and went on sounding —loud, raucous, and continuous. The staff of The Haven knew from past experience that sudden noises such as that can excite a proportion of mental patients and make them almost unmanageable, and the gardener dropped every-thing, left the grille open, and went to help the sister stop it. It was over an hour before they discovered that Derek Marshall was no longer there.

Later that evening they discovered that he had pawned his silver cigarette-case in the city for twenty-five shillings, and had vanished in the rush-hour crowds.

It was bad, any way you looked at it. My first concern, of course, was for the safety of Brenda and her baby, not to mention her mother and the nurse and cook. "I'll sleep here tonight," I said. "You'd better have somebody around."

She shook her head. "There's no need to do that. He won't come home."

"How do you know that?"

"It's the first place they'd look for him. I saw a police-man in the garden just before you came in, down by the summerhouse. Didn't you see him?"

I shook my head.

"He'll keep right away from us," she said. "He's only got to stay free for a fortnight."

"I've heard something about that," I replied. "After a fortnight he's regarded as sane, isn't he?"

"That's right," she said. "If he stays free for a fortnight, then he's got to be re-certified." She paused, and then she added, "I don't think Dr. Somers would certify him—not unless he does something bad."

"Do you think he will?"

She sighed wearily. "I don't know, Johnnie. Not in the next fortnight, anyway."

I asked, "Have you got any idea where he'd be?"

She shook her head. "Anywhere. He may have some old army friend who'd hide him for a fortnight. Even a relation. I don't know."

I took her hand. "Look, dear," I said, "this puts the lid on it. You can't stay here. This is his house, after all, and he'll come back here in a fortnight when he's free to do so. I'll slip down to Oxford tomorrow and find somewhere for you to go—a furnished house, if possible, or else a flat. You'd like Oxford, wouldn't you?"

"It won't do, Johnnie," she said sadly. "It just won't do."

"Why not?" I asked. "It's the only thing we can do."

"I'm his wife," she said. "That's why."

"He agreed to divorce you. You wouldn't have been his wife by this time; you'd have been married to me. But he's not right in the head, and he went back on it. We can't go along on those lines, dear. They're crazy lines."

"I know they are," she said. "Some day perhaps we'll get them straightened out. But in the meantime, I'm his wife, and this is where I'll have to stay till he comes home." I was silent, and presently she said, "Perhaps when I see him I'll be able to talk him round."

I could not move her from that, however hard I tried, and presently I left her and went back to the village. As I drove down the drive of the Manor a dark figure came forward out of the bushes to stop the car, and I pulled up. It was Sergeant Entwhistle, of the police.

"Good evening, sir," he said. "Are there any other guests in the house?"

"No," I said. "I was the only one."

"I'll just go in, then, and make sure the windows on the ground floor are all fastened, and the doors," he remarked. "We don't want any trouble in the night."

"Are you expecting him?" I asked.

He shook his head. "Not unless he's a lot crazier than what they say he is," he replied. "He'd be too cunning to come here. But there's no harm in making sure."

That was the twenty-eighth of April, and the fortnight would be up on May 12th. On May 13th Derek might be expected to show up if they hadn't caught him before, an appropriately unlucky date, it seemed to me. There was absolutely nothing I could do about it, though. I tried once more to make Brenda go away with her mother and the baby, but I only succeeded in annoying her. The nurse, not liking the atmosphere, gave in her notice and left.

She came out to the aerodrome every morning to fly her Moth, and that was good for her, and seemed to ease her mind. She chose the mornings rather than the afternoons because there were seldom any people at the aerodrome on week-day mornings, and there had been a story in the newspapers about Derek's escape from The Haven, with a photograph of him. Apart from these visits to the aerodrome I don't think she left the grounds of the Manor at all. She didn't come on Saturday or Sunday because of the people, but I got her Moth out for her on Monday morning when the club was normally closed. There was so little I could do for her.

Throughout that fortnight the tension grew, till it became nearly unbearable. I know that she was taking sleeping tablets of some sort. I didn't do that myself because drugs and flying don't mix very well, and I used to lie awake most nights till two or three in the morning. On top of the anxiety and the suspense over Derek, I had a terrible feeling that Brenda was growing away from me. Our aims were different. I wanted her to leave her husband and become my wife in fact, if not in law. She wanted to stay with him, not because she loved him but because she had an ethereal sense of duty, almost like a nun. I knew that she was terrified of his return, but she was moving away from me to face it upon planes that I could not reach.

She came out to the aerodrome on the morning of the 11th. She seemed completely normal, went to the club house to change into her boiler suit, and came back to the machine. I had it out upon the tarmac and I was in the cockpit running up the engine for her; I was doing every-thing I possibly could for her at that time, myself. She went into the office for a moment and came out again to the machine. I throttled back and got out, and she got into it without speaking. She fastened her belt, smiled at me, and taxied out to take off.

I watched till she was in the air, and then went back into the office. There was a note there on my desk. It read:

> Dear Johnnie—
> Thank you for everything.
> Brenda.

I dashed out on to the tarmac, with a ghastly feeling of disaster in my throat. She was coming over the aerodrome now at seven or eight hundred feet, flying straight and level. Then, as I watched, she throttled back the engine, pulled the nose of the machine right up, and kicked on full rudder. The Moth hesitated for a moment, and then fell over in a spin.

I breathed, "Oh God . . . please . . . no!"

I stood watching her in horror. At three hundred feet she was still spinning, and I shouted to the men to get the crash wagon. The elevators were still hard up, the rudder hard over. Then she centred the controls and the machine stopped spinning and went into a straight dive, gathering speed quickly. She never made the slightest effort to pull out. She hit the ground near the far hedge with a dull thud and a splintering noise of wood, and as I ran I heard the crash wagon start up behind me.

For the second time that night I woke from a bad dream. I was sweating and trembling, and for a time I didn't know where I was. I thought that I was in the small hotel that I had lived in in New Delhi, where I had woken up in that way practically every night. Brenda was dead, and now the baby was dead, the only part of Brenda that was left to me. I had killed her baby by neglect for I had gone away to India and left her, left Brenda's baby and mine. Mine was the guilt, and my punishment was to go on living in loneliness and shame.

I stirred, and reached out for the letter from Mrs. Duclos to read it for the hundredth time, though I knew every word by heart. It wasn't there, and my torch wasn't there, either. There was something vertical and unfamiliar. As consciousness came back to me I realised my hand was on the standard of a table lamp. In my misery I fumbled about with a trembling hand until I found the switch and got it lit. I lay blinking in the flood of light. I was in Johnnie's Pascoe's room, and everything was quite all right. I hadn't just seen the girl I loved dive in. I wasn't in New Delhi. I hadn't killed her baby by neglect. It was a bad dream, a nightmare. I was Ronnie Clarke, and it was quite all right.

I lay there with the light on, gradually calming down. I

was Ronnie Clarke, and Sheila was waiting for me back at Essendon, and Peter, and Diana. It was all right. Presently I stirred and looked at the wrist-watch on the table by my side. It was only half past twelve, and I had set the alarm clock for five. I had had a few hours of sleep, though whether it had done me much good was another matter. I had a job of hard and difficult flying to do at dawn when I should need to have all my wits about me. There was still time for another spell of sleep, but I knew I shouldn't get it till I had composed my mind. The one thing that I wasn't going to do was to take another Nembutal.

Presently I got out of bed, put on Johnnie Pascoe's dressing gown and bedroom slippers, and pulled the bed-clothes up to the pillow to keep the bed warm. I felt in the pockets of the dressing gown and found his packet of cigarettes and his box of matches. I put a cigarette into my mouth and took the matchbox from the other pocket. There was only one match left in it. I struck that with fingers that were still clumsy and trembling, and the head broke off short.

There was another box on the mantelpiece in the sitting room, that I had used to light the fire. I went through, and stood rooted in the doorway, sick with horror. The fire had been made up and was glowing red, but all the lights were out. And there, in the firelight, in the white boiler suit that she had worn the day she died, curled up in the armchair and asleep, was Brenda Marshall.

Chapter Six

I suppose I made some exclamation, made some noise, because the girl in the armchair stirred and sat up. The white boiler suit melted away and resolved itself into a white starched dress, a sister's dress. The short, curly, reddish brown hair that I had expected wasn't there when she sat up into the firelight; this girl had darkish, wavy hair, shingled at the back. The face was different, too; vaguely familiar, but quite different. It wasn't Brenda Marshall at all, and I had been a fool.

She brushed the hair back from her face, and stood up. "I'm sorry," she said. "I must have dropped asleep. Are you Captain Clarke?"

I nodded. And then I hesitated while I gathered my wits together and composed myself. "You must be the nurse."

"I'm Sister Dawson," she replied. "Dr. Turnbull brought me down here and said it would be all right if I slept here. I hope we didn't wake you when we came in?"

I shook my head. "I never heard you. I thought you were going to sleep in the other room."

She nodded. "We brought down his sleeping bag." She indicated it, draped over a chair. "It's a bit messy in there, though, and very cold. I thought I'd get a better night if I slept in the chair here, by the fire. I hope you don't mind."

"*I* don't mind," I said. "I'm only sorry if I woke you up. I didn't know you were here. I just came in for a match." I reached out and took the box from the mantelpiece and lit my cigarette. It helped to calm my nerves.

And then I recalled my manners and offered her the packet from the pocket of the dressing gown. "I'm so sorry. Will you have a cigarette?"

"Thanks." She took one, and I lit it for her. She glanced at her wrist-watch. "Half past twelve," she said. "I thought you were sleeping through."

"I know," I said. "I woke up."

She frowned, evidently puzzled. "What time are we taking off?"

"If the weather's at all possible I'd like to get into the air soon after six, and be down at the Lewis River at dawn," I said. "I set the alarm for five." I crossed to the window, and pulled the curtain aside. The wind was very strong, but the rain had stopped. There was an overcast at about two thousand feet, eight-tenths, but behind it there was a moon, and there were flying, fitful gleams of moonlight on the countryside. I stood looking out for a few moments, and then let the curtain fall and turned back into the room. I went and tapped the barometer; it had risen in the night, and was still rising. "It's looking better," I said. "Was it raining when you came in?"

She thought for a moment. "No—it wasn't raining then. It had been raining very hard before."

"Was there a moon?"

She shook her head. "It was quite dark."

"Well, it's definitely better now. It's nothing like the forecast, of course, but they don't get any actuals down here from the south-west." This woman had been an air hostess, so I hadn't got to explain things to her. "If it stays like this we shall be taking off soon after six. Did Dr. Turnbull explain about the trip to you?"

"Yes, sir. He told me that there'd be no cabin door, and we'd have to try and jump out on the strip while you held her against the wind."

218

"Is that all right with you?"

"Yes, sir."

I glanced at her. "You can't wear those clothes."

"He gave me a ski suit and ski boots." She indicated them in a corner. "I'll change into those for the flight. But I can't help him at an operation in those. I'll take this dress with me in a bundle. I've got a theatre gown with me."

They seemed to have got their side of it all buttoned up. "Okay," I said. "You'd better try and get a bit more sleep. I'm sorry I woke you up."

She hesitated, and then said, "I thought you were sleeping through, sir, and I'd have to wake you."

"I thought I would," I said. "But I woke up."

She frowned, evidently puzzled. "Dr. Turnbull told me that you were very tired, and you'd taken a Nembutal."

"I did," I told her. "But it didn't work."

"How much did you take?" she asked.

"Just one," I said.

"A grain and a half, or three-quarters?"

"A grain and a half."

She frowned again. "Do you take it very often?"

I shook my head. "I don't suppose I take more than three or four a year. But they're useful to have with you at a time like this."

"I can't understand it," she said. "With a grain and a half of Nembutal you should be sleeping like a log."

"I had a bad dream," I told her.

She nodded. "Would you go to sleep if you went back to bed again?"

"I'll be all right," I said.

She stood in thought. "I'd better get you something. I saw some milk in the kitchen. Would you take a cup of hot cocoa if I can find anything like that?"

"Don't bother." She disregarded that, and went down

the short corridor into the kitchen, very much the nurse. I heard cupboard doors opening and shutting. "There's Ovaltine here," she said. "You'd better have a cup of that. I'll warm up some of this milk."

It seemed that I was to have little say in the matter. A hot drink might not be a bad thing, anyway, if it brought me a few hours' more sleep, for I was still all on edge and the coming flight would be a difficult one. The Auster was a very little aeroplane to fly at night with a full load in bad weather, especially when practically all one side of the cabin was removed. I would have to fly it manually on instruments, of course, over bad country with no lights or navigation aids. I didn't want to start off all tensed up as I was then. Her cup of hot Ovaltine might quite well be the shot.

I threw some more wood on the fire and sat down before it. Presently she came back with a tray of two cups of the hot drink and a few biscuits on a plate. I took one cup and she took the other, and we sat together before the fire waiting for the drink to cool a bit.

"Dr. Turnbull said that you'd been a hostess," I remarked. "With Captain Pascoe."

She nodded. "I was in his crew for about ten months, in AusCan. You know him too, don't you?"

"He taught me to fly," I told her, "back in the dark ages, in England. I've known him off and on since then."

"Is that why you came over here?"

I nodded. "How did you come to be in AusCan?"

"I was trained at the Queen Alexandra Hospital, in Melbourne," she said. "Then I was on Surgical. Then about three years ago I got an itch to get out and go places —you know." I nodded. "AusCan like their senior hostesses to have hospital training," she said. "I put in for it and got it. I was with them for a little over a year."

I smiled. "Get fed up with it?"

"Well—yes. You get it out of your system after a time—just serving meals and drinks. I'm back at the Queen Alexandra now."

"You heard about this, and came over?"

"It was on the wireless," she said. "I thought I'd come over to see him in hospital. I never dreamed there'd be this difficulty in getting him out. I only heard about it when I got to Launceston."

"You're Australian, I suppose?" I asked.

She nodded. "I was brought up in South Yarra." She glanced at me. "You're English, aren't you?"

"I suppose so," I said. "I emigrated out here when I got married, in 1946. I don't suppose I'll ever live anywhere else, now. One gets dug in."

We sat sipping our hot drinks. Presently she said, "There was a woman in the hotel called Mrs. Forbes. Did you meet her?"

"She came here for a few minutes just before I went to bed," I replied. "She seemed rather a queer type."

"I think she's mental," the nurse remarked.

I laughed. "Why do you say that?"

"She was telling everybody that she was his daughter," she said, a little hotly. "Well, that's just not true. On top of that she was telling everybody not to risk their lives by flying in to help Captain Pascoe."

"She came to tell me that," I said. "But she's his daughter all right. At least, I think she is."

She stared at me. "How can that be?" And then she said, "At least . . ." She stopped.

"He was married a long time ago," I said. "In the last year of the First War. His wife was an actress and she left him and went over to America. She divorced him there, at Reno. But I think there was a daughter."

"That's right," she said slowly. "There was."

"There's a photograph here," I remarked. I put my cup down and got up, and showed her the photograph of Johnnie and Judy in front of the rotary-engined fighter. "I think that was his wife."

She glanced over her shoulder at it, but she did not get up; she had evidently seen it before. "That's right," she said. "It didn't last for long." There was a pause, and then she said, "He was so terribly young."

I went back to my chair. "I don't suppose he was much more than twenty-one."

She nodded. "Anyway," she remarked with some satisfaction, "Dr. Turnbull tore her off a strip all right, in front of everyone."

I glanced at her. "The police sergeant told me something about that, over the telephone. Were you there?"

She nodded, smiling. "I'd only just arrived; I landed straight into it. I couldn't quite make out what it was all about, at first. Dr. Turnbull seemed to be in the minority, so I went in with him."

"The others were all saying that it was too dangerous?"

"That's right. The woman didn't know what she was talking about. She seemed to be just spiteful."

I took a drink from my cup. "I'm changing my opinion of Dr. Turnbull," I said presently. "I didn't think a lot of him at first. But I'll say this for him. He's got any amount of guts."

"I think he's very good," she said slowly. "We were talking about the operation, what he's got to do. I've never seen him operate, of course, but I think he'd be very steady . . ." She glanced up at me. "I've seen so many young house surgeons," she said. "And of course, we talk about them in the sisters' home. They seem to get into their stride after they've done a few major operations successfully—if they're the right sort."

"Is he the right sort?" I asked.

"I should think he is. I'd rather see him operate on Captain Pascoe than that Dr. Parkinson."

I finished my drink, and put the cup down. "Well, I'm glad to hear you say that," I said. "All we've got to do now is to keep our fingers crossed and hope that I can put you out upon the airstrip." I crossed to the window and looked at the weather again. "It's getting finer all the time. Thank God for that." I turned back from the window. "I think I'll go back to bed now, and see if I can get a bit more sleep."

"Sit down there for a minute while I make your bed," she said.

"Oh—that'll be all right," I objected.

She went to the door. "Sit down there. You'll sleep better if I make it." She was very much the nurse, and I had no option but to obey her. I sat down again in the warm glow of the fire; in the next room I heard her slamming the pillows about, and the rustle of sheets and bedclothes. Once she appeared in the doorway with a rubber hot water bag in her hand. "This was hanging behind the door," she said. "Shall I fill it for you?"

"No, thanks," I said. "I never use one."

"Are your feet warm?"

I smiled. "Quite."

She nodded. "All right. I shan't be a minute now." She went back into the bedroom. She was an effective girl, I thought, and probably efficient at her job. She was evidently well impressed with the young doctor, as he was with her, and it occurred to me how very fortunate we were that she had happened to turn up at the right moment. Without a good surgical nurse at his side Dr. Turnbull might well have been fumbling and immature, but with this girl beside him as he operated Johnnie Pascoe's chances were a great deal better. A first-class nurse in the theatre, I thought, could almost certainly improve a surgeon's skill by taking all irrelevant responsibilities off his mind. I felt that the surgical side of this thing now was probably as good as we could hope to get it. It only remained for me to get them to the Lewis River and land them safely.

The girl came back into the room. "All ready for you, sir," she said.

I got up and went into the bedroom, and she followed me. The bed was very white and clean and neat, just like a hospital bed, no wrinkle on the folded sheets or on the pillows. It was, in fact, just like being in a hospital because the nurse was waiting there to tuck me up. She took Johnnie Pascoe's dressing gown as I slipped out of it and hung it up behind the door, folded his bedclothes over me and tucked them in professionally as I lay in his bed. Then she stood back. "All right now?" she asked.

"Quite all right," I said meekly. "Thank you very much."

She picked up his alarm clock. "I'll take this with me into the next room. Don't bother about waking up—just let yourself sleep through. I'll come and call you when it's time to get up."

She turned out the light and went out of his room, closing the door softly behind her.

I lay in the darkness, warm and very comfortable, thanks to this efficient girl. The hot drink was still warm inside me and my mind was at ease. The weather was improving and conditions for flying when I woke again would probably be a great deal better than I had anticipated. The wind about the house was less than it had been, and now there was a gleam or two of moonlight in the room through chinks in the curtains. There was a break coming in the weather, and it might well be sunny at dawn for a few hours. We had a good young surgeon and a first-class nurse, and everything was going to be all right.

I lay drifting into sleep, thinking about Johnnie Pascoe whose pyjamas I was wearing and about this nurse who had worked in the same aircrew for ten months in AusCan. The old Canadian senior pilot of the line, due for retirement before long, and the Australian nursing sister who had joined his crew as senior air hostess. Ten months together in a D.C.6b, flying the Pacific route—Vancouver, Honolulu, Fiji, and Sydney. Crews in AusCan are rigorously controlled to prevent pilot fatigue. They fly no more than eight hundred and forty hours in any year; after each twelve hours of flying they must have twenty-four hours free of all duty. From Honolulu to Nandi Airport in Fiji takes about twelve hours, so that a rest there is obligatory; another eight hours flying takes the machine to Sydney. The schedules of the flights each week combined with the necessity to rest the crews necessitate a complicated system of crew changes; in AusCan crews are based at Vancouver and at Nandi in Fiji. For ten months I had lived in close association with this girl, on the flight deck over the great wastes of the Pacific, in the coconut groves and on the coral beaches of Fiji when we were resting as we did for four days out of every week. I had come to know her very well indeed.

She came to me in the Superintendent's office at Vancouver Airport. For three years I had been flying the northern route, Vancouver-Frobisher-London. Now Jock McCreedy's wife had had another baby and had come back to Vancouver, so that it was all rather difficult for him to go on on the southern route. I was unmarried so I didn't care where I went, and the northern route had now become a track so well known and so well provided with navigation aids that it wasn't necessary for me to stay upon it any longer. Nandi would suit me very well for my last year in AusCan; it was warm there, and closer to Tasmania, where I was thinking of retiring. We were reshuffling the crews to make these changes possible, and Bill Myers had lent me his office.

She came in while I was talking to Dick Scott, my new flight engineer. He had been on the southern route before for a time, and as his parents had a property near Cootamundra in New South Wales he wanted to get back on it. I glanced at her as she came in and asked her to sit down for a minute, and went on with Dick Scott. We were taking a machine down to the southern route that had been in the shops for three weeks for a five-thousand-hour check; before that I had had it on the northern route, alternating with Pat Bartlett. The aircraft and the engine log books were in a pile upon the desk before me, and I told Dick to have a look through them while I talked to the girl. He settled down to read them by my side, and I called the girl over.

"Miss Dawson, isn't it?" I said.

"Yes, sir. Peggy Dawson."

I shook hands with her. There was something vaguely familiar about her, and I decided that I must have seen her at Vancouver from time to time. "Sit down, Miss Dawson," I said. "You've been flying Honolulu—San Francisco—Vancouver with Captain Forrest, haven't you?"

"Yes, sir."

"Why do you want to get on to the southern route?"

"It's nearer to my home," she said. "I live in Melbourne."

That was reasonable; once in two months a reserve hostess came on and every hostess got a week's leave in Canada or in Australia. I knew she would know all about that. "You're Australian, are you?"

"Yes, sir."

"You aren't afraid of being based at Nandi? There's nothing much to do there."

"I don't mind Fiji," she said. "I'd rather like it for a time."

"I don't want anyone who's going to get fed up with it after a month or two," I told her. "If you come upon the southern route you'd have to be prepared to stick it for a year."

"I know that," she said.

"And you're quite happy about it?"

"Yes, sir."

She knew the conditions as well as I did, and she seemed to be a responsible person. "I understand you're a qualified nursing sister," I said.

She nodded. "I was trained at the Queen Alexandra Hospital in Melbourne."

"Have you worked anywhere else?"

She shook her head. "I left there to come to AusCan."

I had a good report of her from the Chief Hostess, Mrs. Deakin, or I wouldn't have been interviewing her. "You've been a junior hostess with Captain Forrest, haven't you?"

"Yes."

"How long?"

"Four months. Ever since I joined the company."

I nodded. "Well, if you come with me you'll get upgraded and get a bit more money. I'll be taking you as senior hostess. Think you can manage it?"

"I'm sure I can, sir."

"All right, you're in. This is Mr. Scott."

He raised his head. She smiled. "Mr. Scott and I know each other already."

She knew Pat Petersen, who was to be my first officer, too, because he had been in Forrest's crew with her. It looked as if I was getting a well-knit crew together, all of whom were anxious to come on to the southern route with me. I talked to Miss Dawson a little longer and asked if she had any suggestions for a junior hostess. She mentioned an Australian girl from Ballarat, a Mollie Hamilton, who had two years' hostess experience with Australian Continental Airways, had been with us for about a month, and wanted to get on to the southern route. I saw her that afternoon and took her on, and I took Sam Prescott as my navigator. I had no special views about the wireless operator, and took a lad from Winnipeg called Wolfe. I got a lad called Dixon as third pilot. With him my crew was complete, and two days later we took off for San Francisco and for Honolulu. We rested at the Beachcomber Hotel while the aircraft did another trip to Vancouver and came back to Honolulu, and then took it on with a full load of passengers for Nandi.

I had flown the southern route when AusCan opened it some years before; we had been flying early versions of the D.C.6b in those days and had had to land at Canton Island to refuel. Now with the greater range of the new aircraft we could overfly Canton and go direct to Fiji, and the radio aids were very much better than they had been in those days. In the new machine we had two bunks on the flight deck so that we could get a little sleep in turn when all was going well on a long flight. I took off from Honolulu Airport soon after nine o'clock that evening, local time, and made a wide sweep on the circuit till we were climbing upon course. I stayed in my seat for an hour till we reached operating altitude and had adjusted for the cruise condition. The weather was clear ahead of us and everything was normal on the flight deck; I handed over to Pat and went aft into the cabin to see what was going on there.

Everything seemed normal in the cabin. The passengers were finishing the light meal that we serve after an evening take-off; the girls had taken most of the trays away and were starting to hand out the pillows and the rugs. It was a busy period for them, and I wanted to see how they handled it. We had tourist passengers in the front part of the cabin, some of them Indians going to Fiji, and first class at the rear. I went slowly down the aisle, stopping to chat with a Sikh family, and with a nervous mother with a baby. In the galley everything was reasonably clean considering the dirty trays that were still coming in. In the first-class cabin we had a couple of Australian statesmen, a chap from the World Bank, and a Swedish pianist. I walked to the rear of the cabin stopping now and then to talk to somebody, looked into the toilets and the washrooms, and went back to the galley. I said to my senior hostess, "Everything all right here?"

"I think so, sir. We've got four sleeping berths to pull down. I'll do those in a minute."

"Would you like Mr. Scott to give you a hand with those?" They were high up, and a heavy job for a girl.

She shook her head. "We can manage them."

"All right." I wondered where I had seen her before. "Get the lights out when you've got them all settled down, and call the flight deck when they're out. After that, don't switch them on again without permission from the flight deck."

"Very good, sir."

"I like one of you to be awake at night. Take it in turns to sleep."

I went back to my seat at the controls on the flight deck. Everything was normal, and I sent Pat Petersen off to get some sleep, telling him that I would hand over to him at two in the morning, Honolulu time. I sent the navigator off as well, and sat on in the cockpit alone, with the wireless operator and the engineer at their desks behind me.

I stayed on watch till two o'clock, and then sent Wolfe

229

to call the others. They came to the flight deck and I handed over, and then went back to the bunks that the others had used, to get some sleep. To my surprise the hostess was there. "I'm just giving you a fresh pillow, sir," she said.

"Service!" I laughed. "I've never had that done for me before."

She said seriously, "Would you like a cup of coffee now before you go to sleep?"

"I don't think so."

"What time will you be getting up?"

"We'll be coming up to Canton in a couple of hours. I expect I'll get up then."

She nodded. "I'll bring you a cup of coffee and a biscuit." I saw her go forward and speak to Sam Prescott.

I took off my jacket, loosened my collar and tie, and lay down with my head on the clean pillow that she had provided for me, with a rug pulled over my body. As I lay composing myself for sleep, I wondered if this girl was going to be a nuisance. In thirty years of airline flying the hostess who does everything for an unmarried captain and nothing for the passengers was no novelty to me, though in recent years Mrs. Deakin had weeded most of them out and it was some time since I had been plagued by one of those. I smiled as I lay before sleep; I was probably flattering myself, for I was fifty-nine and due to retire next year.

I slept a little, and then lay resting in the darkness till Sam Prescott came to tell me Canton was abeam, about a hundred miles away to the south-east. I got up and straightened out my clothes and put my jacket on, and went to the navigator's desk with him. Everything was in order. I went the rounds, looked at the radio log, the engineer's log, and the charts. I had a word with Pat at the controls, and went aft again into the cabin.

In the faint blue night-lights everything was quiet and

normal. One or two passengers were reading with their shaded lights, but most were sleeping. I walked quietly down the aisle to the galley, where light showed behind the curtain. The senior hostess was there with a cup. "I was just going to bring you a cup of coffee, sir," she said.

"Thanks. I'll have it here." I stood cup in hand. "Everything all right?"

"The baby in No. 7 started crying about an hour ago," she said. "We warmed up some milk food and gave it a bottle. It's quiet now."

"Many people wake up?"

"Four or five, immediately around," she said. "It didn't cry for long."

I nodded. "Miss Hamilton asleep?"

"I was letting her sleep through till we get busy in the morning," she said.

"You don't want a spell yourself?"

She shook her head. "I'm accustomed to night duty."

I stood drinking my coffee, nibbling a biscuit. "We've got about another five hours to go," I said. "E.T.A. is seven-fifteen, Fiji time. It will be dawn about an hour and a half before that. Tea or coffee and biscuits when they want it." She nodded. "What about the forms?"

"I gave out the health and immigration cards before they went to sleep," she said. "I'll start collecting them as soon as they wake up."

"Customs declaration?"

"Yes, they've got that, too."

"Let Mr. Prescott have them an hour before landing."

"Just the Fiji passengers, or all the lot?"

"No—just the Fiji passengers."

I put down my cup, glanced into the first class, and went back to the flight deck. So far, the cabin work was going pretty smoothly, anyway.

We landed in from the sea upon the long runway

amongst the fields of sugar cane in the warm morning light, and came to rest before the airport buildings. The gangway was wheeled up, the port officials came on board and cleared us, and the ground hostess took charge of the passengers and took them up to the hotel for breakfast. We left the machine refuelling in the sun and walked to the AusCan office where Jim Hanson was waiting with his crew to take over from us, and commenced the handing over. Half an hour later we were walking up towards the AusCan hostel with a Fijian boy wheeling our luggage behind us on a hand truck.

The AusCan hostel at Nandi Airport is nothing very much to look at, though it is comfortable enough. It consists of a light weatherboard building heavily braced with outside cables against hurricanes. There is a central lounge room provided with all the out-of-date periodicals from the aircraft and a radio; one end of this large room is set with tables as a dining room on the cafeteria system. There is a small bar. A long corridor extends from each end of this lounge communicating with the bedrooms, one side for men and the other side for women. The rooms are reasonably furnished, each provided with a firm writing table and a bamboo table and a couple of easy chairs; they are well designed for the tropics with a good through draught and fans. Each room has the same view from the window, over the west end of the airport and the sea. A few of the rooms have private showers, and as a captain I got one of these.

Here we settled down to spend our lives for the next year or so. The schedule that we had to fly was quite a simple one, though liable to be disturbed from time to time when aircraft were delayed. In the normal way we relieved the crew of the machine coming in from Sydney on Tuesday evening and took off for Honolulu at ten o'clock at night. We got to Honolulu about noon next

232

day, but that was also Tuesday for we crossed the date line. We stayed the night at Honolulu in the hotel and left again for Fiji at nine o'clock in the evening of the following day, arriving back at Nandi at seven o'clock on Friday morning, fairly tired after a long night flight. That was our week's work; Saturday, Sunday, and Monday were completely free.

Not a lot of work for people on our scale of salary, perhaps, but quite enough if we were to keep on the top line. One of our duties on the ground was to take plenty of exercise; hard tennis courts were provided and considerable pressure was exerted on the crews to use them, largely through the captains. In a hot and humid place like Fiji that meant getting in a lather of sweat in the first five minutes, but I played three or four sets a day myself and made my aircrew do the same, girls and men alike. It pays off handsomely, of course; if you keep really fit the flying doesn't worry you. And down at the airport club there was a first-class swimming pool to go to after tennis.

The crews play a lot of water polo, but I had not played myself while I was on the northern route, and it was nearly five years since I had had a game. I was still very fit, but age does tell and I didn't take that up again against the younger men. I was still a good diver, however, and won a diving competition at the pool in the second week we were at Nandi, and I began to have a lot of fun around the reefs with an aqualung outfit that I had bought in the United States. At the age of fifty-nine my chest measurement was still nine inches greater than my waist, and I intended it to stay that way.

The trouble that I had anticipated with my senior hostess didn't develop. The cabin work went smoothly and well, and though I still got a clean pillow in the bunk when I lay down and still had my desire for a cup of coffee anticipated, I found that I was getting no more attention than the tourist passengers, which is as I wanted it to be. She did her work and kept her place, and on the ground I didn't see a lot of her. It was not till we had been operating for about three weeks that I had any real conversation with her.

It was by the pool at the airport club at Nandi. I had been in the pool, and had come out and dried myself standing in the sun. Most of the brightly coloured metal tables and chairs beneath the beach umbrellas were occupied, but she was sitting alone at one, reading a novel. I took my lighter and my pack of cigarettes, and towel in hand I walked over to her. "Mind if I join you?"

She laid down her book. "Not a bit. I've been admiring your bathing shorts," she said.

I laughed. "They *are* a bit gaudy. I like them."

She laughed with me. "I think they're wonderful. Wherever did you get them?"

"You can buy them at Honolulu," I said. "There's a place in Kalakaua Avenue just by the Post Office. Ten dollars. You can get women's costumes like them, too. I don't know how much they are."

"I wouldn't dare," she said. "I'm not sure that I know where Kalakaua Avenue is, anyway."

"The main street is Waikiki," I told her. "Half a mile or so from where we stay."

"I don't know Honolulu yet," she said. "I must explore it."

I offered her a cigarette, and lit it for her. "Is this your first time away from Australia?"

She shook her head. "I went to England once, just after I qualified."

"Like it?"

She nodded. "It was marvellous. I'd have liked to have stayed there and worked, but it wasn't possible."

"Why not?"

"My grandmother was getting very old," she said. "It wouldn't have been fair."

"Is she your only relation?"

"She was," she replied. "She died about two years ago, soon after I got back from England." She paused. "She brought me up. My mother and father were killed in a car crash."

"Too bad," I said. "Did that mean a lot to you?"

She shook her head. "I don't remember them at all."

"You live in Melbourne, I think you said?"

She nodded. "In South Yarra. All my friends are there; it's where I was brought up. Grandmother left me all her furniture, so I took a couple of rooms in a friend's house as a sort of flat, and I've kept that on."

"That's a good idea," I said slowly. "You've always got somewhere to go back to, with your own things and people who know you."

She glanced at me curiously. "Where do you live?"

I laughed. "Where I work. Here."

"Haven't you got a flat anywhere?"

I shook my head. "I seem to move around too much. I've got stuff stuck away in stores in London, and in Montreal, and in Vancouver."

"You just live in clubs and airport hostels?"

"That's right. I'll be retiring in about a year, and then I'm going to have a house. A real house, for the first time in my life."

She smiled. "Where's that going to be?"

"In Tasmania, I think. I haven't quite decided."

"Are you a Tasmanian?"

"No," I said. "I was born a Canadian, in Hamilton, Ontario. I've still got some relations there, but I haven't seen them for years."

"You wouldn't want to go back there to live?"

I shook my head. "I haven't lived there since I left

235

home for the First World War. I wouldn't want to go back there. It's either going to be somewhere near Victoria, B.C., or else Tasmania. I rather like Tasmania. There's a little place called Buxton that I've got my eye on."

She wrinkled her brows in thought. "In the north-west, somewhere, isn't it?"

"That's right."

"It's a very *little* place, isn't it?"

I laughed. "I like little places. I've had my fill of seeing the great world."

There was a pause then, while we sat watching the people in the pool. I asked her if she would like a drink and she elected for a Coke, so I went and fetched a couple from the bar. When we were settled down again, she asked me, "Did you ever work in England?"

I nodded. "I was in England in the First War, and I stayed on for twelve years."

"Did you love it?"

"It was all right," I said. "Better than India." She laughed. "As a matter of fact, I've worked there longer than that. I was based in England all through the Second War, and after that." I thought for a moment. "I went to T.C.A. in 1947. But I wasn't living much in England in the war. I was all over the shop."

"Airline flying?"

"Transport Command, mostly. Ferrying Liberators over the Atlantic some of the time. Flying Yorks to Singapore after that. All sorts of things."

"You've been everywhere," she said.

I smiled. "I've never been to South America, or Russia."

We sat in silence for a time. "I did love England," she said at last. "Of course, I'd always want to come back to Melbourne. But England in the spring is just like fairy-land. The primroses, and the bluebells in the woods!"

"Too many people," I remarked.

"I know. But it's—England."

She was very Australian in her outlook; at any moment I expected to hear her speak of going Home to the Old Country. "There's a good bit of England here, of course," I said. "Down in Suva everybody seems to be English."

"I want to go to Suva," she remarked.

"There's not much to see there," I observed. "It's not a very big place. It's worth seeing, though."

"You go there in the little aeroplanes, don't you? Fiji Airways?"

I nodded. "You can drive along the coast, if you like. It takes all day. Some of the buses are quite good. But Fiji Airways might give you a free pass if they've not got a full load. They gave me one, once."

She smiled. "You're a captain."

I laughed. "All the same, they made me pay coming back."

Presently she said, "I'm very ignorant. Is Fiji a mandate or something?"

I glanced at her. "It's a British colony. Most of the Government officials here are English. A few New Zealanders, but mostly English. It's a very English place."

"I'd like to see more of it," she said. "It's silly to be in a country and see nothing but the aerodrome."

"Well," I said, "you've got plenty of time."

"I haven't," she retorted. "You make us play tennis all the time."

I laughed. "I'll accept a certificate from the Governor that you played four sets a day in Suva."

A few days later Charlie Lemaitre was a passenger with us from Honolulu southwards. Mr. Lemaitre had been Minister of Transport in Canada off and on for fifteen years, and I had known him off and on as long as that. He was on his way to Sydney for a conference, but he had brought his wife along with him and he intended to stay three or four days in Fiji on the way for a holiday. Normally, I never invite a passenger to the flight deck; AusCan forbid it and I think it's bad practice. It makes young captains and first officers swollen-headed if they are allowed to bask in the admiration of really important people, and swollen heads bring accidents in their train. Mr. Lemaitre was different because he had a pass from the Head Office and I had him on the flight deck with me for over an hour after we took off, sitting in the second pilot's seat and chatting. He had been a pilot in the First World War, as I had myself, though I never met him then.

When we got to Nandi I took time off to attend to Mr. and Mrs. Lemaitre myself for a few minutes; they were going on to Suva by Fiji Airways. Mrs. Lemaitre apparently didn't very often travel with her husband, and she was absurdly grateful for the little things that I did for the Minister as a matter of course. "So very kind of you, Captain Pascoe," she said. "Charlie will be giving a little dinner for some of the Government people in the hotel on Monday night. Could you come down to Suva for that, and bring Miss Dawson with you?"

I thought quickly. This was in the nature of a Royal Command, and AusCan would probably want me to be there to show the flag. I could charge up the expenses. I didn't know how Bill Myers would feel about expenses for the hostess, but it was not an unreasonable invitation from the Minister's wife, and one which it would be awkward to refuse. The hostess wasn't present so I couldn't bring her into it; I would have to decide this for her, and she would do what she was told. "That's really very kind of you," I said. "I should like to be there very much. You'd like me to bring Miss Dawson?"

"Oh yes," she said. "She told me that she'd never been to Suva, and nor have I."

238

I hoped that Bill Myers would consider this an adequate reason for charging up her expenses. "I'm sure she'd like to come," I said. "It's very kind of you to think of her."

"Oh no," she said. "It will be so nice to have you there, all among these stuffy English people. Charlie had to give a party at Bermuda once, and it was *dreadful*!"

This was another reason that I could put up to Bill Myers, but it didn't seem much better than the first. I thanked them both and saw them off upon the little aeroplane for Suva, and then walked up to my room in the hostel and lay down and slept till lunch, as I usually did on Friday morning after the night flight.

After lunch I went down to our office in the airport buildings and rang up our manager, Stanley McEwen, who was in our office at Suva that day, and told him all about it. He said I'd better come, and then I told him about the hostess. "She asked her, too," I said. "How do you react to that one?"

"Hell," he said. "She can't ask *everybody*."

"We can get out of it," I told him. "Say she's sick, or something. She didn't ask her personally. She just told me to bring her along."

"I see . . ." There was a pause. "Did she ask for her by name?"

"That's right. Miss Dawson. She asked the two of us."

There was another pause. "Was Charlie Lemaitre in on this?" he asked.

"Yes. He was with her at the time."

"All right," he said. "You'd better bring her down."

"Be all right to charge up her expenses?"

"I suppose so," he said reluctantly. "Keep them down as much as possible, or I'll have Billy Myers in a screaming fit. You'd better both come and spend the night with me."

"Two nights," I suggested. "Give us time to do some shopping."

239

"All right," he said. "I'll expect you both on Sunday."

I had laid on tennis that afternoon at four o'clock; our crew of eight was just right for two courts, so that it was difficult for anyone to make an excuse. I played in the mixed doubles that afternoon with Mollie Hamilton against Peggy Dawson and Wolfe; my partner was good and we beat them 6—4, 5—7, 8—6. When we were walking off the court towards our showers, dripping with sweat, I called Peggy Dawson over. "I've got a job for you," I said. "Mrs. Lemaitre wants us both to go down to a dinner party that she's giving in Suva on Monday."

She stared at me. "Wants me to go?"

"That's right. She asked me to go down and bring you, too. I rang Mr. McEwen and we'll be staying in his house. We'll be going down on Sunday."

She asked, "What sort of a party is it? It wouldn't be long dress?"

I hadn't really thought about it. "I suppose it will," I said. "The Governor will probably be there."

"But I've got nothing to wear!"

I smiled. "That's your problem," I said equably. "All I've contracted to do is to deliver you to the party. The company are paying your expenses."

"Are the company paying for a dress for me?"

"I don't suppose so for a moment," I replied. "You'd better try that one on Stanley, though."

That was on Friday night, and she went into an earnest huddle with the other hostesses that night. Lautoka, the second city of Fiji, is fifteen miles from the airport and the Indian tailors and dressmakers there work very quickly. She went in with another girl on the seven o'clock bus on Saturday and was away all day; they came back in a taxi in the evening and I saw her showing them a pastel green gown with a bolero which was apparently the right thing for her to wear. I had found a Suva taxi at the airport with an Indian driver and had kept him overnight to drive us down, and we started off on Sunday morning on the day-long drive through the fields of sugar cane to Singatoka and down the coast and through the groves of coconut palms to Suva.

It was April, and most of the hot humidity of the monsoon season was behind us. When the sun shone it was really hot, of course, but there was much cloud to keep it cool, and an occasional brief shower of rain. I had been in Fiji before and knew it fairly well, but everything was new to her. The Indian driver spoke good English and could answer her questions. He stopped once, laughing, and got her a foot of sugar cane so that she could see what the children were all chewing, and she nibbled it experimentally before we drove on.

It was many years since I had been anywhere with a girl, and I was awkward and constrained. I had put away all thoughts of marriage when I went to India in the early 'thirties. Hostesses on international routes are hand-picked for their courtesy and competence, and in the last twenty years I had been closely associated in my work with many charming and delightful women. I had never taken one of them out. All my interests had been purely masculine, and now at the age of fifty-nine I found that I had wholly lost the knack of entertaining a young woman. I didn't know what would appeal to her, or what would interest her. The brown, dark-eyed children waving to us by the roadside as we drove past did not excite me particularly, but they were fascinating to her. "Just look at that little boy with the big tummy!" she exclaimed once. "Isn't he sweet?"

"Looks to me as if he's got something," I remarked, and felt an awful stiff. I should have been able to enter into her mood.

The system of land tenure in Fiji is quite interesting, because the Indian cane farmers can't buy their land but have to rent it from the Fijians, so that the Fijian has little to do but sit in the sun and scratch. I tried to explain this to her as we drove along but couldn't raise her interest, but a Fijian schoolmistress teaching the children to play net-ball was absorbing to her, and we had to stop the car to look at that. She listened absently while I talked about the village and its part in the feudal system of Fijian government, but when we passed the village where a British film had been made she really got excited. I hadn't seen the picture, so I fell down on that one, too.

I was getting an old man, of course, and she was young. I don't think I had ever realised till then just how old I was. It never intruded itself into my normal life, for I could still do practically all the things that most young men can do, and do some of them a good deal better. I had never thought of myself as an old man when I was dealing with young men; I was just more experienced than they were, less likely to get into a flap in an emergency. My reaction times were still practically as good as theirs. Water polo was the only thing that I had given up, and I glossed that over in my mind, pretending I had never been much interested in it. It needed a day out with a young woman to drive home the inescapable fact that I was getting an old man.

I said something of the sort to her when we stopped for lunch at the small hotel in the little town of Singatoka, feeling that some apology was necessary. We were sitting over short drinks in the lounge that overlooks the river. "I suppose as you get older your interests change," I said. "I'm much more interested now in finding out what makes this country tick than in the physical side of it. This country, or any other country."

She smiled. "Much more interested in that than in

little boys with a grin on their faces and hook-worms in their tummies."

I nodded. "Getting an old man."

She shook her head. "I won't have that."

"I'm fifty-nine," I said. "I've got to come off airline work next year."

"Fifty-nine isn't old," she said. "Not in these days, for a man like you. I've never met anyone who played a harder game of tennis. You wear us all out."

"You can keep the physical side in order if you're careful," I remarked. "I'm not so sure about the mental side. One gets to think like an old man, and there doesn't seem to be a great deal you can do about it. One's interests change." I glanced at her, smiling. "You should have made this trip with someone like Sam Wolfe."

She laughed. "When I want a bit of slap and tickle I'll arrange it for myself, thank you. I'm having a marvellous time just like we are."

"Well, have another drink. The mind of an old man moves on a higher plane. An alcoholic one."

"If I have another I'll probably go to sleep this afternoon."

"That's fine," I said. "You won't see me."

We lunched and drove on in the hot afternoon, and I think I may perhaps have dozed in the car as perhaps she did, because we passed the big beach hotel at Korolevu without seeing it. When I came back to earth we had passed from the sugar cane country into the coconut country where the higher rainfall brings the lusher type of tropical scene. We passed by coral beaches white on the border of a brilliantly blue sea where the surf thunders on the reef some way out. There were dazzling little bays between the promontories where the coconut trees hang slanting forward over the water so that the nuts drop into the sea. She said once, "It's simply marvellous!"

I nodded. "Real South Sea stuff."

"Fancy having a beach party at a place like that, and swimming in the lagoon!"

"Sharks," I said.

"Pat Petersen says the sharks don't come inside the reef."

I laughed. "Famous last words." As a matter of fact, I had good reason to say that, because I had met one a few days previously when I had been spear-fishing with Jim Hanson. I had been fifteen or twenty feet down beside the coral gardens of the reef, and it had come at me from curiosity, I think; a great shadowy thing seven or eight feet long in the pale green water. I poked it on the nose with the spear gun and it went away, and I got out on to the reef damn quick. Jim Hanson was still down and I was terrified for him, not knowing what to do, and I didn't recover until we were in the boat. Jim never saw it at all.

I told her about this incident as we drove on down the coast, and she was very much concerned. "You oughtn't to go taking risks like that," she said. "It's not worth it."

I smiled. "Keeps you young."

"It doesn't if you get taken by a shark."

"I don't intend to be," I said.

"But you might be. Or Captain Hanson might have been. It's frightfully dangerous."

"It's a lot of fun."

"If you won't think of yourself, you might think of your relations."

"I haven't got any," I said. "I've got a sister in Hamilton, but we've not met for years."

"Don't you write to her?"

I shook my head. "I send her a Christmas card, or a short letter then. I've got some cousins, but I never write to them."

"Well, Captain Hanson's got a wife and family."

244

I laughed. "That's a matter that's strictly personal between him and the shark."

We stopped at the hotel at Ndeumba for a cup of tea, and walked down through the garden to the beach. The reef there is a long way out, and the matter of the sharks was still upon her mind, because she asked if there were any there. "I wouldn't know," I said. "It's like the Australian coast, I think. It's not a very good thing to go swimming out to sea."

She nodded. "One never does at home, of course. Only in the Bay."

We drove on to Suva. Stanley McEwen lives in a fair-sized tropical house outside the town up on the hill by the reservoir, and we drove straight there. It would suit him better to live at Nandi but there are no schools there for his children, so he lives at Suva and spends four days of each week at the aerodrome. I know his wife, of course, and introduced the hostess to her, and she showed us to our bedrooms. In the evening light we joined them for short drinks in their big lounge with the magnificent view overlooking Suva Bay and the mountains to the west.

The talk that night, of course, was all of AusCan and the running of the line, and I think we got a lot of useful work done. It's liable to be that way when one can get out of the surroundings of the immediate job; one can take a more detached view of the problems. I said something of the sort to Stanley when we were having a final whisky before bed. "We ought to do more of this," I said. "Get away from the aircraft and stand back and look at them."

He grinned. "Put that to Billy Myers when he comes out next, and see if he'll stand the expenses. I know what the answer will be."

"It's a good idea, all the same. Anyway, put it to him about leaving Sydney an hour earlier. We'd get them through the Customs half an hour quicker at the Honolulu end, and it can be pretty hot in that building. Jim Hanson had a passenger faint there the other day."

He nodded. "I heard about that woman. It's a good idea . . ."

His house is nearly a thousand feet up, and much cooler than the AusCan hostel at Nandi. We slept very well indeed, and I got up thinking of Tasmania. The tropics are all right; I can adjust myself to them and live very comfortably, but there is no denying that there is a freshness in the morning after a good sleep in a cool room that one never gets in a hot place. I dressed thinking of the little town of Buxton with the virtually unused grass aerodrome. I had a week's leave coming to me in a month's time, and I thought I would go there and have another look at it. Victoria in Vancouver Island would be all right, of course, but there were people operating on the field already; there would be hard competition from the start, and I was getting a bit old for that. In Buxton I might well be the king of the castle, a big frog in a very little puddle.

I got a taxi in the middle of the morning and drove the hostess down to the market in the town. Monday is a slack day and half the stalls were vacant, and perhaps it was a better day for her to see it than in the great bustle of a more busy time. She bought a couple of shell necklaces and bracelets from a Fijian woman, whose husband offered us a drink of kava from a coconut shell dipped in a tin basin. We took it for politeness and moved on, looking at the vegetables and the fish. "Tastes like toothpaste," she said.

"That's paying it a compliment."

We found our way slowly through the little town to the Grand Pacific Hotel, and had lunch there. Sitting over coffee after lunch I asked her, "What would you like to do this afternoon?"

246

"I've got to iron my frock some time," she said. "Have you got anything else you want to do down here?"

I shook my head. "You've not seen much of Suva."

"Is there much more to see?"

I thought for a minute. "There's the Botanical Gardens, and the Museum."

She laughed. "I'm not going to wear myself out before this evening. I think we'd be more comfortable back in Mr. McEwen's house, sitting in a long chair looking at the view."

"You can't do that all afternoon."

"I can. If you say I've got to play tennis, I'll hit you with something."

I smiled. "He hasn't got a court. You can play six sets tomorrow to make up for it."

"I know what you can do this afternoon," she said.

"What's that?"

"Write a letter to your sister in Hamilton."

I stared at her. "Why on earth should I do that?"

"Tell her what you were telling me this morning about Buxton." She lit another cigarette. "I think you're going to find it lonely when you retire to a little place like that," she said. "After all this. It wouldn't be a bad thing to keep in touch with what people you've got."

I got up. "Wait there," I said. "I'll just see the porter and see if he can whistle up a taxi." I moved away from the lobby because I didn't want to carry on that conversation. I had been in airline flying of one sort or another for twenty-seven years. For twenty-seven years I had moved about the world, living in hotels and airport hostels and in clubs. For twenty-seven years I had had men of my own sort to talk to and to do things with in all my working and my leisure hours. I was tired of it now, and wanting a house of my own, a settled base where I could hang up all my photographs and souvenirs, have all my toys out of the boxes in the stores of London and of Montreal and of Vancouver, and arrange them all around me. I had wanted that almost more than anything, but deep in my subconscious I had known it would be lonely. I had refused to admit that to myself, refused to face the stark fact that lonely it was going to be, hellishly lonely, utterly divorced from what had been my working life. And now this girl had put her finger straight on to the weak point of my plan. I wasn't very pleased with her for doing it.

I turned the conversation as we got into the car and we talked about the Indians in Fiji, so much more advanced in the Western sense than the Indians of their native land. When we got up to the McEwens' house I made an excuse and went and lay down on my bed, still deeply troubled. Victoria, B.C., might be a better place for me than Buxton in Tasmania. I could retire to either because as a Canadian in AusCan my pension was payable in dollars, and both of them had good fishing. Victoria would be closer to the people that I knew and had made my life with, but at Victoria the competition would be fierce upon the aerodrome, and I was getting an old man. At Buxton I could still do useful work for many years, but nobody that I had ever known would come to see me there. It all wanted a bit of thinking about.

Charlie Lemaitre's dinner party was quite a formal affair, with the Governor and his lady, eight couples from the Secretariat, the McEwens, the hostess, and me. It was still hot in Suva and they had it at a long table laid in one of the cloisters of the hotel, a very pleasant setting overlooking the gardens, the palm trees, and a moonlit sea. We men were in white dinner jackets and the women in evening dress; the table was lit by candles in glass shades, and there were many white-coated, soft-footed Indian waiters moving around behind us. The food was good and the wine passable, and the whole set-up was very, very

248

pleasant. I was about the middle of the table talking to a good-looking woman about the lack of hotel accommodation for New Zealand tourists and the new Mormon church and the spread of Mormon faith through the South Seas, when towards the end of dinner I happened to look down the table to where the air hostess was sitting on the other side near the Governor. She was talking to the Director of the Public Works Department, laughing at something he had said. Something in her attitude rang a bell, and everything clicked into place. I knew now why she had reminded me of someone when I saw her first. She was like Brenda Marshall.

It was only just a momentary flash, a movement of the hand or of the head that put the idea into my mind, and then it was gone. She was nothing like Brenda Marshall, really. She was quite different, in hair, face, figure—everything. She was Peggy Dawson, senior hostess in my aircrew. It must have been the wine, and I was tired, too; worried about Buxton, possibly, and loneliness. Loneliness, and the wine; that added up to Brenda Marshall, and it always had done so, for twenty-seven years. I sat there in a morbid reverie, far away from Suva, and my charming companion rattled on about the tourists and the Mormons till the conversation flagged through my absent-minded answers, and she turned to her partner on the other side. I roused myself then to do my stuff again, and began to talk to the wife of the Colonial Secretary, newly out from England, about Fijian art, a subject that I knew less than nothing about.

From time to time, when my companion was going well and I had my next remark all ready to bring out as soon as she had finished speaking, I stole a glance at Peggy Dawson. I saw no resemblance again to Brenda Marshall. The hostess was what she was, a pleasant, competent Australian girl with quite a marked sense of duty and responsibility. She dressed tidily enough but she wasn't particularly glamorous; even in these surroundings I felt that I could sense the nursing sister in an evening dress. She was different from the English wives of the colonial officials at the table; she was trying hard, but she had no common background with the other women, none of the social experience that was their stock-in-trade. She was from a different world, but Brenda Marshall could have held her place in this colonial society with no effort at all.

The dinner party came to an end at about ten-thirty, for we had started early and there had only been one short speech by Charlie Lemaitre and a shorter reply by the Governor. We got up from the table and strolled about in little groups upon the moonlit lawn until the Governor and Lady Norman said good-bye, and then we all started to go, too. The McEwens drove us back up to their house up on the high ridge above the town and we had a whisky as a nightcap looking out over their view, and then we went to bed. We were to go back to Nandi on the first plane of Fiji Airways in the morning, to take the Tuesday night machine to Honolulu as usual.

I stood at my bedroom window for a time before undressing, looking out over the mountains. I was still a little upset at the reminder of Brenda Marshall that this girl had given me, and that was unreasonable because they were so different. I was unduly sensitive, of course. Many women between the age of twenty-five and thirty must have similar mannerisms; with all the women in the world it would be queer if they had not. At certain ages they would move their hands or turn their heads a certain way; ten years later those attitudes would be forgotten and they would be doing something different, stemming perhaps from an older style in hair-do or in dress.

That was all right, but now that the resemblance was in

my mind it would not be put aside. Tenuous and unsubstantial, there was a definite resemblance to Brenda Marshall. It was nothing physical, nothing to be photographed and set down as a specimen and studied. Since my marriage in the First World War I had led rather a solitary life till Brenda had burst on me for a brief year of glory. In that year for the first time I had known what it was to have somebody really care about me, really care whether I lived or died. After it was over I had lived a very withdrawn life, avoiding contact with women so far as is possible for a man in my position, something of a recluse. Now, the resemblance that had arisen was a resemblance of caring for my welfare, a resemblance of caring whether I lived or died. It was nothing really that I could put my finger on, but after twenty-seven years it came as a bit of a shock. Quite unsought, without any conscious effort on my part, it looked as though that fortune was being given to me again.

I stood looking out over Suva Bay in the moonlight. A Sunderland flying boat on night landing practice flew across almost at eye-level, and I hardly noticed it. It had begun on that first evening when she had put the clean pillow for me in the crew's berth on the D.C.6b; it had gone on unobtrusively like that all the time. Someone must have influenced the cooks in the AusCan hostel to bring my breakfast egg and bacon to the table as I like it, fried on both sides. I had not told them; it could only have been one of the two hostesses. In the first week half my laundry was lost or went astray. I had given up the struggle to find the damn stuff and had bought more in Honolulu, but since then it had returned punctually the next day with nothing ever missing. Was that one of the hostesses? It's not the sort of thing that happens on its own at Nandi Airport. For the first few days I had had one of the dumbest girls in Fiji to do my room, a very

251

jungly type. The Head Girl had succeeded her, a very quick and intelligent part-European, and I had done nothing to arrange the switch. Who had done that for me? And then, on top of everything, had been that very penetrating remark about me being lonely when I went to Buxton. So penetrating, and so true.

The odd thing about it all was that I couldn't feel that this girl, Peggy Dawson, was 'setting her cap at me', as my grandmother used to say. It didn't seem to be like that, somehow. I have had that one before, of course, in twenty-seven years of airline flying, and I have seen it happen many, many times with other officers. They spend time on their hair and face and eyelashes before coming to the flight deck, and then they come with bright and tinkling vivacity until I slam them down. They dress, off duty, rather better than their pay would normally permit; frequently they start to use scent, and to drink a little more, and to stimulate gay parties. One cannot blame them if they do what every human being does at one time or another; one has to grin and bear it and see that their work is done correctly. I couldn't feel, however, that this was one of those. There were none of the usual symptoms, and it didn't feel like that.

The truth of it was that she was just a very decent girl and a good senior hostess, who took it to be one of her duties to see that her captain was made comfortable as well as her passengers. I turned from the window, smiling a little; by God, I thought, she'd make a wife for somebody, some day! I hoped that didn't happen before my time was up with AusCan. I didn't want the jungly girl doing my room again, putting the wet soap in my handkerchief drawer and my clean shoes on the floor of the shower to get filled with water.

We went back to Nandi next morning, played a little tennis, and took the machine on to Honolulu that evening.

Our lives slipped back into the normal groove for several weeks. I took my leave and went to Buxton to have a look round, and stayed at the hotel. That was the worst part of the set-up, because the hotel was horrible, dirty and uncouth. It wasn't a bad little town, however, with good trout streams not much fished within thirty miles or so. I didn't want to stay in the hotel, anyway, and there were several new houses going up, half built. The aerodrome was a grass field of about five hundred acres that had been laid out for training in the last war and not much used since; it was grazed by sheep and the farmer had the one small hangar full of haymaking machinery and stuff of that sort. A bit of money wanted spending on the roof before it could be used for aeroplanes, but the Shire Clerk told me they would do that if I took it on a five years' lease. There seemed to be some charter and instruction work offering and several of the mountain graziers wanted superphosphate spread from the air because they couldn't get it on their rough back country any other way. If I went there I should never make much more than a bare living but on the other hand I shouldn't have to work very hard. I met most of the locals in the four days I was there and thought them a decent sort of a crowd. I told them who I was and just how I was fixed, and that I'd make my mind up within the next three or four months whether I wanted to lease the hangar and come there. But when I left to fly to Melbourne I had practically made up my mind, and I spent a morning at Moorabbin airport before flying on to Sydney and Fiji talking to Arthur Schutt to find out how the prices and availability of little aeroplanes were running.

A fortnight later I was standing on the corner of Beach Walk and Kalakaua in Waikiki one morning waiting to cross the road upon the lights to get a few cigars at the drug store, when Peggy Dawson came along, walking quickly. She stopped, and I greeted her. "Too hot to walk like that," I said. "Where are you off to?"

"I was going back to the hotel," she said. "But now——" She paused. "Could you let me have some dollars?"

"Why, certainly," I said. "How many do you want?" In AusCan on the Pacific route everyone was paid on the same scale, but the Canadians were paid in dollars and the Australians were paid in pounds, and so had difficulty in buying anything in Honolulu under their own steam. In the aircrew this never made any trouble because there were always Canadians who wanted to take holidays in Australia, and anyway at Nandi Airport all currencies got a bit mixed up.

"Could you let me have thirty?" she asked. "I'll give you the pounds back at the hotel. I want to get a dress."

I pulled out my wallet and gave her the money. "Nice dress?"

She took it, smiling. "It's a beaut. Would you like to see it before I buy it?"

I smiled with her. "I was only just going across to the drug store." So we turned and walked along the sidewalk. together in the warm sun, till we got to the shop and saw her dress upon the dummy in the window. She showed it to me. "That's the one. It's only twenty-two fifty."

It was a sort of mottled pastel blue colour, with trimmings of a rather darker blue. It was too old for her, I thought; it seemed to me to be a dress for a woman of fifty. She was so pleased with it that I didn't say so. "It's very quiet and restrained," I remarked. "I think you'd look very nice in it."

She nodded. "I think it's lovely. I don't like things too bright." We went together into the shop and she set about buying it. It would need small alterations which could be done in the back room by the Japanese girls in a couple of hours, but first a fitting would be necessary. "I tell you what," I said. "I'll go and get my cigars while you try it on. Then we'll go and have lunch somewhere and you can pick it up."

She smiled. "I'd like that. But I pay for my own lunch."

"Toss you for that one," I said, and went off for my White Owls. When I came back from the drug store she was waiting for me. "Where are we going to lunch?" she asked.

"The Edgewater's as good as anywhere," I said. It was in our price bracket, too; we were well paid by any standard except that of the largest Waikiki hotels. We went to the terrace of the hotel overlooking the blue swimming pool, and had soft squashes full of fruit and ice before lunch. We had to fly that night, and in AusCan we don't drink the day we fly.

As we sat there smoking she asked me, "How did you get on at Buxton?"

"All right," I told her. "I think I shall go there."

"Will there be enough for you to do there, though?"

"I think so," I said slowly. "I shan't get fat on it, but there'll be something to do every day even from the start. And these things snowball, you know. Once you start up in a place like that, business that you never thought of comes along."

I started in to tell her all about it, and she listened attentively. "Anyway," she said once, "it's not as if you had to work at all, is it? I mean, you'll have your pension."

I nodded. "I could get by on that. But I've got something saved up, of course. Enough for two or three small aircraft. Enough for a house too, I think. I don't want anything big."

"What about furniture?" she asked.

"I'll have to get that. But I shan't need much."

"Who's going to do for you? Cook your meals, and all that sort of thing?"

I laughed. "I haven't got as far as that yet. I haven't even made up my mind if I'm going there at all. I'm not afraid of that one, though. I've managed on my own before now, sometimes for months on end."

She nodded. "You'll have to have somebody. I should think you'd find somebody to come in daily."

"I should think so."

We moved to a table on the dining portion of the terrace and ordered lunch. "When have you got to make your mind up about Buxton?" she asked.

"I told them I'd make up my mind about leasing the hangar by October," I said. "They've got to get the farmer out before I can go into it, and he's got it on a monthly tenancy. And then there's quite a bit of work to be done before I could put aeroplanes in it. The roof leaks pretty badly, but they'd do that for me. And then, I suppose I'd have to do something about a house. The hotel's simply terrible."

She laughed. "They usually are. When would you think of going there?"

"I'll be sixty in February," I told her. "I've got to be out of this by then."

The waitress brought our lunch. When she had gone, the hostess remarked, "I suppose that means there'll be a switch around of aircrew when you leave us."

I hadn't thought about it before, immersed in my own affairs. "I suppose there will," I said. "I know Pat Petersen would rather be upon the northern route."

"It's his wife," she said. "She gets prickly heat."

"I know. When's Mollie Hamilton getting married?" She had got herself engaged on her last leave to a chap who worked for Mobilgas at Kingsford Smith.

"They haven't got a date. She'll stay the year out."

"Wolfe's got a girl in San Francisco," I remarked. "Looks like a General Post after Christmas."

She nodded. "I don't believe I'll stay on when that happens."

I glanced at her. "Getting tired of it?"

"Not exactly," she said thoughtfully. "It's a lovely life in many ways. I'll never be sorry to have seen all this, and worked for AusCan. But one sometimes feels it isn't really important—not like nursing."

"Would you go back to the hospital?"

She nodded. "I think so. Either the Alexandra or some other hospital." There was a pause while we ate. "I think I'd like to try it in an orthopædic hospital," she said. "Polio children."

The blue, brilliant swimming pool lay before us, with the superbly healthy young Americans in and out of it in the bright sunshine. "Kind of an antidote to this," I said.

She smiled. "Well—yes. I wouldn't want this to be any other way. But after all, it's work like that that makes this possible—getting crooked kids straight."

"I know what you mean," I said. I had never felt it personally, of course, because of the responsibilities. Every hour that I spent in the air was spent with the emergency routines upon the threshold of my consciousness. Every change in engine note was a minor shock that jerked me into maximum alertness to check with instruments and cathode ray plug indicator exactly what was happening. So many things can happen to a big four-engined aeroplane, most of which could end up fatally if I fell down upon the job, that I had never felt the need to shoulder any more responsibilities. With the hostesses who came to us from hospital work the case was very different. None of them stayed longer than a year or two;

because they were hand-picked for their qualities of character the hospitals drew them back.

I glanced at her, smiling. "Marriage doesn't come into your programme?"

She laughed. "Not yet, anyway."

"You don't want to leave it too long," I remarked. "Everybody ought to be married."

"You're a fine one to be talking like that," she retorted.

I glanced at her. "I was married once."

"I'm sorry," she said. "I didn't know."

"Nothing for you to be sorry about," I replied. "I was married in the First World War, very nearly forty years ago."

"What happened?" she asked.

"She divorced me," I told her. "In Reno. She was an actress—Judy Lester. Ever hear of her?"

She shook her head.

"Oh well, she was a bit before your time. But she was quite well known. I had rather a dud job in England after the war and she got a film contract in Hollywood. She divorced me from there."

"Why did she do that? Or is it a rude question?"

"Not a bit," I said. "She wanted to marry a band leader in Hollywood. She got it for desertion."

She wrinkled her brows. "I don't understand. Who deserted who?"

I smiled. "I deserted her, because I wouldn't go to Hollywood."

"But could she get a divorce for that?"

"She could then, in Nevada. I believe they've tightened things up a bit since those days."

"Did you have any children?"

I nodded. "There was a daughter, but I never had anything to do with her. We never lived together after she was born. Her mother took her with her to America."

"You didn't keep in touch?"

I shook my head. "I was a bit sore about the whole thing, and anyway I hadn't any money to go to America. It was nearly twenty years before I got there, in the Second War, and then I didn't feel like digging it all up again."

She nodded, slowly. "The girl must have been grown-up."

"That's right. It's better to leave it be when it's like that."

It was many, many years since I had talked to anyone about my marriage. In fact, I can only remember telling two people about it in my life before this girl, Arthur Stuart and Brenda Marshall. Arthur was killed a year later in Ferry Command taking off a Liberator from Prestwick. He had been easy to talk to, so had Brenda Marshall, and now this girl was another. There are some people that you don't mind telling about painful things, but they don't come very often.

That lunch set a pattern of many others. We fell into a habit of strolling out together on our morning in Honolulu after a late, lazy breakfast, to look at the yachts in the yacht harbour, or the sampan fishing boats, or the shops of down-town Honolulu or Waikiki. She had a friend who was at the Queen's Hospital, an ex-hostess of Pan American, and we lunched there once, and once or twice we went together to a concert in the Civic Auditorium. Several times I got a drive-yourself car, and we explored the nearer parts of the main island, lunching at Fisherman's Wharf, Hanauma, or Waimanalo. It became an established habit that we would do something together once a week upon our day in Honolulu, a habit that was only to be interrupted when one or other of us was on leave. At Nandi in Fiji it was different and we didn't go about together; at the airport we seemed more or less on duty all the time; I was the captain and they treated me as

259

one. But in Honolulu we could get lost in the crowd, away from our responsibilities.

I came to look forward to these weekly outings very much indeed; I think she did, too. I never made love to her; perhaps I was too old. Perhaps I told myself that, like the water polo, I just didn't want to do it. Instead of that, a very close companionship grew up between us. I never told her anything about Brenda Marshall; that lay too deep to talk about, but within a couple of months she must have learned practically everything else about me; she was easy to talk to. In return, I learned a good deal about her. Her life had been a simple melody of Melbourne and her grandmother, a melody of school, of visits to the seaside at Portsea and Barwon Heads, of cheerful comradeship within the hospital, of the great adventure of her trip to England. She never told me anything about her love affairs, however; like me, she had her reticences.

Although we didn't see much of each other at Nandi apart from the work and the tennis court, which after all was just another sort of work, she was never much out of my mind. As soon as we had landed and rested on the Friday morning, I usually found myself planning things that we could do together the following week in Honolulu. Very soon, of course, I got wise to myself. I was a silly old fool, for I was coming very close to falling in love with a girl less than half my age, at a time of life when I should certainly have known better. No future in that, I told myself. In all the years that had elapsed since Brenda Marshall nothing like this had happened in my life; that it was happening now was a sure sign of senile decay.

I tried to take a grip upon myself but it wasn't very easy. One morning at Honolulu I told her at breakfast that I had to go down to the maintenance base at the airport, and I didn't know how long I'd be; she'd better not wait in for me. She was surprised and obviously disappointed, which didn't make it any easier, and I drove down to the base sick and angry with myself for hurting her. They were a bit surprised to see me at the base; I milled around there for an hour and asked a lot of damfool questions till I thought she would have gone out, and then went back to the hotel. I found her sitting disconsolately in the lounge reading a copy of *Time*, terribly pleased to see me, as I was to see her. I backslid then, of course. I had the car outside and we drove out to Kualoa on the east coast for lunch, and had a grand time together.

October came, and towards the end of the month I went on a week's leave again. I went to Buxton and put up at the hotel. Nothing had changed since I was there before, either at the aerodrome or in my own affairs; my deadline for getting out of AusCan was now January the 31st. It was time that I made up my mind, with only three months left to go. I made it up. It was spring in northern Tasmania and the country was very lovely, fresh and cool and sunny after the hot humidity of Fiji, with wattles in bloom everywhere and everybody going trout fishing. I got myself one of the two solicitors in the town and the Shire Clerk got the other and we set them to draw up a lease of the hangar and the flying rights upon the aerodrome, the latter based upon a very small percentage of my turnover. When that was all in train, I set myself to organise a house.

There were houses on the other side of the town available, but I wanted one upon the road that led to the aerodrome. I bought the last lot of a row of building sites, the one nearest to the hangar, and started my negotiations with the local builder. I wanted to buy three aeroplanes, and tools, and spares, and a reasonable second-hand car; that meant that there wouldn't be a great deal of money left for a house. It would have to be a fairly small house of nine or ten squares, but I didn't want a big one anyway. He had a book of designs of small weatherboard houses, and we went into a huddle together over that. I picked a house that was within my price bracket, and started to consider it in detail.

It had a large lounge, a kitchen, and two bedrooms, one very small and the other not a great deal bigger. Without admitting to myself why I was making the alterations I decided on meals in the kitchen as a regular thing, cut the lounge down till it was quite a small room, and doubled the size of the main bedroom. That made a reasonable house for an elderly bachelor, I thought, and the builder agreed with me. A weatherboard house goes up very quickly, and he was confident that he could get it finished in the time. I had a small camera with me and took a photograph of the amended plan so that I could think it over back at Nandi, and fixed with him that I would come on leave again about the end of December, by which time the house would be nearing completion and we could settle details of the fixtures and the decoration. Then we got on to the money side, and he told me who to see about a loan at the State Savings Bank in Hobart. I got an estimate in writing from him and signed a contract in the solicitor's office, and paid him five hundred pounds deposit. I signed the lease for the hangar and the aero-drome, and then my business in Buxton was over for the time being.

I had the afternoon to spare before the bus left for Hobart at four o'clock. I wandered round upon the aerodrome with my camera, snapping everything I could think of, the hangar, the site of my house, the view from where the house would be, the shopping street of the small town—everything. I knew that next week when I was in Honolulu I should want to tell Peggy Dawson all about it, and that she would want to know; the Indian photographer in Lautoka would get this film developed and printed for me before Tuesday so that I could take the photographs to Honolulu with me to show her. With the views that I had taken and with the photographed plan of the house she should be able to get a very good idea how I was going to live, I thought.

I got to Hobart at eleven o'clock that night after seven hours of sitting in various buses or waiting at bus stops, changing at Devonport and Launceston. I got into a hotel and went to the State Savings Bank next morning, and put in my application for a loan. Then I went round Hobart looking at furniture, new and second-hand, and getting estimates. The bedroom furniture bothered me a bit because I was a silly old fool and nothing could ever come of it, but there was no harm in looking and finding out what the stuff cost.

I flew to Melbourne on an afternoon plane and saw Arthur Schutt again that night, and told him that I'd write to him with definite orders about Christmas time. After I had done with him I took a tram out to South Yarra, and walked around in the warm night, trying to visualise what her life had been among these quiet streets and houses. I found the house in which she had her flat, her *pied-à-terre*, and stood in the lamplit road looking at it from the outside for ten minutes. I was a silly old fool, of course, but I asked my way to the Queen Alexandra Hospital and went and had a look at the outside of that, too.

Next morning I flew to Sydney on the eight o'clock service of Australian Continental Airways. When I was in my seat I saw a list of the aircrew posted on the door into the flight deck, and the captain was R. Clarke, Ronnie Clarke, that I had taught to fly at Leacaster so many years ago, in that wonderful year. I had been very happy then, and I was happy now, and here was Ronnie Clarke again. When we were airborne and the notice about seat belts had gone out and we were climbing upon course, I asked one of the hostesses to tell the captain that Johnnie Pascoe was on board and she went forward to the flight deck.

She came back at once with an invitation to me to go up forward. Ronnie made his second pilot get out of his seat, and I settled down by my old pupil, and the hostess brought me a cup of coffee. I was glad to see Ronnie again. He had been a commercial pilot practically all the time since I taught him to fly, first with John Sword and then with British Airways. In the war he had been in the R.A.F. for a time, anyway, because I remember flying him home from Burma in 1944 or 45. He joined Australian Continental soon after the war; he was married with two children. It was some years since I had seen him to talk to, and I enjoyed it. Sitting there together at the controls of the Viscount we exchanged news as we slid along past Eildon and Canberra towards Kingsford Smith. He was well dug in with Continental now, unlikely to make any change. I told him about my coming retirement and about Buxton, and what I hoped to do there. "Like going back to Duffington again," he said.

"That's right," I replied shortly. I hoped it wasn't going to be like going back to Duffington again.

We both had about three hours to kill at Sydney before he left to take the lunch-time flight back to Melbourne, before I got on to the AusCan flight to Nandi. He asked me to come up to the pilots' room at Kingsford Smith and I said I would, and went back to my seat in the cabin as he started to lose height.

When we landed I went and made my number with AusCan on the overseas side, and then went back to have another chat with Ronnie Clarke. I always liked Ronnie, and now he was one of the oldest friends I had; moreover he lived in a Melbourne suburb and I could see him from time to time when I went over to the mainland from Buxton. I wondered, as I walked back to the domestic side, how much he ever knew about my love for Brenda Marshall. I had a vague idea that he probably knew quite a lot, because he was always at Duffington in those months and he went to the inquest with his father. Another thing was that in all the years that I had known him, off and on, he had never spoken of her.

I had a cup of coffee and a plate of sandwiches with him in the pilots' room, because I had missed my breakfast on the Viscount through sitting up front talking to him. As we sat together we glanced over the morning papers. There was a case going on in England against an unmarried girl and the newspapers were full of it in all its details. Essentially, it was quite a simple matter. The girl had borne an illegitimate baby. Wanting to get rid of it, she had left it on the steps of a Foundling Hospital in the traditional style; she had done that about midnight to escape attention. It was in a little basket with one thin cloth over it. It snowed in the early hours and then froze hard; when they found it in the morning it was dead from exposure. They were trying the girl for murder.

"Looks like they'll pin it on her," Ronnie said. "But she'll get a reprieve."

"I hope she doesn't," I said bitterly. "I hope she bloody well hangs." It ought to have been me, of course, and I should have hung, too, for I had gone to India.

"That seems a bit severe," he said mildly.

I threw down the paper, for it had upset me. When you do a thing like that it's done for ever, and you can't undo it. You've got to live with your guilt for the rest of your life, even if no one ever knows. "People who do that sort of thing to their illegitimate kids ought to hang," I said vehemently. "The kids have a hard enough row to hoe anyway, without being neglected. Without being just chucked away in the gutter because their parents don't want them. I hope they throw the whole book at that bloody girl." As, of course, they should have thrown the book at me.

He didn't answer that outburst, but turned the page. I sat gradually collecting myself, recovering from my temper and my shame. I lit a cigarette and sat staring at the runways outside the window, at a Skymaster taking off and a Dakota coming in. If Ronnie Clarke knew about Brenda and myself I had probably told him a bit more, but I didn't really care. He was a very old friend now, and there are some things that a friend ought to know.

I left him presently, and went back to the AusCan office over the road. We landed back at Nandi about ten o'clock that night, and I was very glad to be there, hot and humid though it was after the southern spring. I walked up from the terminal buildings to the hostel. There was a light on in her room and I thought perhaps she might come out and talk to me, and so I went and had a whisky at the bar and sat for half an hour looking at the ancient magazines that I had seen before. But she must have been too far towards her bed because she didn't come, and presently I went to bed myself, thinking of the photographs that I would have to show her in three days' time at Honolulu.

I showed them to her next week, sitting on the terrace of the Edgewater Hotel with our soft drinks. She was very interested, as I thought she would be, and examined each of them quite closely. I showed her the alterations I had made to the design of the house upon the enlargement of the photographed plan. "The kitchen's quite a decent size," she remarked. "Twelve feet by fourteen feet—from here to that chair . . ." She measured with her eye. "That ought to be big enough. The lounge doesn't look to be much bigger than that, though."

"Fourteen feet square," I said. "It's easy to keep a room that size warm."

"It's not very big. And then you've got a great big bedroom."

"I like a big bedroom," I said. "And you haven't got to keep that warm."

"I suppose not. And one tiny little spare room."

"I'm not expecting visitors," I said. "Something had to be cut down, so I cut that."

She turned to the other photographs. "It's a pretty little place, I should think. What do they do there?"

"They farm," I told her. "Mostly sheep and beef cattle. It's a bit far from a town for dairying. Some of them do that, but not very many. They used to have a market there at one time, but now everybody sells at Devonport."

"What happens if you get ill?" she asked. "Is there a doctor there?"

"There isn't yet," I told her, "but they say that there's one coming. A young chap just qualified. He's going to put up his plate after the New Year. But anyway, I don't intend to get ill."

She laughed. "Nobody ever does."

I offered her a cigarette and lit it for her. "You've got it all worked out," she said presently. "You're going to get the sort of a retirement that will suit you best, I think. You'd never be really happy now away from flying, would you?"

"I don't think I should," I replied. "I've been at it so long."

"I know. I wish you weren't starting in quite such a new place. It's going to be lonely for you, just at first."

It was the second time that she had said that. "I make friends fairly easily," I said. "As a matter of fact, I know some people in Melbourne, and I shall be going over there fairly often, I expect."

She glanced at me, surprised. "Who do you know in Melbourne—besides me?"

"A chap called Ronnie Clarke," I said. I went on to tell her about Ronnie, how I had taught him to fly back in England in the dark ages, how I had bumped up against him in the small world of aviation throughout my life, how I had travelled in the cockpit of his Viscount with him from Essendon to Sydney. "It was good meeting Ronnie again," I said. "I always liked him. He's a trout fisherman, too."

She smiled. "It must be funny, flying with somebody you taught to fly yourself."

"He was born to be a pilot," I told her. "Never wanted to be anything else, right from the start."

She went on leave soon after I got back, and when she was away I had time to think things over. She was right in saying that I should be lonely when I went to Buxton, but not the way she meant. I wasn't a bit afraid of being lonely for the company of men. I had lived for so long with men alone that making friends came naturally to me. In the saloon bar or the golf club I got on all right with people; I suppose I was good company, for I was never without friends. I should be lonely all right, because when I left AusCan a close friendship that I had grown to depend on would be interrupted, probably for good. I should be lonely, very lonely indeed, but my loneliness would be for her.

In that week I faced up to what would happen if I asked her to marry me, with all its implications. I knew it was a silly thing to do at my age, and I knew that she would probably laugh it off, and there would be an end of the companionship that meant so much to me. For that reason I must put it off till I was nearly out of AusCan, in fairness to both of us. Yet if I didn't do it, this companionship must come to an end anyway when I retired, and

I should be left kicking myself for a fool that I hadn't reached out to take the love she might have offered me.

It would have been an easy decision to make for I didn't stand to lose much either way, but for one thing. I didn't particularly want her as a woman, and I had never made love to her. That was very serious indeed. It was my age, I thought; I was still fit and virile but I was just on sixty years old and my interests were probably beginning to wane. Yet if I married her, a woman in her middle twenties, she had a right to have a family, and I must marry her with that intention or else leave her alone. The thought of bringing up an adolescent family when I was nearing the age of eighty and probably hard-up rocked me a bit, but that was what I had to face if I went on with this. On the other hand, I was one of the fittest men of sixty in the world; they could not fault me at the medical examination I took every three months. At sixty I still had the physique of an average man of forty. If I went on like this, at eighty I might still have the physique of a man of sixty, able to enjoy the vagaries of adolescent children. It would be a new experience for me and one that I looked forward to in a way; new experiences keep one young.

By the end of the week I had come to the conclusion that I must try my luck. If she accepted me, it would be an unusual marriage, but there was no earthly reason why it shouldn't turn out very happily for both of us. If she didn't, well that would be too bad, but not so bad as failing without ever trying. I would do it about Christmas time, I thought. That would leave a month before I retired from AusCan and left Nandi for good, and my crew broke up. She might well want time to think about so unusual a proposal, and that month would give her all the time she needed to make up her mind before we had to separate. If she refused me, as she probably would, a month of awkwardness would lie before us, but only a month; there was an end to it.

She came back from her leave and we went on doing things together in Honolulu every week. It wasn't quite the same, because now there were fresh circumstances of my retirement in my mind that I couldn't possibly discuss with her till this got straightened out; I was very conscious of evasions and constraints that had not been there before. We enjoyed our days together, perhaps more than ever, but there was no doubt that our relationship was changing. Once or twice I caught her looking at me with a sort of wonder, and in turn I wondered how much she knew.

The weather in Fiji got very hot and sticky in December; it rained almost every day and on some days even walking from the hostel to the terminal brought us out in a sweat, fit though we were. Our day in Honolulu then was a real relief; it was much cooler there. At Nandi I cut down the tennis; three sets was trying for us men on some days and altogether too much for the girls. The object was to keep us on the top line for flying all night through, and that wasn't achieved by sheer exhaustion in the afternoon. Instead of tennis on the worst days, I made them all go swimming at Saweni beach, and when they got there I made sure that they *did* swim and swim reasonably long distances. I wasn't going to have them all getting pot-bellied just because it was the monsoon season.

Saweni is a very lovely little land-locked bay half way between the airport and Lautoka. It used to be a sea-plane station in the Second War but it has been out of use since then; only a concrete slipway shows now where the Catalinas were pulled up. It has a long, gently shelving coral beach that runs down into clear, calm water; coconut trees shade the shore.and grow right down on to the beach, so that they lean out over the sea. There are shelters for men and for women to change in; at the week-end it tends to be crowded, but on week-days there is a seldom anybody there except the aircrews like ourselves.

I used to take them down there in one of the AusCan station waggons for their disciplinary swim, or else Pat Petersen would drive them. I had a half share in a little Austin car myself at that time. Jim Hanson and I owned it together, and as we were only at Nandi together for two days in each week the joint ownership worked very well. Sometimes I used to go down in that and so be independent of the crew.

We landed in from Honolulu on Friday morning just before Christmas. It had been a tiring and a troublesome flight through monsoon weather all the way from Canton. The thunderheads were up to forty thousand feet so we had to go through the stuff and there were quite a lot of electrical discharges at times all around us. I had to reduce speed to under two hundred knots in the turbulence and once I went down as low as three thousand feet in an attempt to get through underneath it. There was never any danger, of course, because the aircraft was all right and Canton was in the clear behind us, but a lot of the passengers were sick and the hostesses had quite a busy time. Nobody got any sleep that night, of course, and when we came to Nandi it was in a cloudburst. The Control kept us in the holding position for a quarter of an hour before they brought us in, and when we finally put down we had been in the air for nearly fifteen hours.

It was like a Turkish bath out on the tarmac. We were all tired but not unreasonably so, because that's what the tennis is for. The girls had had the worst of it, and they were looking white and strained. When we had cleared and handed over to the fresh crew in the office I told them we'd all go down to the beach at three o'clock if it was reasonably fine, and fixed up for the station waggon to be at the hostel for us then.

I walked up to the hostel with my senior hostess. It was hot and steamy, but the frangipani was fragrant in the rain. "Nice to be out in the fresh air, anyway," she said once. "I'm tired of vomit."

"Get a bit of sleep and then a swim," I replied. And then I said, "I tell you what. Would you like to stay down on the beach this evening if it's fine, and have a supper picnic?"

"Not everyone? Just us?"

"That's right," I said. "I'll get the cook to make us up a supper. Something cold and light. Crayfish salad and ice cream, and a bottle of hock."

She smiled. "That'd be marvellous. But it'll probably rain."

"I don't think it will," I told her. "The Met say this one's passing, and we're going to get a spell."

It was very lovely on the beach that evening. The clouds had cleared away but for a storm down on the horizon, and the sun set in a clear sky. The crew went back to Nandi in the station waggon and we stayed on upon the beach, alone but for another party of four about a couple of hundred yards away. We sat on the white, coarse sand in our bathing things luxuriating in the coolness and the beauty of it all, enjoying the little whispers of warm wind about our bodies after the strain and effort of the night. I undid our supper and the bottle of chilled hock wrapped in a wet cloth, and we ate together in the fading light. A coconut fell once with a plump on to the sand only a few yards away from us, and a little Fijian girl appeared out of the shadows of the bush, and smiled at us, and carried it away.

Presently I started in to say my piece. It would have been easier if I had ever held her in my arms, ever kissed her, but I had never done that. "I'll be retiring in about a month from now," I said. "There's something that I wanted to say to you before then, but I don't know if you'll want to hear it."

"What's that, Johnnie?" she asked quietly.

"It was just a crazy idea I had," I told her. "We get on so well together that I'm going to miss you terribly when we have to break it up. I was wondering if you could ever bring yourself to think of marrying me."

She was silent.

I reached out and took her hand. "It's a May and December sort of a proposal, this," I said. "People will laugh at you if you accept it, because I'm an old man. But I do love you very truly, Peggy, and I think I could give you a very happy life." I paused. "I suppose I'm doing this very badly. I don't do it every tick of the clock. But I would like you to think it over, if you would."

She sat silent, motionless. At last she said, "How often do you do this, Johnnie? How often have you done it?"

"You mean, in my whole life?"

She nodded.

"Twice," I said. "Only twice."

She turned to me. "Was one of them Brenda Marshall?"

I stared at her, amazed. "Who told you about her?"

"Was it?" she asked gently.

Somebody must have told her, but I couldn't think who it could be. "Yes," I replied. "Brenda was the last one. But that was a long time ago."

"I know," she said. We sat silent together on the warm sand in the fading light. At last she said, "I've been playing a trick on you, Johnnie, and I'm feeling very badly about it. I want you to try and forgive me." She hesitated, and then said, "It's been wonderful to hear you say this. How wonderful, you just don't know. But I couldn't marry you."

"That's all right," I said a little thickly. "It was just a silly idea I had."

She turned to me. "It's not that, Johnnie. It's not that at all." She paused, and then she said, "You see, if everybody had their rights, I should be Brenda Pascoe."

Chapter Seven

I stared at her. "I'm sorry, but I don't get that," I said. "Is your name Brenda?"

"My names are Brenda Margaret," she said quietly. "That's how my birth was registered, at Cannes, in France." I sat speechless. "Grannie always called me Peggy," she remarked. "I don't think I ever did get christened properly. There was some trouble about it."

I turned to her. "Let me get this straight. Are you trying to tell me that you're Brenda Marshall's daughter?"

She faced me. "That's right, Johnnie. I'm Brenda Marshall's daughter, and yours."

"What was your grandmother's name?"

"Duclos," she said. "She was married twice. Her first husband was my grandfather, Henry Dawson."

"But Brenda's baby died!"

She smiled gently. "She didn't, Johnnie. She grew up a very ordinary child, and finished up as an air hostess in her father's crew."

I sat back and stared out over the dark sea. I had made the most colossal fool of myself, and I needed a little time to recover from what this girl had done to me before I spoke again.

Presently she said in a low tone, "Don't be angry."

"I'm not angry," I replied. "But Mrs. Duclos wrote to me from Cannes. She said the baby died there."

She nodded. "I know. She did what she thought was the right thing."

"Why did she tell me that?" I asked resentfully.

"I'm not sure that I know the whole story," she said. "Probably you know the bits I don't. My mother committed suicide, didn't she?"

"I think she did," I said painfully. "She spun her Moth into the deck at Duffington."

"Why did she do that, Johnnie?"

I was silent. Even with this girl it was difficult to talk of that bad time. "Her husband got out of The Haven," I said at last. "He'd have been coming home to live with her in a few days. He was a mental case, you know. And she was in love with me."

She nodded slowly. "Is that why Grannie took me back to Cannes?"

"That's right," I said. "She left directly the funeral was over, before Derek Marshall came home. She was afraid that if he saw you he might do you an injury."

"That's what she told me." We were getting on better now. "Why did she go back to Cannes?"

"She'd just come from there," I said. "She knew the hotel, and they knew her. It was the easiest thing for her to do."

"Well, when did you go to India?" she asked.

"Almost at once," I said. "I had to get away from Duffington, and Imperial Airways wanted pilots for the East. I stopped in Cannes on the way out and spent a day with Mrs. Duclos, and saw the baby."

"Me," she said.

"I suppose so." I paused. "There wasn't anything that I could do. Your grandmother had plenty of money and everything was under control. I couldn't have interfered if I'd wanted to, legally. But everything was going on all right."

She said slowly, "You mean, I wasn't legally your child?"

I nodded. "Legally, you hadn't got a father."

She smiled gently. "And now I've found one, he doesn't care about me much."

"That's not true," I said. "I always cared about you. You were Brenda's child."

We sat together in silence on the beach. A moon was coming up in the palm trees behind us, and the point of land a mile away was bathed in light. We sat in the half-light each busy with our own thoughts. It was quite true what I said; away in the heat and dust of Delhi Airport I had loved that child, because she was a part of Brenda.

Presently she asked, "How did you get on with Grannie?"

"Not very well," I told her slowly. "We never quarrelled, but she never liked me much. You see, it was because of me that it all happened. It was really because of me that Brenda died."

"Oh, I see," she breathed. "That does explain a lot."

"What does it explain?"

She turned to me. "When she invented this story that I died. It seemed a bit hard on you, if you *had* minded. I asked her that once, and she said it would have been a relief to you. She said it was the best thing, if you married somebody—not to have an illegitimate child round your neck."

"I never wanted to marry anybody after Brenda," I remarked. "Anyway, not till now."

"Oh dear."

"All right," I laughed. "I'm a bit old for marrying, anyway."

We laughed together about that, and eased the tension. "Why did she do it?" I asked presently. "When did you first know that you'd got a father living?"

"When I was twenty-one," she said. "She told me then. Before that, all I knew was that my father and

mother were killed together in a car accident in England."
She paused. "Of course, I knew that wasn't right. I came
to that conclusion when I was about fourteen. Whenever
I asked her about my father and mother she told me
something a bit different—she was getting old, you see. I
knew I must be illegitimate, and of course I thought it
must be nastier than it was, because she wouldn't tell
me." She paused. "It wasn't very happy, in my school
days."

"There wasn't anything nasty about it," I said. "You
can forget about that." I thought about it for a minute,
and then said, "I still don't understand why she told me
you were dead."

"It wasn't only you," she replied. "She told everybody." She paused, and then she said, "It was all such a
mess, you see. She was afraid of Derek Marshall, for one
thing. She was afraid he'd come to Cannes and do me
some harm. She was afraid he might claim me, and take
me away from her to Duffington and try to bring me up
there—when he was a mental case."

"That would have been a bad one," I said quietly.

She nodded. "She was afraid of all sorts of things. She
thought that you'd marry somebody, and if you had to
look after me I wouldn't get a square deal. She was afraid
of me knowing when I was too young that my mother
committed suicide, and that I was illegitimate." She
paused. "Tell me one thing, Johnnie. Did you ever know
my mother's maiden name was Dawson?"

I shook my head. "It never occurred to me to question
that it was Duclos."

"That's what Grannie said. She said you never knew
my mother was her child by her first marriage. But you
see, when my mother registered my birth at Cannes, she
told the registrar that her husband was in a mental home
and that he wasn't the father. I was registered in her

maiden name as illegitimate, and there was a note against the entry of her married name."

I glanced at her. "I never saw the entry. You were registered as Brenda Margaret Dawson?"

She nodded. "That's my name."

"Well, when did you go to Australia?"

"Grannie took me straight there from Cannes," she said. "You see, she had relations there."

"Had she?"

She nodded. "My grandfather's brother Ernest—Grannie's brother-in-law,—he married a girl at Colac with five thousand acres. The family's there still, Coniston Station." She paused. "I'm pretty sure we went there right away, because I can remember living there when I was little. Then when I was five or six and had to go to school, Grannie took a house in South Yarra, and we lived there all the time."

"I see," I said slowly. "She made a clean break, and started you off somewhere fresh."

"She thought it was the best thing to do," she said.

I sat looking out over the moonlit sea. "Probably it was." I turned to her. "How did you come to be here?"

"I was curious," she said simply.

"About me?"

She nodded. "You see, Grannie told me everything she knew when I was twenty-one. I was training at the Alexandra then, so it wasn't quite the shock it might have been. And anyway, I'd guessed that it was something like that. She hadn't kept in touch with you, but she thought you might be still alive somewhere."

"She vanished into the blue," I remarked. "I tried to find her when I was on leave, but I never got a line on her at all. She never even kept in touch with old George Marshall up at Halifax. She just vanished."

"I know. She thought it was the best thing to do. She was afraid of Derek Marshall."

"Well, what happened then?"

She said, "As soon as I was qualified, I went to England."

"To look for me?"

"Partly," she said. "Only partly." She turned to me. "Try and understand, Johnnie. I wanted to know how I'd been born, what really happened." She stared out over the sea. "What Grannie told me was such a confused sort of a story, so unlikely in some ways. It could have been wonderfully good, or it could have been—just smutty. I didn't mind much about being illegitimate, but I wanted to know how it all happened."

"It was wonderfully good" I said. "Good enough to keep me single all these years, anyway. Do you want me to tell you about it?"

"If you will."

"Finish your story first. What did you find out in England?"

"Very little," she said. "I went to see the Marshalls up at Halifax. George Marshall—the one you knew—he died about ten years ago. I saw his son, John Marshall, and told him who I was. He knew hardly anything. His uncle, Derek Marshall, blew his brains out with a shot gun soon after we got to Australia. That must have been while you were still in India."

"I heard that," I said.

"I was just one of a whole lot of unsavoury scandals that the Marshalls wanted to forget," she remarked. "John Marshall didn't introduce me to his family."

"I'm very sorry," I said, and I was.

She smiled quietly. "I hadn't expected much else. So then I went to Duffington."

"You went there?"

. She nodded. "That was no good either. There's no flying club there now."

"The aerodrome's a big place, isn't it?"

"That's right," she said. "It's got runways about two miles long, and the American Air Force are there. And Duffington Manor's been turned into a girls' school."

I sat thinking back about those distant days upon the far side of the world. "Peter Woodhouse could have told you something," I remarked. "He should be in the district still. You didn't talk to him?"

She shook her head.

"Well, what did you do then?"

"I went back to London and went to the Royal Aero Club. The secretary there was awfully nice and I think he knew you, but he couldn't or wouldn't tell me where you were. He told me to go to a public library and look you up in *Who's Who in Aviation*. So I did that, and found that you were with AusCan."

Up the beach at the old Catalina slipway three Fijians had launched a boat. They came paddling slowly down the shore in the darkness with a brilliant acetylene lamp hanging on a pole over the bows, spearing fish as they came to the light. We watched them in silence as they crept along. London seemed very far away.

"That's how you came to know I was in AusCan," I said thoughtfully.

She nodded, watching the boat. "I went to the AusCan office in Piccadilly and got a time-table," she said. "I asked the girl who gave it me if Captain Pascoe was still flying for them, and she knew all about you. She said you were in London every week, because you brought in the machine from Vancouver over the North Pole and took it back again. It was quite a new service then—just one machine a week. She said you were training younger captains on the route."

281

I grinned. "She told you a damn sight too much. Bloody gossip."

The boat before us paused, and there was a lot of excited chatter from it, because one of the men had speared a fish. It was quite a big one, but I couldn't tell her what sort of fish it was. We sat looking at the spectacle, talking about it; then as the boat moved on we came back to our conversation.

"Is that when you decided to become a hostess?" I asked.

"Not quite," she said. "I went down to London Airport a couple of days later and stood in the public enclosure to see the AusCan machine come in from Vancouver. Before it landed, I asked at the AusCan office who the captain was, and they told me it was you. When the machine came in and all the passengers got off, you came off with the other officers—an awful lot of them. There must have been eight or nine. You passed quite close to me."

I sat there in my bathing trunks in the warm night, trying to put myself in this girl's place when first she saw her father. "What did you think?" I asked.

She said seriously, "I thought you looked rather nice. Very strict, but rather nice."

I didn't like the very strict part much, but it was probably justified. "I may have been tired," I said. "It's a long flight from Vancouver, and we didn't know the route well, just at first."

She nodded. "I went to bed much happier that night."

I was glad of that, but I didn't know how to say it. "Then did you go back to Australia?"

She smiled. "I flew back with you."

"Flew back with *me*?" I was dumbfounded. "As a passenger?"

282

"I was so terribly curious," she said. "I wasn't at all sure if I wanted to know you, or to let you know who I was. There wasn't any reason why I should, after all. I wanted to know all about you first—what sort of a person you were." She paused. "What sort of a person I am," she said thoughtfully.

"I understand that," I replied.

She stared after the boat, now moving away from us and coming out of the shadow of the palm trees into the moonlight. "I couldn't really afford to fly back to Australia, but I had to," she said. "I went tourist, of course, and I made quite sure that you'd be the captain before I confirmed the booking." I smiled, and she smiled with me. "You came down the cabin once and asked me if I was comfortable, and told me when we'd be landing at Frobisher. That was the first time I ever spoke to you."

I sat trying to recollect that evening, one of so many similar flights. I couldn't place it. "When I took you on in Billy Myers' office in Vancouver," I said slowly, "I thought I'd seen you before. I wonder if that was it."

"I saw you several times at Vancouver when I was in Captain Forrest's crew," she remarked. "I don't know if you saw me. We never spoke."

"That might have been it. How did you come to be in AusCan, then?"

"I flew on back to Sydney down this route," she said. "You handed over at Vancouver, of course. It was after that that the idea came to me. I talked to the senior hostess, Mary Barrett, about hostess work."

"I remember Mary Barrett," I said. "She got married."

She nodded. "When I told her about my nursing experience, she said that I could get to be a hostess on this line quite easily. She told me what to do, and all about it. By the time I got to Sydney I wanted to do that more than

283

anything. I thought if I could get to be in your aircrew I could really get to know about you. I wanted to find out everything I could about you, and then make up my mind whether I'd tell you who I was, or not." She paused. "I couldn't do it while Grannie was alive. It wouldn't have been fair to leave her. I had to put it out of my mind. But then she died. After that I couldn't do it at once, till the estate was settled up. But then I was quite free to do whatever I wanted to." She stared after the boat. "And what I wanted to do was—this."

We sat together in silence on the beach in the warm night. I was thinking how much I had missed, in all these years. And yet, I couldn't have done much more for her if I had been around during her adolescence. Mrs. Duclos had done a good job of bringing her up, and though I never got on well with the old lady, I was grateful to her. For better or worse, I had an adult daughter ready-made. I should never, perhaps, be very close to her for I had seen nothing of her childhood. Perhaps I should never really understand her, as perhaps I had never really understood her mother.

I sat for a long time thinking of these things. Presently she said gently, "Will you tell me about my mother?"

"I'll do what I can to tell you," I said heavily. "I only know it from my side, of course. She came to learn to fly at Duffington, and we fell in love. But there was more to it than that on her side, much, much more. I never got to understand her side of it, not properly." I turned to her. "We wanted to get married. But we never had more than a day or so together. She did things that I never really understood, because I never had the chance to get to understand *her*." I paused. "We were just in love."

"Tell me what actually happened," she said quietly. "Perhaps I'll understand better than you."

"You mean, from the beginning?"

She nodded. "Tell me everything that happened, right from the beginning."

I sat for a few moments in silence, thinking back over the years. "I was the pilot-instructor at the flying club," I said at last. "The aerodrome was on her husband's land, and he was in The Haven. The land had been re-quisitioned in the war, and had never been de-re-quisitioned. We paid rent to the Air Ministry, and they paid rent to Derek Marshall. So your mother was our landlord in a kind of way, and one day she came along to see the club."

She asked, "Did she come to fly?"

I shook my head. "Not at first. She just came to see what was going on. She never bothered about it till the doctor's daughter joined the club."

I went on talking to her in the night on that calm beach of Viti Levu, and it came more easily as I went on talking. She asked a good many questions and I answered them as well as I could. Sometimes I had to stop and think about the sequence of the things that happened nearly thirty years before, sometimes she asked me things about her mother that I could not answer. I must have talked to her for well over an hour in the calm night, perhaps for nearly two, telling her everything I knew. At last I came to the final scene when she had spun into the deck. "She was still alive," I said painfully. "She was still living, terribly smashed up, when we got her on the stretcher."

"Did she say anything?"

I shook my head. "She wasn't conscious. She died in the hangar about ten minutes later, before the doctor came."

"You were with her, Johnnie?"

"All the time." I paused, and stared out over the sea. "We'd only got blankets and a first aid box—nothing for shock. We didn't know so much about the treatment of shock as we do now. I sometimes think we might have saved her if we'd had the modern one-shot dopes. I don't know."

"It was deliberate, though, wasn't it? She wanted to die?"

"She never even hinted that to me," I said. "I wouldn't have let her fly. But—yes, I think she did."

"She chose to die rather than go away and live with you, unmarried? Even with me?"

"I think she did," I said. "She left a note about you for her mother, but I never saw it."

"I've seen it," she said. "Grannie gave it to me. I've got it at home, now."

I glanced at her. "Is there anything about me in it?"

"Nothing," she said gently. "I'll show it you one day."

We sat in silence for a long time on the beach. It had grown cooler and we had pulled shirts over our bare shoulders while I had been talking of those far-off, painful days in England. The fishing boat had gone a long time before, and we were quite alone upon the beach. The moon had worked around, and we were now sitting in the silvery light on the white sand under the coconut palms. I glanced at my wrist-watch presently, and it was after midnight. "Time we went back to the hostel," I said presently.

"I know." She sat thoughtful, not moving. "There's one more thing I want to say before we go."

"What's that?" I asked.

"When we started doing things together, in Honolulu," she said, "I was playing a sort of trick on you, because I knew all about you and you knew nothing about me. I want you to try and understand why I did it."

I smiled. "That's all right," I said. "But you might have given me a hint before I went so far."

"I know . . ." She sat staring at the distant, moonlit

point, not looking at me. "I wanted to be friends with you before I told you who I was," she said. "I wanted you to know everything about me, too, before I told you. I thought that it would make it kind of easier to tell you . . ." She paused. "Then, when I realised what was happening, I didn't know what to do." She sat silent, and then turned to me. "Tell me. Am I like my mother?"

"Just once or twice, when I've been tired and had a bit to drink, I've thought that you *were* her," I said slowly. "You're not very like her in the normal way. Not in appearance, I mean. But in character—I think you're very like her." I glanced at her. "I think that's been the trouble."

"I wouldn't call it trouble," she said softly. She turned to me. "Did you know I looked like you?"

I laughed. "No, I didn't. Do you?"

"Mollie Hamilton says so. There's been quite a bit of gossip since we started going about together in Honolulu."

I stirred. "Better not let me hear them at it. It's probably a good thing I'm retiring."

"They'll all be very sorry to see you go," she said. "It's been nice gossip."

"Make any trouble for you?"

She shook her head. "No. If they've been saying I'm your daughter, I've been proud of it."

She turned to me. "I shouldn't have let you go on and ask me to marry you," she said. "I should have turned it off, somehow. I could have done. I want you to forgive me for letting you go on."

"That's all right," I said again.

"It seemed so incredible," she said. "I knew by that time that there'd been no one in your life since my mother died. And I knew that there must be a good deal of my mother in me . . ." She paused. "If you were falling in love with me, it could only be that you were falling in love again with what was in me of my mother. I couldn't resist letting it happen, Johnnie. Because you see, it was the final, absolute proof that everything was quite all right when I was born—but for bad luck."

"Bad luck or bad management," I said slowly.

"What do you mean by that?"

I sat silent for a time. "I've had a long time to think this over, and now I'm an old man," I said at last. "And what I think is this. When you get to wanting something that doesn't belong to you so badly that you've just got to have it, and you take it—well, that's stealing. You don't let yourself get into that state of mind with other things—with money or motor cars or gold cigarette-cases. And you mustn't do it with love. That's stealing, just the same. But that's what we didn't understand." I paused. "I think your mother understood it a bit better than I did. We kidded ourselves that love was something different, because it says so on the pop tunes."

She laughed. "If you hadn't kidded yourselves, I shouldn't be here."

"That's true. Are you glad or sorry?"

"Glad," she said. "Very, very glad."

I got to my feet, stiff after sitting for so long. "Time we were going back," I said. "If we stay much longer I'll have to write a confidential note about you to Mrs. Deakin—staying out too late upon the beach with men."

She stretched out her hand and I pulled her up beside me. We gathered our things up from the beach to take them to the car. "When you're at Buxton and I'm back at the Alexandra again, we shan't be very far away from each other," she said. "May I come over and see you when I get a holiday?"

"Sure," I said. "Come and start a bit of gossip for me there." We laughed together.

288

She turned to me. "I've been so happy tonight. Everything's quite all right now, isn't it?"

"Yes," I said quietly. "Everything's come good at last. It's quite all right, now."

We walked slowly from the moonlit coral beach into the deep shadows of the palm tree groves. Our feet made no sound on the ground; we were gliding along as if suspended in the air, floating along. Everything had come good at last, after so many years. I had reached the happy ending of the story, and I was quietly, serenely happy. In the soft, velvety darkness I lay utterly at peace for I had finished with all heartaches, with all pains and worries; nothing could touch me now. I had finished the book but I could take it up and read it over and over again, and I would do so, secure in the knowledge of the happiness in the last chapter. There would be no more misery ahead of me, for everything had come good. Everything was all right now.

There was light all around me, and she was by my side. She was dressed in a blue combination suit of smooth denim cloth over a heavy white polo-necked sweater, stifling in Fiji. I blinked my eyes and muttered, "You'll be much too hot. Whatever are you wearing that for?"

She glanced at me curiously. "It's five o'clock, sir. There's a cup of tea here." I saw she had it in her hand, and she put it down upon the table by my side, beside the lamp that she had lit. She stood back from the bed, and she was in ski-ing clothes, with heavy ski-boots on her feet. "I can get you some breakfast while you're getting up," she said. "Would you like bacon and eggs? It's about all there seems to be."

I rubbed my hand over my eyes. I had been dreaming. This was Johnnie Pascoe's room and I was in his bed, in his pyjamas. I was Ronnie Clarke, and I had work to do for him. I rose upon one elbow. "What's the weather like?"

She crossed to the window and pulled up the blind. It was quite dark outside. "The sky is clear," she said. "It's all starry. The wind has dropped a lot."

I was still happy, and this confirmed my happiness, for everything was going to be all right this time. "Has the doctor turned up yet?"

She shook her head. "He said he'd be here by ten to six. How did you sleep?"

"Never better," I said. I was Ronnie Clarke, and she had made me a hot drink in the middle of the night. "That's thanks to your Ovaltine."

She smiled. "How many eggs? I'll do them while you're getting up."

She was the nurse, and she had been a hostess with AusCan; I was awake now. "Not bacon and eggs," I said. "It's too heavy so early in the morning." She nodded. "I'd like a couple of boiled eggs, lightly boiled, and some toast."

"I'll have it ready in the kitchen by the time you're dressed," she said, and went out of the room.

I got up in the chilly, spartan bedroom, so much larger than it need have been, and put on Johnnie Pascoe's dressing gown, and thrust my feet into his slippers. I went to the window and looked out. The night was as she said. There was not a scrap of cloud in sight, and very little wind. In Tasmania they get no actuals from the south-west, and a high had come along that the Met had not been able to forecast. It might well last for a few hours, long enough for me to put the doctor and the nurse down at the Lewis River. Everything was coming good at last. Everything was going to be all right.

Chapter Eight

The doctor came while I was having breakfast with the nurse at the kitchen table. We heard his car outside, and I got up with my mouth full and went to let him in. He was in ski-ing clothes as he had been before. "The weather's looking better, isn't it?" he asked.

I nodded. "It's going to be perishing cold for you without the cabin door," I said. "But if it's like this when we get there I think we might be able to put down and land it properly."

He smiled. "Is Sister Dawson up yet?"

"She's in the kitchen. She didn't go to bed. She slept in the chair before the fire."

"She told me she was going to do that. It looked a great deal more comfortable than the bedroom."

He came with me to the kitchen and had a cup of tea while I was finishing my breakfast. As I got up from the table we heard the engine of the Auster start up from the direction of the hangar; Billy Monkhouse was there and on the job, running her up for me. Everything was under control now and coming good. Everything was going to be all right this time.

We went the few hundred yards to the hangar in the doctor's car. It was cold and frosty in the night with the extra bit of chill that always seems to come before the dawn. We parked the car and got out by the hangar, the nurse carrying a little bundle of clothes tied around with string. There was a Proctor in the hangar, dimly visible in the half-light. Outside, Billy Monkhouse was sitting in the Auster still running it up; four equal blue flames streamed from the exhausts beneath the engine cowling. The two boys were at the tailplane, their clothes blown and buffeted by the slipstream.

I led the doctor and the nurse round behind the hangar, a little out of the noise, so that we could talk. "Now look," I said. "This wind's not very strong. If it's like this when we get down to the Lewis River we may be in trouble again. It may be too strong for me to land upon that little strip cross-wind, and at the same time not quite strong enough for me to hold her stationary across it, like I did yesterday. In that case I'd be moving forward ten or fifteen miles an hour across the strip, and you'll have to get out damn quick."

The doctor nodded. "I understand that. But I could pretty well fall out, since there's no door."

"That's what I want you to do," I said. "I hope we shan't have to perform like that. But if we should, I want you to fall flat on the ground, so that the tailplane will pass over you. I don't want that to hit you, for my sake as well as yours."

"I understand," he said again. "I've got to go down flat upon the ground as soon as I'm out of the machine."

"That's the shot. Think you can do it? I'm afraid it's a bit acrobatic."

"I can do that all right," he said. "You think we may be going forward fifteen miles an hour?"

"It could be twenty," I said. "I hope it won't be so fast as that. It could be like getting off a tram going a good bat, and falling down."

"Fall limp, and try to guard one's head," he said thoughtfully. "Look, Captain Clarke, I'll do my best with it. If I think there's not a hope that I'd get up without broken bones, then I won't do it. There's no sense in loading up the woman with another patient."

"Fair enough," I said. "I hope it won't be like that.

But if it is, I shan't think any the worse of you if you don't jump."

I turned to the nurse. "Sister Dawson, I'll have you in the back seat, and the doctor beside me. If he succeeds in making it, then we'll go up again a few hundred feet, and you get out of the back seat and sit beside me, where he was sitting. Then we come in again when you're quite ready. Before we take off, now, I want you to sit in that seat and just practise getting out."

She nodded. "I'd like to do that."

I thought for a moment. "If it looks too difficult, or if the doctor has a very rough landing, I won't ask you to jump," I said. "We'll try again later in the day, when there's a bit more wind."

She said, "If the doctor jumps, I jump."

There was a sudden resemblance to Johnnie Pascoe in the set of her chin, the line of her jaw, the wrinkling of her eyes. "All right," I said. "I'll tell you the right moment when I'm going as slowly as I can, and then you decide for yourself, like the doctor."

The roar of the engine slowed to a tick-over as I was speaking, and then stopped as the engineer switched off. "That'll be best," she said. "I'd like to practise getting out a few times, before we start."

We walked round the hangar to the machine. Billy Monkhouse was getting out of the cabin. "Morning," he said in the darkness. "She's all ready for you."

"Flares?" I asked.

"I got them laid down on the aerodrome. They're up-wind from the thorn tree in the far hedge. I'll nip out in the car and put a match to them when you're ready."

I nodded. "Thanks. How much petrol did you use for running up?"

"Gallon. Maybe a gallon and a half."

"Get a can and top her up," I said.

He went off for a can, and I put the nurse in the back seat, and got into the left hand seat in front of her myself. I made her practise climbing over into the front seat, and then practise getting out of the machine. The doctor helped her. "Right foot out upon the step. Swing round. Hold the door frame—*there*, and the seat—*there*. Change feet. Now, left foot on the step, swing round, and face forward. That's right. Now, jump out and let yourself fall limp on your right side. That's fine."

I watched this going on in deep concern. It looked horrible, but they knew what they were in for and they were both quite prepared to do it. The final decision lay with me, however; if it seemed to me too dangerous I could veto it by not going near the ground. Only if I put the aircraft on the little runway could they do this thing. Mine was the responsibility, and mine alone. The feeling was still strong in me, however, that everything was all right now. Everything was going to be all right this time.

The girl practised it half a dozen times, the doctor once or twice. The extra petrol was put in, and we were ready to start. It was still dark, but a paler tinge was showing in the black sky over to the east. "Okay," I said. "Let's go."

They got into their seats, and I got into mine, shutting my door beside me. Billy Monkhouse swung the little propeller and the engine caught; I sat there studying the instruments in the dashboard lights while he drove out to light the flares. When the first flare flamed up I waved the chocks away and turned, and taxied out to the far hedge.

The wind was light now, no more than a gentle breeze. I took the full length of the aerodrome, for the little aeroplane was heavily loaded and it was pitch-dark beyond the line of the flares; I could not even see the hedge I had to take off over. I lined up beside the line of flares, checked everything once again, and satisfied myself that both my passengers were strapped in and comfortable. Then I opened up the throttle steadily, and we moved off.

I got the tail up as soon as I could and trimmed her so, and then I sat and let her fly herself off the ground. She took quite a long run but we came unstuck at the fourth flare and we were a few feet up at the fifth. The hedge flashed by twenty feet below. I trimmed her for seventy and got on course, for it was all clear ahead of us for fifteen miles or so, and presently I throttled back to cruising revs.

It was pretty dark still, for the moon had set, but as we gained altitude the grey light to the east increased and I could see the line of mountains stretching out ahead of me in a clear sky. I could go over everything this time, and there would be no creeping round the coast in the grey muck. The Gipsy engine only had to keep on turning and I had no fear of that, and we should be okay. Everything was going to be all right, this time.

I kept her on a steady climb up to about five thousand feet. It was terribly cold at that height without the door on the starboard side. It must have been way down below freezing, and the wind beat and whistled around us in the cabin. There was no icing on the aircraft for there were no clouds, but ice formed from my breath upon the muffler round my throat and on my eyebrows. I became seriously concerned about this jumping out of the machine if my passengers were frozen stiff with cold; as soon as possible I must get down to a lower altitude and give them a chance to thaw out before they had to do their stuff. Yet we must take the most direct course that we could, lest we should be in trouble over petrol again before getting back to Buxton.

I compromised, and deviated slightly to the west and began to let down before we got to Macquarie Harbour, scraping the bush-covered hills with only a hundred feet to spare. It was full daylight by the time we passed over the east end of the harbour and the mountains were high above us on our port hand; we were down to two thousand feet or so and it was getting warmer, though the sun was not yet up. I headed for the coast ahead of us, and presently I checked her at a thousand feet, and we went on like that.

Presently I saw the Lewis River and the house, and at the same moment the doctor pointed it out to me. We went on looking for some indication of the wind, and seeing none. There was heavy surf against the rocks upon the coast but I judged this to be more from a ground swell than from any wind. I saw no white horses on the sea out from the shore; if there was wind, as there must be, it was impossible to say from which direction it was coming.

When we were a mile from the house I saw the woman come out of the door and look towards us; she had heard our motor. She went back, and came out again carrying a bundle that must be the windsock, and I was grateful for her intelligence. She hurried with it up the hill to that desperate little airstrip that looked more like a very short length of cart track than ever, and as I turned upon a circuit she was busy with it at the flagstaff. She hoisted it, and it hung limp and vertical along the spar. There was no wind at all.

I stared at it for half a minute, incredulous, watching for the gust to blow it out. No gust came; the sock hung motionless. I turned to my passengers, elated. "Money for jam," I said. "I'll make one dummy run, and if it looks all right I'll land upon the strip. Keep your belts done up."

The sun was coming up over the mountains to the east as I turned on to final. There was no wind at all to hinder us in landing. The only problem now before me lay in coming in slow enough to put the wheels down within a few feet of the near end of that short strip, and so to stop her before running off the far end of it. But Austers had landed there before in good conditions like we had, and I was feeling fine. I had had a good sleep and I was right on the top line. Everything was going to be all right, this time.

I lined up on the strip to come in for my dummy run, throttled back a bit, and put my hand up to pull down half flap. I brought her in upon the throttle, watching it ahead of me. There was a little stunted tree with a bush beside it about seventy yards from the end of the strip; if I pulled down full flap there when I was about six feet up, ready to catch her with a burst of throttle, I should just about make it. I shot a quick glance at the flagstaff and the sock to make sure there was no sudden gust of wind.

There was something funny there. I took my attention from the runway and looked at the sock properly. It was hanging vertical, but it was only half way up the mast. Then the woman caught my attention. She was standing by the mast and waving both arms horizontally.

I turned back to my flying, and moved the throttle forward. We passed over the strip twenty feet up as I gently raised the flaps. I turned to the doctor by my side. "See that?" I asked.

"You mean, the sock? It was at half mast, wasn't it?" I nodded.

"Was she trying to tell us not to land?"

"I think so. She seemed to be waving us off."

I put the machine on a climbing turn and turned to the nurse in the seat behind the doctor. "It doesn't look so good," I said. "I'm very sorry."

She had gone rather white. "That's all right," she muttered.

We circled round. "What would you like to do?" I asked the doctor. "I can land there normally, but I don't

297

suppose that I can stay there very long. This calm won't last longer than an hour, at most."

"I think I ought to have a look at him, perhaps," he said. "It wouldn't take very long."

The girl leaned forward at my shoulder. "I want to land, please, Captain Clarke."

I nodded. "Okay. I'll do another dummy run, and then run in."

I turned on final again and brought her in. It was still calm; I used half flap, touched my wheels a few feet from the near end of the strip, and took off again. There was plenty of room to pull her up if I did it like that again. I brought her round, lined up again on final, put full flap down at the little tree, and plumped her well and truly down in the right spot. We came to rest about thirty yards from the far end. I glanced at the windsock; there was still no wind. The woman was running towards us.

I turned to the doctor and the nurse. "Be as quick as you can," I said. "I'll stay with the machine."

I left the engine ticking over, and we all got out. The woman, Mrs. Hoskins, came panting up. "I tried to stop you landing," she said breathlessly. "I suppose you didn't see."

The doctor asked, "He's dead, is he?"

"I'm sorry to say so. You took off before the radio schedule, or I'd have let you know. I told them, so they're not sending the Lincoln."

"What time did he die?"

"A little after four, it must have been," she said. "A quarter past, perhaps. It's hard to say exactly when he went, you know."

"I'll just come down with you and have a look at him," he said.

Beside me, Sister Dawson stirred. "Have you got any news of the ground party?"

"They're a little way this side of Gordon River," she said. "They don't think they'll be here today—tomorrow dinner time, they thought. Some of them, the doctor and another, I think they'll go back now. But I said I'd like someone to come on." She hesitated. "I mean, there's things to be done."

The girl asked, "Is there a burial ground here?"

The woman hesitated, and then said, "Well, there's a nice little place where we put Grandpa, looking out over the sea. It's not consecrated, of course, but he could lie there, by Grandpa, if you think that'd do. Or they could take him out . . . But it's a long way."

The girl said, "We'll bury him here." She had taken charge completely of the situation. She turned to the doctor. "I'd like to go down now. Then you can get away with Captain Clarke, and I'll stay here and do what's necessary."

They all went down to the house and I was left alone with the Auster, its engine still ticking over, on the little airstrip on the ridge above the sea. The sun had come up and it was very beautiful there between the mountains and the Southern Ocean in the blue dawn. I walked a little way back along the strip and stood looking down upon the wreckage of the other Auster at the foot of the little cliff; then I climbed down to it. The engine was worth salvaging, but there was nothing else worth bothering about in that locality. I stood sadly for a few minutes, thinking back. He had been a great influence upon me in my youth; he had been part of my whole life. I would have said I knew him pretty well, if I had thought about it at all, but now it seemed to me I knew him much, much better.

I climbed back to the little gravel runway. The strip was too narrow for me to turn the Auster in the normal way, so I carried the tail round and taxied down to the lee end. I turned her in the same way there and carried the tail back till the main wheels were at the extreme end of the strip, gave the motor a burst to clear the plugs, and shut down to wait.

The doctor came up from the house presently, just as I was beginning to get worried about a little rising air that moved the limp windsock. He was carrying the battered suitcase that we had dropped on the scrub the day before. I took it from him. "Did anything get broken?"

"One bottle," he said. "It doesn't matter now, of course."

"Is Sister Dawson coming back with us?" I asked.

"No. We're taking the child back to hospital, for observation. There's not much wrong with her now. The mother's just dressing her up in warm clothes."

"She'll have to hurry up," I said. "I can't stay here much longer."

"She knows that. She'll be here in a minute." And as he spoke I saw the woman leave the house carrying the child, and come hurrying up the hill.

"How is Sister Dawson going to get out?" I asked.

"She'll come out with the ground party, or else by sea. Probably the ground party. She wants to stay here for the burial." He hesitated, and then asked, "Is she a relation, do you know?"

I faced him. "She's his illegitimate daughter," I said. "Don't go telling everyone."

"Are you quite sure of that?" he exclaimed.

"Quite sure," I said.

"However did you find that out? You only met her this morning!"

"I knew her mother," I said. "She was a fine woman. I remember when this girl was born. They had pretty bad luck." I paused. "I've known Johnnie Pascoe a great many years. We were old friends. There are some things

300

a friend ought to know." And then I wondered why I had said that, and where I had heard it before.

I turned to the aircraft. "Here she comes. Let's get in now, and get going before the wind gets up again."

I started the motor, and we got into the machine. The woman came up and handed the child to the doctor, who took her on his lap, wrapped in about three blankets. I ran the engine up, checked everything, and took off down that appalling little strip. We made it all right with a bit to spare; I turned over the house and set a course for Buxton. We flew back up the coast without incident though the weather was closing in and the wind getting up again, and landed back upon the aerodrome under a grey sky at about half past eight.

I taxied to the hangar and stopped the motor. Billy Monkhouse, the ground engineer, came up to the machine as I was undoing my belt. "You heard the news?" I asked.

He nodded. "They got it from the Lewis River soon after you took off. Too bad it had to happen."

I nodded, and got out of the machine, and looked around. Something was missing. I asked, "What's happened to the Proctor?"

"They took off about an hour ago for Hobart," he said. "Wanted to get down while the good weather lasted. The woman, Mrs. Forbes, she went with them."

"Damn good job," I said.

"You left the nurse there?" he asked.

I nodded. One of the boys was near us, and I took the old ground engineer to one side. "Look, Mr. Monkhouse," I said. "I don't know what's going to happen here now. I mean, about these two aircraft, and the house, and all the rest of his stuff. I don't know if he made a will, or if so, where it is."

"Mr. Dobson would have it, if there is one," he remarked. "He's the solicitor."

"You'd better go and ask him if he's got one. If there is, I wouldn't be surprised to hear that he's left everything to Sister Dawson."

He stared at me. "You mean—this nurse—here?"

I nodded. "She's visited him before, hasn't she?"

"Yes. She's been here two or three times." He hesitated. "Looks a bit like him."

"Well, there you are," I said. "That's none of my business, and none of yours. But she'll probably be telling you what she wants done here."

He asked, "What's the other machine like—the one he piled up in, at Lewis River?"

"The airframe's a write-off," I said. "It wouldn't be worth trying to bring that out. The engine didn't look too bad. It would be worth going in for that some time, and bring it out by sea."

We talked about that for a minute or two. Then he said, "What will you be doing now, sir?"

"I'll get some breakfast somewhere and pick up my haversack," I said. "Then I'll get back to Melbourne. There's nothing else that I can do here."

"Mrs. Lawrence is over in the house, waiting to cook you breakfast," he said. "I got that fixed for you."

"You've told her about Captain Pascoe?"

"Aye, I went over and told her. It'll be better if you have your breakfast in the house. They're a nosy kind of party, up at that hotel."

The doctor joined us, and I told him what I was going to do. "I think there's a plane from Devonport today about the middle of the morning." The old ground engineer nodded, and said, "Eleven thirty-five." The doctor said, "I'll run you over in my car."

"That's very kind of you." I paused and then I said, "I understand that there's some breakfast going in Johnnie's house. Would you like to join me?" So we

302

went together to the little house by the aerodrome that I had left so full of quiet hope before the dawn, only a few hours before.

Mrs. Lawrence was in the kitchen, looking as if she had been crying. I told her we'd be glad of breakfast for two, and she started in to get it. The doctor and I threw off our coats and went to wash and clean up, and presently we were sitting down to breakfast at the kitchen table.

Mrs. Lawrence had gone over to her own house next door taking the child with her, after telling us to leave everything as it was. She would come in later to wash up the breakfast and clean up the house. We said little while we ate, but after we had finished and were smoking at the table over a final cup of coffee, the doctor brought the subject up that was on both our minds.

"I've been thinking over what you told me about Sister Dawson," he said. "After I've taken you to Devonport, I think I'll go on home. I'll leave Betty in Hobart with her father on my way through. We've got a place down on the Huon. Then when the ground party come out from the Lewis River I could meet Sister Dawson with my car at Kallista and bring her back up here."

It seemed to me that that meant leaving his practice to look after itself for three or four days, but that was his affair, not mine. "That would certainly be a help to her," I remarked. "I think she'll want to come back here."

"She'll have to," he said. "She left a suitcase at the Vicarage." He thought for a moment. "Of course, I could take that down with me in the car."

"I should do that," I observed. "By the time you meet her she won't have had a change of clothes for three or four days, and she'll have walked about forty miles through the bush."

"Of course. I'll take it with me."

"I think she'll want to come back here, in any case," I

said. "There's probably a will, and Johnnie probably left everything to her. She'll have to come and settle up what's to be done."

He nodded slowly. "I hadn't thought of that . . ."

I glanced at him. "You'll be seeing a good deal of her?"

He met my eyes. "Probably."

"Well—look," I said. "She won't have a lot of money to throw around. She'll want to sell the two aircraft that are here. She doesn't have to pay a pilot to fly them away. I can get over here for nothing, any time, and I'd be very glad to fly them to Moorabbin to be sold. I shan't be seeing her again, but will you tell her that? I'd like to do that for her."

"That's really very kind of you," he said. "That's a very generous offer."

I flushed a little. "Her father was a very old friend," I said. "It was he who taught me to fly, back in the dark ages. And the girl's a good type, too."

He said quietly, "I think she's a very wonderful person."

"She's going to be a very lonely one now," I said practically. "I don't think she's got a single relation left in the world. Except, perhaps, some second cousins up at Colac." I grinned at him. "Good luck."

He smiled, a little self-consciously. "Thank you."

I got up from the table. "I'll give you a ring in a few days' time when you've got back here, and you can tell me what the form is."

He drove me to Devonport and put me down at the aerodrome. Then he went on southwards, while I waited for the midday plane. I got back to Essendon about half past one, reported at the office, and told them what the form had been at Buxton. They had a crew fixed up to do my flight to Sydney that afternoon, Flight 82, so I got the day off; I had a late lunch in the restaurant and walked out to my car. It was only about thirty-six hours since I had left it in the park, but when I unlocked the door and got into it, it seemed like so many years.

There was nobody at home when I got back to my house in Essendon. Sheila sometimes did the shopping in the afternoon before fetching the children home from school, and I guessed that that was where she was now. She must be walking, because I had had the car locked up in the car park, and I was sorry about that. I put down my haversack and leather coat and wandered round the house, fingering the children's toys, Sheila's fur stole that I had saved up for for so long, the small tools in my workshop. Johnnie Pascoe had been a better man than I, but he had never had the little benisons of life that I had got. I hoped his daughter would be luckier. She would be, I thought, if the doctor had anything to do with it.

I got the cutter, the half-moon thing with the long handle, and began to trim the edges of the lawn.

Sheila came home with the children before I got it finished. They were surprised and glad to see me, and came running to hug me. When the children were sent into the house to take their coats off, Sheila said, "He died, didn't he? They said so on the wireless."

I nodded. "We couldn't get in to him yesterday. It clamped right down. I got a doctor and a nurse in there at dawn today, but they were just too late."

"I'm so sorry," she said softly. Peter came running from the house towards us. "Tell me about it after they're in bed."

We went into the house together because it was a bit cold in the garden for the children, and I lit the fire in the sitting room, and we had tea. Then Diana showed me her latest paintings and Peter showed me the arrows he was making for the bow that he had made, and I helped him a bit with that. Bed-time was coming near and it was time for me to read to them, and I took Diana on my knee and read to her from *Doctor Dolittle* as we always did on Fridays, my day off, till it was time for her to go with Mummy to her bath, and after that I read *Coot Club* to Peter. When he was off to bed I laid the supper table and got a glass of sherry for us both, and sat on the edge of the kitchen table talking to Sheila while she grilled the steak. Somehow, I felt that evening that I had never appreciated my home so much.

We ate our steak and apple pie, and washed the dishes up. Then in the sitting room, smoking by the fire, I told her everything factual that had happened in Tasmania. I didn't tell her anything about my dreams because people who insist on telling you what they dreamed are a bit of a bore, and anyway, they didn't mean a thing.

When I had told her everything, and we had discussed it all, I said, "I'll probably have to go over there again, and fly the aircraft to Moorabbin to be sold. I offered to do that. I'd like to do that for him."

She nodded. Then she said, "You'd known him a long time, hadn't you?"

"Nearly thirty years," I said. "I never knew till now that we were such close friends."